INSIDE A HAUNTED MIND

INSIDE A HAUNTED MIND

By
K. PATRICK MALONE

A Better Be Write Publisher
New Jersey

INSIDE A HAUNTED MIND

All Rights Reserved © 2007
By K. Patrick Malone

No part of this book may be reproduced or transmitted
in any form or by any means, graphic, electronic, or
mechanical, including photocopying, recording, taping, or
by any information storage retrieval system, without the
permission in writing from the publisher.

A Better Be Write Publisher, LLC

For information:
A Better Be Write Publisher, LLC
1100 Buck Street, Suite 110
Millville, NJ 08332
www.abetterbewrite.com

ISBN: 978-0-9788985-0-2
ISBN: 0-9788985-0-8

Book Cover designed by Carl Cone

Printed in the United States of America

~Dedication~

Dedicated to the loving memory of my mother, who, from my earliest memories instilled in me, as her legacy, the reflective conscience of a thinking man, and, in the end, comforted me with the knowledge that love never dies. I love you. KPM

"And she said --
"Tell me are you a Christian, child?"
And I said "Ma'am, I am tonight"

Walking in Memphis
Marc Cohn

˜Thank You˜

To "My English" for struggling so tirelessly and so valiantly to keep me from degenerating into a caveman while I did this; to Trisha Moore for her insight and experience in rescuing "Inside A Haunted Mind" from the no-talent hands of hack editors who tried to turn it into "Little House on the Prairie;" and last, but certainly not least, to Maggie Stapperfenne for embodying the courageous spirit of independent publishing in letting this voice be heard when so many sought to silence it. You are a remarkable woman, Maggie, and my muse. I'll never forget you as long as I live. Thank you. KPM

PREFACE

A Journal Found

By way of introduction, I feel I should explain how the enclosed text came into my possession. I've also included a few additional notes which explain what was necessary to bring it to completion. First, I am an accountant by trade and training, but I've been a junk hound for most of my adult life having spent years rummaging through flea markets, garage sales and junk shops as a means of release from the tedium of the numbers I've dealt with for more than twenty-five years. What I look for mostly are pieces of antique jewelry, china, pottery and glass, small items that can be easily placed in the house or resold on eBay. It was during one of these events that I came across the enclosed document. The following are the particulars.

I was on a weekend treasure hunt in northeastern Pennsylvania in the fall of 2004 to attend a "Giant Flea Market," not looking for anything in particular, but nevertheless hopeful of coming across the ever elusive "flea market find." By midday, I had found a Carltonware pot, an early Christian Dior brooch and a Mdina Maltese paperweight from 1934 (hallmarked and dated on the bottom). The Mdina paperweight was in a box lot, which I rarely have any interest in, but it was clear that no one recognized the value of it, so I bought the whole thing knowing the paperweight alone was worth no less than fifty or seventy-five dollars. The box itself was approximately two feet long, two feet deep, one and a half feet wide and had the name of an egg company printed on the sides. The other items in the box included a few tattered men's garments, some dishes and other commonplace household odds and ends, but since I was only interested in the paperweight, I didn't pay much attention to the other items until I got home later that afternoon and unpacked the box.

When I went through the remainder of its contents, I discovered the manuscript at the bottom of the box tied with twine and wrapped in a dusty, regional New York State newspaper dated June 2002. The pages it contained were handwritten in blue and black ink. Not quite as big as an average telephone book nor as heavy, it was bound by what appeared to be the remains of a three-hole binder notebook of the kind typically used by college students a decade or so ago, but with the binding clasps removed from the inside.

Ordinarily, I have no interest in documents and this one was certainly not old, but for the sake of thoroughness, I unwrapped the parcel and thumbed through the contents thinking I might come across some rare stamps or postcards. One really never knows what one may find, even in the most unlikely of places. What I found, however, were not old postcards or stamps, but what appeared, at first glance, to be a journal...but not just any journal. I was riveted from the very first words on the opening page, and took it out on my front porch to read the entire document. I became so consumed by what it contained that it wasn't until I had finished the entire volume well on into the night (or more accurately, close to the next morning), that I realized I was drenched in my own sweat, my hands having given in to a slight tremble by what just simply could not be real. I didn't sleep at all that night and had only uneasy sleep for several nights after.

It was during one of those nights of uneasy sleep that I finally realized what I had to do. I had to go public with it. The following text is the result. But before continuing, there are a few things the reader should understand. First, for the sake of my respect for humanity and avoidance of any legal trouble, my conscience has required me to change the names of people and places named in the original document, along with some minor details regarding a number of specific events in order to maintain the privacy of those involved, both dead and alive. Above all considerations, it's important that their memories, as well as their families, are protected. The last thing I would want to result by doing what I have done here would be for droves of reporters, paranormal investigators or wannabe ghouls to converge on the parties involved or their loved ones. It has always been a standard of my life that my conscience takes precedence over the lure of dollars so not even America's Mysteries, the Sci-Fi Channel, or Oprah Winfrey herself, could ever make me divulge the true details.

Secondly, I've had to restructure the text to make it readable to the average person in areas of dialogue, formatting, paragraphing, spelling, etc. I did this with the indispensable aid of a professional editor to whom I will forever be indebted for his help in bringing the text to life. In its original form, each smaller notebook contained in the larger manuscript seemed to have been written as one long "stream of consciousness" type of work over a short period of time and was evident throughout that, at the time of its writing, the writer did not intend the thoughts, ideas and events contained therein to be made available for public consumption. Thus, the reformatting, as well as the other editorial actions, was absolutely necessary to bring the manuscript to its current state.

The original text also contained numerous scratch outs, illegible words (giving the impression that they were written in a state of extreme haste) and, in places, was marred to a blur by numerous large water stains. As such, certain substitutions were required to maintain both the flow of the dialogue and the continuity of the story, but please be advised that these substitutions were made only where absolutely necessary to the completion of the project, with careful attention and every effort made to retain the integrity of the original. I have also divided the text into chapters with titles that seemed appropriate to the content. Then, to further highlight the complexity of emotions portrayed in the original text, I have added selected quotations culled from both contemporary and historical sources to these chapter headings (as well as the opening and closing pages) as they would be reflected from my point of view, rather than that of the participants themselves. In the end, I can only say that I have already drawn my own conclusions about the content of the journal. Now it is up to the individual reader to decide for themselves but, upon my advice, hopefully not at night and especially not alone.

Daniel Vincent Carruthers, C.P.A.
Montclair, New Jersey
May 2005

BOOK ONE

THE PRECIPICE

All day, staring at the ceiling
Making friends with shadows on my walls
All night, hearing voices telling
That I should get some sleep
Because tomorrow may be good for something
Hold on,
Feeling like I'm heading for a . . . breakdown
And I don't know why
But I'm not crazy, I'm just a little unwell
I know, right now you can't tell
But stay awhile and maybe then you'll see
A different side of me
I'm not crazy, I'm just a little impaired
I know, right now you don't care
But soon enough, you're gonna think of me
And how I used to be . . . me.

Unwell--Rob Thomas

CHAPTER 1

Unwell

"...then black despair. The shadow of a starless night was thrown over the world in which I moved alone."

-Percy Bysshe Shelley,
Early 19th Century Romantic Poet &
husband of Mary Shelley, author of "Frankenstein," from
The Revolt of Islam-Dedication (st.6)

January 2002

God, I'm so afraid! I can hardly breathe. I don't know what to do anymore or where to turn for help, or even if there can be any help for me. Could there be anyone out there who knows fear the way I do? Are they still alive? If they are, they'll know the hell I've lived in these past months, every day, every second and at this very moment as I struggle to hold my pen straight to keep it from shaking out of control, someone to know what it's like to live with the kind of relentless panic that makes me want to run and hide, knowing full well there is nowhere to run, nowhere to hide. But that would be incredibly selfish, wouldn't it? Inhuman, really. My conscience would never let me wish this even on my worst enemy. Martin is the closet thing I have to someone who might understand, but I've kept so much from him to try and protect him. Then what little he does know, he doesn't remember. I guess that's for the best. It's all just like one long nightmare for him, fading day by day as he gets better, and poor Jenny, the brief glimpse of it that she saw almost sent her over the edge. I could never burden her life any further with this. She's done so much for Martin already. It would be unconscionable, beyond unforgivable.

I've been cursed by so many things, not the least being an unfailing ability to hold everything tightly inside myself. It's served me well lately, though. Up 'til now, I've managed to protect those around me that I hold so close, even at the cost of my own sanity. I'm sweating so hard right now. It's running down the back of my neck, dripping down my forehead, running into my eyes, stinging them, mixing with my own shameful tears as they run down my face, droplets of myself splashing the page as I try to get this all down, or are they tears? I just don't know anymore. I don't know who I am, or even if I am. I'm so cold, chills of an invisible current from somewhere beyond myself running over my flesh making the hair stand up on my arms, and my nerves...twitching through my brain as this unholy current works its way down through every inch of my being making the nerve endings snap like tiny light bulbs bursting from a sudden surge of high voltage electricity. It's like this all the time and has been for so long that I have to keep my bowels on constant guard, afraid they'll get away from me like a small child in the night, terrified of the unknown thing in the bottom of the closet, or the monster under the bed that may not stay there...but I'm not a child. I'm an adult, and for me, the thing won't go away when the sun comes up. It'll be waiting for me, waiting until I'm dead, and possibly even beyond.

I've been such a fool, taken so much for granted. I just want to be normal again, or as normal as I ever was. I watch people on the street, soccer moms, businessmen, teenagers, little old ladies with blue hair, and find myself wishing more than anything that I was one of them...any of them...anyone but myself. I'm jealous of what they don't know. In their everyday lives they have the luxury of ordinary kinds of fear, car wrecks, plane crashes...disease. They routinely think that the worst they have to fear is death, but that's not true. There's more. I know...much more. God! I feel so abandoned...so alone, clinging to my gun...just in case.

I used to think that grief was the worst of all human emotions, back in the days when I thought it would swallow me whole. I know better now. At least my father is safe and at peace, but for me, having managed to come this far, I realize I was so very deadly wrong. Fear is the cruelest feeling in the human vocabulary of emotions. It's the cancer of the mind, of the soul, black cells multiplying by the thousands inside me every day, gnawing away at what's left of whatever made me feel like I was a man. I can feel them again now, thick black clots breaking off inside me, dissolving in my blood, running through my veins, seeping from my pores, choking me with that awful smell, the smell of my own fear.

From the first time I saw that house, I should've known. Some primal instinct inside tried to warn me, but I didn't listen. Maybe somewhere in the back of my mind, I knew all the time it would come to a showdown between us. It was going to be either it or me, and as I sit here wallowing in my own sweat, it looks like it, or my gun, will win. I'm so tired of living with an unknown that takes such delight in having shown its ugliness to me, wanting me to know it as if we were lovers discovering each other's bodies for the first time, making me feel dirty and...violated as if it were raping my sanity and my humanity. I think I must feel fear as only the rarest of human beings can. I pity them...and myself for having discovered an evil more base than any human being should ever have to face...and letting it beat me, making me a prisoner in my own mind, alone with the knowledge of things that transcend the human soul and the monstrous acts committed by men who create them.

It knows I'm writing about it. The hair on the back of my neck just stood up. It's here again, toying with me. I can't stop my teeth from clattering no matter how tightly I clench my jaw. I'm not sure what to do right now. Oddly enough, when I know it's here, I still try to convince myself that it's not real, that somehow I've found myself in some cosmic 'reality TV' episode of *The Twilight Zone* or *The Outer Limits,* but in the darkest spaces of everything that still makes me human, I know I'm not. This is no movie. It's all too horribly real. There'll no safe haven when the lights come up. For me, there'll only be the cold reality of mind-bending, body-numbing fear; fear for my immortal soul. I have to stop here, close my eyes and wait until it goes away—if it goes away. It tends to come and go these days. I don't think it has what it wants yet, or I wouldn't be here to write this.

❋ ❋ ❋

It's gone away again...for now, but it's left me drifting back to the idea of the soul. Since this all began, I've realized that most people go through their daily lives completely unaware. They never consider things such as the human soul, theirs or anyone else's for that matter. Even the most devout have only the most abstract concepts of it, as if it were a wisp of air, ethereal and fleeting. I don't think I particularly blame them. I've come to believe that their fanciful ideas are simply a result of the limitations of our mortal selves, our bodily beings, but at least that's something, and they're safe. I'm not. After all, not everyone has had the privilege of crossing the barriers between life and death, heaven and hell, the way I have. Lucky me!

Others don't believe in the human soul at all. Having had my own faith run through the meat grinder by the randomness of life on earth, I used to be one of those, but I'm a true believer now. I know it exists. I live every day in fear for my soul and the souls of those I love because I know now what souls can become. I've seen them, heard their voices. I've felt their touch on my skin, but it's even worse than that...much worse, because not all of them are harmless or good. Casper, the friendly ghost, yeah right! I'd laugh if I weren't so afraid I'd cry again and I can't afford to break down right now. But make no mistake there are those that are here for no other reason than to hurt us. Malignant and rotted, they thrive on the evil they create as they seek to consume the souls of others and make them suffer. They delight in the suffering of others because it sustains them. My skin crawls even to write about it. Then when I feel it near me and can smell its breath as I have for months now, constantly hammering at my senses, I have to doubt every sound, every movement, every thought and perception. It's even forced me to doubt my own sanity because it's easier to think that I've gone stark raving mad than to believe what I know to be true: that evil exists right beside us every day, surrounding us, waiting patiently in the cold, dark recesses of the human soul. Even more than that, what happens when evil bound in human form is released from the body? What then? God help me, I know the answer now. I need another drink. I still have to exist, at least for now, even if I'm reduced to clinging to the barest, most elemental animal instinct in nature to sustain me—the will to survive.

❋ ❋ ❋

I'm calmer now and have some sensibility about me. With a clear head, I still can't help but try to think it through, get my head around it all as best as I can. No matter what I do, I keep coming back to the same thing—the fear. Fear has got to be the evil soul's strongest weapon, the way it can use it against you, driving you beyond all rationality. Then when you've become consumed by it body and soul, you realize, as I did at first, that there are really only two options of escape for someone in its grip...like I am right now. Suicide, or true, drooling, howling insanity.

Once you've come that far and your mind and spirit are bent so far out of shape from your ordinary reality that you don't even recognize yourself, it becomes clear how someone living under the pressure of such an unrelenting fear can be forced to choose between the two. I've had time to reflect on the suffocating feeling of a trapped animal it creates, understanding it like no one else. I guess that's why I'm writing this, grasping wildly in the dark for a third option that may offer some hope for my survival, even if only for a little while. It's my pressure valve opening in one last desperate bid to keep myself from the other two.

I need to put this down, what I've felt, seen, what I've done and why...or lose my mind. It's my only focus, my only concentration. Whether it's ever read by anyone else is unimportant. I just want to keep from putting my gun in my mouth or having the state take me away in a straightjacket. I'm not sure which would be worse, but I don't know how much longer I can stand this. The way I feel right now, I know it can't be long, maybe only weeks, possibly only days. Then I worry about what would happen to Martin. The thought of him alone and at its mercy terrifies me, even more than it does for myself. I just know one thing. I will not give up his soul...or mine...not without a fight. If I have to die, I'll die fighting in a way that'll deprive it of its final victory over me. If it goes that way, I just pray that it'll be in a state of grace. I have to believe that even if I have to do us both, God'll understand that we died a good death and finally embrace me in a blanket of light, because I've learned in these last few months that there are worse things than death. I've seen the face of it and know its true nature. Worst of all, I know it's here and it's coming for me again, for both of us, coming back to get whatever it is that it wants, so time is not on my side. I'm having another panic attack. I have to put my head down for awhile. I'll come back to this when I wake up—assuming I do wake up.

Morning is here and I guess I managed to sleep a little. It's hard to tell sometimes. I may have just been lying there in a narcotic- and alcohol-induced trance, afraid to let go. I can't really tell, but I can see the light of the winter sun through the window, feel its warmth on my face, so I guess I'm must still be alive. It doesn't seem to show itself in the mornings, small miracles I guess. Sleep for me these days is like a double-edged sword. I'm afraid to go to sleep thinking I might not ever wake up again; then I'm afraid of waking up to find that nothing has changed. But let me get back to where I left off in the best way I know how.

I'm going to have to take this one step at a time. My mind has been so fractured from months of struggling with a knowledge that no human should ever be forced to comprehend that the focus a thorough, methodical approach would afford is all I can think of to get it down before it's too late. I suppose I should start with who I am, how I got to this place and how I became its prisoner. Maybe if I put it all down and go over it again in writing, I'll find something I've missed, something I failed to do when I tried to destroy it, but then...can one ever really destroy evil?

Maybe I'll see something in my life to this point that has made me the target I've become. No matter what the end result, it'll help me to collect myself, even if only temporarily, and allow me to breathe for a while, to relive what good memories I have, brief moments of love and freedom, pride and accomplishment, "Putting my effects in order," so to speak. It can help remind me of times before the darkness overcame my life and my mind making me break into cold sweats when there's a creak in the floorboards thinking that it's coming for me, tremble when there's a noise in the house thinking that it's beside me, and shake uncontrollably when the wind is at the windows thinking I can hear it call my name.

Evil is the most insidious creature imaginable because it can live forever. It has all the patience it needs to lie in wait until it's ready to strike, and it always strikes when its prey is at its weakest and most vulnerable to its tricks. It seems only now, in hindsight, that the traumas and tragedies of everyday life that I always took for granted as the worst that could happen to me seem so insignificant. Unfortunately, it's only now that I've felt the breath of the foulest, most godless evil imaginable on the back of my neck that I realize it but, of course, now it's too late.

※ ※ ※

My name is Terrence Arthur Chagford and I'm the Chief of Police of Jennisburg, New York, a quiet, unassuming little burg. Just another one of those small upstate towns of under a thousand people named after its founder back in seventeen hundred and something, famous for nothing more than its maple syrup, apples, peaches and cows. I was born here forty-one years ago to very loving parents. My mother, God love her, is a psychiatric nurse at the hospital about ten miles over in the nearest large town of Henriston, just about to retire, and not a moment too soon if you ask me.

My father was a state police officer, a good man and a great cop, not one of those miscreants with a gun and a badge who get off on bullying people under color of law just because they can. He always said that those kinds of cops were only trying to make up for their own personal deficiencies and the job was the only thing that made them feel that they had any power. The whole big gun-little dick sort of theory. It was always, "To Protect and Serve," with Arthur Chagford, and do it with respect and a sense of dignity that let people know they were in good hands. He was a decent man who respected people and was respected by them for it. I remember him teaching me that from my earliest memories when we'd go fishing together on the river or hiking in the mountains. Even just walking down a street in town with him, people would stop to put their hands out for him to shake, smiling the kind of smile that can't be faked, no matter how hard one might try, genuine, real, warm. I can see it so clearly in my mind now. They would take his hand in theirs to shake it then put their other hand over top of his so that they were holding his hand in both of theirs. People just don't do that unless they think you're special. Their eyes would always shine as they looked into his, honest and unafraid, open and accepting. I always got the feeling that they felt he'd done them a good turn or had protected them in some way that they'd never forget.

That was my dad. I loved him very much. I guess I probably shouldn't use the past tense here because I still do, and I miss him terribly, even after all these years. Especially now. As I sit here I can't help but wonder what kind of man I might've become had he not been killed leaving me the half-formed human being that I am. Would this even be happening to me? *Focus, Terry, Focus.* I have to keep saying that to myself. I can feel it welling up inside me again, the panic, the anxiety. I can't let it get to me here or I'll never finish this. If I do, it'll paralyze me. I can't let that happen, not now that I've finally found the balls to do it. I've got to beat it down and move on.

❋ ❋ ❋

I was just a regular kid of the times, not particularly special in any obvious way. I ate peanut butter and jelly or bologna and cheese sandwiches on Wonder bread out of my Batman lunch box, watched Wonderama and Soupy Sales on a black and white TV. You know, that kind of kid, just bigger than most my age, a little chubby and kind of clumsy. It wasn't until high school that I seem to have surprised everyone, including myself, and became…not so ordinary anymore. It's what put me on the path I've stumbled down ever since. I call it "my metamorphosis." It seemed like, almost overnight, I wasn't chubby anymore or clumsy, or shy and backward. I also seemed to have found my voice and, to my utter amazement, people started to listen, my teachers, my friends, my parents. That was when my grades began to soar and what would later become my athletic gifts started becoming apparent. I remember when the track and field coach came to my house to speak to my parents about joining the team. He told them that my regular gym teacher had asked him to come and watch me in class to see if he thought he could develop my potential. I remember thinking to myself then, *What potential?*

The whole thing mystified me so I just did what they told me, pleased for the attention. Looking back now, I can't shake the idea that it left me with an insatiable hunger for accomplishment, craving approval at every turn, while at the same time setting me up for the feelings of failure that would follow my life with an all too alarming consistency. I ended up graduating high school with the second highest grades in my class. "Bringing up the rear," I call it. I still got both academic and athletic scholarships, though, and decided on the State University at Albany. I guess I could have gone anywhere. I had plenty of offers, but I wanted to stay as close to my mother as I could, for both our sakes. It was a bad time then. It would have been for anyone who'd lost someone they loved so suddenly and so senselessly.

The unimaginable had found its way to our door in the form of two uniformed state troopers. My father had been killed in a high speed car chase, and my mother needed me, so I wanted…needed to stay close to home. We needed each other, really. I don't think either of us ever really recovered from it. People don't recover from things like that. It just lives inside you in a little box, opening up every now and again to remind you that it'll hurt you until the day you die. Time seemed to have stood still so long for me then, like my head was encased in concrete. Months went by before I realized I was still alive and that it was real, not just a bad dream. I have my mother to thank for bringing me out of it...by force, her hands pushing me out of the front door when the day came for me to leave, pulling me by my arm to the bus that would take me to Albany.

"I don't want to go. Please, Ma, I'm not ready yet...don't make me go!" I begged, sobbing like a child half my age. "I'm afraid!"

"You have to do this, Terry. You're all I have now and he wants so much for you to make something of yourself. It's his dream for you. Do it for me...and for him. He loves you so much, Terry. Get on that bus!" she cried as pushed me up the steps. It wasn't until I looked out of the window as the bus was pulling away that it dawned on me. She wasn't able to speak of him in the past tense,yet...

❋ ❋ ❋

I must have drifted off somewhere for a while. I don't remember writing that last bit. But that's just the way it happened. I'm soaking wet now, all down the front of my shirt. I have to change into dry clothes and throw some cold water on my face if I'm going to continue. I don't even know what time it is. Time just seems to shift under my feet, like an undertow in a storm, eroding reality into something I no longer recognize. Maybe I took one pill too many. All I know is that it's still light out; I need to get a grip on myself and keep anyone else from knowing what's been going on. Martin should be coming down soon anyway. I can't let him see me this way.

❋ ❋ ❋

Martin has gone to bed early. He does almost every night. He's still on the mend, so by 9:00 P.M. he's worn out by the day's struggles. It was a quiet day in town, and even quieter yet since I got home—alarmingly quiet. It sounds like what I imagine a tightly wound rubber band must sound like right before it snaps in your face. I'm going to try and get as much done as I can tonight because no one knows better than I do the potential for unexpected events that tomorrow may bring. My head is still clear. I can thank the cold weather for that, nothing like a bracingly cold wind to pull you out of a haze, substance induced or otherwise. I guess I'll pick up with my years at school. That seems to be the time when I was closest to reaching my goals, but even then, it all came crashing down around my head. Anyway...once I'd come out of the shock my father's death, the only thing left for me to do was to try to be the best that I could to make him proud of me. I chose Criminal Justice as my major in his honor. Although, looking back now, maybe it was more to see if I could be him, replacing his loss with myself.

❋ ❋ ❋

My first year away was a hard road to acceptance, alternately rocky and pocked with deep trenches of blackness that forced me to take to my bed every few weeks, staying there with the lights off until it passed. After that, I decided that the only way I would survive would be to channel all my grief, anger and loneliness into school work and sports. I got that idea from a book I read on coping with grief. Sometimes I think that book saved my life, although for what it was saved, I'm still at loss to understand.

I kept as much of it from my mother as I could. She had her own grief to deal with. I felt guilty enough having to leave her alone, so the idea of making her cope with my grief on top of her own was unthinkable. Funny, sometimes, how one's love for others can block out whatever else they might be feeling. I guess that was the first time I felt like a 'protector.' It made me feel good. I found strength in it that helped me make it through, probably seeming to the outside world like an 'All American' success story, while on the inside being nothing more than a hollow, pointless, directionless, empty shell of not quite a man.

I did have my rewards during those years, though. As it turned out, my channeling exercises led me to being chosen for the 1980 Summer Olympics team for the pole vault and broad jump. My mother was so proud when she read it in the newspaper. I could hardly understand her through her tears when she called to tell me about the article. I didn't even know the final decisions had been made, but more importantly, it was the last time I heard or saw her cry. To me, that was my real accomplishment. It's not that she didn't cry when I wasn't around. I'm sure she did, and often. It's just that it made me feel that I'd given her at least one reason not to cry.

❀ ❀ ❀

I'm drifting again, losing time, like I'm not really here but somehow hovering above my own life, watching it but completely powerless to change it. It's strange how the past can come back to you and seem so vividly alive when the present seems so hopeless and the future seems non-existent. I saw the same thing happen to Grace when we had our 'little talk.' Now I know how she felt. I can empathize with the wisdom of her age, but I'll get to that later. If I can get that far. For now, I'd better move on, back to the Olympics.

❀ ❀ ❀

It was 1980 and the world was in a particularly tense state of self-induced political distress. The Cold War was still arctic, even though the threat of nuclear war had taken a back seat. Mexican stand-offs, posturing and boycotts were the current trend so participation by the United States and fifty other countries from the Moscow Olympiad ended up being withdrawn because of the Soviet invasion of Afghanistan. Do I have the best fucking luck in the world or what? You really gotta laugh sometimes because I was having an increasingly rare good spell then. I even had the nerve to dare and think I could win, but fate apparently had other ideas. I did eventually end up going to Los Angeles with the team in '84, but by then I was older, not in as good a shape and suffering one of the blackest spells I'd had up to that point. I managed to rally for a little while right before the events, but the coach and I both knew it was too late.

Ironically, I came back home to a hero's welcome for my two bronze medals. Go figure, third place. Like I said, it's the story of my sad fucking life to 'bring up the rear.' No Wheaties box covers for me. Endorsements went to superstars and I was only...well...an 'also ran' or a 'has been' or a changeling of something in-between the two, and in events nobody really cared about anyway. After that I decided that I wouldn't try again. Sports achievements were a useless accomplishment. So many things felt useless to me after that. I just said, "Fuck it!" and gave up. The black spells, although less frequent from then on, became longer in duration. But when they did come, they were more like 'black holes' than 'black spells.' They got so bad sometimes that I couldn't really tell if they would ever end, much less when. The only positive thing I can say about that time was that, by then, I'd at least learned how to hide them from almost everyone, except my mother. We didn't talk about it for along time, but I know she knew. Mothers always do—particularly mine.

With my Los Angeles 'triumph' behind me, I managed to summon up the last shred of what my mother, in trying to dissuade me, called my "… youthful idealism and enthusiasm." But, stubborn as I've been all my life, I held fast and fierce to the feeling that I could still make myself useful in some way. It seemed like it was all I had left to keep me breathing. I figured that if I made some real impact on other people's lives, it might make me a worthwhile human being instead of the walking, breathing carcass I'd become. If I couldn't be happy for myself, I had to at least offer myself up and do the best I could for others, thinking that maybe their lives might fare a little better through me so that the dwindling core of goodness I still felt inside wouldn't be completely wasted. I'd hoped I might find some salvation in that, by being a 'protector' again.

My father never wanted me to be a trooper like he was. He wanted better for me as any parent would, so I tried to get into the FBI. The upshot of that was—that's right, you guessed it— they didn't want me. Who knows, maybe my psychological exam gave them a glimpse of what was to come. Whatever it was, the 'other' federal police didn't seem to have a problem with it, so there I was, an 'also ran' yet again. You've really got to laugh at it all. I'm nothing if not consistent. Nevertheless, the ATF gave me confidence again, and a purpose, and a reason to live. Little did I or anyone else at the time know, but in those next few years, my 'quiet' agency was just about to heat up to white hot and, not least of all, for me, nothing would ever be the same again because of it.

※ ※ ※

David Koresh and his Branch Davidians had created a compound of allegedly 'dangerous subversives' in a place called Waco, Texas. It was said that they had an arsenal of weapons in a compound there and were hurting children. The shameful fiasco that later became euphemistically known as "The Waco Incident" was approaching its deadly and disastrous conclusion while the rest of the south was ablaze with flames from the burning of black churches being set by one or more racist lunatics on a rampage of hate. True to form, I wasn't assigned to that primary Waco project, thank God, but pulled what was thought to be at the time, a lower priority assignment, investigating the burning of the churches.

I still don't understand the logic there. Sketchy allegations of guns and white parents supposedly hurting their children justified the government burning and killing them all, but the random burning out of decent, hardworking, churchgoing people on a routine basis by a lunatic fringe hardly made a ripple, left to back page news and tail end stories. It's a funny thing about 'threats' in a multi-media world, either real or imagined. They can become so subjective and prime for being worked out of all reality by 'spin doctors' who spend their lives turning truth into lies and lies into truth to the point where no one can tell the difference anymore. I guess, in some minds, the life of a little white child is still more valuable that of a little black one, so no one ever really heard about the little black one. Did they? Gotta love it don'tcha? Jeeze, I just got such a bitter taste in my mouth. I'm gonna get a drink to wash it out before it gets too comfortable in there.

Anyway…my team and I traveled throughout the south for months, always seeming to be one step behind the arsonists. My men were good men, but the frustration we were all feeling kept building until it had us all at the boiling point. Then, one night while we were staying in a tiny town in southwestern Tennessee not far from Memphis, they struck right under our noses. Less than five miles away from where we had stopped for the night, another church was torched. For the first time, we were on the spot and leapt on it with all we had. That night, and the crushing baggage I'd carry away from it, would change my life forever...again.

As we approached the site, the dark night sky was already glowing with the surreal light of the white clapboard church, simple and small, being devoured by flames like a legion of demons spewing forth from hell, dancing gaily at their newfound freedom. But even worse than the sight of it were the sounds. When I got out of the car, all I could hear were voices, shouting, screaming to us that there were people still in there. God, it still hurts me so badly I can't breathe. Each time I think of it my heart bleeds out into a river of sorrow, flowing from a half-healed wound of guilt and loss, tearing it open daily so that it can continue to live inside me.

There was a young woman named Cordelia Weston, a victim of domestic abuse, and her eight-year-old daughter, Angelica, still in the burning building. They'd been left homeless and were living there in a few unused rooms upstairs in exchange for maintenance work. They were trapped upstairs in the back when the fire was set underneath them. Just as my men and I approached the action, I could see the woman being carried out by one of the few local firefighters who'd arrived not long before we did. They'd found her after she'd managed to make her way as far as the stairs. Blinded by smoke and covered with soot, she was screaming and crying with the kind of unrestrained abandon that could only mean one thing—her child was still in there. As long as I live, I will never...never forget the pleading sound of her voice, her anguished, shrill cries. "My baby! My baby! Somebody, please save my baby!" she screamed, smoke streaming from her singed hair and blackened nightgown as she fought her rescuer to get back into the blazing building.

That poor woman. It seems that when the fire broke out, the little girl ran and hid out of...fear. Without even giving myself a second to think, I did the one thing I had been so rigorously trained not to do, but what I knew my father would have done. I ran in. I could hear my men shouting at me from behind as they followed with our equipment, but I was too fast. Fueled with an eruption of energy I didn't know I still had, I flew through that door. When I got to the bottom of the stairs, I heard the little girl's voice crying with a terror she should've never had to know.

"Mama! Mama!" Using muscles I'd forgotten I had for ten years, I shot up the stairs, taking them three at a time until I was more than halfway up. The last thing I remember was getting the briefest glimpse of her frightened little face illuminated by the flames that had imprisoned her as she hid in the back of the linen closet, seeing the helpless panic in her eyes as she saw me. I reached out my hand out to her. Just as I opened my mouth to call to her, "I'm coming, baby," I felt the burning rafter come crashing down on me, catching me between my neck and shoulder, the stairs giving way beneath my feet and that horrible dreamlike feeling of falling further and further into darkness with the certain knowledge that I'd failed her, failed us both.

When I woke up in the hospital, the little girl was dead. As I laid there with my broken right collarbone, right hand and forearm, broken left ankle and foot, fractured right knee and scattered spots of second and third degree burns all over my upper body and legs, with a concussion thrown in for good measure, I wished I had died in there with her. But it wouldn't be that easy for me. I was doomed to live the rest of my life with the big L on my forehead . . . branded forever . . . *Loser!*

I'll always believe in my heart that her death was my fault. I can't get away from it. I should have done more, run faster, been...better. That poor little girl. Her death has burned a cavernous, bottomless pit in my soul that will last until the day I die. I relive it at least once every day, usually at night when I'm alone and can hear the echoes of her tiny voice crying out, over and over, "Mama, Mama." I couldn't sleep in the days that followed, dreaming that I could still see the terror in her eyes, beckoning me to save her, pleading. That makes two now. My father's death was the first. He did what he thought was best to feed us, keep a roof over our heads and live like a man of honor the only way he knew how, and he died because of it. I wanted so much to be like him. Now there was Angelica. Her death was my own personal failure, an everlasting mark of inadequacy on my conscience. My shirt is wet again. My head hurts...and my eyes, but I've got to get past this tonight.

Cordelia Weston came to the hospital a few days after the funeral. She was a thin, frail-looking woman of no more than thirty-five with smooth cocoa skin, spotted in places by scorch marks left by the spitting sparks. She wore a black turban to cover the places where the fire had burned her hair to the scalp. Her face was a portrait of blinding grief and pointless, endless loss. A portrait that I knew all too well. My mother wore it for years after my father was killed. I still wear it myself when no one is around. She brought me flowers and a school picture of Angelica, a pretty, bright eyed, smiling little girl with dark skin, pigtails and brightly colored barrettes. As I looked at it, I knew that her senseless loss, the waste of her human goodness, had broken my spirit in ways that the rafter could never have broken my body.

"I want to...thank you...for trying to save...my baby," she said haltingly with a light southern accent, taking my hand as she fought back tears through eyes nearly swollen shut from days of them, "...and tell you...how very sorry I am that you got hurt so badly tryin'. You're a very brave man, Mr. Chagford. I will never forget you." The unselfishness of her words and the kindness in her voice shattered whatever was left of my already brittle composure. This woman who had lost the most precious gift life had to give her had the presence of mind and generosity of heart to come see me, even though I'd failed. I didn't know what I could say to her that would give her any peace.

"I will hold her smile in my heart until the day I die, Mrs. Weston. I promise," I said, my throat sore and swollen from the smoke and the heat, my voice little more than a groaning whisper. I can still feel the soft pressure of her hand on mine, her warm tears on my skin as she held me to her. I had to be sedated after she left, but I've kept that promise to this day...unflinchingly, unfailingly everyday. That was when I first started drinking. It offered me only the slightest relief from the pain, but it allowed me to sleep some. When you're desperate, you have to take what you can get.

The pill-taking thing has been more gradual, in cases of extreme pain. I've only begun taking them regularly in the last few months, on and off mostly, but more and more since the first time it came after me. I'm sure it loves when I'm in pain and I've got more than enough to feed its hunger. Maybe that's why it's waited for me. I know it's not a new evil. It's been around for a while, at least a hundred years, but it could be older. It had to come from somewhere before this...had to learn its tricks somewhere.

❄ ❄ ❄

An analyst told me once that my drinking and taking pills "isn't the answer," but when I asked him what the answer was, what do you think he said? "I don't have any answers," while charging me a hundred dollars an hour for his sage advice, the thieving son of a bitch. I could've got that damn advice from Oprah on TV...for free. "Then don't mother fucking tell me my way isn't the answer unless you have something better to offer to replace it. I'm in pain, you fucking asshole, so if you don't have any goddamn answers what the hell do I need you for? Booze and pills are cheaper...and at least they do the job without taking Caribbean vacations on my hard-earned money, jerk off! " is what I told him in return, kicking the chair over as I stomped out of his priggish, over-decorated office, slamming the door behind me.

I'm going to put my head in my hands and sob now for a while. The wound is open again and it's...killing me. I need a pill and a drink, too. I'll pick up where I left off when I can, when I'm feeling better, maybe later on tonight. What little sleep I've been getting lately hasn't been serving me well, hardly at all really. I can't put my head down or I'll lose track again. I can't afford to lose any time just in case it comes back tonight. I've started to think that it's trying to wear me down to the point that when I do sleep, it'll be unshakable so that it can go after Martin and I won't be there to protect him. The hourglass never stops running for me and I've got to keep an ever watchful eye out for signs. It's the only plan I have.

❄ ❄ ❄

I'm better now. I've taken my pills and had a good, long drink. I stood out in the cold for a while without my coat. It revived me some, so I guess I'd better get on with this before my head gets too heavy and my eyes get too clouded to write.

❄ ❄ ❄

I was in the hospital for a few weeks before they released me to my own devices, such as they were, with my disability and pension still intact, even though what I did broke the rules. There I was, thirty-five years old and out of a job. They said my injuries were too severe to expect a full duty recovery because I'd never be able to run as fast, lift as much or move as quickly as the job required. They were right, I couldn't. Not without enormous effort and grimacing discomfort. But by then I'd lost my heart for it anyway, and the thought of being chained to a desk like a wounded animal in a cage, alone with my misery, was out of the question.

I must confess here, I've always wished we'd caught the rotten son-of-a-bitch responsible for that fire. Watching him fry for it would've at least given me some sense of justice. I think that was the first time in my life I'd ever truly had a taste of hate, the thick bile of festering injustice welling up from my guts into my throat, ready to spew itself out at those who turn their heads away from it. They did recover an unidentified male body in the ruins, burned beyond identification. I'll never know if it was the arsonist or just another poor soul seeking shelter unobserved for the night. Marginal lives can be that way. I've learned that, having become one of them myself, and "...seeking out the poorer quarters where the ragged people go..." The worst part is that I'll never get my chance to spit on his grave, or even have the satisfaction of knowing that he's really dead. The way my luck runs, the dead man they found probably was just another lonely soul with no where else to go, like me, and the real murderer is still out there somewhere having a beer and laughing at me.

After a few more weeks of climbing the walls in some dump of a motel in Memphis, letting it all weigh on me, I looked over my resources, found that I enough money to feel as secure as I needed to be and decided to do the one truly selfish thing I think I've ever done in my life. I couldn't go home and face those I loved and respected looking at me, judging me, only to find me lacking or worse yet, pitying me like a three-legged dog with an ear torn off, so I ran away from it all...from my guilt...from my pain. It wasn't until later that I realized that there'd still be my own judgments to face when I looked at myself in the mirror and found myself lacking, seeing everyday for myself what a three-legged dog that I was.

When I got to Europe I decided to try and drink it all away. It worried my mother half to death. That's something I'll always regret, but at the time, I was just too blinded by self-pity and vacancy of purpose to care anymore. I went to London first and drank their strong beer until it drained from my body of its own accord. I was a dirty, unshaven, ale-soaked wretch by the time I got to Paris a few months later, which is still little more than one big blur. I'm not really sure when or how I left Paris. All I know is that I landed in Spain where the booze was so cheap I could drown myself in it and almost did, literally. I was in a hospital there in Seville for a while. It seems I hadn't eaten in days and was floating in alcohol when I collapsed on the floor of some dive bar on the fringe of the city weighing twenty pounds lighter than when I had left home. *...running scared, laying low, seeking out the poorer quarters where the ragged people go, looking for the places only they would know...* I remember the words from the old Simon and Garfunkel song played in my head as I went down, signaling me, as it has for years, that there was another black hole looming beyond the horizon, waiting to pull me in head first.

When I woke up a few days later, after having been sufficiently medicated, I got a message from the States. The doctor in Seville had contacted the U.S. Embassy in Madrid. They, in turn, contacted my mother through channels in New York City. She'd called the hospital and left word for me to contact her immediately.

When I was released a week later, my conscience got the better of me. I called her and was carefully and calmly informed in her most professionally practiced voice that she'd spoken to the Police Chief in Jennisburg, who just happened to be a buddy of my father's. They'd agreed that it would be best if I came home immediately to take a recently vacated officer's position. It seems that one of my old buddies from high school was leaving the force and moving to Florida to raise his family near his in-laws and they needed someone to fill the spot. It was agreed beforehand that, although my injuries may have disqualified me from federal duty, I would still be perfectly qualified for a small town job and it was hinted that I might move up quickly because of my experience and my father's connections. As much as she tried to contain it, the tone of her voice was one I'd heard only one other time before, after that knock on the door eighteen years earlier. Overwhelmed by guilt for having worried her so badly and leaving her alone again, I agreed to come home and take the job. By then guilt was like a Siamese twin attached to my side at all times, reminding me constantly that it had its needs, too. That's how I got here, who I was and who I am.

❀ ❀ ❀

I spent the next three years patrolling the eight-square-mile area that comprises my quiet, postcard picturesque little town of Jennisburg, looking out for under-age drinking, the smell of marijuana, graffiti and other sorts of vandalism, speeding and various traffic violations, not to mention the usual sundry domestic violence calls, but personally living in a self-imposed exile of the soul, a vacuum of the heart and a void of the...mind. Then, when Chief Oberson retired a couple of years later, the Mayor and Town Council, a number of whom were also friends of my father, appointed me to be the new Police Chief citing my long years of experience in high level law enforcement as my qualifications. I expected some resentment from the ranks but surprisingly enough, everyone was on board, which made me feel even more like a cripple than I already did. But since I was rapidly approaching forty and felt seventy when it got cold or rained, I wasn't in any position to make waves.

I took the job. I was long past anything resembling pride or dignity by then. But the real story, and the reason I'm writing this, was just about to begin. Even now, as I begin to think about what I'm about to say and how I'll ever say it, I can feel my stomach squeeze itself into a knot the size of a fist, beads of sweat already beginning to build on my forehead, upper lip and back of my neck getting ready to join hundreds of others like them for their trip down the rest of my body as I force myself to relive these last few months. The panic is already growing inside me, starting to make my hands shake. I'm weakening. I can't control it anymore. It's getting more difficult to write. I'm going to take half a pill and a good, long drink to steel myself. I cannot allow myself to falter here. The house is quiet now; I haven't felt it near me since yesterday, but I can't guarantee how long that'll last. I've got to begin in earnest. The time has come for me to put blinders on my fear, remember what it felt like to be a 'protector,' and let the devil have his due.

CHAPTER 2

Rough Remnants

"It is a miserable state of mind to have few things to desire, and many things to fear."
                                                    - Sir Francis Bacon,
                                        Renaissance Author and Courtier

This is where it begins, my descent, step by step, into places lain dormant inside us all for centuries, millennia, the eons since we left the caves, places cultured and bred completely out of us in this modern, twentieth-century age of science and computers...into the core of our worst fear, that place beyond death and what awaits us there. Writing about it now has given me perspective. Looking back, things that didn't seem so important at the time have taken on a whole new meaning, so maybe my doing this will have some benefit after all.

The waking nightmare that's become whatever is left of my already wearied life began in late October of 2001, although from where I sit now, it seems like an eternity since I first stepped over the line into the...unreal. It began with the rain, the rain and the pain. Rhyming, that's the first sign of schizophrenia. Isn't it?

It'd been raining for days and we were waiting for the chill of late autumn to descend on us up in this neck of the woods as it did every year. I came home from work that night like any other night, watched some TV, had a few drinks and went to bed. The next morning my alarm went off at 6:00 A.M. like any other day, but something was different...and not in a good way. When I went to hit the snooze bar with my right hand, my shoulder screamed with an electric pain that shot right down to my fingertips. It hit me that the temperature must've dropped some twenty degrees overnight and combined with the rain, created a chilling dampness that sank straight into my bones. My old injuries made themselves known in a very big way.

I let my arm drop where it was, took a deep breath and, with my head still a bit hazy from the night before, struggled to make a plan. Still sitting on the edge of the bed, I reached for the bottle of Advil I kept stored in the bedside table and took two tablets with a glass of stale water that had been sitting there for who knows how long. Keeping my bad leg straight, I pushed myself up with my remaining good arm, all the while being careful not to put any pressure on my left leg. I got up as slowly as I could, ambling from pillar to post as I limped gingerly away from the bed, across the room and down the stairs, still keeping my bad leg extended so not to aggravate the twinging ache in my knee and ankle. It took awhile, but I finally got to the kitchen counter. Soaked around my head and neck with the sweat of the pain and effort, I stood there motionless, listening to the wind beat at the glass in the windows, reminding me that it was a force of nature and I wasn't. It was the worst 'left over' pain I'd felt in years.

After I recovered myself a few minutes later, I poured myself a half cup of coffee from my coffee maker with the automatic timer—my favorite modern invention, no waiting—and filled the half empty cup with cold water to make it easier to take. I reached for the kitchen cabinet to get to the heavy-duty drugs. I didn't use them as much back then, not as often as I do now. Actually at the time, I couldn't remember the last time I had used them. It could have been weeks. I took out the two bottles, one a muscle relaxer and the other a pain killer, took a tablet of each, broke them in half and swallowed half of each, then refilled my cup and worked my way over to a chair at the kitchen table. As I sat there waiting impatiently for the meds to take effect, I engaged in what'd become my favorite pastime, beating myself up over my limitations, letting it gnaw at my insides again, rehashing my losses and failures in my mind all over again. I took a cigarette from a pack on the table, lit it, and with my head propped up on my good hand, smoked as I stared out of the window, growing increasingly desperate for the relief I knew the drugs would bring.

A few minutes later, I felt the hypnotic wave that signaled my rescue. I learned a long time ago that drugs always work faster on an empty stomach, so I passed on the idea of food. Instead, I sat and drank more coffee, allowing the increasing comfort of the pills to wash over me in a rippling tide as they were absorbed. Wave after glorious wave, I sat watching as the wind blew a continuous rotation of leaves onto the window, then blew them off again as the rain beat against the glass. After a bit, the pain receded, leaving me with only shadows of aching stiffness. It was time to try and make it to the shower where I hoped that the hot water would soothe away the remaining edge of the pain.

Notwithstanding the favored security I knew I had in my job, I still didn't want anyone to know the extent of my old injuries. Call it vanity or ego, but I always made my best efforts to cover them up whenever they reared their ugly heads. Feeling a little steadier, I made my way back up to the shower and turned on the hot water tempered with only a little cold, set my coffee cup on the edge of the sink as I normally did, and got in. The hot, streaming water felt wonderfully soothing on my aching body. I stood there motionless for a few minutes, letting the water run over the tightness of my muscles, relaxing their rebellion against the pain that held them captive. But, as I stood there encased in my comforting cocoon of healing steam, letting it console me, what I didn't know...couldn't have known...was that in the next few short seconds, the boundaries of my reality would be changed forever.

Feeling some of my old flexibility return to me, I reached out of the break in the shower curtain for my coffee cup, a common habit I had. Just as my fingers grasped the handle, I felt something like the light touch of a small, cool hand gently stroke my wrist, startling me out of my comfortable daze. I jumped, dropping the cup, shattering it in the sink as I tore back the shower curtain with my other hand, my eyes darting suspiciously around the room. Nothing. No one. Then I noticed out of the corner of my eye that the bathroom window was open about four inches and felt the cold wind blowing through it. *That must have been it!* I thought to myself, but what I couldn't rationalize was the faint but unmistakable smell of baby powder that permeated the room. I never used baby powder, never owned any, but it made me think of Angelica. The amazing thing was that when I stepped out of the shower, I was completely pain free, like none of it had ever happened.

Although the pain was gone, my mood was still as dark as ever, having been reminded out of sequence about Angelica. I put my uniform on in the dark, letting the dull, rainy morning light have its way, enhancing my already gloomy mood as I strapped on my gun. I hadn't ever used my gun at that point, not as part of the Jennisburg force anyway. Then, just as I had refilled a new coffee cup for the road and headed toward the living room to go out the front door as I would any other day, I saw a dim glow over the top of the back of the sofa. As I got closer, I could see that the TV was still on. I could've sworn I'd shut it off before I went to bed. At the time, I just thought I must have hit the 'mute' button instead of the 'off' button but my eyes were too bleary to notice.

As I headed for the remote on the end table next to the sofa, I glanced at the screen. What I saw there made my blood run to ice in my veins. It was like I'd been kicked in the stomach, wanting to crawl into myself like a homely, unpopular teenager who's just found out they've been made the butt of a cruel joke. The hair stood up the back of my neck and I froze where I stood, caught somewhere between blinding rage and tears of helplessness. The scene on the screen was of a woman news reporter with short blonde hair and four names like Maria James Marshall Smith or something like that, but what tore me open was the scene going on behind her, the smoldering remains of a white clapboard church. She was interviewing a tall, distinguished looking black man with graying hair and a clerical collar. He was trembling as he spoke. Behind them were small groups of people gathering around, men shaking their heads, women wiping tears from their eyes.

The caption below the action read, "Montgomery, Alabama-Our Savior Baptist Church." As hard as I tried, I couldn't seem to tear my eyes from the screen. It didn't occur to me at the time, but I've since come to believe that Angelica was there with me that morning. The church fire had brought her back to me. She touched my wrist in the shower. It was her scent in the bathroom. She took away my pain. She turned on the TV because she wanted me to 'see' and know she was there. I know now that there was something she wanted to tell me, something she wanted me to do and that was her way of telling me. What I didn't know then was that I was going to find out what that 'something' was...that night.

At the time, none of this supernatural hokum would have ever occurred to me. Things like that didn't really happen. It was just fodder for the cheesy Roger Corman and Hammer films I'd loved so much at drive-ins while I was growing up. Things like that couldn't happen in real life, and if by some bizarre chance they did, they happened to other people not to 'Joe Nobody Police Chiefs of Nowherevilles' like me. Common sense told me to pass it off as an odd coincidence combined with the drugs I had taken affecting my perspective and I went to work. I just remember feeling odd. Sad. Hopeless. *What a way to start the day!*

About ten minutes later I was at work, a little way over the river on the far side of town and although I had no pain, I must have still looked shaky when I arrived because my dispatcher, Lila Horn, jumped up when she saw me and rushed to fix me a cup of coffee. She acted like that around me sometimes, but even more so on damp, rainy or cold days. Lila is one of the few people who knew all about my injuries because she keeps the books and maintains the personnel records. A real multi-tasker that Lila, and as solicitous toward me as she can be. With her shoulder length blonde hair, gray eyes and petite figure, she's never failed to be a bright spot in my otherwise overcast days, enlivening me with her seemingly endless reserve of youthful energy.

Oddly enough, I can't help but feel that Lila looks on me as a tower of strength, when the truth is, I don't know what I'd ever do without her. She was pregnant and on the run from that bastard wife beater of a husband, Randy Horn, when she came back to her mother's from another small town about twenty-five miles away and he'd followed her. I'd only just become Chief a few weeks before, so when the call of a domestic disturbance came into the station, my first thought was to take it myself.

When I got there, he was still banging on the door and yelling, "Open the fuckin' door you stupid bitch or I'll kill you and that cow of a mother of yours, too!" I didn't like that at all and could feel the stalking animal rise up inside me as I snuck up on him from behind. He was drunk and stupid, but oddly good looking in a white trash sort of way, dark haired with a sinister looking goatee, a skull and cross bones tattooed on his neck, colored graphics up and down his arms from wrist to elbow and a ton of silver rings on all of his fingers. He wasn't quite six foot and a little on the scrawny side. I could see how she might have been attracted to him at first, like young girls can be to that type, but I could never understand why she married him. He never felt me coming as I grabbed him up by his jacket collar, swung him around and landed a good one square in his left eye. The expression on his face was…priceless. He flew back so hard his head smashed on the side of the house before he slumped down on the porch.

"Who's the bigger dog now, tough guy? How's it feel to be afraid, you fucking piece of shit?" I bellowed at the top of my lungs as I grabbed him up by the back of the neck again, dragging him off the porch and down the steps, kicking him in the ass every step of the way. You should've heard him.

"Stop! You're hurting me!" he whined like a school girl as I shook him by the scruff of the neck as violently as I knew how.

"Don't you ever let me fucking catch you back here again, you son of a bitch, or I'll really give you something to yelp about!" I roared as I pulled him toward his car and threw him in the seat. I was still yelling as I watched him drive off, looking back in a wide-eyed panic thinking I might still be coming after him. As I stood there watching the dust fly from under his wheels, I couldn't help thinking, *What in the world raised that?* Well, no matter what creatures can claim responsibility for him, I knew one thing for sure. He'd never forget me, or that night, and I'm glad. I don't like wife beaters.

I probably went too far that night. Actually, I'm sure I did, but don't care because we've never heard from him again, other than through his lawyer to finalize the divorce and by then, I'd already hired Lila as my office secretary. She was going to have another mouth to feed soon and 'Joe Dirt' certainly wasn't going to be coming across anytime soon. She turned out to be a real winner though, my Lila. Within a month, she was running the office and cleaning the station on weekends. A real 'price above rubies,' she is. I've never regretted doing what I did and she's taken good care of me ever since. The only thing I can really say I regretted about that night was that I kicked him with my bad leg and paid for it for days afterwards, but I've gotten off the track...back to that day.

I spent the rest of that day dealing with the flooding caused by the seemingly endless rainfall. It wasn't uncommon to have some flooding problems in our area because the town is bordered on three sides by a snake bend in a small river, but the amount of rain those past few days, and that day in particular, was worrying because it was getting to be well more than the river could comfortably absorb. By two in the afternoon, the first of the three bridges leading away from town had flooded out. I had to send a man out to the site to cordon the area off, close the road to through traffic and create a detour. I counted that as substantial because I only have five cars and five men total, including myself, and I only have three men on duty at a time.

There was nothing approaching panic in town, so I was still well within my comfort zone, but I couldn't be sure for how long. Everyone was out and about collecting food and other supplies, just in case. Hearty stock, my people, but I had to keep going out on foot every now and again to let them see me and know that everything was under control. I had my other man out patrolling town for the odd fender bender or slide off of the road. That left Lila to man the helm by herself for most of the day.

By four, the rain still hadn't let up. In fact, it got heavier by the hour and when a tractor trailer slid broadside off the road just outside of the town limits, I had to call in my off-duty men and lend them to the neighboring township along with our towing facilities to clear the area. It was a very long, very busy day and before I knew it, it was ten at night, I was exhausted and more than ready to go home. Before I left, I called over to Margie at the diner and ordered my usual cheeseburger deluxe with fries 'to go' and was looking forward to a Creature Feature film I had coming on at eleven. I'd waited all week for that, a ghost story of all things, *The Uninvited* with Ray Milland and Gail Russell from the forties. Thinking about it now, it's laughably ironic. Little did I know at the time that I would be living in my own horror show, and in very short order. What I learned there was reality always trumps 'make believe' and there is no guarantee of a Hollywood ending in real life.

❄ ❄ ❄

As I came around by the diner on my way out Main Street, I could see Margie waiting for me outside with her umbrella and my dinner in a paper bag. It would be hard to miss her, really. She's as big as a house with a chimney full of peroxide blonde hair. A mother of five kids, she's a real asset to the town as far as PTA queens go and has a heart and a smile to match her broad ass and high hair. Nobody can fry up a burger with onions like Margie can. I pulled up close to the door and rolled down my window. She handed me the bag, braying over the sound of the pouring rain and water rushing down the street.

"Lila just called, Chief. She wants me to tell ya that the Orchard Road Bridge just flooded out and that she sent Gunner Bjornstrand over to close it up so ya gotta take the Overmill Bridge to get home."

"Thanks, hon…" I said, almost in a swoon from the smell of her fried onions. "your burgers are food fit for the gods and you are the undisputed goddess of fried onions."

"Awww, Chief. You do say the sweetest things," she replied, laughing as she turned to go.

"Oh and Marg, thanks for coming out in the rain for me," I said, grateful for not having to get out of the car.

"Anything for you, Chief…anything at all," she said and gave me a sly wink.

"Arrrgggg. You're a saucy wench, mah dear!" I replied in my comic pirate's voice, giving her an appreciative wink back. She let loose a cackle that could splinter wood, waving me off as I rolled up my window to head out.

I'd only gotten past the ten blocks of the downtown area

when I began thinking, a dangerous thing for me to do most of the time. There I was, in the so called 'prime of my life,' forty-one years old, educated, traveled, decent, still in reasonably good shape, and the best I could do for myself was to be a small town police chief in a place no one had ever heard of, much less cared about, looking forward to going home alone to my big, empty house with a cheeseburger deluxe to watch an old horror film on the TV. Pathetic. A failure to all the potential I'd dreamed of all my life and that'd once been expected of me. I was finished. Done. Waiting to die and hoping it would be soon.

By then, I knew that it had a name, depression, but no cure. How could there ever be a cure for what ails a life? And, as it had so often done in the past, it began in the pit of my stomach and welled up from there, that sinking feeling of hopelessness again. I'd gotten to know that feeling all too well over the years and knew what it meant. God knows I'd felt it enough in my life, in college, in the hospitals, in Europe, and so many times since. In the background of my mind, I could hear that old Simon and Garfunkel song from when I was growing up play again, trumpeting yet another of its victorious arrivals and announcing to me yet another humiliating defeat. *I am just a poor boy, though my story's seldom told I have squandered my resistance for a pocket full of mumbles such are promises...*

There was a tidal wave of it out there waiting for me, building its monumental strength until it was ready to come crashing down on my head like a ton of bricks of the size used to build the Pyramids. Its sole purpose being to overwhelm me with a power I knew it was useless to resist, choking me with my own insignificance, dragging me down into its black heart to drown me there in yet another suffocating swamp of bottom-scraping despair. Even worse than the depression itself, if that's at all possible, is being able to recognize what it feels like on its way in, the helplessness, the futility of even breathing. You wish you could just die on the spot so you wouldn't have to feel it anymore, and there it was again, in my stomach, growing every second and me knowing it was coming.

Not long after, its distant cousin, panic, joined the party to celebrate my humiliation. *God! You are such a FAILURE OF A MAN*, drummed in my head. I was so ashamed of myself. *You are*

NOBODY...NOTHING! it screamed at me like a vulture about to dive and make a feast of my exposed entrails. At that moment I just wished I could die and I remember thinking of the peace the gun at my side held. I don't know what triggered it at that particular moment. Maybe it was the effect of the rain or the repetition of the windshield wiper blades going back and forth, back and forth. I guess it could've been anything. It didn't really need a reason to torture me. After all, it was the story of my sad-ass life and had been with increasing frequency and severity since I was a teenager.

Then, just as I was looking down to squeeze the water out of my eyes in one of my seemingly endless moments of self-pity, struggling with all my might not to let my hand feel the quiet of the cold metal in my holster, I had, for the briefest instant, the strangest impression of not being alone and thought I could smell faint the scent of baby powder pass under my nose. I looked up. That's when I saw it, the blink of headlights off in the distance less than a mile away approaching the opposite side of the Overmill Bridge, but something was wrong. They were moving much too fast for the weather conditions. Suddenly, the lights strayed from what I knew to be the ramp of the bridge and disappeared. I knew what that meant. I blinked for a moment, not believing what I'd seen.

An overpowering surge of urgency jolted through my head like a hot poker pushing aside all previous thoughts of myself. The twisting feeling I had in my guts was suddenly replaced with a driving sense of purpose as my foot pressed down on the gas pedal. I sped up as much as I dared with the rain and poor road surface, while at the same time somehow managing to reach Lila at home to send help in one of those rare instances when I actually used my cell phone. I hardly knew how to turn the damn thing on.

In no more than two or three minutes, I'd crossed the bridge and pulled over. By then, the adrenaline of my days with the agency was riding full throttle. I wasn't thinking. I was just moving, acting. I ran over to the guard rail of the bridge and looked down. There it was, a car, a black mid-sized with its nose down in the water, tail lights creating an eerie glow in the dark, stuck in the mud at the bottom of the river like a spoon in a murky pudding. I ran to the trunk of my car and grabbed a tow rope, tying it to the nearest strong looking tree, an old oak about twenty feet from the edge of the river, and worked my way down the side of the slippery edge. Most of the bank was already on its way to being submerged by the rising tide of the river. I used the rope for balance, but still slid most of the way down. Once in the water, I regained my footing and managed to wade against the rush of the tide out to the car. The river was only about three hundred feet in width so, for the most part, I could wade the distance to the car with the water coming only up to my chest, but the tide seemed so strong and the water seemed to be rising at a furious rate. There was no time to lose. I had to hurry.

By the time I reached the car, the water was almost up to my shoulders. The rain was coming down in sheets, slapping my face with stinging pellets, making it hard to see through more than a squint. When I looked inside, I saw a man in the driver's seat slumped over the wheel with more than half his body covered by the dark water. He was unconscious, his face covered in blood. My training told me I had one quick decision to make. If he had any spinal injuries and I moved him, I could cripple him for life, but if I didn't move him, he would drown for sure with the rising tide or be swept away by the increasing rush of the current. I had to move quickly or it would be too late.

I smashed out the driver's side window with the hook on the end of the rope, opened the door and secured the rope around the window frame, then took hold of him and pulled him out of the car as forcefully as I could to fight the suction effect created by the in-rush of the water. He wasn't wearing a seat belt, which I guess was a good thing for a change. Had he been buckled in, I'd have had to fight that too, losing valuable time in the bargain. Just as I had him, the car shifted from the momentum of the rushing water, but I held my nerve. Grabbing him under the arm in a lifeguard hold with my one arm and wrapping my other forearm around the taut rope, I awkwardly started dragging us both back toward the bank, struggling to keep his head above water.

It was slow and steady for the first few feet with the rain battering my face, forcing me to fly blind. I slipped in the mud a few times, our heads going under, but I never let go of him or the rope, somehow always managing to find my footing and keep my wits about me against the threat of the water rising around my neck. The next movement of the rope let me know the car was shifting again, tipping from the force of the rushing water. *You only have a few minutes before it gives way,* I thought to myself, and gave it my all to pull ahead.

Although it couldn't have lasted more than a few minutes at most, it seemed like an eternity before we hit the bank and I could drag him up into the tall grass and reeds. As I looked up and around, I saw head lights coming from the direction of town. *Thank God!* I thought with a sigh. Once I had us secured on the muddy edge of the bank, I tried to drag him up over the bank to flat ground. That was the first time I actually looked at him. His eyes were open, looking at me. Before I could say anything, he had my hand in his and was looking in my eyes. "Please don't let me die…alone," he sputtered in a weak, raspy voice.

It caught me off guard and I responded the best I knew how, "Don't worry. I'm not gonna let you die at all, buddy. I promise." A look of relief came over his face. He took a deep, heaving breath, his eyelids fluttering briefly, and closed his eyes. Waiting breathlessly for help to come, his blood all over my hands, I knelt over him, helpless to do anything but watch as the life slowly pumped out of the gaping gash in the side of his head and pray that I wasn't too late…again.

The next thing I knew, one of my cops, Joe Rogan, was calling to me as he lumbered toward us, "Chief! Chief!" The EMS crash wagon was parked behind him.

Thank God for Joe Rogan! I thought, relieved that it wasn't one of my smaller men. Joe is as big as an ox and just as strong. He pulled us both over the top of the bank and onto the flat ground in a flash. I never thought I'd be so glad to see anyone in my life. The paramedics were right behind him with the stretcher. It wasn't until they had him on the stretcher that I saw that one of the EMS guys had an open wallet in his hand and I heard him read the name out loud, "Martin Welliver, New York City."

By that time, the adrenaline rush or whatever it was that'd numbed my body was gone and I was racked with the most God-awful pain I'd ever had. Layered with the chill from my wet clothes, my muscles started constricting around my aching joints, rippling through my entire body like a string of dominoes slapping each other down. Although I probably hadn't felt it through and through yet, I must have been shaking pretty good because Joe took off his coat and gave it to me, taking my wet one and throwing it in his car. I left Joe with the car and instructions to have it towed into town for inspection and followed the crash wagon the ten or so miles over to the hospital in Henriston.

I've come to realize in retrospect, now that I'm writing this, that the hand I felt on my wrist that morning was real. It was Angelica Weston. She knew I would need everything I had to pull that guy out of the river that night, and it was only with her help that I managed it. Without it, I know I would've folded, crumbling under the pressure, and Martin Welliver would've died then and there with me helpless to do anything to save him.

That was when I first actually gave brief pause to the possibility of the supernatural. It was somewhere inside me that day. I felt it. I know I did. She'd put it there that morning so I would be prepared. But, of course, later during the daylight, I played the whole thing off by convincing myself that what I'd experienced the night before was the same sort of 'rush' they talk about in stories of little old ladies lifting cars off of run down kids, and I did what any normal person would've done. I rationalized it out of my mind and let it go.

❈ ❈ ❈

Stop. Jesus Christ Almighty! What the hell was that? I've just heard something in the house, a rattling of a door knob, somewhere out back. Something is trying to get in. I have to break here. I've got to go do a walk through of the house, check the doors and look in on Martin to make sure he's alright.

❈ ❈ ❈

Okay…I'm back now. I didn't find anything but that doesn't mean that it wasn't anything or that there was nothing there. I've learned that much from those first days of the accident and every day since then. I don't know how I go on anymore. I'm just so tired, but I have to go on for Martin. If it were just for myself I'd just as soon lie down and die before it comes for me again. I don't want to see it again. I couldn't bear it.

I can't let it touch me again. I just can't…but I will not let it get to Martin. I will not let it have him! I know that after it gets rid of me, it'll come for him and both our souls would be lost, but I've got to concentrate. *Focus Terry! You've got to focus! Don't let it distract you.*

Where did I leave off? I've got to get back where I was. God, I'm sweating again. I can feel it around my neck, dripping down my chest. My tee shirt is soaked with it. I probably smell bad, too. I don't know when the last time I showered was. It'll just have to wait until Lila or Martin tell me I smell. I've got to go on while I still can. I don't think it wants me to be doing this but, for some reason, it can't stop me just yet. Still, it knows it's gaining and I'm losing. Time…time…time.

※ ※ ※

The hospital. Oh yes, I was on my way to the hospital. I followed the crash wagon to the hospital in Henriston. It's the only one in the county and it's where my mother works. I remember taking four Advil from my mobile stash as soon as I got in the car and swallowing them with a slug of Wild Turkey from a bottle I keep in the side pocket of my driver's door, just in case. I followed as closely as I dared given the intense rain conditions still going on. We arrived at the Emergency entrance about twenty-five minutes later. I prayed the whole time that the EMS guys would at least be able to stabilize him during the trip. I couldn't lose another one. I just couldn't and after I'd promised him. I promised him!

By the time I got to the Emergency desk, they'd already taken him into the trauma area. I spoke to a young nurse at the desk, told her who I was and was starting to tell her what happened when she cut me off. "I know Chief. I had a call from the EMS crew that you'd be coming in," she said as she came around the desk. I just cut to the chase.

"I'm gonna wait as long as it takes," I said defiantly, making my stand. She took me by the arm and led me toward the men's room not far down the hall.

"I thought you might feel that way, but you've got blood all over you. You've got to wash it off, and you're soaked to the skin. You go wash up. I'll go look in the lost and found to see if I can find something for you to wear. Just wait here for me when you're done," she ordered kindly, pushing me toward the door and hurrying back down the hall.

The first thing I saw when I went in was the last thing I wanted to see, a mirror. I wasn't ready to look at myself yet, not until I knew, one way or the other, so I looked down...at my hands. They still had his blood on them. I wasn't ready for what I felt then, either. I didn't want to wash it off. I thought of Angelica and remembered how I reached out to touch her, but never did. It was different this time. This time, I'd touched him and he was still alive. A disquieting rush of superstitious dread came over me telling me that if I washed him off me he might die, but if I kept him on me, he might live. I got lost in that feeling, only coming around when I heard the loud knock on the door.

"Chief! Are you done yet?" the nurse called out.

"Just a minute!" I called back nervously as I went over to the sink and turned on the water. Then putting my hands under the running water coming out of the tap, I watched it mix with his blood, washing it off me, swirling together as it ran down the drain, letting it hypnotize me. I started to drift off again, suddenly feeling myself going down the drain with it. A strange impulse from somewhere inside came over me, telling me to look up, into the mirror. When I did, what I saw there made my knees buckle. My face was streaked with blood, as if I'd drawn my bloody fingers over my face leaving trails of it behind, marking me. Horrified by the sight of it, I closed my eyes, squeezing them tight, and waited for it to go away. When I opened them again a few seconds later, I was still staring down at the swirl of blood going down the drain. I hadn't looked up after all. It was just my mind playing tricks on me. To be sure, I looked up into the mirror again. I was clean. It'd never happened. I went back to staring down into the sink again, his blood still swirling down the drain, and said quietly to myself without thinking, "I'm coming with you." There was another knock at the door.

"Chief, are you alright in there? Are you hurt?" the nurse called in.

"No, I'm okay. Coming out now," I called back, grabbing for the paper towels to dry off as I tried to get a grip on myself. She was waiting for me when I came out with a big denim shirt in one hand, a pair of heavy white gym socks in the other, and a hospital blanket over her shoulder.

"Here, put these on. It's the best I could do . . . and let me have your boots. I'll put them by the heater to dry out." So I went back in and changed my shirt and socks and gave her my boots, but, in a voice that let her know I meant business, I made her promise to notify me as soon as she knew anything. I wasn't in the mood for equivocating.

By the time I got to the waiting room, I was desperate for a seat. The pain in my leg was so intense I could hardly stand. The Advil took the edge off, but it was still tremendous, from hip to toe and from shoulder to fingertips. I needed more. That was when I remembered the little pill box in my pocket and wondered if it was watertight. I took it out and opened it. Apparently it was. *Hallelujah! Luck be a Tylenol-3 with Codeine tonight,* I thought with a sad-ass laugh. The two halves I'd left there from the morning were still intact so I took them, dry, and as my life would have it, when I turned on the TV in the waiting room, my ghost story was on. I sat there for about an hour and a half watching Ray Milland chasing ghosts in some English seaside mansion when I started getting hungry and remembered the burger in the car. I was feeling steady enough by then, so I went and got it, wet boots and all, and ate the cold food while the film ended. My stomach full, it seemed like the tension in my nerves had dropped through the floor and I got sleepy, letting my head hang for what seemed like only a few minutes. The next thing I knew, I felt a light tap on the shoulder. Another nurse was standing in front of me.

"Chief..." she said softly and smiled. "Sorry to disturb you. I know how tired you must be." I wiped my face with my hands and looked at her. She was middle aged with dark hair streaked with gray but still very pretty. She had fine features and expressive blue eyes. Her skin was smooth and, with almost no make up, she had a youthful countenance that made you forget her gray streaks.

She sat down next to me and began to tell me about the man I now knew to be Martin Welliver. He was still alive, but in critical condition. She told me that he'd suffered some broken bones, a forearm and wrist, a dislocated shoulder, a broken leg and ankle. Of the more serious injuries, she told me he had some internal bleeding, but that they'd gotten it under control after some emergency surgery. The next twenty-four hours would tell more. He'd also suffered a serious head injury, a fractured skull, and that there'd been some swelling of the brain so the doctors thought it best to keep him in a medically induced coma until the threat of brain damage from the swelling had passed. I'm just paraphrasing that part. I'm sure no doctor and grasped as much of it as I could under the circumstances.

Shit, he must've been going at some speed to get those injuries, I thought to myself as I listened to what she had to say.

The bottom line was that it would be 'touch and go' for a while, but since he was in good general health, they were being "...cautiously optimistic." She told me that she and the doctors wanted me to know that any chance of survival he had was due to my being in the right place at the right time and acting as quickly as I had.

"Another fifteen minutes," she said with a serious sort of look that only doctors and nurses get, "and he wouldn't have survived. Either the internal bleeding or the head injury alone would have proven fatal." Then she shook my hand, smiled earnestly, and told me I should go home and get some sleep. It was after three in the morning. As she turned to go, she said with another smile, "...and please say hello to your mother for me. We work different wards and don't get to see each other as much as we'd like anymore." I smiled back and said that I would as I headed out the door back to my car, not thinking that she didn't tell me her name.

It was still raining when I left and I was just too tired to drive all the way back to my place. On top of that, I admit I was tilting emotionally from the whole episode, so I went to stay over at my mother's as I've been known to do every now and again, when my mind gets worn down. I had my own key so there was no need to disturb her. It was so late when I got there, I just slipped in quietly, making my way to the sofa, kicking off my boots and collapsing. When I opened my eyes again, I was walking down a winding dirt road, long and narrow, that ran through a field of seemingly endless wildflowers leading into a faded, blurry horizon. The sun was shining, the sky was bright and the fields were full of vibrant colors, reds...blues...yellows...pinks and purples. After a few steps, I felt a slight pressure on the fingers of my right hand and looked down. It was Angelica. She was holding my hand, looking up at me and smiling, just like in her picture.

"I am so proud of you, Terrence," she said brightly, her big, brown eyes shining. We walked in peaceful silence for a while before coming to a bench along side of the road.

"Angelica, I'm so tired, and my leg hurts. Can I sit for a little bit?" I asked her. Then I realized she was still dead and tears began to flow down my face in a constant stream, quiet, soft, calm tears of resigned sadness. She stood before me as I sat down on the bench, gently putting her hands on both sides of my face, holding it up to look at her.

"There's no need to cry, Terrence. I've been living in your heart all this time, and I've been safe and happy there with you...but now it's time for me to go," she said, her sweet little voice revealing a depth well beyond her years.

"Where?...Why?" I asked, already feeling terribly alone.

"To a good place where you won't have to worry about me anymore...but I had to see you one more time, to say good-bye and tell you how proud I am of you," she said, and I felt a warm breeze blow. I let my head slump gently into her hands, sobbing.

"Please don't go. I'll be so alone," I pleaded, sounding more like a child than she did. She picked my head up again, stroking the side of my face with the back of her hand.

"I'm sorry, Terrence, but it's time. Time for me and for you," she said, still stroking my face.

"Please don't go. I don't know what I'll do. Can't I go with you? I'm so tired, and I hurt so badly...all the time." I crumbled.

"You still have things to do, important things. Always remember your promises, Terrence. They make you the man that you are," she said, her eyes beginning to fill with tears. "It's because of your promise to me that I've been able to stay with you so long...but there's something important I have to tell you before I go." She leaned in close, whispering in my ear, "Not all games are fun, Terrence...be strong and... please...please be careful." Tears were running down her beautiful little face as she drew back. My heart felt like it was breaking in a million pieces. She leaned over again and kissed my cheek, then turned and began walking down the road alone. As I watched her disappear into the horizon, I felt another warm breeze on my face and smelled the scent of baby powder. It carried with it her little girl voice. "I'll hold you in my heart forever, Terrence and...I'll miss you...so much." Then it faded into the sky.

I held my head in my hands and cried for what seemed like hours before I felt I could go back. Then, when I put my hand on the bench to help lift myself up, I felt something, a small, square block of some sort of odd heavy plastic under it, yellow and aged looking with strange symbols engraved on it that I didn't understand. Not knowing what else to do, I just put it in my pocket and turned back down the road in the direction we'd come from.

I woke up to the aroma of freshly brewed coffee, the sound of something frying in the kitchen and my mother's voice humming. Soaked with sweat, my face still wet with tears, at that moment I can't say I really knew which part was real and which was a dream. That was when I first realized I might be in real trouble, the crack in my mind was widening into a fissure. My mother must've heard me stir because the next thing I knew, she was calling to me from the kitchen.

"Good morning, sweetheart! How's my hero this morning? I had a call from Hannah Dyer a little while ago...she couldn't wait to tell me all about it," she called out from the kitchen, sounding even more cheerful than usual.

I got up and went into the downstairs bathroom to wash my face and hands, still not having what it took to look in the mirror. When I was done, I yelled into the kitchen that I was going upstairs to my old room to change my clothes and I'd be right down. I came down a few minutes later in my old pajamas and robe and sat down at the kitchen table. She came over, kissed me on the cheek and set a huge mug of steaming coffee in front of me. A second later she was back with a plate full of fried eggs with cheese, sausage and toast.

"You must be starved," she said as she lit a cigarette for herself, leaning, arms crossed, in her usual place in the corner against the kitchen counter. Rude as it may seem to strangers, I dug right in and spoke to her with my mouth full.

"Starved! Thanks, Ma," I mumbled appreciatively. She looked supremely pleased at that, smoking her cigarette and smiling at me lovingly.

"That's my boy! So how are you?" she asked in a tone that I knew meant she was reaching well beyond my physical well being. She knew all too well about my depressions and Angelica. She knew pretty much everything.

"Don't know yet," I replied still stuffing my face, hoping to deflect what I knew was coming.

"So, tell me what happened," she asked. I gave her the details while I ate. She lit another cigarette and poured herself another cup of coffee.

"I told you everything would be alright," she said in a tone only mothers use. "Your mother always knows best," she continued, referring to the days when I first came back to town and laid my head on her table too depressed to move, telling her my life was over and that my usefulness as a human being was finished.

"You saved another life...that little girl was not the end of you. It was not your fault. You did your best, honey, and risked your own life doing it. No one blames you for her loss but you, not even her own mother. Your father and I raised a good, strong boy. You can be proud of yourself again, because without you, that young man wouldn't be alive now." She walked over and put her hand on my shoulder.

"By the way," she went on, "Hannah was on the night shift last night. She called me right before her shift ended. She checked on his condition and said that he's been stable all night," she said, refilling my coffee cup then asked, "So...are you going to see him when he comes out of it?"

I knew where this was going. *You betcha!* Mom hadn't been a psychiatric nurse for thirty-five years for nothing, and could be as cagey as they come.

"I don't know, yet," I replied. I knew that she was hinting that I should see him as a way of resolving my feelings about losing Angelica.

"I think it would be good for you and for him. It gives him a chance to thank you, which is good for him, and it gives you a chance to see that your efforts have had real meaning for someone. It would be a good thing for both of you," she said, doing her best to sound supportive while still making her point in the face of my increasingly touchy mood.

"I don't know, Ma," I said, growing weary of the pressure when I was still feeling so…unwell.

"You know that when he's conscious again and learns what happened he's going to want to see you. He'll ask for you," she said, letting me know she wasn't going to give up easily.

"I'll deal with that when it happens," I said grouchily, lighting myself a cigarette from her pack on the table. She took another tack then.

"You know, it wouldn't do you any harm to have someone to talk to, maybe give Catherine a call?" I just kept still, not knowing quite how to respond. She went on.

"I still get Christmas and birthday cards from her every year. She really is a sweet girl and she seems lonely out there in California…and she always asks about you. You do know that she's divorced almost three years now, don't you? I think she really loved you, Terry." That was it. She hit the nerve she should have stayed away from and I spoke before I could think.

"Loved me? You think she loved me? She never loved me, Ma. She just wanted a Ken Doll she could polish off and dress up to show off at Daddy's Country Club…and when I needed her to show some understanding and actually feel something for me, she ran off with the first guy with a foreign accent she could lay her hands on. Well, as far as I'm concerned, she's made her own bed and now she can lay in it…but it'll never be with me!"

She backed away from the sore spot she'd touched, but ever the professional looking to have her way, she tried a lateral move. "Well, how about I introduce you to some of the girls from the hospital. I'm sure any number of them would love to go out with my handsome son." I just let my head slump into my hands, signaling that I'd had enough.

"The last thing I need right now, Ma, is the responsibility for someone's every happiness forced on me, turning to wheedling, nagging, weeping discontent when I don't live up to it. You can't get blood out of a stone, Ma, and I'm as stony as they come. I can't find any peace for myself, so how the hell am I ever gonna be able to offer it to someone else? Let's face it, that ship has sailed, and at my age, it's clear that I wasn't meant to be on it. I'm an old dog, too tired for new tricks, especially the emotional hoop-jumping kind." I barked at her, my head throbbing, my body aching and screaming for drugs.

"I know, sweetheart. I just thought...well...maybe if you had someone to talk to about things, someone who could appreciate you as you are...it might help you to see yourself in a different light...and not be so hard on yourself," she said, reaching up to take her raincoat from the rack. When I didn't respond she moved on.

"Well, I have to go out and do some things this morning before I get ready for work, so I'd better get going. I'm on the three-to-eleven shift again this week. What are you going to do today? It's your day off, isn't it?" she asked, knowing her child well enough to know when to change the subject.

I looked at the clock on the wall. It was 9:30 A.M. "I think I'll take a shower and then maybe get some more sleep. I feel like I've been hit by a Mack truck," I said, my head starting to swim from it all.

"I'm sure you do, sweetheart. You know where the Advil is," she said with a slight smile, putting on her coat.

"Yes, Mother," I replied in a subdued voice, like I was fourteen again and had talked back to her, "and don't worry about dinner. I'll bring in a pizza and leave it for you in the oven for when you get home from work tonight," I said, awash with shame and regret for being so cranky with her and raising my voice.

"Thanks, hon," she said and kissed me on the cheek again. "Sausage, peppers and mushrooms would be great and, Terry...I'm so very proud of you, sweetheart," and she was out the door.

CHAPTER 3

Lost and Found

"The oldest and strongest emotion of mankind is fear. And the oldest and strongest kind of fear is fear of the unknown."

-H.P. Lovecraft
-20th Century Horror/Sci Fi Author

I'd just gotten out of the shower at Mom's when the phone rang. It was Lila. It seems that there was a call to the station from a Nurse Denton at the hospital asking me to stop by, and a second call from Tom Wuchowitz at the garage wanting to know what to do with the car. I told her I'd stop by the hospital by Noon and that she should call Tom and ask him to check the car for any mechanical malfunctions and get back to me. I still had to account for what happened that night and with the victim being unconscious for who knows how long, I figured I'd better start working on it from the other end, so I put on one of the extra uniforms that I kept there and got ready to head out. *So much for your day off,* I thought to myself.

I arrived at the Emergency desk about eleven thirty and asked for Nurse Denton. It's a small hospital by modern standards, so I knew I wouldn't have to wait long and yes, I was still popping Advil like crazy. A chubby desk attendant with rosy cheeks and curly black hair picked up the phone and spoke into it briefly,

"There's a police officer here at the Emergency desk to see Jenny Denton," she said, turning her head to cover the receiver with her hand and whisper, "…and he's a handsome one, too," she giggled.

A few minutes later, the nurse who had spoken to me the night before came walking down the corridor, looking a bit more tired than she had then. She smiled as she saw me, "Hello, Chief," she said, holding out her hand to shake mine. "I'm Jenny Denton. I'm so sorry for not introducing myself properly last night. It was just that I'd heard so much about you from Charlotte over the years, it seemed like I already knew you." Her smile was as youthful as I'm sure it ever was, but her eyes had the glazed look of long hours. The poor girl was dead on her feet.

"Are you still here?" I asked, genuinely pleased to see her again.

"Yes," she replied, sounding exhausted. "I volunteered for a double shift last night because of all the extra activity from the accident and with two teenagers and a toddler at home, the extra money never hurts. I'm off duty now, but I wanted to speak to you before I left," she smiled and went on. "The reason I called is that we've run into a bit of a problem. No…please don't worry. Mr. Welliver has been stable all night. He seems to be responding nicely, as a matter of fact. The problem is that we've checked his driver's license for an emergency contact and all we could find was a Manhattan address. When we checked the phone number to notify any family members, it had been disconnected and there's nothing else in his wallet indicating anyone to contact. I'm sure you understand, Chief, how important it is to have a family member on hand in these cases. We're at a complete loss about what to do, so I was wondering if there was something you could do. There must be someone we can contact," she said, giving me a slight push with her eyes and manner.

I smiled the crooked smile I have when I'm in pain and leaned on the counter to take the weight off of my leg. "Yes, of course, I'll do whatever I can. If I can have a copy of the driver's license, I'll see what I can find out," I said, taking my cue from her approach.

"Oh, I knew I could count on you," she said, sounding relieved and pulling a folded piece of paper out of her pastel flowered smock pocket, handing it to me.

"I have it right here," she said, putting her hand on mine

over the desk, squeezing it. She looked me in the eyes then and said, "He's our special patient, isn't he? We'll take good care of him, won't we?" and gave my hand another squeeze. "Well, I've really got to run now. Jeff is a great husband and very understanding but I'm sure he's pretty fed up by now so I'd better get home soon. I'll be on again at 7:00 A.M. tomorrow. You can reach me here or at home if you find out anything. If you find anyone, it would be best to bring them back with you if you can. Thank you so much, Chief," she said and winked at me before rushing away back down the hall.

❊ ❊ ❊

I've got to take a break now. I think I hear Martin upstairs and the sun is coming up. I have to check in at the station and spend a few hours there. Thank God for Lila. She's been covering for me more than usual this week, well above the call of duty. Anyway, I hear Martin upstairs again. It sounds like he's having another nightmare. I need to check and make sure he's alright. I'll pick up where I left off when I can.

❊ ❊ ❊

It's 5:30 P.M. now and it's already dark out. I brought some books home for Martin, mostly innocuous junk, but good for a laugh which is so rare after all he's been through. He gets a kick out of Jacqueline Susann, *Valley of the Dolls* and that kind of stuff. Jenny got him hooked on it in the hospital. I got some historical dramas and things about exotic places, too. He likes those. I had to handle a stupid road rage matter while I was out. Two fucking idiots fighting over a parking space of all things…and in Jennisburg of all places! Nitwits. I gave them both a summons for disorderly conduct. Tourists! Go figure! Gotta get that last goddamn bottle of maple syrup before the other guy! The whole county is only fucking loaded with the crap. What is this world coming to? I don't know. One of the pitfalls of human nature, I guess, is the ability to think, but only use it halfway most of the time.

I brought in fried chicken and French fries from Margie's for dinner. We'll eat soon, then I have to go around and secure the house without letting him know what I'm doing. I noticed yesterday when we got home from sending Grace off that the coffee jar was turned upside down on the counter. It's been fucking with me again, trying to make me crash. I can feel it in my gut, but I'm feeling better now. Writing this has kept me focused enough to be able to back it off my mind for awhile, maybe take away some of its power until it's ready to kill me.

The kitchen chairs were pulled out from the table, too. That almost tipped me over. I know they weren't like that when we left. When things start to move it means it's getting stronger—I'd better hurry. I don't know how long I can hold on, even with my new found hobby. Today is a good day, but tomorrow may not be. I try to keep acting as normal as possible but it's getting harder and harder to maintain, so I'd better get on with this. Martin doesn't know about anything that's happened here in this house and I want to keep it from him as long as I can. My palms are sweating again and my heart is working overtime. I can hear it beat in my ears. That means it's here again. I think I can hear it breathe. It sounds like it's coming from inside the walls. I know what that means. It's begun again. It's getting ready. *What do you want from him, you fucking bastard? Whatever it is, you'll have to kill me first to get it!* I'd better get back to this while I still can. It's not going to like that I've challenged it again, so I'd better get prepared.

After I left the hospital, I went home and changed into my street clothes—khakis, white Oxford shirt, jacket and boots—then caught the 1:00 P.M. bus to Manhattan arriving at the Port Authority about four. I took a cab directly to the address on the license. It was a doorman building on East 68th Street. I spoke to the doorman first, a middle-aged black man with shocks of grey hair at his temples, a well trimmed mustache and horn rimmed glasses. He wore a slate grey uniform with silver epaulets, a porter's cap and a name tag that read "Marcus R." When I asked him if he knew of a tenant named Martin Welliver his face brightened instantly and he smiled.

"Oh, yes! I know Mr. Welliver. Considerate young man and a good tipper too. Always treated me right at Christmas...but he's not a tenant here anymore. He left about...oh, 'round 'bout two months ago, I guess," he said, rubbing his chin with his hand. I showed him my badge and explained that Mr. Welliver had been in a serious accident. I told him that I was trying to find his family and asked if he had left a forwarding address. He looked down and shook his head.

"Oh, I'm so sorry to hear that. I hope he's going to be alright. Such a nice young man. What a shame," he said sincerely, continuing to shake his head as we walked inside to a directory-like book at the front desk. He turned a few pages then looked up at me. "He only left a post office box number. No real address," he said disappointedly. I took the box number and thanked him with a five dollar bill.

"Much obliged, sir," he said nodding then stopped me. "You know, sir, you might want to check with some of his neighbors up on Nine. They might be able to help you more. I know I used to see him talking to Miss Hasher up in Nine C quite a bit. Maybe she could tell you something. She came in only about a half an hour ago, so I know she's in," he said pointing to the elevator and telling me to take it to the ninth floor, turn left when I got out then go to the second door on the right. I flipped him another five for going the extra mile. It's a rare quality in people these days.

I arrived at the door of apartment Nine C a few minutes later and rang the bell. A young woman opened the door. She was wet in a thin, white cotton bathrobe. Before I could say a word she smiled tartly and said, "You're early. I wasn't expecting you for another half hour...but come on in anyway." She was beautiful, a redhead with long, wavy, thick hair, green, almond-shaped eyes with an impish twinkle, and long lashes. Her figure had the look like it may have been...'augmented,' I believe is the polite term they use these days. She was very tall. I remember thinking that she reminded me of the movie actress, Nicole Kidman. I could see the delicate, pink nipples of her dessert cup sized breasts begin to push through the damp, flimsy cotton of her robe as she looked me up and down. Then turning and waving me in, she rambled on, "I don't usually take clients at home, but when Leona called and said she had someone who needed some 'special attention' I said to myself, 'Oh, what the hell.' Boy, she wasn't kidding. You're a real doll. I can't believe a big, strapping guy like you with a face like that would have to...uh...'make arrangements,' but it takes all kinds, I guess. Married I suppose? Need something your wifey won't give you, handsome?" she purred as she opened her bath robe, letting it drop to the floor as she came up close to me. "Wanna talk dirty to me, stud? Maybe rough me up a little? After all, I can be a veerrryyy baaaddd girl."

I backed away at that. "Whoa!"

"Come on. Don't be shy, honey," she cooed as she came toward me. "It's not often I get a client that looks like you..."

I was sort of flattered, I guess, in a schoolboy sort of way, and hoped I wasn't blushing, but then she said, "...and I can tell by the way you walk that you're packin' so let's make the most of that rifle of yours," and grabbed at my belt buckle. With things having gone so far, the best I could do was to pull out my badge and hold it in front of her face. I'm sure by then I was as red as a beet.

"Why you slick son of a bitch! I should have known it was too good to be true," she yowled like an alley cat that's had its tail stepped on and bent over to pick up her robe in just such a way to make sure I got a good look at what I was missing before she put it on. "Just give me a minute to put on some clothes and we can get this fucking shit over with. Damn, Leona! Damn her! Stupid fucking bitch! A bust is the last thing I need." I couldn't help but smile.

"Take a closer look, Miss Hasher," I said, holding up my badge so she could see it more closely. "I'm not a city cop. I'm not here to interfere in your life and I don't know anyone named Leona. I'm just here for some information." She looked at it, hands on her hips, then back at me still half angry, rolled her eyes and let out a sigh of relief.

"I don't rat on my friends either!" she spat back, softening from alley cat to spurned kitten.

"I'm not looking for anything like that. I'm here about a man named Martin Welliver. I understand he used to be your neighbor."

She looked surprised and her expression softened even more. "Martin? Oh, yes. He lived next door to me for a few years, close to five, I think. Is he in some kind of trouble? Doesn't sound like him," she said absently, having finally come to the realization that she wasn't under any threat.

"No, he's not in any trouble, miss. Not that kind of trouble anyway. He's been in an accident, a serious accident upstate. I'm trying to locate his family to notify them," I said, doing my best to sound official in the face of an otherwise steamy situation. After all, she may have put her robe back on but she sure didn't use it to cover herself much.

"Oh, my God!" she cried, putting her hand over her mouth and finally pulling the flaps of her robe closed with the other. "He's going to be alright, isn't he? He's not going to die or anything is he?" She seemed genuinely concerned for a girl in her line of work, not that I would know much about girls in her line of work, but I was touched by her concern. I actually thought I could see her eyes fill with tears.

"I don't know, miss. He's stable now, but it's very important that I contact his family as soon as possible."

"What kind of an accident was it? Oh, the poor guy! Of all the people for something like that to happen to." she rambled on. I had to interrupt.

"It was a car accident, Miss Hasher, but please, I need to know if you know anything about his family or how I might contact them," I said, working to keep some firmness in my voice.

She walked over to a wet bar on the other side of the room and pulled a bottle of beer from the refrigerator underneath, opened it and took a long swallow the way a man would, then asked, "Can I offer you a drink, Officer... ?"

"Chagford, Terrence Chagford and actually, yes, a beer would be great. It's been a long trip...and it's Chief...but Miss Hasher, the information?"

"Oh, yes..." she said as she handed me a bottle. "Martin and I were friends," and looked at me slyly, "...and not like that either. Martin was, uh...is a gorgeous guy. He'd never have to...well...'make arrangements' and I don't do freebies...but, yeah, we were close," she said guardedly. "We talked almost every day. He was pretty much of a workaholic, which I can understand. He didn't grow up a spoiled rotten kid with a silver spoon shoved up his ass. We made our own way, him and me. That's why I think we got along so well. It's a sad story, though." She turned around briefly to look in the mirror on the wall behind the bar, a quick primp and then back to me.

"His mother was pregnant when she got married just before his father went off to Vietnam. He never came back, and she died having Martin. Martin was a self-made man for the most part, and a lawyer, Wall Street, no less. I always admired him for that. It made me think that he was always channeling his energies into his career to make up for, you know, not having parents, since he never had a chance to know either of them." Her eyes got deep as she shook her head sadly, betraying the fact that she really must have been touched by this guy in some way. She went on.

"He was raised by his aunt somewhere in Jersey. She died just a few years ago, of breast cancer. He took it hard. I let him sleep on my couch for a few days until he got himself back together, but that's it. He never talked about anyone else. I guess there could be some cousins out there or something, but he never mentioned it, poor guy. Now for this to happen. God, my heart goes out to him. He must have been born under a dark star or something." She took a breath, drank more of her beer and lit a cigarette. I took that as a sign that I could do the same and lit one of my own.

She was a real chatterer that one. It's a wonder that she actually got any real work done. Then she was at it again. "He was a survivor of the World Trade Center attacks, ya know."

That caught my attention. I was interested to know more, so I let her go on with it. *Damn, this girl can talk a blue streak,* I thought and wondered what her specialty was.

"Oh, of course not. You couldn't know…but he was." The only time she stopped talking was to sip her beer. "Yeah, he barely got out with his life before the whole thing went down…killed most of the people in his firm." The more she spoke, the more interested in listening I got, so I let her go on uninterrupted.

"Yeah, he was running late that morning. I saw him in the

hallway hurrying to the elevator. I said, 'Good Morning.' He just said, 'Running late, Cash. Can't talk. I'll see ya later.' Cashmere, that's my name...uh...well...it's my stage name anyway. He wasn't the same after that. When I saw him again later that afternoon, he'd been wandering the streets for hours in some kind of shock. His clothes were all ripped and filthy. His face and hands were all dirty and scraped up. It was about five, I think. He wouldn't go to a hospital. He just asked me to come over and bring him a bottle of booze and some Valium then he just shut the door."

"After that I didn't see him for days. Every time I called over to his place he told me that he was alright and just wanted to sleep. Finally, I went down to the corner deli and got a ton of food, took it over there and banged on the door until he let me in. He was a mess in a ratty old robe, sweat pants and socks, his hair sticking up, unshaven. I've never seen him so unkempt. He was always so well put together, ya know? Well, I just barged right in and insisted that he shower. I waited there until he did. After that I got him to come and sit down with me to eat something and talk. He told me that he was just on his way up to his office when he felt the building shake." She stopped there for a second to take out another beer for each of us before she went on.

"I could see him start to sweat and tremble as he talked about it. He got real pale, and clammy looking, too. It scared me. He told me that he'd just gone into the second tower when the first tower got hit but didn't realize what was going on. Then, when he felt his building shake and heard all the sirens and screaming, and saw people running everywhere, he just ran out with them. Just in the nick of time, too. He'd only gotten about a block away when first the tower came down. The rush of wind hit him in the back and blew him right down on his face. He told me he stayed there for a few seconds, stunned, then got up and ran like hell. He wandered around aimlessly for hours before he ended up somewhere in the East Village, and kept walking until he got back here."

"Like I said, after that he was never the same. He never went out...not even to shop for groceries. He had me set up a delivery account for him at the Gourmet Garage over on 64th, but I have my doubts as to whether he ever used it. It went on like that for a few weeks. He completely shut himself off from the world. I think I was probably the only one who saw him. He got such dark circles under his eyes it worried me. I tried to get him to find some help. All he said was, 'I can't take this anymore. I gotta get outta here before it kills me. It didn't this time...but I feel like it did. I'm not gonna wait around to give it another chance. I give up.' That was when he told me that he was selling his place and leaving the City. 'Where ya gonna go?' I asked him. 'Anywhere but here, Cash. I'd rather leave now while I still can and find somewhere to...hide. With any luck, it'll be somewhere I can breathe, quiet...and peaceful...and green. No more for me. I'm beat,' he said. The next thing I knew he was gone and the place was up for sale. He must have set the whole thing up before he even told me about it."

"That's why, when you said he had an accident, I thought he might have...well...decided to end it all for himself, poor guy. He was acting so freaky. I thought that maybe it was all just too much for him. On the outside he seemed to have everything going for him but, on the inside, I guess he felt he had nothing. Even stupid whores like me have families to love them," she said, sniffing back a tear. I felt bad for her. Then, the doorbell rang and startled her.

"Oh, I can't do this now...not today. Do your stuff for me, will ya?" she asked, wiping her eyes with the tail of her robe. I walked over to the door and opened it to find a short, greasy, middle-aged man standing there in a five thousand dollar suit and more gold on his hands than in Fort Knox. He looked at me suspiciously and asked if this was Cashmere's apartment.

I responded by flashing my badge at him saying, "Yeah, and she's going on a long vacation. Wanna join her, pal?" giving him my 'tough cop' routine. He beat it out of there like a comic gangster on the lam. She laughed out loud, "Thanks, handsome." I gave her two fifties for her time, putting it down as investigatory expenses, and left.

❋ ❋ ❋

Well, I'd gotten what I went there for and knew then why he

didn't want to die alone. He'd been alone and isolated for most of his life, must have felt left out and abandoned all the way around, just wanting some connection with another human being at the time when it mattered most. *Poor fucking slob,* I thought. *Too goddamned damaged to form any kind of connection in life,* resounded heavily with me for reasons of my own. *Sad bastard!* He was just like me, but at least I still had my mother. I always count my blessings on that one.

Just as I was leaving the building it occurred to me that he must have been running away when he went off the bridge, just happening to land in Jennisburg. What I still didn't know was if he intended it. That's when I decided. As I walked down the street looking for a bar, desperate to have a real drink, I remembered how I felt when I looked down and saw his blood on my hands and thought to myself, *Don't worry, pal. We'll look after ya. You have us now, such as we are. Jenny, Lila, Mom and me. We'll take care of ya.* I've never been able to turn my back on a stray, particularly this one. We had a common thread between us. We were both a couple of sad-ass bastards. Then I wondered to myself, *Does he see the big 'L' on his forehead when he looks in the mirror, too?*

❄ ❄ ❄

I've just had dinner with Martin and watched some TV with him. We only watch the quiet, gentle English shows on PBS anymore, *Last of the Summer Wine, As Time Goes By, Waiting For God* and the BBC period pieces. He flinches and goes pale when there's any sort of violence in a show. With all that's been going on, I really shouldn't leave him alone so much. He told me when I came home today that he'd dreamed he heard something scratching at the door, sounding like it wanted to come in. God, I only hope it was a dream, but I just can't be sure. I thought I heard scratching in the house a few times myself this week, and I wasn't sleeping. I try to tell myself it could always be squirrels, but squirrels don't move coffee cans or chairs. I guess I'm just kidding myself that it could be anything as ordinary as that just so I can get through this. I know it's here. Now it's just a question of waiting. It's funny how, when you know your days are numbered, you have moments of lucidity and calmness. I imagine it's the same way for men on Death Row. The shows are off for tonight now so I'd better continue on while I can still think straight. I get so little sleep these days. I'm so tired.

*** * ***

When I got back home from Manhattan, I called Jenny Denton from the bus station. I was lucky she was in the book. She and her husband invited me over. It was only about nine thirty and the kids were in bed so I accepted. They have a lovely home, very well kept, which Jenny attributes to her husband. Jeff Denton is a professional gardener for the wealthy families over in Victory Hill and apparently does very well at it.

We sat and had coffee and brandy while I told them what I'd learned about Martin Welliver from the hooker. I could see in her eyes that Jenny was moved by it all, which I'm sure reinforced her already existing feeling that Mr. Welliver would be 'our special patient.' Her husband, Jeff, looked to be a big, burly kind of guy in his early fifties, balding slightly with a short buzz haircut, a well trimmed dark brown beard and a deep, friendly voice. I saw him discretely give her a subtle 'ok' the way happily married people do with each other. He took her hand on the table, gave it a gentle squeeze, looked at her and said that under the circumstances, she might "...keep an eye on our fellow and do what you can to make him feel at home here while he recovers." It made me think that, under the right circumstances and with the right people, marriage could be a truly wonderful thing... a communion of hearts where making each other happy came as naturally as breathing.

Although I don't know why I should have been, I was surprised to find out from Jenny that the buzz of the accident had gone around town like a bad rash and had brought in a call that afternoon from the local realtor and resident busybody, Sylvia Hadrada. It seems Sylvia'd left a message saying that she'd heard about the accident and apparently believed that the 'injured man' was the same man she'd sold a house to only a few weeks earlier because he was from the City. She said she was calling because she'd heard that the hospital was looking to give notice to the next of kin and thought that there might be someone at the house they could contact.

We both agreed that, based on the information I had gotten in New York, it was unlikely that anyone would be at the house, even assuming Sylvia's information was good to begin with. I took the address anyway and left, saying I'd contact Sylvia in the morning and take a ride out there to see if we could find out anything. In the meantime, I told Jenny I'd stop by the hospital to check on things when I had the time. From there I went home, my head hanging down, feeling even lonelier than usual for what I now call one of the few remaining good nights of sleep I'd ever have and taking a pill just for the hell of it.

✳ ✳ ✳

The next day I had Lila call Sylvia Hadrada from the station and set up a time when we could go over to the house. After the call, Lila came into my office with a cup of coffee for me, sat down looking at me expectantly and said "So give!"

I told her all I knew up until that point, keeping most of the personal details of Martin's life out of it. I kept to the facts that there was a possibility that he was a transplant from New York City; that as far as I could find out, he had no family and although his condition had been stable, it was still critical. I could tell by the expression on her face that she was going to get involved, too. No surprise there. Even though she'd recently gotten engaged to one of my men, Eli Beauchamps, and had a toddler to worry about, she has more energy than anyone I've ever known. She's really gone all out to become an active force in the community since she came back. She has her hands in everything from church bake sales and flea markets to organizing the local parades and is becoming very well regarded for her efforts. She's a real 'citizen' in the making, my Lila is. Between her mother and the dozens of stay-at-home moms around, she never has a problem finding child care. It's a good thing, too, since she practically lives at the station, which is fine by me, and since it allows her to spend some extra time with Eli, it must work for her, too. But I could tell at this point that she was about to take on yet another project, 'the mysterious Mr. Welliver from

New York.' Not only did the glint in her eye give her intentions away, but on the way out she tipped her hand.

"By the way, Chief, I called over to Marchand's and had them send over some 'Get Well' flowers on behalf of all of us here at the station and as soon as he's well enough, I'll go over and bring him a cake or something." It was time to add another name to the growing list of the local Martin Welliver Rescue Society! Small towns can be that way.

Humorously, I replied in a false, whiney voice, "What about me, Lila? I want a cake, too!" She laughed at that, but I had a nice big piece of chocolate cake on my desk by lunch. *That's my girl!*

I spent the rest of that morning going over reports from the prior two days and completing my own report of the accident. By then it was time to go over and pick up Sylvia. *What a joy!*

Sylvia Hadrada, with her basket of black lacquer hair, tons of gaudy jewelry, red fingernails and matching lipstick, hadn't changed much in thirty years except for maybe a little work around the eyes and the chin. Had she not become one of the most successful businesswomen in town, she would certainly have become the town character. She knew everything about everyone and usually found a way to make a buck off of it. *Barking mad, she is!* But a man's gotta do what a man's gotta do, so I went over to her office and picked her up.

"Oh, Chief!" she screeched at me in a voice worse than fingernails across a chalkboard. "What an honor!...and on official police business, too! I'm so delighted."

Well, before she got too delighted, I had to ask her to show me some of the paperwork of the house sale she'd referred to in her message. She was right. A house had been sold to a Mr. Martin Welliver of New York City a few weeks earlier. Oddly enough, I wasn't familiar with the place but Sylvia eagerly filled me in that it was in the very far northwest end of the town by the town limit close to the Hamilton Township border, tucked away in the woods at the end of a quarter-mile dirt drive so no one would notice it unless they were looking for it. At that point I felt obliged to ask her if she could show it to me, official business, you know.

After about ten minutes of useless chatter in-between orders of unnecessary directions she said, "Did you know that I went to

high school with your mother and father?" and "Oh my! Your
father was such a handsome man?" and "Oh, I would have loved
to have gone out with him back then, but he and Charlotte were
high school sweethearts from the minute they met, so I never
really had a chance."

Thank God for that! I thought then felt a little guilty
afterwards. I was still in too much pain, feeling rough as a
badger's ass, grouchy as hell and none too charitable. I took a
half a pain pill…dry…to keep the two slugs of Turkey that I had
had on the way over company and did my best to be patient. She
really wasn't that bad. Actually, after you got used to her, she
could be really kind of endearing in a bizarre sort of way. I think
she just channeled her energies into everyone else's life to make
up for the fact that she and Harry never had any children to
occupy them.

We eventually turned into a dirt drive that cut through a
grove of thick brush and trees that led into a clearing where the
house stood. I should've known it was trouble the minute I laid
eyes on it, looming before us like an enormous, towering skull
bleached white by a desert sun, its outline distinct against the
backdrop of the brightly colored autumn leaves that still clung to
the surrounding trees.

It was a large place for the area, larger than anything we had
in town—at least fifteen rooms, I figured. Whoever built it must
have had more money than brains…and more imagination than
could be considered healthy. Maybe it was just my small town
mind, but it gave me the sense that it'd been picked out of a
legend from an ancient civilization, completely out of kilter with
anything else for hundreds of miles around, and dropped there
by some cataclysm, doomed to exile among the fields of crops
and cows.

Two stories high, three if you counted the two pitched attic
spaces that held small windows giving them a tower-like effect
on each side of the vaulted central roof. The eaves were lined
with intricate lattice work that reminded me of a child's paper cut
outs. Below the towers, a few feet inward toward the center of
the house, were larger pitched overhangs with more latticework
above two large windows. Two more windows on the first floor
were overshadowed by a second roof with matching lattice to

cover the porch space surrounding the house on three sides. The front door and the stairs leading down to the drive created the only break in the stair rail of the porch, the dark oak of the door and the gray of the broad steps and porch being the only deviation from the sheet of white that was the house. Before I could even turn off the engine Sylvia started her 'pitch' routine.

"A lovely, charming place isn't it? Pure Victorian. It's a real gem, but so far removed from anywhere that no one really knows it's here. It's in marvelous shape for its age...built in 1901," she ranted as we got out of the car. "I rented it to the pastor of...what was it now?...oh some Evangelical Church over in Hamilton Common in the early sixties. He spent close to twenty years raising his family here. They had a big family...six or seven children, I think. I guess when the last one went off to college, he and his wife decided their calling was to do some missionary work in the jungles of South America, or Africa, or something like that. The house has hardly been touched since they left, except for some general upkeep to hold its value. I've had a hell of a time getting anyone to look at it," she said as we got out of the car, waving her hands about as if she were going to take flight. Sylvia always uses her hands for high drama when she speaks, like a cock-eyed opera singer.

With Sylvia trailing behind me, still shouting, I walked up to the front door. No one answered when I knocked, not that I expected anyone, knowing what I did. She took the lead then and began to walk around the outside of the house, rattling on, still flapping her hands for emphasis as if I might be a potential buyer.

"Oh! And did I tell you? I got it for a steal from some widow from California who used it as a getaway in the fifties. I had it modernized before I rented it to the church people and you know what? The rent they paid in the first ten years paid off the mortgage and the repairs so the rest was gravy, as they say. I think it was in 1982 or '83 that they left."

By then, we'd walked around to the back of the house while she chattered on with hardly a breath. "And isn't the garden house lovely, so clever of them to model it on the big house. Don't you think, Chief?" Actually, it was way too cutesie for my tastes, to build a garden house to look like an oversized doll house version of the main house is like housing a stunted child's mind in an adult body, more creepy than charming, but what do I know about Victorians? Too much time on their hands and no television to entertain them. If it were up to me, I'd have just built a log cabin and left it at that.

Oblivious to my lack of response, Sylvia just continued on with the energy of a rapid fire machine gun. "Anyway, one day this young man just walked into my office about three or four weeks ago and asked about it, a nice looking boy, too. It seems he was touring the area when his car broke down not far over on the other side of the Hamilton line. He told me that he'd wandered up the dirt path looking for a phone. Of course, the house was empty, but he seemed to have fallen in love with it. Didn't seem to mind the isolation at all. He hitchhiked his way into town, got a room over at Dunham's and came straight over to see me about it. I even let him call over to the garage from my office to have his car towed into town. While that was being taken care of, I brought him out here in my car to have a walk-through. He seemed like a nice young man, quiet, shy, I'd say, but very pale with dark circles under his eyes. I got the feeling he was very unhappy. He told me he'd just gotten tired of city life and wanted somewhere quiet. After I showed him that everything in the house, though old, was still in excellent working order, he asked how much I wanted for it. Well, it's been costing me a small fortune to maintain the place for the last few years, yard men to mow, cleaning women to come in every few months or so to dust off the place, an outside paint job every two years or so. It adds up." She was waving her hands all around again, like she was swatting at flies.

Red fingernails at her age, Good God! I thought as we came back around to the front and she stopped to continue her saga.

"I offered to sell it to the County Historical Society" she said, "but they turned me down because it was so remote and all. 'No tourists would ever come out here just to see an old house,' they said, so I gave him a low-ball price, but where I could still come away with a nice tidy profit, of course. I'm not as young as I used to be, after all, not that I haven't aged well," she said pulling a compact out of her purse and looking in it admiringly as she pushed up her hair and made a smooch face in the mirror.

As I stood there with the din of her voice constantly ringing in my ears, I couldn't help but look over her shoulder at the front of the house and notice that the sun was setting. It made me nervous, edgy. I was cold and in pain and just wanted to leave, so I took her gently by the arm and tried to get her to move. That's when I started feeling really uncomfortable. It seemed to me then that the more we moved away from the house, the more I felt the need to look back over my shoulder at it. It made me uneasy, the way a good oil portrait can when you walk back and forth in front of it, like its eyes are following you. About halfway to the car, Sylvia stopped again, resisting my efforts to keep her going.

"I do think it's time to unload some of my more difficult properties and reinvest in something more liquid. Anyway," she continued, beginning to sound winded. "He called me the next day and told me that he'd have it. Wanted to pay cash, too, if you can believe it. No negotiating or anything. But I'll tell you, there was one funny thing, not funny really, just odd," she said, nodding and squinting her eyes to see me through the rapidly approaching dusk.

"I could've sworn that I'd gone through this entire house two or three times since the pastor left and it was empty. There were only the appliances, a chrome-and-enamel kitchen set and some dusty old things in the attic and basement, but when I showed him the hall closet under the stairs next to the basement door, a glimmer of light came through a crack in the stairs and I saw something shiny in the back corner under the first stair."

"Mr. Welliver reached in and took it out, looked at me and smiled. 'Antiques?' he asked. 'Not that I know of,' I said and shrugged. It was a dusty, old engraved silver box. I took the box from him and opened it. There was nothing much in it, just a few old-style Mahjong tiles. You know, the old Chinese game that was popular forever ago? 'Who knows?' I said, 'not worth anything, I'm sure,' I said, but I took the box anyway and handed him the tiles. •There! A house warming gift,' I said, and we laughed."

"I guess that when the old pastor and his wife weren't preaching or making babies, they liked to play Mahjong. Not nearly as exhausting as the first two activities, I'm sure,' I said, and had a good laugh to myself, and lucky we found it when I was there before the papers were signed. I sold that box to the owner of Monique's Unique Frantique Boutique over in Hamilton Common for two hundred dollars. Monique told me it was made in the early Art Nouveau style and had the hallmark of a London silversmith," she said with a self-satisfied grin, obviously impressed with herself for remembering the artistic terms. "I thought that was kind of strange though, an old silver box from London finding its way to our little cow-town. But two hundred bucks is two hundred bucks," she said with a shrug.

Sensing the end of her story was near I took her by the arm again and began guiding her toward the car. The sun had almost completely set by then and I'd had enough for one day. I needed to get away from there and sit down...soon. I had no sooner gotten her into the car and shut the door when I felt a cold wind, like the fingers on a hand, blow up the back of my jacket. I turned to look at the house one last time, feeling as if somewhere deep inside me something primal was trying to warn me.

At the time I thought that maybe it was the pill starting to kick in with the drinks or the effect of the sun almost gone behind us, but as I looked at the house, it seemed to take on a presence of its own. The low glow of the sun reflecting through the autumn leaves seemed to give it color and motion...and expression, some sort of...life...like some surreal carnival funhouse where the entrance was made up to look like the face of clown, except this was no clown. The peaked windows became arched glaring eyes, the door gave the impression of the hole of a nose, the break in the porch turned into a gaping mouth, the steps rippled like a tongue and the tower peaks stood out defiantly against the background of the setting sun like...horns. As I sit here writing this now, I'm sure it was grinning at me...mocking me...like it knew what was to come and I didn't. But back then nothing like that would have ever occurred to me. I just passed it off as another of my roaming anxieties like the 'sundowning' Alzheimer's patients get, and drove off. I was unsure of so many things then. But I know better now. I know enough to be afraid.

✳ ✳ ✳

After I dropped Sylvia off back at her office, I went by the hospital. Jenny Denton was there. I told her what I'd learned from Sylvia. It wasn't much only that Martin Welliver had come to Jennisburg alone and had bought the house on Randolph Road just this side of the Hamilton Township border. She looked as bright as I'd seen her before in her white nurse's uniform and pastel flowered smock. 'Our patient' was doing as well as could be expected, she told me, then asked if I wanted to see him. That gave the knot of anxiety in my stomach a good wrench, but I agreed, not wanting my 'standoffishness' to become too apparent.

The room number was seventy-six. It's funny the things that you remember sometimes. He was in the bed nearest the window with the curtain drawn. The first thing I saw was his encased leg and foot protruding out from behind the drawn curtain in a sling hanging from a trapeze over the bed. The anxiety rose to my throat from the pit of my stomach, squeezing me like a vice grip with each step that I took. I must've looked just like that when I was recovering from the church incident. The next thing I noticed were the flowers Lila had sent and a second bunch on the window sill, home grown and fresh cut, and assumed Jenny had brought them. Then I turned the corner and saw the whole scene. There he was, lying very much like I had all those years ago, an arm in a cast to the hand, his shoulder in a brace to the neck. His head was wrapped in bandages, face all bruised, looking like he was asleep, quiet, peaceful. I felt sorry for him, but at the same time I was glad for him. With the calm look on his face, he couldn't have been in any pain. There'd be plenty of time for that later.

When Jenny spoke to him directly, it startled me and I took a step back. It must've shown on my face because when she looked up at me she said, "It's okay. The jury is still out on whether coma patients can still hear what goes on around them. There have been plenty of cases where patients respond to familiar voices and music. It's okay, Terry, really. Come closer. Talk to him. "

She turned to him. "Mr. Welliver...Martin. Chief Chagford is here to see you. He's the man who saved you," she said, embarrassing me right off the bat. "He came by to see how you were doing and I told him you're doing just fine," she said quietly as she ran her hand gently down the side of his face. "You're quite the celebrity here these days. All the girls have come in to see you. You already have so many friends here you don't even know about." The sweat began beading up on my forehead and upper lip.

"Go ahead, Chief, shake his good hand. It's okay." I wasn't ready for that, but I didn't want Jenny to know what a coward I was either, so I went over to the side of the bed and took his good hand, giving it a gentle squeeze. I couldn't help thinking back to when he took my hand by the river.

"I'm Terrence Chagford, Martin. Good to see you're still with us," I said and looked at Jenny for approval. She nodded, smiling. I'd never really seen his face clearly before. It was so bruised, but even through the bruising, I could see the thick dark eyebrows, well-chiseled features, full lips and cleft chin that would undoubtedly make 'all the girls' fuss over him, and knew he'd get the best of nursing care for the duration of his stay there because of it. I can only assume that Jenny saw the distress dripping down the sides of my face because she came over to me and walked me back out of the room. As soon as we were in the hallway and I could breathe again, I asked if the doctors had said anything about his recovery, struggling desperately to act as normal as possible.

"Well…" she said, "Dr. Barton said that the danger of brain swelling should be over soon and if all goes well he would take him off the coma medication at the end of the week. He should start to regain consciousness a few days after that. He'll need some physical therapy for a while, but it if there are no complications, he should be able to go home sometime around Thanksgiving. Only time will tell, really. But then the question becomes, go home to what? There won't be anyone there for him. He'll definitely need some in-home care for a while, not to mention someone to talk to." I could tell by the look in her eyes and the inflection in her voice that something was coming and had a feeling that it wouldn't be long before I found out what it was.

"I was thinking that, once he comes out of it, we might try and get someone local in Jennisburg to act as a live-in housekeeper for him for a while to cook and clean, and keep him company until he can get around better on his own. If you can think of anyone, it would be a great help," she said, more than hinting that I should do something about it.

"Yes, ma'am," I said, automatically reaching for the comfort of Lila's 'can do' abilities. "If Lila can't find someone, no one can."

"Yes, I should think so. I've met her a couple of times. Our kids are in the same Gymboree class. She's a real go getter. I like her. That'll do," Jenny said approvingly. Then as we got back into the elevator, she asked me, "Any news on the cause yet, or the car?" I told her what I knew, that Lila had a call from Tom Wuchowitz over at the garage, that he couldn't find any mechanical explanation for the accident and that it was his opinion that it must have been the rain and mud that made the car slide off the ramp.

Then she asked, "You gonna come by and see him when he comes to?"

"I don't know if that's really a good idea. It'd probably be kind of awkward. Guys deal with things differently than women do. He'd probably just rather forget it and move on," I said, hoping my awkwardness wasn't showing, then asked her with a half smile, "but I can tell that you've been burning up the lines with my mother. Haven't you?" Her eyes twinkled and she gave me a knowing smile as the elevator door opened.

"I told you. Charlotte and I have been friends for years. We've worked a lot of shifts together," she said, confirming my suspicions on the subject. I let it drop, but not without wondering how much my mother had told her about me, my past and my problems. More than I'd be comfortable with I was sure, but at that point, what was I gonna do? I just let it ride.

When I got back to the station, I called Lila into my office and got her working on the housekeeper angle. I told her if all went well, he'd need someone by Thanksgiving then I got back to doing my own job of keeping the peace in Jennisburg, such as it was. I made out the schedule for the next two weeks of duty, went over to the diner for a tuna salad sandwich and walked around Main Street just to show my presence. It was Halloween, it was dark, and there were kids in costumes everywhere. It was important that I be seen, at least until the kid's curfew. I'd made plans with my mother for later that night, spaghetti with meatballs and American Movie Classic's Monsterfest. That would be after I'd had a nice hot Epsom salts bath and dipped into my own stash of that 'green leafy substance' everyone talks about. *Whoopeee!* It was Halloween, I'd done my part in keeping the balance of justice in the universe and it was time to relax for an evening. I figured even guys like me deserve a break every once in a while.

❋ ❋ ❋

It's raining out now, and the house seems quiet. There are only a few more hours before the sun comes up and I'm aching all over. It's time for my pills again. I hope I can keep my head up long enough to continue on until sunrise. I'm off tomorrow, so I can spend the day sleeping. It's easier to sleep in the daytime when there are no shadows to lurk over my bed, no voices to whisper in my ear. The house has been quiet tonight, but that business about scratching sounds has got me nervous. I'm going to take a walk around the house now to stretch my legs, check on Martin and inspect the bottoms of the doors for scratch marks. If I find any, I think I'll scream. It's a funny thing about screaming, something I've learned from experience. Once you scream, you're afraid to stop because once you stop, you know you'll be all alone again with the fear and nothing will have changed. So what's the point? You can't keep on screaming forever, can you? There must be some resolve to it, some end. As I've said before, fear is the cancer of the mind, the incurable kind, no modern medicine for this strain. The only resolution is just to let it eat away at you, but at least once it's done, you know it's over for good.

❋ ❋ ❋

Everything seems fine. Martin is sleeping quietly, but I could've sworn the window in his room was closed when I left him and it was open a few inches when I checked just now. Maybe he opened it himself if it got warm in there. Maybe it's just my nerves cracking under the pressure of it all, but after all we've been through, no one could ever blame me if my imagination got the better of me. Maybe I did put the coffee jar upside down in my distraction. I don't know anymore, but I know I didn't leave those chairs out. It's a horrible thing when your mind is so preoccupied with fear that you don't remember if you did something or not. I just do not know anymore. Maybe...Maybe not...Maybe...

※ ※ ※

My head is getting a little heavy now. Where was I? Oh, yes! Halloween. I passed Halloween quietly at my mother's. She gave out the Trick or Treat candy to the kids that came by. I've never been really all that fond of kids...other than for Angelica and recently, the Denton boys. I don't understand why. Maybe they remind me of the chances I'll never have again and I envy them, subconsciously resenting them for it. I guess it doesn't matter much anymore but back then, I'd have been just as happy to hide behind a bush with a monster mask and jump out with a thundering BOO! to scare the hell out of them. But that was before I knew what I know now about fear, and suddenly it doesn't seem so funny anymore.

Other than for the local Halloween festivities, life went on as it had before for a while. I stopped by the hospital a few times to check on things and catch up with Jenny. Time seemed to go by quickly with few incidents out of the usual, a few fender benders, a few domestic violence calls, a few prowler calls that didn't turn up anything . . . probably just a bunch of bored kids raising hell over at The Old Settler's Cemetery. A pot bust here, a DWI there...but my men handled most of those things. Lila and I really just coordinated.

I did the usual politic thing and met with the Mayor and Town Council on matters no one really cared about but them anyway. Then I got a call at the station from Jenny. He was awake. She told me she was sitting there reading to him, some Jackie Collins crap of all things, and when she looked up, there he was. His eyes were open, staring at her.

She said she'd been wondering the whole time whether he'd be as nice a guy as he looked while he was out or if he'd be some loud mouthed, self-absorbed city shit screaming for his lawyer and a specialist to be flown in from Los Angeles. But she was pleased to report to that he was very polite, quiet and shy, and a little scared, which was to be expected since he was at a complete loss as to what happened, no memory of it at all or the few weeks that passed before. She said the doctor told her that it was very common with serious head injuries and then told me that she knew that long before he'd told her. "Doctors!" she said with a whiff. 'So much for doctors,' was the impression I got.

She told me that she had to tell Martin basically everything but his name. He knew that much and that he lived in an apartment on East 68th Street, that he'd put his apartment up for sale and left the city to look for quiet place to settle down. The last cogent memory he had was of his car breaking down on Randolph Road. He had no memory of buying the house, the furniture he'd put in it or the accident itself, just the sensation of being cold, wet...feeling like he was falling, and hearing the vague sound of a man's voice from somewhere off in the distance.

She told me she dared go the bit further, asking him if there was anyone he wanted her to contact that could come and be with him, even though she already knew better, but he said there wasn't and thanked her for her concern. She went on to say that he was amazed by the number of flowers in the room. There were the earlier ones that Lila sent already beginning to fade and the ones Jenny brought twice a week from her husband's hothouse. There was a lovely arrangement sent by Sylvia Hadrada and a small bowl of red tea roses from my mother. Then there was a rather expensive looking arrangement sent by someone she didn't know with a card signed with a bunch of 'xxxs and ooos' and the name Cash Hasher. *A hooker with a heart of gold*, I thought and smiled to myself. She must have remembered the name of Jennisburg from my badge and researched the rest herself. I had to give her credit for that. *Not bad, Red!* I thought to myself and smiled. Jenny said that he seemed genuinely moved by it all, but she could tell he didn't feel much like talking, completely understandable under the circumstances. He told her that he was in a good deal of pain and very hungry so she gave him his pain medicine, some scrambled eggs, toast and tea and let him go back to sleep for a while. That's why she was calling me just then.

She said he had sad eyes. "Huge, sad, lonely, deep brown eyes," was how she put it. She said they brought out the mother in her and it was all she could do to keep herself from putting her arms around him. She didn't tell him about my trip to New York, or that I was on the spot when the accident happened, but she did warn me that he would probably ask about it when his mind cleared. I told her to just tell him the truth, but try and play down my part in it. It's never good for someone to feel beholden to another, especially when I was only doing my job. I was sure it would only make us both feel more than a little uncomfortable.

I never told anyone about what he said to me before his lights went out that night. *Better left alone,* I thought. *It's a man thing.* Then she asked if I was going to come up and see him. I lied telling her I had my hands full over at the station, but that I'd try to get over when he was feeling better, in a day or so. She accepted it grudgingly, leaving me with the laughing threat, "Don't make me call your mother on you!" as she hung up.

❄ ❄ ❄

I had dinner with my mother that night and, as I expected, she wanted to discuss it. "Closure," she said as she shoveled a load of her famous spinach and walnut pasta bake onto my plate. "That's all it's about, sweetheart...closure. You can finally put that little girl's death behind you now. He's your absolution, not that you ever needed it. Take it as a gift from God, sweetheart. You never have to forget about her. You just don't have to wear her loss around your neck like a glaring badge of dishonor anymore. It wasn't your fault. It wasn't that you weren't brave enough, or skilled enough, or didn't try hard enough. You proved that when you pulled that man out of the river. Things just happen, honey! You've earned the right to have your dignity back if that's the way you have to look at it. Go and see him. Let him thank you. You'll feel better, I promise...and besides, he lives here now. You'll run into him all over town once he's well enough, and the whole town is abuzz over my son the hero, so it's not like it's a grand secret or anything. You can't avoid him forever now, can you? And who knows? He may just come and see you when he's well enough. What then?" she said with a sigh of exasperation from her corner by the kitchen counter.

"I'll deal with it when it happens, Ma," I said, getting a little exasperated myself by it all.

"Men! I love them to death, but as long as I live, I'll never understand them," she said and smiled as she came over and kissed my forehead. "Your father was just like that too, God bless him. Stubborn as the day is long! At least you come by it honestly," she finished as she put her cigarette out and sat down to her plate. "Now eat!"

The next day Lila told me that she'd finally found someone to take on the housekeeper job for 'our patient' as he was increasingly being called by all the women involved. "Martha Portensky said she'd do it, but on her own terms, of course. She'll live in with him and take care of him for the first few weeks until his casts come off. After that, when he's able to get around pretty much by himself, she'll go by and do three weekdays to cook, clean and do laundry. On Sunday afternoons, she'll go over after church until he can get on by himself. She'll discuss a once-a-week housekeeping day with him then. So, we've got that under control. She just needs to know a few days before he's due to be released so she can go in there and get things ready." Lila said, looking exceedingly pleased with herself and as usual, I couldn't have been more pleased with her.

I gave her Jenny's home number and asked if she could coordinate the thing with her. "I'd be ever so grateful if you could handle this for me, Lila," I told her, which meant she could get her hair and nails done during any work day that she wanted...on me. Lila's salary was never enough for what she did for me, so I gave her as many perks as I could to make her life easier. Pretty much every shop owner and merchant in town owed me more than one favor and knew if they comp'd Lila with little things every now and again, I'd be •ever so grateful' in return when they needed me, especially if they wanted to keep something quiet. My Lila is a gem. My heart can't help but bloom whenever I think of how much she does to show she cares for me.

❋ ❋ ❋

Things were quiet in the run up to Thanksgiving when my mother stopped into the station unexpectedly, looking very much like the cat who ate the canary. "Guess what came in the mail today, Chief?" she said excitedly as she handed me a formal looking envelope made of ivory parchment and addressed to "Mrs. Charlotte Chagford & Son."

"Go ahead, open it," she chirped.

It was an invitation to Thanksgiving dinner given by Mr. and Mrs. Jeffrey Denton. I looked at her suspiciously. Her face was shining and nodding.

Well?" she asked. "It sounds like fun. Doesn't it? I'd love to go and see their house. I hear Jeff has done wonderful things with it since the last time I was there, and I won't have to cook for a change. Oh! And I can go out and get a new outfit too, and it wouldn't hurt you to put on a regular shirt and tie for a change either," she said with a grin and an elbow to my side.

"Yes, Mother. Of course, go ahead. RSVP that we'll be there if it'll make you happy," I said grudgingly, but not meaning to sound that way. She deserved all the happiness she could get, so if it was a dinner party she wanted, it would be a dinner party she would have.

"It would," she replied, kissed me on the cheek, then turned and rushed out of the door as if I'd change my mind if I had the chance to think about it. As I stood there alone, all I could do was shake my head and smile. *Women! Waddaya gonna do with 'em. Can't live with 'em, can't lock 'em up.*

Thanksgiving Day came. We were due to arrive at the Denton's for hors d'oeuvres and cocktails at three o'clock, dinner to be served at five. By the time we got there, the street was lined with cars on both sides. I recognized Lila's car which meant Eli was there, too. At least there would be someone there I could buddy up with.

Mom had made a large baked brie stuffed with sun-dried tomatoes and wrapped in puff pastry. She's always very proud of it, and rightly so. There was never a crumb left whenever she made it. She really looked lovely that evening too, with her graying, sandy hair done professionally. She'd bought a new coffee-colored dress, a new scarf printed with autumn leaves and leaf patterned earrings with matching scarf pin. She does love her themes, my mom. I put on a white shirt, the Stewart plaid tie that I got as a gift from the Mayor's trip to Scotland last year, a new pair of blue jeans and a navy cable-knit cardigan. I even got my hair freshly buzzed for the occasion.

When we walked in, there were a lot of faces I recognized from around town and not too many kids. I was so relieved. They can be so noisy and rough on one's nerves. There weren't more than twenty people in all, I'd guess. Jenny took Mom immediately under her arm into the kitchen. Jeff, looking very 'Lord of the Manor' in a tweed jacket and matching vest, ushered me to the bar and began mixing up some pink vodka drink in a shaker that he called a "Cosmopolitan."

"It's what all the upper class ladies up on Victory Hill were serving last season," he said with a hearty laugh. "They do like their drink and they pay damn well. Hell, this whole party is pretty much on them!" he laughed again. His laugh was contagious. The better I knew him the more I liked him. "And ya know what?" he continued. "Nobody has to worry about getting a ticket...and ya know why?" I knew what was coming next. "Because I'm serving our very own Chief of Police the first drink!" That one got a big belly laugh all around and, of course, I agreed and laughed like hell with him. •Membership does have its privileges,' so to speak.

"Not a problem, Lord Denton," I said and took a bow. "Be assured, I will attend to everything."

"I knew you would, my dear gentleman constable!" It was clear to me that Lord Denton had tested his concoction more than once before the guests arrived and was in a ripe entertaining mood. He's such a good-hearted guy and I knew he was a hard-working man. I'd seen him and his van with the business name on the side all over town. I just hadn't make the connection with Jenny until I saw him the night I came back from New York...and he was one hell of a bartender, that was for sure. Who could ask for more? They even had their two teenage boys, about thirteen and fourteen, dressed in jackets and ties, walking around with trays of hors d' oeuvres to serve the guests and feeling more adult than not. I guess it was a sign that they wouldn't be sitting at the kids' table anymore.

A few minutes later, Jenny reappeared with Mom and a tray of her baked brie cut neatly into wedges. She was wearing a plush, black velvet hostess skirt with lots of frilly layers underneath and a waist-hugging, high collared, black and gold jacket that was very...low cut and daring in the front. Her was hair done up like the blonde woman from Dynasty...what was her name? Evans, I think. She was really a knockout that night, not a trace of the weariness I'd seen at the hospital.

She kissed me on the cheek and thanked me for coming, her eyes twinkling with a hinting mischief of the 'party girl' she must have been before she was married. Meanwhile, Jeff was getting Mom to experiment with his drink. She took a sip and crinkled her nose, took another one and grinned, "Naughty!" Before I knew it, Jenny had me by the arm and was giving me a tour of the lower floor of the house, introducing me to those I didn't know, mostly from the hospital and the guys who worked with Jeff and their wives. I said my 'good to see yous' and 'Happy Thanksgivings' to those I did know as we went along.

After working through the crowd, she pulled me into the den area or TV room, whatever people call it these days, and there I was, face to face for the first time with a fully conscious Martin Welliver. You could've knocked me over with a feather. It happened so fast, I didn't even have time to get anxious. *Jenny-1, Anxiety-0*. There he was propped up on the sofa with pillows, wearing oversized sweat pants cut up to hang over the cast on his leg and an oversized shirt cut up to hang over the cast on his arm and braced shoulder. Jenny, ever the hostess, broke the ice.

"Chief Terrence Chagford, I'd like you to meet my prized patient, Mr. Martin Welliver. Martin, this is Chief Chagford." In the next second, before I could say a word, Jenny was shouting loudly through the door,
"Jeff, send Jordan in here with another Cosmo for the Chief...and make it a double, will ya?"

I walked over to the sofa and put out my hand, took his and shook it. "Nice to meet you," I said, sounding stiffer than I'd intended.

"Same here...Jenny has told me so much about you," he said. He looked at me strangely at first then, in a low, slow voice said, "I've seen you before..." He paused, clouds coming over his eyes. "It was you...at the river. I remember now. That voice...."

Jordan came to the door with the drink. Jenny took it from him, handed it to me and said quickly, "Sorry guys. I've gotta run. My guests need me," and was gone, leaving me standing there like a dunce.

"It just came back to me this minute...when I saw your face and...that voice," he said, still looking straight at me or, I don't know, maybe into me.

"Yes, I was there," I answered flatly, feeling that old knot start again in my stomach.

"I remember now," he said again, his eyes filling. "How can I ever thank you?..." and then trailed off.

"Here. Take this. A sip won't kill you," I said and handed him the drink, fumbling for something to say that wouldn't sound too lame or make me look like a dolt while he worked through it.

"I was just doing my job. I was at the right place at the right time, but thanks to Jenny and the others at the hospital, you're on the mend now. Everything will be fine. But how in the world did she get you out of the hospital to come here?" I asked, sounding like a cardboard cut out, undeniably losing my struggle with both lameness and dolt-hood. He looked back up at me with eyes that were just as Jenny had described, large, brown, sad and deep. I could see the patch of his scalp where they'd shaved off a hank of his hair that was just then starting to grow in, and the three inch scar forming beneath it. His face was still badly bruised, although by then it was showing signs of healing in shades of purple, yellow and green. My heart thumped deep in my chest at the sight of it all.

"She didn't want me to spend Thanksgiving alone. I guess she pulled some strings. I'm due to be released at the end of the week anyway, so there's really no harm to be done. People have been milling in and out of here for an hour now to say 'hello.' It's been nice. Jenny is very kind, so is Jeff. He came to get me in his van, wheelchair and all, but I've got to be back by ten. Jenny's got the EMS guys on hand waiting to take me back. Apparently, she's got some serious pull with the medical people around here," he said, impressed.

I took a good slug of my drink and was going to make a polite exit when he put out his hand again. When I took it, he pulled me close, our heads side by side so we couldn't look directly at each other and said in a soft, wavering voice, "Thank you for keeping your promise, Chief. I'll never forget it." My eyes filled then. I gave his hand a firm squeeze and let go.

"Anytime, pal. You can count on me," I said, for lack of a better response, but meaning it all the same. Cashmere Hasher's words ran through my mind in a flood about who this guy was and I knew it was time I went back out to the party, quickly. I was just in time too. My mother and Lila were heading in with plates of hors d'oeuvres, looking prepared to have a little visit with him.

Feeling the twinges of anxiety winding themselves up into a full blown attack, I gulped the rest of my drink to fight it off and headed out to the main dining room to find Jeff and the boys setting up the table. They had a nice set-up going, putting the everyday dining table horizontal in the dining room then adding another, second dining table to abut the horizontal one forming a "T" so it extended through the open shutter doors into the living room space. Very creative of them. Then with dinner still at least an hour off, I decided to grab another drink, mingle a bit and take a breath to recover after meeting Martin Welliver for the first time…alive and kicking . . . more or less.

Jenny and Jeff were really hosting themselves to the limit. He walked around with his shaker, filling glasses and trying his best to get everyone into a 'festive' mood. She introduced people around encouraging new conversation in a flirty manner I hadn't seen her do before, but that she was very successful at. Everyone seemed to be having a great time. I really don't know how they manage it—house, family, jobs—and they're still able to pull together such a really fine gathering. I found myself admiring them more and more for their togetherness and unity of purpose. *Why couldn't I ever have found that?* I thought to myself as I meandered around aimlessly, hoping Jeff would pass my way with the shaker…soon.

Out of the corner of my eye, I spotted Eli looking out of

sorts, standing over in the far corner of the dining room looking out of the window. It was obvious Lila had dressed him. He had his straight, black hair cut short and wore a tie with a print that picked up the colors in his hazel eyes. I think he was kind of lost without Lila to drag him around, so I went over and put my hand on his shoulder. "Hey, Buddy."

"Oh, I'm glad it's you, Chief. I'm just no good at these types of social things," he sighed, shuffling his feet nervously.

I agreed with him. We talked about things around town and other nonsense for a few minutes. I had just started teasing him a little about his upcoming wedding when I heard a light, lilting voice come from behind me. "Terrence Chagford! I was wondering when we would get around meeting again." We both turned around to find this very refined looking old woman standing before us.

"You don't remember me?" she said with a quizzically devilish smile. Of course, I knew her instantly.

"Mrs. Coutraire !" I said with a genuine voice of delight. "Well...I'll be."

"Please, Terry...call me Grace. We're all adults now," she said, holding out her hand, very ladylike, to be taken. Grace Coutraire had been the local librarian when I was growing up and without question the most beautiful woman in town in her day. Hell, she was still a looker when I knew her back when I was a teenager and she must have been in her fifties then. All the local teenaged boys got their first lesson in the wonders of female anatomy from Mrs. Coutraire's snug fitting skirt sets with the slits up the back and her high heels. She wore the kind of things our mothers would never have worn, in a manner they never would have worn them, and although there was never a cross word said about her because she was a hometown girl and a war widow, there was never any mistake that Grace Coutraire was the height of small town anomaly, and everyone knew it. The talk was that she brought her style back from her early days of living in New York as a model during the war and left it at that. *God...she must be in her eighties by now, at least,* I thought. I don't think I'd seen her since I graduated high school.

"You look beautiful," I said before I could stop myself. She had her hair done up in a French roll at the back of her head like Grace Kelly wore in the fifties, a style she adopted then and stuck with ever since, although her hair was no longer red but completely white. I guess she was of the philosophy 'if it ain't broke, don't fix it,' and she was right. It still suited her. She was wearing a very elegant green suit made of raw silk over a smooth, white silk blouse with the collar over the lapel, but what struck me most was her jewelry. She had on an emerald necklace and matching earrings. The emeralds were large center stones connected end to end around her neck, each stone surrounded alternately by small diamonds and pearls and, although I'm no expert, from the look of them, I knew they had to be real.

"You don't look too bad yourself, Terry," she said smiling. "I always knew that you'd grow up to be a big, strong, handsome man just like your father." Across the room, Eli spotted Lila waving to him to come over, so he excused himself from the conversation and maneuvered himself around the room to where Lila was waiting.

"Why don't we sit down and catch up a while?" Grace asked. "I've seen you so often since you came back, dashing around town here and there, but you've always been so busy we haven't had a chance to talk...and I've heard so much about you," she said, and we took two chairs over in an unoccupied corner of the room.

"Really?" I said, caught off guard by the genuine interest apparent in her voice.

"Oh, yes. Your mother is so proud of you. She still comes into the library regularly. We chat all the time. She loves her true crime books, that Charlotte. I don't know how she does it. All that blood and gore...but to each his own," she said with a wave of her hand. "I still work part-time at the library, you know, and still hold the Director's position. Sheila Woolf is the Head Librarian now, and with that we still need two assistants. I have one full time and then I have a girl from the high school for school credit."

"I'm so glad, Mrs....uh...ah...Grace. I'm so pleased to see you're doing so well," I said sincerely.

"Thank you, dear boy," she said putting her hand over mine on the arm of the chair, "and I'm glad to see you doing well, too. Your mother told me about your accident some years ago. She was so upset. Charlotte is really a lovely woman. Such a shame about your father, but I'm glad she has her consolation in you. She was so thrilled when you decided to come back and take the job with the police and here you are now, the Chief! Your father would be so pleased," she said and squeezed my hand.

Just then Jared, Jenny's other son, came by with a plate of crab puffs announcing like a real pro that we would be seating for dinner at five. I looked at Grace and said, "It's remarkable. You've hardly changed a bit." She just waved me off.

"Oh, you flatterer!" she said obviously still able to appreciate the attentions of a younger man.

"No, really." I said. "What's it been? Almost twenty years since I've seen you and you've hardly changed at all."

"Well, I'm officially old now, but I guess it's better than the alternative," she said with a sardonic grin. "But I've heard you've been involved with some excitement lately, Terry. A car crash, I understand...saved a man's life over by the Overmill Bridge. It's been all over town. There was even a bit about it in the paper," she said, her eyes shining with interest.

"Oh, it was nothing," I said, feeling very 'aw shucks,' like when I was fourteen years old again and Sharon Bartlett told me I was a good kisser.

"Now, Terry,'" she admonished, "the whole town was talking about it. I was so pleased for you when I heard...and the young man too, of course. I know what a hard time you must have had after you left the government." I knew then that my mother had been at it again.

Grace went on, completely oblivious to my growing discomfort on the subject. "I understand that the man is here tonight. Jenny's got him stashed away somewhere so he could enjoy the party but not be too tired by all the excitement. She says his injuries were rather severe. That Jenny is really quite a girl. She's got a heart as big as all outdoors and the support of a wonderful husband too. I was so pleased when they were allowed to adopt that little Russian baby. She was afraid that the agency would think she was too old to be a new mother. I was so happy when it worked out for them. I wish I'd had a daughter like her but, as I'm sure you know, I've never had any children of my own. It's one of my greatest regrets, but that's water long

under a very old bridge at this point. But I do have Sheila, a real
darling of a girl. I couldn't get along without her…literally," she
said, and turned her head away with a melancholy expression.
Just then, Jenny came walking over toward us with a huge smile
and more than a little sway in her hips from a cocktail or two.

"So there you are, you two! We're about to sit down for
dinner soon and I wanted to take Grace in to meet Martin before
we start seating," she said giving me another of her knowing
smiles to let me know she had set me up earlier. "So, if I could
steal her away for a while," and she put her hand out to help
Grace up out of the deep chair.

"Of course, dear," Grace said politely. "I'd love to. Terry and
I were just catching up. I don't think we've seen each other since
he was little more than a boy," and put out her hand to allow
herself to be helped up.

It was when Grace lifted her hand toward Jenny and the
sleeve of her blouse fell back that I noticed the bracelet. The
sight of it startled me, to say the least. I got the feeling I imagine
one gets when they think they've had a deja vu. It was a chunky
sort of thing made of small, aged, yellow blocks, each with
different markings or symbols in red, black and green, and
separated by little green glass or plastic marbled beads. Some of
the symbols on the blocks looked like Chinese characters, I
thought.

I spoke before I could think. "What an unusual bracelet. I
don't think I've ever seen anything like it."

"Oh! Do you like it?" Grace asked.

"Yes. Very much," I said. "It really does suit you. It looks
old. Is it?" I didn't mean it the way it sounded but no one seemed
to have noticed, so I let it go. Then Jenny chimed in.

"Yes, it's lovely. Mahjong tiles, aren't they?"

"Yes," Grace answered, pleased for the attention once again.
"I can't believe you recognize it, my dear. Mahjong went out of
fashion so many years ago. I didn't think anyone outside of China
played it anymore." She looked at me intently then and said, "It
was a gift from…an admirer, many years ago, a young man I
loved dearly. I wear it whenever I go out," and for a moment
there I could swear she was drifting away to another place in
time. A second later she was back with us. "It used to be sort of a

trademark of mine along with the slit skirts and high heels." She looked directly at me then, raising a single eyebrow. "Didn't think I knew about you boys and your fascination with them, did you?" she asked, her eyes aglow with satisfaction. My eyes must have gotten like marbles at that. She gave me a mischievous wink. "Thank you so much for noticing, Terry. You're a dear young man," she said, touching my cheek softly before letting Jenny lead her into the other room. I'm not sure, but I think I blushed.

As I sat there finishing my drink and waiting for the dinner seating to begin, it hit me like an epiphany in a rapid flashback to the dream I had of walking with Angelica and holding her hand. The thing she left for me on the bench when she went away was one of those blocks, like the ones in Grace's bracelet. Next, like a slap in the face, Sylvia Hadrada's face and words jumped into my mind, "...nothing much in it, just a few old style Mahjong tiles. You know the old Chinese game that was popular early in the century. Who knows? I said, not worth anything I'm sure, but I took the box anyway and handed him the tiles. There! A house warming gift."

I didn't make the connection between what Sylvia had told me about the Mahjong tiles in the house and the piece that Angelica had left me in the dream because I hadn't seen the things Sylvia described, but after seeing Grace's bracelet it hit me like a sledge hammer. Something. Something about them. There was something about them that made the small hairs on the back of neck bristle. To this day I'm not sure I understand the meaning of the tiles. All I know is that they're a link, a frightening heirloom linking Grace, the house, and me. Then, just as I was trying to put it together, losing myself in thought, I had the honor of both Jared and Jordan Denton standing in front of me smiling, holding out another drink and announcing that,

"Mom says it's time to come to the table, Chief."

❋ ❋ ❋

As I sat down in my assigned seat, I noticed that my mother and Lila were conspicuously absent and I was seated next to Eli. Before she sat down, Jenny came over and whispered in our ears, "Charlotte and Lila are eating with Martin. I hope you two don't mind. I didn't want him to feel left out and they each volunteered."

"I'm not going to have anything to be jealous about, am I?" Eli said, trying to sound as much like a tough guy as he could manage, but since it wasn't in his nature, he didn't do it well.

"Of course not, silly boy," Jenny said with a sigh of mild exasperation. "It'll be months before he can even put on his own shoes and by then, you two will be on your honeymoon. Just look at it as Christian charity or since it's Thanksgiving, American hospitality...and by the way, Lila has already let me know me that, in your case, the size of a man's feet is in direct correlation to his other appendage and she's quiet happy where she is, thank you very much...girl talk, you know," she snickered.

I half choked on a piece of bread. "Nurse Jenny!" I croaked. "You dirty little girl!" Eli turned ten shades of red but didn't say a word. After all, he did have big feet.

From there the dinner went off easily. Lila had made a Cajun-style turkey. Jeff made his in the traditional style with sausage, onion and mushroom stuffing. One of Jenny's nurse friends, a very stylish West Indian woman named Pierra, brought a beautiful turkey with whole sage leaves in a pattern under the skin stuffed with a sage and oyster dressing that was out of this world. She was very dark skinned with tight little black curls, bright, shining, inviting eyes and a warm laugh. There were times that evening that I could even swear that she was flirting with me, but since I noticed she was wearing a wedding ring, I didn't think anything of it. It seemed a harmless flirtation, so I did the honorable thing. I flirted back. She really was lovely.

There was plenty of food and drink, good company and laughs. After the dinner dishes were cleared, the boys took one table into the living room area, setting it up against the front bay window for dessert and coffee to be served there buffet style. Some of the guests followed them in and took comfortable seats. Others, mostly the older ones, didn't stay for the dessert and the boys were let off to go upstairs. Grace said that there was not a chance that she would pass up one of those rare opportunities to have a rich dessert and some brandy in her coffee, although she would have to leave shortly afterwards. So, after helping her to a comfortable chair and leaving Jeff to serve as a bon vivant maitre d' of the dessert table, Jenny maneuvered the remaining guests into seats around the dining room table, leaving Pierra at the head. Then she discretely disappeared to oversee Martin Welliver's return to the hospital through the garage door. A few minutes later, I watched from the front window as the EMS unit backed into the driveway and could see Jenny waving her hands in a frenzy like an overwrought orchestra conductor. When the symphony was safely over, I gave my seat to my mother and wandered back to the dining room to see what was going on in there that was attracting so much attention.

The first thing I noticed when I got there was Pierra seated at the head of the table with a symmetrical setting of cards splayed out in front of her, like she was playing solitaire. Everyone else around the table was craning their necks, watching her move the cards, hanging on her every word. Curious, I moved in closer to get a better look. About half way to the table, I saw that the cards she was playing with weren't your average deck of fifty two. I stopped in my tracks. They were Tarot cards. I couldn't believe it. She was telling fortunes! I recognized them from *Dark Shadows*, the spooky old soap opera from when I was a kid, and on that show, they never said anything good.

Just then Pierra looked up at me. "Would you like to be next, Chief?" she smiled, her dark eyes sparkling with amusement.

"No, no, no, no," I said, exaggeratedly waving my hands and shaking my head, trying not offend her. "I think I'd rather not know, thanks," I laughed in a veiled attempt to mask my discomfort with humor.

"No problem, Chief," she said with a glimmering wink that let me know she'd pierced my veil. What she couldn't know was that I'd been struggling daily to keep that little fissure in my mind from widening into a gap I couldn't control. I didn't need another wedge to crack it further, so the last thing I wanted to know was my future, even if it was only a parlor game. I headed back to the living room for dessert and another drink...like pronto.

After I reached a comfortable distance, I got another chair and went over to where my mother was chatting with Grace. As I sat down, they were talking about the topic of the month, the mysterious Mr. Welliver from New York. I heard my mother say to Grace, "Oh yes. He's going to be with us for a while. Terry told me that he'd bought a house here just before the accident, somewhere on the northwest end of Randolph Road, near the town limits. Isn't that right sweetheart?" she asked, looking to me to confirm it.

"Yes, a big old Victorian-looking thing set back from the road. I was just out there the other day with Sylvia Hadrada checking it out," I answered, trying to sound like I knew something about architecture, failing miserably and sounding a little silly.

"Oh, really?" Grace said, looking suddenly distracted, almost stricken, and taking a long sip of her brandy laced coffee.

"Yeah, a real white elephant," I said and laughed. "I didn't even know it was there until Sylvia took me out there. Kind of isolated though," I said, not really paying attention. I had had more than a few Cosmos, wine with dinner and at that moment was working on a very large brandy, finding myself becoming increasingly distracted as we chatted. I couldn't take my eyes off Grace's bracelet. It was having an almost hypnotic effect on me. She kept turning it and touching it when she wasn't finishing her coffee or frosted carrot cake. Turning it and touching it. Then Eli and Lila came over to say goodnight and ask if they could take Grace home.

She accepted with her usual politeness and Lila reached out her hand to help her up. As she did, I heard Lila say, "Oh Grace! What a beautiful scent. Do I know it?" sniffing at the air around her for a better take on it.

"Why thank you, dear." Grace said, flattered yet once again that evening. I went out of my way to catch a whiff of it myself then. It was beautiful, but I'm certainly no expert.

"...it's called My Sin by Lanvin Paris. It's a very old brand, as so many of my things are these days, not quiet Chanel #5 but I've always preferred it," she said and turned to smile at me again. As they walked away, I heard Grace tell Lila that she would make sure she had some for her honeymoon. I don't think I really had a full realization of Grace as a woman until that moment, not young, not old, but a true woman of the world living in our own little town. *A rare bird, indeed,* I thought as I walked them to the door. Just then Jenny arrived back on the scene looking flustered, more than a little tipsy but none the worse for wear, and still in time to say good night to her guests.

When she saw me and asked, "You're not leaving yet are you?"

"Nah," I responded, "just helping the lovebirds walk Grace out to the car."

"You're not going to " she asked me with a raised eyebrow.

"Yes, I am," I answered, raising my own.

"Oh, Terry, don't. I was only kidding!" she said, blushing and touching my arm.

"We'll see about that," I said, smiling wickedly as I closed the door behind me to walk behind with Eli as Lila went arm-in-arm with Grace down the path to the car. Then, just as Lila had gotten Grace settled in the backseat and shut the door, she stood up, looked at me smiling innocently, completely unaware. I looked at Eli, shook his hand, looked down and said, in my driest tone and a voice only Eli and she could hear, "Nice feet!" then looked back to Lila. Her eyes got as wide as saucers. I turned quickly, laughing like hell as I headed back up the path, leaving them to work it out. I was drunk and damn happy to be that way.

Feeling warm and comfortably anaesthetized, I got back to the house to find Jenny waiting there for me with a large box in her hands and Pierra standing behind her, smiling at me with her shining black eyes and holding another large box.

"Be a darling, will you, Chief, and use those muscles of yours to help Pierra take her things out to her car?"

"Sure, no problem," I said, knowing my time as lifter and lugger had arrived.

"Thank you so much, Chief," Pierra said, handing me her box then leaning over to kiss Jenny on both cheeks and taking the other box from her. "Thank you so much, Jen, for a lovely time and a chance to meet such interesting people. I'll see you at work during the week," Pierra said to Jenny, then turned to me with a twinkling smile that seemed to hold a significance that went straight over my head. As we walked out to her car, avoiding scattered puddles as we went, Pierra told me that she and her husband were moving back to Haiti in a few weeks to look after her sister and her nieces and nephews, and how much she'd miss her life in America.

Once at her car, we stopped and she put down her box to open the trunk. I put my box in first then bent over to pick up the second box and put it in the trunk. When I stood up the second time, she was facing me. The look in her eyes and the expression on her face had changed, no longer bright and smiling, but somber and serious, almost ominous in the dim light of the street lamp not too far away. She sought my eyes, probing them with hers and held up a card. I could see it was one of her Tarots, the one with a hanging man dangling upside down by one leg, the other leg crossed behind it, "Le Pendu..." I looked back into her eyes, puzzled.

"You have the heart of a warrior, my Chief, a quality highly valued among my people. Use it. Follow your destiny, and meet it with the fire I've seen burning inside you," she said, her sing song island accent taking on a deep, almost echoing quality. Then she stood up on her toes and kissed me, hard on the lips. Stunned, I just stood there like a dope as she jumped in her car and started the engine, giving me a backward glance of fondness, the brightness having returned to her eyes as she drove off. I stood there for a few seconds before going back to the house, my head spinning from the drink mixed with the strange passion I felt in her kiss. It was weird, like she was trying to transfer something of herself to me and I had no choice but to accept it. As I walked back, I couldn't help but feel her words etching themselves into my mind, wondering about what she could've meant by the card. *Was I dangling?*

Not long after I got back to the house, I grabbed up my mother, who'd also had a cocktail or two over her limit, we said our 'thank yous' and 'good-byes' and left. *Dangling?. . . above what?*

By the time we got to my mother's house about ten minutes later, it'd started raining again. She suggested that I stay over and, in my state I readily agreed that was best. I got into my ragged, comfortable old robe and settled myself on the sofa, not wanting to bother with the stairs since the dampness had given me a good case of the creaks. Between the alcohol and my half-and-half combo, I was asleep in an instant. When I opened my eyes, I was standing naked in a blackened room. There were two people sitting at a table off in the distance, a man and a woman. The man was dressed in old-fashioned evening clothes, a black beard covering his corpse-like pale face, a black silk top hat on the chair next to him. Across from him was the woman, an Asian woman, Chinese I think, dressed in an ornate red silk dress with a gold dragon embroidered on the back and wearing elaborate make-up. A prostitute was the impression I got, not a lady. They had something that looked like sheet music stands next to them, but without any sheet music.

I couldn't see much of the detail from where I stood, so I went in closer. The man began to pour a pale green liquid from a bottle over a spoon-like object with holes that looked like it was draining into a glass. He laughed as he poured. *Absinthe*, I thought to myself. I'd never seen it but had heard about it in Paris. He pushed the first glass over to the woman. She smiled at him as he went about making another for himself. When he'd finished, they tapped glasses and drank. I felt drawn to them against my will and moved in closer.

The man took out a small box and pinched something out of it. He placed whatever it was onto the pouch between his thumb and first finger, brought it up to his nose and inhaled. He offered some to the woman who took some with the tip of the nail on her little finger and did the same. *Cocaine?* I couldn't tell for sure. As I moved closer, I could see them shifting the little yellow tiles in turn on the surface of the table. He had one hand moving between her legs underneath her skirt. She was smiling. He kept his head down. As I edged in closer to the table, I could see more tiles on the stands. I stood there naked before them and for some unknown reason was not embarrassed by my nakedness. They didn't seem to know I was there. I spoke, the words coming out of my mouth involuntarily.

"What is this?" I asked, hearing my own voice ring with a childlike wonderment. The woman looked up at me. Her red rimmed eyes were filled with a frightening hunger.

"Mahjong," she said and smiled revealing teeth rife with the beginnings of decay. "Would you like to join us?" she asked, foam starting to form in the corners of her mouth.

I looked to the man who raised his head at that. His eyes were a startling, icy blue, rimmed with red and bulging with rage, blazing at the woman. He rose from the table and walked around to her, putting his hands on her shoulders. He took one of the tiles from her stand, dipped it in her drink and playfully put it in her mouth. I felt something was about to happen, but before I could move he'd clamped his hand over her mouth and pulled her head back violently against his body shouting,

"Shut your mouth, you stinking, filthy slut. This is my game! How dare you invite the pig into MY GAME! MY GAME! Do you understand me? All mine, FOREVER!" he screamed wildly as the woman struggled frantically against his grip, her arms and legs flailing in all directions, kicking over the table, sending everything on it flying in into the air. In the next second, he pulled a long, gilt handled knife from somewhere in his jacket, yanked her head back and, in one swift movement, cut her throat, screaming,

"Gaping, diseased cunt! All MINE! Don't you ever forget that!" Spittle flew from his lips as he raged. Blood sprayed everywhere. The woman stopped struggling. He let her fall to the floor. He turned to face me covered with her blood and wiped his mouth with the back of his hand leaving a trail of blood to contrast starkly against the pallor of his face. His expression was nothing less than...orgasmic as he groaned, licking his lips, his eyes rolling up into his head. Then he looked back at me, the rage returning to his bulging eyes.

He grinned at me, his sharp teeth colored pink with her blood, and held his hand out to me, flat, palm up. I could see there was something lying there. It started to move, raising itself upright in the palm of his hand, lifting itself to face me. It was "Le Pendu," the hanging man card. I looked up into his eyes, still glaring at me hypnotically, and followed his gaze back down to the card as it turned itself slowly in the palm of his hand until the back of it came to face me. Somewhere outside the darkness I heard Pierra's echoing voice call to me. "Don't look, Chief. Don't look at it!" But I couldn't take my eyes off it. It was too late. I saw it. It was the picture of a horned, winged creature sitting in the center of an inverted, five pointed star. At the bottom of the card, it read, "Le Diable," the devil. Then it burst into flames. "Get away, pig! This is MY game!" the man hissed at me, pink foam sputtering into the air. He threw his head back, laughing wildly as if he'd won some demonic triumph over me, crushing the ashes of the burnt card in his fist. When he turned his glance back to me again, the mirth in his eyes was gone leaving only the pure, unvarnished hatred of evil personified. He opened his hand and, with an exaggerated expression, blew the ashes at me in a cloud that reeked of what I can only describe as the stench of thousands years of human misery and death.

I reeled back as if I had been hit with the force of a full body blow, my blood spattered body struggling to keep balanced against the force of it. Choking from the smell, my eyes burning from the ashes of the card, I turned and ran into the darkness. In the distance I saw the silhouette of a woman and a man embracing. I ran toward them. I could hear his thundering footsteps behind me as he chased me, laughing at me again as he shouted, "Run, pig, run away!"

"Help! Help me!" I shouted to the couple in the distance. They turned their faces toward me. I saw that the woman was Grace Coutraire but not the current Grace a twenty-five or thirty-year-old Grace and she was wearing the bracelet. I saw it as she rested her wrist on his shoulder.

"Grace!" I cried out. "Help me!" But before she could answer, I saw his face, the man she was embracing. The same red rimmed, blazing, bulging blue eyes glared at me.

"Get AWAY or I'll kill the bitch! I swear I'll kill her this time. This is my game!" he spat at me as he tore the bracelet from her wrist, scattering the tiles on the ground at my feet. Before I could stop him, he grabbed the young Grace by the throat and squeezed. "No! Stop!" I yelled, lunging at him. He disappeared from my grip as if he were never there. Grace was gone, too.

I looked around for anything real, then down on the ground for the tiles around my feet. When I looked up again, I saw Martin Welliver in front of me, hanging by a rope around his neck, his hands tied behind his back, his face already gone ashen gray. I ran over to hoist him up from the tension of the rope, calling out to him. "Martin! Martin! It's me. I'm here!" When I looked up at his face, I saw a raised mark on his forehead, red, like a scar, or a brand, in the shape of an inverted, five pointed star and he was staring at me, his large, sad, half-dead eyes bulging. "Please don't let me die alone," he begged. I dropped to my knees screaming like I never remember screaming before in my life, and I went on screaming until I felt my mother's hands on my shoulders shaking me.

"Terry! Wake up, Terry! Honey?"

When I opened my eyes and saw her face, I knew it had only been a dream. Drenched with sweat, I sat up and put my head in my hands. I had a splitting headache and my hands were shaking. Through the pounding in my head I heard my mother say, "It was only a dream, sweetheart. All that rich food and drink. We both should have known better. I haven't had an easy time of it either tonight, tossing and turning. I'll make us a nice cup of chamomile tea and we'll try it again in a little while Okay, sweetheart?"

"Sure, Ma. Thanks," I said, but denied remembering what the dream was about when she asked. No one would ever believe anything but that I was losing my mind, including myself. Because if it was only a dream, why could I still smell the unexplainable, yet unmistakable, scent of flowers on my hands?

CHAPTER 4

A Charming Victorian Place

"Fear is only as deep as the mind allows."
Japanese Proverb

The next day I got up and dressed for work in my spare uniform. There was no more discussion about the previous night's troubles. The following week or so went on like any other. Lila prepped 'thank you' notes to Jenny and Jeff for all of us. All I had to do was sign. As usual, she took care of all the loose ends of my life.

I seemed a little more tired than usual. I didn't sleep as well as I ought to have done that week, but didn't remember anything that should have disturbed it. My aches and pains settled back into their usual mild twinges and for that I was grateful. It was the first time since the river accident that I got through my days without the aid of more than my Advil bottle. I'm sure the fact that I had the Convention of State Law Enforcement Officials coming up in Florida soon to look forward to helped. With all that'd been going on, I'd completely forgotten about it until Lila reminded me a few days after the party saying, "I've made all your travel plans for the Convention, Chief. I typed up the details and left them on your desk along with your tickets."

Ah! Five days in Florida. No rain, no accidents and no hospitals, no pain. Only fresh faces, drinks and sun by the pool. Heavenly! I thought. I don't usually go in for these types of things, but the Mayor and Town Council thought it might be a good way to be politic and get some leads on how we could get some state dollars to fight 'the war on terrorism.' Yeah, right! I can see it now, a group of Middle Eastern religious fanatics descending on Jennisburg, bent on blowing up Main Street. I had a real N'yuk, N'yuk, N'yuk over that one but thought, *What the hell. I could use a break* In the meantime I bought some khaki shorts and tank shirts, some new socks and a pair of sandals. I figured I could get some sunglasses and tanning lotion when I got there. Lila, as usual, was already ahead of me with the scheduling of shifts for the men.

I had a call from Jenny a few days before I left updating me on 'our patient.' He was due to be discharged the next day and Mrs. Portensky had been going over to the house getting it ready for his arrival. She told me that she'd been over to see the house when she gave Martha the keys and thought it was lovely and in excellent shape for its age. "It's so charming," she gushed, "too bad it's so far away from town. It would really be a nice attraction for the tourists looking for local color."

Then, being the Jenny that I was coming to know her to be, she talked about having a small house-warming party over there after Martin had time to settle in, "Just a few people, you know, Jeff and me, the kids, Lila and Eli, you and Charlotte…and Mrs. Portensky, of course. We can't leave her out. She'd be highly insulted if we didn't ask her, even though I'm sure she would rather have the day off," she said with the same excitement she'd had in her voice on Thanksgiving. She sure likes her parties, our Jen, but at that point, I'd have agreed to anything.

"Sure," I said. "Just let me know," and changed the subject telling her about my trip.

"Oh, yes, Lila told me. It sounds great. A break wouldn't do you any harm either," she said in a good-humored voice.

"So I take it you and Lila have gotten pretty chummy," I said slyly.

"Oh, yes, she's a doll, a sweet girl and she thinks the world of you. Charlotte and I have already been talking about throwing her a wedding shower after the holidays. Oh yeah! That reminds me. When you get back, I'm going to give you a really hard pinch for that 'Nice Feet' comment you made to Lila, you devil!" she said and laughed loudly. "You can bet the next time I see you, I'll check out yours," and she giggled like a school girl.

"Save yourself the trouble, darlin'. I'm a 13 EE," I said with a hearty belly laugh. "See ya when I get back," and put down the phone.

❀ ❀ ❀

The plane ride down gave me time to think, clear my head, and try to piece together the last dream with what I actually knew. First, I thought of the tile Angelica left for me in the dream and Sylvia telling me about the tiles she'd found in the house, then Grace wearing the tile bracelet and finally, that fucking weird-ass dream with the tiles and the Tarot cards.

This is where I need to explain myself, to talk about what must seem like an unbelievably unrealistic approach to whatever events were happening around me. I need to talk a bit about what I've learned about the human psyche and denial in my failed attempts at therapy. It may sound simple on paper, but you really have to think about it and what it means to the limitations of the human mind.

Women live in denial of their husband's infidelities. Parents live in denial of a missing child, probably dead. People routinely deny traumatic events like abuse and abandonment. They repress feelings of all kinds, things that are shameful or socially unacceptable, dark fantasies and forbidden desires. Denial is the mechanism the human mind employs when something is too sad or tragic, hurtful or terrifying to live with and still survive as a functioning human being. It's a safe haven for the mentally weak or confused and those too exhausted by grief or, the most frightening of all, their fear of the unknown. There are times when it's simply just easier, safer, more comforting not to see something rather than to see what may be under one's very nose . . . and fears most. That's how I got through the earlier parts of my ordeal, stupid, blind, garden variety denial!

In my case, I considered my own baggage using the few years of secret counseling it took me to come to terms with it. Then only to find out that my only hope for survival was to accept the fact that I would be spending the rest of my life as an emotional cripple. My lost ambitions, grief over losing my father, my guilt for failing to save Angelica...all came into play. My hopes of redemption in having pulled Martin Welliver out of that car, my anticipated fear of losing my mother and being left adrift and totally alone in the world, all these things were whirling around in my psyche, playing tricks on my subconscious, then spouting themselves up into my consciousness like a geyser, setting off emotional fire alarms at increasingly frequent intervals.

It would make anyone wonder. *Is it real? Is it my imagination? Could I be creating all this?* I came to the conclusion that it just couldn't be real. It had to be me and I couldn't let go of my already tenuous hold on reality, no matter what. It's like the nightmare that terrifies you in the dark, but when the sun comes up becomes so much nonsense that you laugh at yourself, but still keep one eye on what may be lurking behind you, just in case. This is where I was mentally as I headed to Florida.

The trip itself was refreshingly routine and ordinary, just what I wanted and needed sun, sand and frozen drinks by the pool punctuated by a few seminars on terrorist awareness, color coded alerts and equipment to combat gases, bio toxins and the like. I went out with the younger guys the last night to party at the clubs but soon discovered that, since I was practically old enough to be everyone's father, discretion would be the better part of valor and I discretely left early.

Looking back now, something strange did happen that night, sort of. It didn't mean anything to me then, but now...I'm not so sure. As I was walking back to the hotel, I passed an arcade. Out front was one of those old fashioned fortune telling machines, the kind with the mechanical gypsy inside. The old Hollies classic, "She was a long cool woman in a black dress..." blared from a speaker overhead. For some reason, that song played in my head the rest of the way back and continued to run until I was asleep. By the time I woke up the next morning, it'd somehow morphed itself into, "She was a strong black woman in a cool dress..." with a barely audible voice repeating in the background, whispering to me, "Go home!"

In the end, I played it off on the tropical drinks, spicy food and the fact that I missed my mother. But, knowing what I know now, I'm not so sure I didn't get a message from somewhere closer to...Port-au-Prince that night. It seems just too pat to have been a coincidence or the result of a plate of bad mussels.

❀ ❀ ❀

I have to break here and go into the station today. God help me, I need a break to breathe before I descend back into the abyss. Martin has been doing well lately, for which I'm so grateful. Since that night by the river it seems that, somewhere in the hollow of my soul, I've known that we'd be inextricably linked forever by the hand of God, Fate or the Devil...and I'm not sorry for that, either. A man can never be sorry when he follows his conscience, for in the end, he'll always know that he kept his promises. Martin has his night out tonight with Jenny and Jeff   dinner over in Henriston   curry. He loves curry and so do I. I'll be back before nightfall to check the house again.

❀ ❀ ❀

I'm running out of time. I can hardly breathe, much less write now. I can't stop my hands from shaking. God! My head feels like its going to explode. I want to run away, but there is nowhere to go. I want to scream, but there is no one to hear it, or care, or believe me. *Oh, God, just let me finish this or just take us to you heart right now, both of us. I'll go and he'd go too, but please don't let it start all over again. How could you have created such a thing and let it thrive? Is this some sort of metaphysical chess game between good and evil? And am I the good...or the evil? Could this thing be some terrible angel of God sent down to destroy the evil in...me, like it saw the evil in those women? What have I done to displease you? It just can't be.* That can't be true. I'm the good one, *me*, not it. I need a pill. I'll be back as soon as I can, but time has just taken a huge leap against me and I don't know what I may be forced to do, or how soon. "Our Father, who art in Heaven, hallowed be thy name, thy kingdom come, thy will be done, on earth as it is in Heaven. Give us this day our daily bread and forgive us our trespasses as we forgive those who trespass against us. Lead us not into temptation but deliver us from evil for thine is the Kingdom and the power, and the glory, forever and ever. Amen." I'm afraid, God! Help me!

❊ ❊ ❊

Okay. I've had my pill. I've had my shakes. I've had my cry and I'm as much of a man as I can be again, for the time being. When I came home this evening, Martin had already gone. Jenny and Jeff must have come early. There isn't anything I wouldn't do to protect him, not anything. For all that, I could have just let him die safe and at peace in the river, but he's been my responsibility since that day. I will not give in as long as there is a breath left in my body. The monster will not have him! I will not let that happen! I will not let him go the way I let Angelica slip away. The house was empty when I got here. I checked everything as I always do and found nothing. I was so relieved. Then I went into my bathroom to wash up. When I looked at the mirror it was there, written in dust on the mirror, "Game over!" It was as if someone cleaned the mirror but had dusted around the letters, leaving the message in dust on the otherwise clean mirror. My heart sank and my stomach lurched. I felt my knees give way beneath me, shaking so furiously I had to hold on to the sink to keep from collapsing, my head swirling so badly I thought I'd be sick. It's here. It's coming after him. It's coming after me. There's no doubt now...against all hope...it's not in my mind. I've got to hurry.

❊ ❊ ❊

When I got back from Florida, it was already snowing. Just a light dusting, but we get quite a bit of snow up here and it starts early. It felt good on my face when I got off the plane and, as I knew I could count on, Eli was there to pick me up. It was just before dinner time when I got back to the house, so I took a shower and called my mother telling her I'd be over with a pizza in an hour. There were only two messages waiting for me on my answering machine, the first from my mother asking me to call her when I got in, the other from Jenny telling me that they'd set the date for the housewarming party, December twenty-first, but that I should call her when I got in. She sounded out of sorts, anxious, very unlike her. I called and ordered the pizza, then returned her call.

After the usual niceties about rest and tan and such, she told me that in my absence, "there's been some trouble with Mrs. Portensky over at Martin's." Then she launched into it. "She started out just fine. The house was in ship shape when we moved him in and they seemed to get on with each other just fine…" she said, referring to Martin and Martha. "Then I stopped by there two days ago. He was alone and looked terrible, Terry. He said he wasn't sleeping well and had been in constant pain for days, so I asked where Martha was. He hobbled into the kitchen, sat down, put his head in his hands and said 'She left.' 'She left!' I repeated almost shouting. 'What does that mean, *She left?*' I asked him. 'She just left,' he told me.

"It seems that he came home from having his casts removed the other day and she had just gone. Gone! At first he thought she may have gone to the market or something, but when she didn't show up again the next day, he called her and got her answering machine. After a few more messages and no return calls, he just stopped calling. So I asked him, 'Why didn't you call me?'" Jenny said, her agitation level rising by the second. Apparently, he told her that after all she and her husband and everyone had done for him, had been so kind to him and patient with him, he knew he was beginning to become a burden on them. He told her he would always be grateful for all that everyone had done for him, but he realized that her time was already stretched between her job and her kids…especially the four-year-old, Jonah, and he couldn't in good conscience ask her for more than she had already so graciously given.

He told her that now that his casts were off, he could get around pretty well on his own with the crutches and that Martha had filled the house with all he would need for a while so he'd be okay. He just needed some time to heal. "But what about the party?" she asked him. He admitted, "It would be great. I'd love for everyone to see me standing up and walking for a change, even if it is on crutches, and I wouldn't want to miss Charlotte Chagford's cooking for the world." She closed off by telling me that she'd made lunch for him before she left, but that when she kissed him on the cheek on the way out, she could swear she smelled alcohol on him.

"Be the darling that you are and go over and check on him, will ya?" she asked me.

"Yes, dear," I answered, like an exasperated husband would to an endearing but nagging wife. But I must confess, it did sound strange to me. Martha Portensky used to run the high school cafeteria like a white-gloved general. She may be quirky, but she was nothing if not 'starch' dependable. I made a mental note to speak to her about it when I saw her, then headed out to pick up the pizza. I was already late.

I arrived at my mother's a little later, pizza in hand just the way we like it and an hour before our spook movie was due to begin on cable. It was *The House on Haunted Hill*, of all things, the one with Vincent Price and that cheesy blonde actress with those god awful pointy features.

"I love your tan, sweetheart. I wish I could tan like that, but you have your father's ruddy complexion. Oh...and look...it brought out your freckles. How sweet. I just turn red, burn, and then it's gone, you know. You did use at least some sun block, didn't you?" she asked, brimming with excitement that I was home.

"Yes, Ma," I replied as I dished out the pizza.

"Did you have a good time?"

"Yes, Ma."

"You look so healthy," she said, sounding satisfied.

I've never really been good at small talk, even with my mother, so I made a quick segue in pure small town fashion to the tale of my conversation with Jenny and, in pure small town fashion, Mom was ahead of me with her own spin on the same event.

"Funny you should mention that," she said. "I just ran into Martha over at the market the other day. We chatted some about the weather and the holidays coming. It seems her son, the stockbroker, had just had a new washer and dryer delivered to her in advance of Christmas." She took another slice and continued, "She was so excited by the new appliances, but I could also tell she was disappointed by the card that came with them saying that he wouldn't be able to make it home for the holidays. Apparently he gave her some excuse about business keeping him too busy to travel.

"I could see it was upsetting her to talk about it, so I changed the subject and asked her about how she was making out over at Martin's. Well, you should have seen the way the color drained out of her face. It happened so fast it was almost funny. She went as pale as a sheet. She stammered telling me that she wasn't there anymore. She said something about it not working out because it was too far for her to travel at her age and with the bad weather coming and all, and her sons doing so well, she really didn't need the money. Then she rushed off saying she'd see me at church for the holidays and was gone.

"It was very strange, even for Martha. She acted like Martin had tried to seduce her or was into child pornography or something equally shocking. She's probably in the early stages of Alzheimer's or something. I used to hear when I was a girl that her mother was carted away to a sanatorium when her father ran off with that Tavistock girl, so maybe it runs in the family. Martha has always been very high strung, even in high school. That's why everyone thought she kept such an extra tight grip on herself, her boys and her place here in town."

"Mother!" I said to her with mock chastisement, "with all your training and experience...to talk like that. It's not very charitable of you."

She laughed. "Honey," she said, "when you've seen the things I've seen and as much as I've seen of it, from men telling you they're everyone from Julius Caesar to the Devil himself and then carving themselves like spring lamb, you've earned your liberties," and waved her hand dismissing my comment, laughing to herself.

"Lord knows, Martha ran that cafeteria like a clock for more than thirty years and raised three successful sons practically all by herself. It's no wonder if it's time for her to unwind. I guess it's no different than my blowing kisses to your father's picture every night before I go to bed, or talking to my cats like they understand me," she said and nonchalantly dropped a large piece of sausage on the floor for the two stray cats she'd adopted over the years, a calico she calls Mrs. Ellis, and a big grey tabby she calls Theodore, who were waiting patiently under the table, then having the nerve to smile at me like I didn't see her. I admit the bit about Martha's three successful sons pinched me, but it's not her fault. *The fault lies not in our stars but in ourselves,* I thought, and I dropped a piece of sausage under the table myself.

I thought for a moment and took another slice. Childish as it may seem, I decided then that there was not a snowball's chance in hell that I was going to let that two-bit horse trader Randall Portensky out-do me. The next day, I ordered a new washer and dryer, new matching refrigerator/freezer and a new thirty-two inch color TV from Dave Phillips' appliance store to be delivered to my mother's house the day before Christmas Eve.

I got a great deal too, being that Joe Rogan caught Dave's pride and joy, Errol, careening through a stop sign well over the speed limit last year. Drunk as a skunk he was and on his way into town coming home from some titty bar over in Henriston at five in the morning. When Joe called me, I got out of my bed to personally deliver the kid into his father's hands. Dave and I were close in school, two parts of a four-man relay, and have stayed pretty close ever since. Whenever we see each other, it's like we're still the same youthful, gangly, uncombed teenagers we were back then so, of course, he always gets special treatment from me whenever I can do anything for him.

When I got there, I just shook Dave's hand earnestly, had a quick chuckle about when we used to do the same thing and told him where to pick up the car. I got my first bit of satisfaction when I saw Dave holding the kid's head over the front porch, puking his guts up as I drove away. I got my second thinking about the tongue lashing the kid would get in the morning when Holly Phillips saw what he'd done, and I had my final satisfaction when I got all the appliances at cost, with free delivery to boot. Small towns are like that. The conversation then turned to the house-warming party Mom and Jenny were planning for the twenty-first.

"I'm so excited to see the house. Jenny says it's just beautiful, and covered with that intricate old latticework," she said in her lively 'I'm so glad you're home' voice. "I can't believe I've never seen it. I thought I knew every inch of this town."

"Well, it's not really part of town, Ma," I said. "It's just about spitting distance from the Hamilton Township line and set way back off the road. Sylvia Hadrada told me that the people who lived there before, a pastor and his family, were associated with a church in Hamilton Common so they probably wouldn't have had any real connection to Jennisburg, or had any reason to come here when it would be so much more convenient to go to the Common." I finished with my mouth half full.

"Jenny says we can expect ten for dinner. We've already chipped in for a set of dishes, glasses and flatware as a house-warming gift. I thought I'd make meatballs and sauce earlier in the day, then just cook the pasta and throw together a salad when we get there. We're expecting to all meet there about four, so could you pick me up around three thirty, honey, so we'll have time to load up?" she said, trying to corral me into joining in her enthusiasm.

"Yes, of course, Ma," I said absently.

"Oh, …and could your pick up some fresh Italian bread from the market on your way? I have everything else I need here."

"Sure, Ma." This time with my mouth full. After all that was settled, I stepped out for a smoke, actually one of each kind…the legal and the not so legal, before the movie started.

Just as the opening credits began to roll, she finally said it. "I'm so glad you're home, Terry. Even when you're across town at your own place, I always feel better when you're close."

"Me too, Ma," I said and meant it.

❅ ❅ ❅

I'd just gotten back into the groove of my usual routine by the twenty-first. I thought a party at that time was kind of cutting it close to the holidays, but what do I know? Not much, apparently. I picked up the bread my mother asked for along with a case of Bud and a fifth of Wild Turkey, just in case, went by her place, got the car loaded and we were off. It started to snow again, but it was light and not expected to get heavy for days. When we arrived at the house just before four, Jenny's SUV was already there.

As we pulled in the drive and came through to the clearing around the house my mother sighed out loud. "Oh, my!" she said breathlessly. "Whoever built it must have been very well off…and probably well off his rocker. It's beautiful, but much too grand for this area. Why would anyone want to build a house like this and hide it way out here where no one would ever see it?" she asked curiously.

"Probably just wanted to be left alone, Ma. Idle rich, maybe," I replied, trying to suppress the memory of the hackles it raised on me the last time I was there.

"I can't wait to get a good look around the inside. I wonder if it still has its original interior woodwork. Oh, I hope so," she said fascinated. I pulled around to the front door and began unloading the stuff onto the porch.

In her excitement, Mom didn't even bother knocking. She just opened the front door and yelled in, "Martin? Jenny? We're here!"

Jenny came to the entry hall, took the grocery bag from my mother's hands and led her into the recesses of the house. To the kitchen, I supposed.

After I unloaded onto the porch, I pulled the car around and parked, then walked back to the porch. I picked up the box with the sauce pot and headed toward the door. Jordan Denton was right there to open the door and I thought to myself, *Boy, those Dentons sure know how to raise a kid.*

"Thanks, Jordan," I said, following him into the kitchen. After I put the box down on the chrome and enamel table Sylvia had described, I turned to go back and retrieve the rest of the stuff. Jordan and Jared were already heading toward me, each with a bag in hand.

"We got it covered, Chief. Dad and Martin are in the other room trying to tire Jonah out so we can eat in peace later," Jared said, rolling his eyes up and smiling.

Good boy! I thought and went into the kitchen.

"Just go through that door and try to stay out from under our feet for a while," Jenny said, pointing her head in the direction of a second swinging kitchen door to the right as she took the bags from the boys and put them on the counter. Mom was already busy getting familiar with the stove and chattering to Jenny. I let them have at it and went through the swinging door.

Martin was sitting in an overstuffed chair set close to the fireplace on the far side of the room in partial shadow. The first thing I noticed as I approached him were the dark, hollow circles under his eyes and I remember thinking, *God, he's so pale.* Jeff Denton was on all fours on the floor like a pony with a small, thin child on his back. Jonah, I presumed. I saw that they didn't have a fire going, so after shaking hands all around, Jonah's too, I volunteered to get one going. The guys agreed that it was a good idea and since I was feeling okay that day, I got started at it. The weather was cold and snowy but the atmosphere was dry, so I was only in a standard state of small aches and pains which I'd pretty much learned to ignore long ago.

The wood pile was on the porch just outside of the front door in a black wrought-iron frame. It was already darkening quickly as I bent over to grab some log quarters with my back turned and got the strangest feeling that there was someone behind me. I turned around slowly, holding my breath. There they were, standing there smiling. Jordan and Jared Denton. *Whew!*

"Need some help, Chief?" Jordan asked.

"You guys are too good. You're starting to scare me. What are you guys, robots or Superkids from another planet? " I asked them. What I actually wanted to ask was if they were from Stepford, but I kept that comment to myself knowing the reference would be completely lost on them. Then, hoping to cover my feeble attempt to pull their legs a little, I followed up by asking them, "Who raised you anyway?"

"Oh, Chief!" was Jordan's response, accompanied by more eye rolling.

Yup, They're real kids alright, I thought and loaded them up with wood, grabbing some kindling under my arm to follow them into the house. This time I opened the door. Once we were inside, the boys and I built a nice pile in the fireplace and lit it. Jeff was giving my mother a tour of the house and Jenny had Jonah in the kitchen. I sat down in the rocking chair on the opposite side of the fireplace from Martin. He smiled at me, seeming to brighten up.

I spoke first. "So, how ya been makin' out, pal?" I asked, putting out my hand for another shake.

"Oh, not bad, actually. Much better now that I'm not hauling around a ton of plaster," he said, taking my hand and giving me a nice, broad, friendly smile.

Man, he looks rough, I thought. He was thinner than I remembered, and weaker. His hair was getting shaggy, he hadn't been shaving and he had those deep, dark circles under his eyes. I knew that look. I'd had it myself. It was pain, lots of pain and pain medication, combined with the loss of a reason for living. I knew from experience that he was probably thinking, *I'm going to spend the rest of my life this way.* Maybe I was just projecting my own experiences on him, but I don't think so, not this time. One lame animal recognizes another. It was a bad time of year to be recovering from bone injuries. For a moment I thought I could feel it again myself, just from looking at him.

Before either of us could say anything else there was a knock at the door. I got up, yelling toward the kitchen, "I'll get it!" and headed toward the door. Eli was standing there balancing a small box on top of a larger one and wearing that 'put upon' husband face he would eventually get to know all too well. Lila was holding a small, flat box, going "Brrrr," and smiling.

"Hurry up, Chief! It's freezing out here!" she said, so I let them in.

"Hey, Chief," was all I got from Eli. I took that to mean that they'd just had a premarital 'disagreement.'

"Hey, Buddy," I said, taking the top box from him and nodding with my head to Lila. "Jenny's in the kitchen. Thataway." I told Eli to put his box down on the entry table to the right of the kitchen doorway. I sat the other box on top of it. Lila'd already gone into the kitchen, so I said to Eli, "You don't wanna go in there. Come with me," and led him into the living room where Martin was sitting, staring into the fire. A moment later, Jeff came downstairs with my mother. She went straight into the kitchen and Jeff came into the room with us. More hand shaking all around. Then the boys came up looking expectantly at Jeff, but remarkably silent.

"Okay, boys, you're off duty. You can go into the other room and watch TV or play with your Gameboys, or read a book or something...whatever, as long as it's quiet...until dinner is ready. Is that alright with you Martin?" Jeff asked, looking in Martin's direction. He was lost in thought, staring into the fire again.

"Martin!" Jeff repeated, touching him on the shoulder.

"Huh?" He looked up at Jeff.

"Is it okay if the boys go entertain themselves in the TV room?" Jeff asked again.

"Oh, sure. Yes, of course. Please help yourselves," Martin replied, having brought himself back to the rest of us in the room.

"Okay, boys" Jeff said with a wave of his hand, "be gone!" and they disappeared in a flash into the TV room on the opposite side of the entry hall.

I recognized the look on Martin's face as he gazed back into the fire. It was the hypnotic effect of the pain killer/muscle relaxer combo. I could only hazard to imagine the other baggage that backed them up and thought again about what the hooker had told me. I needed a drink. Not a second later, as if she'd read my mind, Lila sauntered through the swinging kitchen door with four beers and four water glasses on a tray in one hand and the bottle of Wild Turkey in the other.

"Cocktails, gentlemen?" she asked with a girlish giggle as she waved the bottle in the air.

"Perfect," I said. Lila bent over and put the tray and bottle on the table in front of the sofa, making the conscious effort to wag her tail in front of where Eli was sitting. *So much for premarital discord,* I thought. I'm sure she ended up getting whatever it was that she wanted.

"Serve yourselves, guys" she said, "dinner will be ready in about forty minutes. We're having our own 'hen party' in the kitchen," and sauntered back out, making sure we all got a gander at the swing in her hips along the way. Eli, Jeff and I helped ourselves to a beer. I handed one to Martin. Just at that second, Jenny poked her head out of the swinging door and shouted across the room.

"Only one beer for Martin…and no liquor. He's on medication!" and then disappeared again.

Another mind reader, I thought. The men looked toward the door, shrugged and then went back to the business at hand. There was some football talk, some discussion about Lila's rear as compared to J Lo's and some teasing Eli about his upcoming surrender to marital bliss. Eli, Jeff and I each poured ourselves a shot of varying sizes. Needless to say, mine was the largest. I fielded questions about the Mayor. Was he having an affair with the girl from the beauty shop? Did I think the proposed effect of the new highway would cut off local commerce, and did I think that bribes were involved in the construction contracts?

I started to pour another round of shots when Martin caught my eye. "Please," he mouthed without sound. Then and there I knew he recognized in me the same lame animal I recognized in him. That knowledge gave me butterflies, but it also let me know that, with my conscience, I couldn't let him suffer.

I poured a triple shot into my own glass, sipped a shot's worth myself, then got up with the glass in my hand and picked up the fireplace poker. I set the glass down on the end table next to his chair and turned my body to shield it from view as I poked at the fire. When I was done, I put the poker back in its stand, picked up my glass and went back to my rocking chair. The glass was empty. I did the same thing one more time before dinner was served.

Martin got up only once during that time, using a single crutch to make his way to the bathroom. He still had a brace on his leg and shoulder. I'm sure all of us wanted to lend an arm, but it was pretty clear that he wanted to show everyone that he could do it himself, so we let him. After all, it really was the first time any of us had seen him walk. I was surprised to see he was almost as tall as I am, but of a much slighter build. He'd only just returned, not yet having had the chance to sit back down when my mother came in announcing proudly,

"Dinner is served!"

By that point, I guess Martin thought he'd proven his point to the men and let the professionals, Jenny and Mom, help him into the dining room on the opposite side of the kitchen, not that he had any real choice. They wouldn't have had it any other way. Then, just as they each had an arm, I thought I saw something in his eyes that troubled me, I didn't recognize it then, but I wouldn't miss it now. It was a glimpse of the thing we would both be on much more intimate terms with later on…fear.

❀ ❀ ❀

Before we got seated, Jenny filled plates for the boys and let them go into the TV room to eat while they watched some movie or other. Jonah, all worn out from playing, the excitement of a new environment and a full stomach from being fed in the kitchen, was snoozing on the love seat in the TV room with the boys.

Once the adults were settled at the table, the food was passed around. Mom's spaghetti and meatballs were a hit, great as usual. Everyone raved...no surprise there. Jeff brought some good red wine and kept everyone's glass full. Then the conversation started. It began with the weather. Everyone weighed in on whether there would be any significant snow fall for the holidays, agreeing that it would probably be mild, but you could never really tell in this neck of the woods, the Great Lakes not being all that far away. It's always best to expect the unexpected when it comes to rain and snow around here.

The conversation then turned to my trip. By that time, I'd had a few drinks and decided it would be best to be as entertaining as possible, so I regaled the company with tales of poolside bars, frozen margaritas, palm trees and all you can eat buffets. Next, it was on to Lila and Eli's wedding plans. They had set the date for early spring so the weather might be with them, April first, of all things. The women all agreed that Jenny, Mom and Lila's sister, Sara, would give her a shower some time in mid March. Then all the women looked at me with a sense of expectancy, which I grasped to mean that this would be a good time for me to offer to give Eli a bachelor party.

I was feeling good and had known Eli since he was a child. His older brother, Aaron, and I went to grade school together before he was shipped off to prep school. He's a doctor now in either Rochester or Buffalo. And since I'd always felt a closeness to Eli, kind of like the little brother I never had, I thought, *Why not?* I knew I could count on Joe Rogan to help.

Joe and Eli had been practically inseparable since they were kids. They even went through the academy together, but two more different personalities you couldn't imagine. Joe was the big, tough, take charge kind of guy and Eli had always been a shyer, more reserved and thoughtful type. He would make a good husband for Lila. Joe, on the other hand, was on his third wife, the first being a 'shot-gun wedding' and the second to an ex go-go dancer from Henriston. The current Mrs. Rogan, was just like him though, not the type to let him push her around, so they seemed evenly matched.

I made the offer with sincere good-hearted wishes for the both of them. Then it was on to Martin. No one really knew anything about him other than what I had gathered in New York, and then I had really only told Jenny what I knew.

The women started in on him in an obvious fashion. Jenny was first. "So, Martin, with all that's been going on, you haven't told us much about yourself," she said, smiling at him almost deviously. He seemed uncomfortable at first, shifting around in his chair and fumbling with his fingers, but in the end was good spirited about it and rallied with a charm I got the feeling he could turn on and off like a light bulb. He was a lawyer, after all.

"So what would you like to know, my dear Nurse Jenny? Ask me anything, anything at all."

"Well, we know you're from New York City. Were you born there?" she asked, like she was just getting warmed up.

"Nah," he shook his head, "but not far from it. I grew up around a seaside resort area in New Jersey until I went New York University. I was raised by my Aunt Cecilia. My mother died having me, so I don't remember her at all and my father died in Vietnam, so I never knew him, either."

"Oh, you poor dear!" my mother chimed in loudly and reached across Eli to touch Martin's hand.

"Not really," he said stoically.

He'd probably had a lot of experience with that sort of thing wherever he went and people wanted to know about him so he knew enough to get it over with early. Then he looked at Mom calmly and said in a voice that couldn't be anything else but real, "People say that you don't miss something you've never had, and it's true. Don't get me wrong, I carry the knowledge of them with me along with their pictures, but please believe me, I was never poor in love. I had plenty from my Aunt CeCe. She was a wonderful woman. I loved her with all my heart…still do…always will. There wasn't ever a time that I didn't feel loved in her house.

"Sometimes I think the reason she never married was because she had me to take care of, but she never once ever complained, never took it out on me or seemed unhappy with her choice. She died of breast cancer a few years ago." His color started to change then, and his eyes got dark. That particular subject was probably still a little too raw for him, but he came through it and continued with his story. I'm sure by then he knew he was among friends and didn't need a game face.

"I made sure she had the best care money could buy while we fought it. She wasn't only my aunt and my mother she was also my best friend. I did all I could to make sure she knew how much I loved her."

He got a little misty then and started fumbling with his fingers again. Lila looked as if she was about to cry and took Eli's hand.

"Thanks to her" he continued, "I had a great education...became a lawyer. Wow! I don't think I've told anyone here that yet. Yes, I'm a lawyer...or I was...once."

"A lawyer!" all the women said at once, looking at each other as they said it, all sounding very impressed.

"How nice! We only have a few actually working out of Jennisburg. Most of them are in Henriston. That's where the business is," Mom chimed in again, coming to the rescue by shifting the conversation somewhere else. She knew pain when she saw it. We all did.

"Well, I guess whatever plans I had but can't remember now will have to be put on hold for a while, for obvious reasons, but let's see how things go," he said with an awkward chuckle. I could tell he was trying to end the inquiry, but at least he seemed to have snapped out of his haze for a while and began to eat more.

"Delicious meatballs, Mrs. Chagford," he said to Mom in an obvious attempt to change the subject with a boyish smile that I'm sure he'd used on women more than a few times in his life, but Jenny wasn't having it.

"So, why did you leave New York?" she asked, leaning in toward him with her chin on her hand.

He hedged. "Eh...well, I just got fed up with the crowds, the crime, the stress, the dirt, and after the World Trade Center attacks and the business with the anthrax in the mail going on about four blocks from my apartment, I just figured it was time to go. I've made enough money to carry me for a while, so I decided to take a chance and try for a different kind of life." Then he leaned back and began to sing in a drawn sort of twang,

"Greeeeen Acres is the place to be, Faaaaarm livin' is the life for me…"

By then I was on it and helped. "Land spreadin' out so far and wide." Then the entire bunch joined in, "Keep Manhattan, just give me that country side…" and everyone laughed and clapped.

Hurt, drugged and drunk, the man still sure knew how to work a crowd. Jenny winked at me across the table. She knew it, too, but was satisfied, at least for the moment, that he wanted to be as straight with us as he could allow himself to be. Just then she started as if she'd just remembered something she'd forgotten. "Oh, my goodness, Jonah. I hope we didn't wake him up. Jeff, honey, could you check on the boys?" she said in a loud whisper, pointing to the door.

He came back to the table looking, at first embarrassed then worried. "He's not there!"

Everyone looked at each other as if to say, "What do we do?" Jenny and I stood up at the same time. She shouted into the other room for the boys to start looking for him. I told Eli to check the front door to see if it was locked to narrow down the search. A minute later Eli shouted back that the front door was unlocked but there were no footprints in the snow on the porch, so he must still be in the house, but he'd check outside anyway just to be sure. By that time everyone was calling around the house, "Jonah! Jonah, where are you?"

Martin looked to me and asked, "Do you think he can he manage the stairs?"

I thought about it and called for Lila. "Lila, you go up the front staircase. I'll take the servant's stairs off the kitchen. We can meet in the middle." Although I hadn't had the benefit of a tour, I was sure I could wing it, so we went our separate ways to search the upstairs.

There were five rooms upstairs off of a central corridor, not counting a water closet. I looked in two empty rooms and the closets, no Jonah. Then I saw an odd shaped door on the wall midway through the corridor. I could hear Lila calling, "Jonah! Jonah!" from the other end.

The odd door was smaller, shorter, almost like it was an afterthought. When I opened it, a small set of stairs led upward. Realizing that it must be the attic, I flipped the light switch casting a gray dimness to the unfinished, cobwebbed walls as I went up. I looked around. There was nothing there but some dusty old boxes and a few clothes racks, still no Jonah.

Then, just as I was looking in the best hiding place, behind the clothes racks, I heard a noise behind me and caught the glimpse of a shadow move out of the corner of my eye. Startled, my heart skipped a beat. I swerved around instinctively. "Jonah?" No response.

With my lighter lit, I walked over to the corner where I thought the sound emanated and searched behind the packing cases...nothing. *Must have been a mouse,* I thought. It's only natural for field mice to look for a nice, warm home given the season and the place. Then, just as I was heading back down to meet up with Lila, I was struck by a scent I could swear was lavender, the old fashioned kind that reminded me of the stuff my grandmother used in her closets. I hadn't noticed it on my way in, maybe because I had Jonah on my mind, but it was unmistakable, almost like it'd been blown in my face. 'Sachets' are what I think my grandmother called them.

When I met up with Lila again, she looked worried and shrugged her shoulders as if to say, 'nothing.' I responded verbally. "Me either. Let's go back downstairs. They've probably found him already," and put my arm around her heading down the front staircase. As we descended, everyone was there waiting, anxious anticipation on their faces. When Jenny saw we didn't have Jonah with us she understandably panicked and shouted,

"Oh, my God! Jeff, we've got to call the police," and looked to him for support.

He put his arm around her and said as calmly as he could manage, "Terry *is* the police, hon," but I could see the panic growing in his eyes, too. I came off the stairs into the room and looked at Eli.

He looked back and said, "Nothing outside, Chief. No

footprints in the snow either. He's gotta be in the house somewhere."

I looked to Martin. "Is there a basement?"

"Yes" he answered, looking worried, "the door is off the entry hall under the stairs, but it's locked. I'm sure of it."

I could have kicked myself then. I hadn't even noticed it. "Damn!"

Just then I saw the worry and panic ease itself from Jenny's face as she looked past me. I turned my head to look behind me. "Jonah!" we said simultaneously as he stood there on the landing before the last set of steps.

I stepped out of the way to let Jenny rush past me up the few steps onto the landing and snatch him up in her arms. "Oh, my baby!" she cried, "I was so worried. Where have you been?" As she came back down everyone gathered around letting loose sighs of relief in varying pitches, casually taking seats around the living room.

Jenny took Jonah and sat on the sofa. In a matter of seconds I saw the expression in her face change to anger and frustration, thinking for a moment she might give the kid a good shake, but she didn't. She just hugged him hard and asked again, "Where have you been? You had Mommy and Daddy so worried!" the tone of her voice high with concern.

"Upstairs . . ." he said in a small, scared voice, pointing behind him to the front stairwell. Lila and I were standing next to each other. I looked at her and she at me. We shrugged at the same time, watching the kid as his hands fidgeted nervously in his pockets.

"What were you doing up there?" Jenny asked him, calm coming back into her voice.

"Talkin' to the man," he said, taking his hands out of his pockets to fiddle with the hooks on his little overalls.

"What man?" The pitch of her voice went up again.

"The man upstairs," the kid said, looking down at his shoes and sounding like maybe he shouldn't be telling her this.

Jenny looked at me. I shook my head and mouthed to her without sound so as not to contradict or alarm the kid. "There is no one upstairs." Lila looked at Jenny nodding her head and shrugging in agreement with me. Jenny looked back at Jonah and asked with some concern in her eyes,

"Was this a real man, like Daddy or Martin or Chief, Jonah?"

Jonah just kept looking down at his shoes, finally shaking his head.

"Was this a make-believe man?" she asked him looking down, trying to catch his eye. To that, Jonah just shrugged his little shoulders guiltily and nodded.

"Oh, Jonah!" she cried out in exasperation. "You scared the life out of Daddy and me. Don't ever do that again! Please, promise me, Jonah!"

"Yes, Mommy," he said and put his arms out to be held. She hugged him tightly. Jeff looked at the boys sternly as if to say, "Why weren't you watching him?" and as if they could read his mind, they looked back at him sheepishly and said in virtual unison, "Sorry, Dad."

Once things calmed down, everyone went back to the dining room for coffee and dessert. Jenny left Jonah on Mom's lap while she, Lila and the boys began clearing the dinner dishes. Jeff's color was still too hectic for comfort, so I took the opportunity to try and smooth things over saying to him, "You know your boys really were a big help in unloading the car and building the fire earlier...and without being told or asked." I felt like I had to go out of my way to sound as impressed as I really was without sounding phony. "They're good kids and that's no small accomplishment with all that's going on these days. Real little gentlemen, they are. You and Jen must be terrific parents," I said, trying to keep the boys out of the doghouse for letting Jonah slip away. They really were good kids, probably the most genuinely helpful and polite kids I'd ever met, and Jonah slipping away really wasn't their fault. Sometimes things just...happen.

"Thanks, Chief ...that means more than I can say. We worry so much about them and don't let anybody kid ya. It's a full time job, and if anyone tells ya different, they're lying or doing something wrong. I'm just glad my work is seasonal so I get to do my part and have a real hands-on influence."

I gave Jeff a hearty slap him on the back and went for the Wild Turkey bottle. I could tell he was still more than a little tense over the situation and thought it was time we had another drink, both of us.

When I went into the living room to get the bottle, Jenny was there bending over the coffee table, nervously picking up the drink glasses and beer cans. "Thank you, Terry," she said without looking up at me.

"For what?" I asked.

"For saying those nice things to Jeff in there...about the boys," she said as she stood up.

"No problem, Jen. They really are great kids. I meant every word." She looked at me then like she was searching behind my eyes. "I'm glad you think so. They think you're 'the coolest' and always stick to their best behavior whenever you're around, but there is something I want to tell you because I know you'll understand," she said, then stopped for a few seconds to choose her words carefully.

"People think we got Jonah because I was feeling broody over my last chance at more children...but it wasn't me. It was Jeff," she said seriously, working to keep her voice down. "He wanted more but I couldn't do it and I love my husband very much," she said, pausing to take a deep breath before going on. "He had a brother once. His name was Jonah, too." I caught the phrase "had a brother once," and immediately had a feeling where this might be going.

"When Jeff was ten and his Jonah was six, they were out walking. They lived in Hartford then and were crossing the street not far from their house. Jeff was holding his brother's hand when a car came speeding around the corner and caught Jonah and dragged him down the street. The impact threw Jeff to the curb. He hit his head and was knocked out, but his brother was killed. He carries tremendous guilt over it, Terry, for not being able to protect him. I don't think a day goes by that he doesn't think about it. Sometimes, when he locks himself in his study telling me he just wants some alone time, I swear I can hear him crying...for hours. I think those days are probably his Jonah's birthday and the anniversary of the accident.

"That's why we got our Jonah. Jeff lives and breathes for those kids, so when someone who doesn't know about his brother says good things like you just did about our kids...it really means the world to him. Maybe it even takes away his guilt for a little while. He works so hard to be the best, most loving and responsible father he can be, living every day through our kids to try and make up for losing his brother. The guilt he feels has got to be enormous. I can only imagine it, but I see it in him so often and I love him like crazy. There isn't anything in the world I wouldn't do for him, so if it meant having another baby for him at forty-four years old, well, then that's what I did, and I'm not sorry."

I was at a loss for words at what she told me but, looking back, it made a lot of sense. The boys were just too well behaved to have been the product of the current trend of 'laissez faire' parenting, or the 'it takes a village' shifting of parental responsibility. It took years of loving, hand-raised care to get those boys to where they were. I just took a deep breath and held her hand. "God, I'm so sorry, Jen."

"I just wanted you to know," she said solemnly. "I…we…know how you feel about some things and I just wanted to say thanks for making Jeff feel good, particularly after our Jonah's disappearing act earlier." She smiled at me sadly and I knew then she was referring to Angelica.

Then Mom's voice rang out from the kitchen. "Jenny…We're ready for dessert in here. Leave the clean-up for later and I'll help." Jenny touched my face fleetingly with her free hand and went back to the kitchen. By the time I got back to the table, Lila was putting a cherry cheese cake on the table. Jenny had started pouring coffee, and Mom was having a ball entertaining Jonah on her lap. Looking at her then, I could tell she missed not having grandchildren and all I could think of was that it was, *Time to chalk up another one for 'good old' Terry being less than he should be.* On my bad days, I couldn't look after a gold fish much less a child. After that, it was time for a half of a pill.

From there, dessert went off without a hitch and in all the fuss over Jenny's baking skills I managed to pour some Wild Turkey into my coffee cup and switch it with Martin's, unnoticed. Jenny had said the other day that he'd complained about not sleeping well. *Well, he'll sure sleep well tonight,* I thought, but I also knew from experience that he was going to have serious trouble with pain management. That was when I asked myself for the first time, *Where do his problems end and mine begin, and conversely, where do my problems end and his begin? When we*

look at each other, is it like looking into a mirror? What a club!
"Physical and emotional cripples unite!" could be our battle cry
and would make a hell of a good banner, I thought, and smiled
ironically to myself. What a couple of sad-ass bastards we were,
with me officially becoming what the professionals call an
'enabler' and not far down the line adding 'co- dependent' to that
list.

As the party broke up, I got Mom into the car and went back
for the box of empty pots. Martin was waiting for me in the entry
hall, leaning on the stair rail for support. "Cash must have really
spilled her guts to you when you spoke to her," he said, clearly
having put two and two together from the flowers she'd sent. I
didn't say anything. "So…you must know all about me then," he
said as a statement rather than a question, deliberately trying to
avoid looking at me, "…and know that I haven't been a well man
since the disaster. Actually, I'm not all that convinced that I
haven't lost my mind," he said, shaking his head sadly.

"I know what she had to tell me," I said, putting my hand
out close enough for him to see it. "…and you didn't lose your
mind. They call it 'Post Traumatic Stress Syndrome.' Soldiers
who've seen combat get it, so you're not alone." He finally took
my hand and shook it, then slowly looked up at me, searching
for the truth in what I'd said, his eyelids drooping from the pills
and drink. "Everything will be alright. I promise, and I always
keep my promises, don't I?" I said, stressing the word 'promises,'
remembering what Angelica had said to me in the dream.

He smiled weakly and nodded. "Yes, you do, Chief." The
poor guy could hardly hold himself up by then.

"Now go get some sleep. Sleep time is healing time. Take it
from an expert," I said heading toward the door then stopping. I
wanted to say more but couldn't find the words. So, I just closed
the door behind me.

❋ ❋ ❋

With the holidays only a few days away, it seemed like all
hell was breaking loose. Lila's baby got a stomach flu, so she was
out. Jenny's mother fell and fractured a hip, so she had to go to
Rochester to do her duty there and leave Jeff home alone with

the kids, a mountain of unwrapped presents in the house and an undressed tree. I volunteered to take Mom over there for the day to lend a hand in helping un-stress the situation over on that side of town. Then I had to send Eli and my newest cop, Gunner Bjornstrand, over to the Rogan residence on a domestic disturbance call. It seems the third Mrs. Rogan found out that Joe had kept some nudie pictures of the second Mrs. Rogan in a copy of *Field and Stream* in the basement while she was taking out their artificial Christmas tree. During the 'discussion' about it, she apparently clipped him with a heavy glass ashtray from across the room splitting his head wide open, so he was out of commission for the week and staying at the Old Colonial Motel on the highway. What an embarrassment. *Ain't love grand?* I asked myself, and even though I managed to keep it out of the "Police Beat" section of the paper, I couldn't stop tongues from wagging. I'm only a human boy, after all.

Then, to add insult to injury, so to speak, the Mayor had been chewing my ass out over a rash of cemetery vandalism episodes that were happening at The Old Settler's burial ground. It seems it'd recently become fashionable among a certain species of teenager to conduct black magic rituals over there by knocking over headstones and trying to dig up bodies, and during Christmas week of all times. *What the fuck is the world coming to? Who, in God's name, is raising these children? Rosemary's fucking baby?*

Then on top of it all, against all predictions made around Martin's table, there was a nor'easter on us looking to drop a couple feet of snow everywhere in its path. Thank God, Mom always takes a few days of her vacation time during Christmas week. That meant that after I got around to doing her shopping, she would stay 'snug as a bug' as they say, and wouldn't leave the house for a while. At least that would be one worry I wouldn't have. We'd already been through a twisted ankle the year before and I wasn't looking forward to her having a broken hip this year. But before I could even get to that, I had to make sure the plows, salt, sand and tow trucks were ready. People were always sliding into or onto one thing or another during a storm.

I put my two off-duty guys on one-hour notice for the week

just in case. They were so thrilled. *Not!* My bones hurt like the bejezzuz from the decreasing barometric pressure of the storm, so I was just about at the end of my goddamn rope. The one positive thing that happened was that Lila called and told me that the baby was much better and if I brought the extra dispatch radio equipment over to her place, she would work with whoever she got to cover the station and coordinate with me through my cell or car radio. *Lila,* I thought to myself, *you are a true miracle of modern womanhood.* But I must confess the thought of actually using my cell phone again when my nerves were so fucking ragged sent shivers of techno terror down my spine.

Having taken care of all of that, I found the time to go over to the Cozy Cupboard Market with my mother's list while she was over at the Denton's figuring I could swing by and pick her up when I was done. By that time, it'd been snowing for close to twenty-four hours. There was already about a foot of snow on the ground and, as human nature would have it, the place was heaving with everyone who'd waited until the last minute to do their storm and holiday shopping, running around in a frenzy. It was a madhouse, so I grabbed a cart and went at it with the rest of them.

Just as I pulled up to the deli counter, I saw a wiry little figure in an oversized coat and long springs of gray hair poking out from the sides of her head. Lo and behold, who did I run into but Martha Portensky. My first feeling was guilt because with all I had going on, I hadn't even thought of Martin out there by himself with the storm coming until I saw Martha's face. My second thought was to give her holy hell for leaving him alone the way she did. "Martha!" I said, about to let it rip. "I've been meaning to run into you. How are things going over there at the Welliver place?" I asked, baiting her.

"Oh, Chief Terry! I ain't been there for weeks," she said in her quivery voice then went into her sob story about too far, too old, whatever.

I lost my temper some then. "How could you leave an injured man alone, without notice, or a call, or making arrangements for someone else to take over?" I said, gritting my teeth.

"Please don't be sore with me, Chief Terry. I jus' couldn't stay no longer. I jus' couldn't," she said, wringing her bony hands and looking from side to side to see who might be watching us or listening. I pulled her out of line over to the snack section.

"Cut the crap, Martha! Did he do something to you? Did he offend you in some way to justify your running out on him like that?" I asked snarling at her, not really believing it but using it to narrow her excuses.

"Oh, no!" she said. "Mr. Welliver was a perfect gentleman. A sad young man...but very kind, very polite. He even paid me in advance."

"So you just took the money and took off, is that it?" I barked at her, my patience getting paper thin.

"You wouldn't believe me if I told you anyway. You'd think I was crazy," she said defensively, clutching her purse to her chest like a shield.

"I already think you're crazy, Martha," I said tight lipped. That one was very unlike me. I've never been intentionally cruel to anyone in my life, but I was tired, racked with pain and in a hurry. I'm only a human boy after all, but I regretted it the minute it left my mouth, so I took a breath, wiped my forehead with my hand and tried again in a calmer voice. "Please tell me what happened, Martha."

"I will, Chief Terry, but only you...and only 'cause you're pressin' me so hard. If anyone ever asks me again...I'll deny it, to my dyin' day, I'll deny it," she said defiantly, a flush of pink rising up in her wrinkled white cheeks.

"Please, Martha, what? What is it?" I asked again, softening my tone yet further, still struggling to hold on to the last of my increasingly shredded patience.

She looked at me wide eyed. "There's somethin' *wrong* in that house, Chief Terry. It's *not right* out there," she said, stressing the words 'wrong' and 'not right,' poking her finger at my chest to show her conviction. I put my hands on my hips and stepped back, dumbfounded.

"Things moved," she said, sounding spooky and looking around again to see if anyone was listening or watching us.

"Whaddya mean things moved?" I asked her, feeling what was left of my patience about to snap.

"Things moved," she repeated, then added "by themselves."
I was like, *Huh? What the fuck?*

"I swear, Chief Terry. At firs' I thought it was jus' me gettin'
old and not rememberin' where I put things," she said, looking at
me intently with her watery blue eyes. "But then they started to
move...right before my very eyes. I seen a glass salt shaker move
from one end of the kitchen table to the other...all by itself!" Her
voice went up with the last bit. "an'...an' doors opened an'
closed...all by themselves!...an' I heard things, strange things like
whisperin' an' breathin' in the walls...an' cryin'!" she said, getting
more agitated and shaky as she spoke. My mouth must have
dropped a mile in disbelief. "'An' I could smell flowers...in the
dead of winter, followin' me everywhere." Her eyes were bulging
then.

"Jesus H. Christ, Martha!" I said, my mind boggled with the
thought of what she was suggesting.

"I knew you wouldn't believe me," she said. "No one would.
That's why I kept my mouth shut. You think I'm crazy don't
you?" she asked on the verge of bursting into tears, her wispy
voice wavering and trembling.

I thought for a moment and the incident with Jonah and 'the
man' came into my head. "No Martha, I don't think you're crazy
at all," I said with all the patience I could muster, reminding
myself of what my mother said about what a hard life Martha's
had, but thinking, *Oh for God's sake...* "It's just an old house,
Martha. More than a hundred years old. It has drafts, uneven
doorframes and floors that aren't even close to being level, that's
all it was, the wind blowing through the rafters, and old lavender
sachets. I smelled it myself when I was in the attic the other
day," I said, trying to put her mind at ease after I'd rousted her so
badly.

She put her hand on my arm. "Are you sure, Chief Terry? I
been terribly worried about Mr. Welliver out there all by
himself...an' guilty, too," she said, sounding less convinced of
what she'd just told me. I guess the badge gave my words
enough credibility in her eyes for her to believe me. "I didn't
wanna leave him all alone out there, really, I didn't. But what
else could I do? I was so afraid...an' after taking his money and
all. D'ya think I should send it back?" she asked sincerely, her

eyes starting to water.

I just shook my head and put my hand over hers. "No, Martha. I'm sure you did a good job while you were there and I'm sure Mr. Welliver appreciates it. You keep the money and have a good Christmas for yourself." God, I felt awful about being so rough with her. Lord knows, a new washer and dryer weren't going to make up for the fact that her sons rarely, if ever, came home to see her. Ashamed of their humble beginnings I suppose...like they could ever have more than one mother. *Bastards*.

"You have a good Christmas too, Chief Terry. Will I be seein' Charlotte at church for the holiday?" she asked placidly.

"I don't know," I said contritely, "probably not this year, Martha. With the storm here and me with my hands full, I think it'd be best if she stayed home and you might do the same. God will hear your prayers wherever you are, and you can bet he doesn't want you to get a broken hip over it." She smiled at that and I felt just a little bit better.

I went on with my cart completely forgetting that I hadn't picked up anything from the deli counter. Before I'd gotten through the next aisle, I could feel the cold sweat on my forehead, upper lip and the palms of my hands. As I've said before, denial is a comfortable place to be and, believe me, I stayed there as long as I could, but things were beginning to mount up.

I was feeling trapped in my own mind and when that happens, it seems that my way of dealing with it is to let them go physically. I tried to get a grip on myself as I went on my way, but then I got to thinking about Martin out there alone at the house and it being Christmas and all.

In the end, my conscience won out. I doubled back around the store and loaded up on more basic supplies, then went back to the deli counter and ordered up extra bunches of sliced meats, cheeses and a couple of pounds of pasta and potato salad. I had no idea what Martha had stocked up before her hasty departure, so I just had to wing it. On the way out, I picked up a garish, cheap and cheerful, plastic, pre-decorated, two foot musical Christmas tree to take for Martin. It had to be God awful lonely out there for him, especially after all he'd been through, and even more so at Christmas time. I had to do what I could to help. I thought that, at the very least, the tree would make him laugh.

By the time I got out of the store, the visibility had gotten worse. I radioed in to Lila to check on things. As usual she was on top of it. Joe Rogan came in to man the station. Eli was patrolling in the four-wheeler. My oldest and most experienced cop, Warren Newman, was coordinating the sanding, plowing and towing from the town yard with Lila. Joe said he'd do a double shift until morning since he really had nowhere else to be anyway. She put Eli on a double. He had no choice or there'd no nookie, and she had Bjornstrand ready to come in at midnight to relieve Warren over at the yard.

I told her I had to drop off the groceries before I picked my mother up from the Denton's and, once I dropped Mom off at home, I was heading over to Martin's to drop off his supplies. Before I rang off, I asked her if she could call up Big Bill Keller and ask him to load up two cords of quartered firewood and meet me at Martin's in an hour. "Tell him that he can to look on it as a 'personal favor' to me," which meant I would overlook the 'green leafy substance' I knew he grew behind his barn, and that I pilfered from, for yet another year. I told her once I got Martin secured, I'd go over to the station and relieve Joe and take over for her so she could get some sleep.

She told me not to worry about her because, in her words, she would enjoy being the "Snow Queen for the day" and that she and Eli would call in their marker "Oh...around honeymoon time," she giggled. "Oh, and by the way, the Mayor called to tell you what a great job you were doing. He had no trouble at all getting home from town hall," she said, laughing out loud. "That translates into the fact that he had no trouble stopping by Marissa Kamen's place for a quickie and still make it home in time for dinner," she said, laughing out loud again. "I had Warren direct that both their neighborhoods be plowed and sanded first...just in case. I'm nothin' if not politic, eh, Chief?"

I laughed out loud myself at that. "Lila, where did I ever find you?" I asked rhetorically.

"On the balls of my ass, Chief. On...the...balls...of...my...ass!" she answered, laughing again.

"Gotta love ya, Lila," I said. "Thanks."

"Yeah, I know. Over and out," she said and rang off. *She's some sassy piece, that Lila,* I thought to myself. Eli's gonna have his hands full for the rest of his life with that one.

With that done, I got back out of the car and walked over to the liquor store to pick up a case of Bud and a bottle of Hennessy before going my merry way. The streets in town were in good shape on the way over to the Denton's, but when I got there the roads on their far end of town were still snowy. I guess the plows hadn't gotten that far yet. I still had no trouble managing it, but I had to keep on my guard nonetheless.

I told Mom my plan before dropping her off at her house. Luckily enough, I'd had time to meet Dave's men to deliver the new appliances late that morning after I'd dropped her off at Jenny's before the storm got too bad, so she had quite a surprise coming to her when she got in.

I kissed her cheek and sent her off telling her, "Please, let the first kid who comes by and wants to shovel the path do it. I'm too old, Ma. Don't tell him your son will do it. It's only twenty bucks for God's sake and I *am* gettin' too old."

"Yes, dear," she said with a placating smile, clearly humoring me. "I know you have your hands full. Will I see you for breakfast in the morning?"

"There's no telling, Ma, but if you can't reach me, just check with Lila. She always knows where I am." I waited until I saw her shut the door behind her to make sure she got in all right and I was off again. I must confess here, I'd already had four Advil by lunch time and took my half-and-half combo before I went into the market. There was no way in the world I was ever going to shovel any fucking snow. The best I could hope for was that the excitement of new appliances would force her to let me have my way this year and hire the kid. *God I hate this weather,* I thought.

CHAPTER 5

bagatelle (noun);
1.) a game in which small balls are
hit into numbered holes on a board.
2.) something unimportant.

"Fear of monsters attracts monsters."

Unknown

The drive down Randolph Road, especially the bridge section, was slow going the further out from town I got, so I had time to ponder. I couldn't shake what Martha had said to me about the house. The earnest conviction in her voice asking me to believe...the unbelievable. The words, "there's something wrong in that house," and "things moved," rang in my ears, backed up by Jonah Denton's voice saying he was, "talking to the man...the man upstairs." It just could not be what my mind was trying to make me think it was. As I've said before, my only excuse for not believing anything so outlandish was my strong sense of denial combined with the possibility of my own instability creating the perception of things that just weren't really what they seemed. Ultimately, the only thing I could come up with was to toss it off as an old woman's superstition and young child's fantasy. The only spooks I had to be afraid of were those running around inside my own head and achy joints, or that was what I used to think. But before that night was over things would change, and not in a 'good way.'

By the time I got to the dirt path leading to the house, Big Bill was already pulled to the side of the road waiting for me. The drifts in the surrounding fields were already well over two feet high out there. Snow whirled around our heads like a cloud as we spoke outside his truck. It must have been 8:00 P.M. by then. We agreed that I would drive up first, then he would back in so we could unload. Bill was a great bear of a man with a big black beard in a red and black buffalo plaid coat and hat over Carhartt overalls. To give him space, I pulled up the path where it ended alongside the house. He backed right up to the front of the porch near the existing wood pile.

As I slugged my way up to the front door, I could see Martin peering out from behind the curtain. He must have heard the rumble of Bill's engine. He poked his head out of the door a moment later. I shouted to him from the back of the truck that I'd come in after we unloaded the wood. He looked dazed, like he didn't know who I was, or didn't understand what I said, and shut the door again. It took Bill and me almost a half an hour to unload the whole thing and before I knew it, he was back in his truck.

I went over to his window and shook his hand, "Thanks Bill, I owe ya one," I said.

He just winked at me and said, "No problem, Chief," in acknowledgment of my obligation to him next harvest season and pulled out of the drive. Bill Keller was a man of few words, but he sure grew some great 'buds.'

After Bill left, I went over to my car and opened the door to take out the bags of supplies, then thought better of it. *Pull the car around front and save your already howling leg some steps.* So I got in and pulled the car up forward toward the porch, then threw it into reverse to back up, intending to straighten out and go forward in a k turn sort of way. Well, I guess I hit the gas a little too hard because the back end of the car slid straight off the fucking path into a goddamn ditch.

Maybe it was fate. Maybe it was the combination of pills I took earlier mixing up with the two slugs of Hennessy I took on the way over, but when I put the car back into drive and attempted to pull up out of the ditch, I just spun wheels, going nowhere. Snow flew everywhere. "Mother fucker!" I shouted into the air. "Fuck you!" I bellowed at the car, kicking the bumper when I got out, mumbling, "Son of a Bitch!" to myself. I was definitely stuck, so I did the only constructive thing I could think of. I grabbed the bags out of the passenger side of my car, balancing them on the case of beer, and stormed toward the front door. Martin must have heard me stomp the snow off of my boots when I got to the porch, because when I looked up he was standing there with the door open. He'd combed his hair back, looking a little more alert and aware than when I first came. My fault really, he wasn't expecting anyone. I should have had Lila call ahead.

I went straight to the kitchen to put the bags down on the table and started to rub my temples with one hand, wincing. Losing my temper always gives me a really nice headache.

"What's all this?" he asked.

"Supplies," I said, almost growling. "There's a snow storm out there, if you haven't noticed." He looked surprised.

"Oh, yeah, that. It's not going to be that bad is it?" he asked, sounding none too bothered by it.

"Well, it's not like you'd be snowed in under a hundred feet of snow in some hotel in the Colorado mountains," I said, struggling not to sound mean spirited, "but it's gonna tie things up for a while, and under the circumstances, I thought it would be best for you to be prepared."

I was tense, tired, achy and sounded all of it, not at all meaning to. "You got a glass for me, Martin?" I asked gruffly. He turned around without moving much and took a water glass out of the kitchen cabinet. I took the bottle of Hennessy out of one of the bags and poured myself a double slug, then reached into my pants pocket for the couple of Advil I had left rolling around in there and chased 'em down. That done, I went back out to the entry hall, took off my coat and boots, tossing them in the corner, and turned around to find him staring at me blankly.

"Care for some company tonight?" I asked, holding my arms out in a gesture of abject frustration.

"Sure," he said, "but I don't understand."

I gave a big groaning sigh and said, "Nah, I'm sure you don't. Well...I've just spent all fucking day prepping town and my near and dear to weather out the storm in relative comfort and you, my friend, were the last stop. Literally, the last stop." I put my hand to my head again and squeezed. "And now I'm stuck. I backed the goddamn car into a goddamn ditch and I'm stuck until I can get someone from town to fucking tow me out." He just looked at me from the kitchen doorway with a perplexed expression on his face without saying a word. I guess a grown man having a tantrum right there in his entry hall was a new experience for him.

"Of course you're welcome to stay. The company would be great," he said, trying to stave off the storm brewing in his hallway, but not knowing quite how. I must have looked like a wild man or raving madman. Actually, an oversized raving man-child was probably more like it. After a few deep breaths, I realized how foolish I must have looked, got a grip on myself and went back into the kitchen to start putting the groceries away.

"Do you mind if I join you?" he asked, holding up a can of beer.

"Help yourself," I said off handedly. He reached and got himself a beer and poured himself a shot to go with it. He downed the shot chasing it with the beer, then sat down in one of the kitchen chairs and started talking as I was about to put the last few items in the fridge. "Chief?" he said as I kept working. "Chief!...Terry!" He raised his voice insistently, clearly wanting my undivided attention. I turned around with my hands still full. "Chief, put the stuff down and come sit for a minute. I want to talk to you." He flipped the top on another beer and pushed it toward me on the table.

"You got a cigarette?" he asked. I pulled the pack out of my shirt pocket, took one and handed him the pack. I lit us both up with my lighter. He took a long draw and exhaled followed by another deep exhale.

I sat down across the table from him. "Okay...Shoot."

"Chief...Terry...listen to me," he began, looking like a train wreck in the bright kitchen light. His face was shallower than it had been the other day. The circles under his eyes were deeper and darker, and his skin had gone beyond merely pale into a sickly pallor. He took another drag of his cigarette.

"I know whatever Cash Hasher said to you about me had to

be more than I'd ever want you to know," he said with a look of sour dismay, waving his hand as if he were pushing it away to the side, "but I've wanted to talk about you for a while now, anyway." He stopped, took a long drag on the cigarette, then started again.

"I've learned a good bit about you too, lately. I heard about your Olympic medals from the old librarian, Grace. I heard about you losing your father and your government work from your mother. She's enormously proud of you...and she should be. She raised a decent, caring son."

He stopped, took another swallow of beer and poured himself another shot. I just sat there rubbing my forehead. I should have known that in their moments alone they were all talking about me.

"Jenny told me about the little black girl who died in the fire. She says they've been hoping that pulling me from the car would give you some sense of peace so that you might begin to forgive yourself for losing her," he said quietly.

"Good God...she didn't!" I thought, not realizing I'd actually said it out loud.

"...and Lila told me how much you've done for her and how you fill your life taking care of other people. You've got a real fan in that Lila. I wouldn't be surprised if she was a little in love with you. Actually, if the truth be told, I think they are all a little in love with you," he said, never taking his eyes off me. I started to sway slightly back and forth in my chair the way I used to after my father and Angelica died, rubbing my temples with my hand while he spoke.

"But, Terry, I'm not your responsibility, no more than I am Jenny's or anyone else's. I'm sinking faster everyday, like I'm drowning, dying inside. I'm not getting any better. The pain is killing me and I don't know how long I can live this way. I'm getting worse and you can't help me. No one can. These last few months, I've felt like I'm living for all of you and not for myself. I'm a sad, weak son-of-a-bitch trying to hide away from the world, and since the accident I've been in so much pain, I find myself going to sleep every night wishing...hoping...praying that I don't wake up. I'd probably have been better off if you hadn't come along that night."

Red lights started flashing in my head, sirens blasting in my ears. That was enough. I'd had it. I looked up at him, slamming my hand on the table so hard that he jumped in his seat. "Enough!" I shouted. "Enough! So, you came here to die, is that it?" I barked and laughed a sad ironic laugh, lit another smoke and took a long swallow of beer before turning back to him. "I let a little girl die who wanted to live and helped a man live who wants to die. Is that it? Huh? Jesus H. Christ! If I didn't have bad luck, I'd have no goddamn luck at all!" I bellowed at him, holding my hands to the sky as if looking for an answer. I could feel a roll coming on that I couldn't control. I turned back to him.

"Now, you listen to me, boy!" I said, pointing my finger at him. "You think that you're the only one who lives with pain. I know you've had some in your life, probably more than your share, but it's not always about you. You think you're the only one who suffers? Do you? Did you know that my mother blows kisses every night at a picture of a husband who's been dead for twenty-five years? Or that Lila flinches every time there's a sudden movement or loud sound around her, expecting it to land a blow on her...still...all these years later?"

"You want to know what pain is, Martin? Pain is that 'little black girl,' whose name was Angelica Weston by the way, choking to death on thick smoke, struggling to live in a blazing inferno. Pain is her mother, Cordelia Weston, screaming, 'Save my baby. Please save my baby,' and living with her loss every single day of her life like it was yesterday. It's Jeff Denton looking at his kids and thinking about the speeding car that ran his little brother down in the street while he watched when he was no more than their age and...and...and...that doesn't even count what I go through every single day of my own sad-ass fucking life...just to survive. And why? Why? I do it for them...and for you...every fucking day...which you can't begin to understand." My eyes must have looked like they were about to leap out of my head. My hands trembled with anger, clenching and unclenching my fists, like a psycho Robert Mitchum in *The Night of the Hunter*.

"We all live with pain, Martin. Why the hell should you be any different than the rest of us poor suffering slobs?" I knew I was over the line then, losing it.

"Life *is* pain, Martin. To be human is to suffer. I risked my life to save yours, pal! Had the current in that river been a little stronger, or the towrope a little weaker, we'd both be dead right now. I gave you back your life, so don't ever tell me I made a mistake!" I shouted, jabbing my finger at him. "Don't ever fucking tell me that you'd rather be dead! Don't you ever tell me that!"

I huffed and puffed glaring at him like a bull who'd just had a red cape waved in front of his face. He drew his head back, his eyes widening well beyond their natural state. I could see the emotions shift over his face in seconds like a sliding palette of paint. He didn't know whether to laugh, cry or tell me to get the fuck out. I don't think anyone had ever spoken to him like that before and, by that point, he must have realized that he'd picked the wrong time and the wrong person for that particular discussion.

Martin took a deep breath, struggled up to the counter and began pulling out plates and things from the fridge asking calmly, "I'll bet you haven't eaten today have you, Chief?"

I didn't answer. I just went on huffing and puffing and rubbing my head. By then, my legs had gone from trembling to bouncing up and down with nervous tension.

"Well, I'll tell you what. You're my guest tonight, even though you brought the food." He turned his head to me and smiled. "You let me take care of you for a little while."

It was the first time I'd seen a spark of life in his eyes, but as with Martha at the market earlier, a rush of guilt came over me for blowing up at him like that. It's not my nature, or I didn't used to think it was. As I sat there stewing in my own juices, I thought to myself, *You big, drunken bully. You're a big, stupid, fat-headed, drunken bully, and you're a hypocrite, too. Weren't you thinking the exact same way when you found him only a few weeks before? And now listen to you. What the hell has happened to you? You must be losing your fucking mind. You should be ashamed of yourself for beating up on a man in pain. You...of all people...should know better."* And I was, terribly ashamed.

A moment later, the telephone on the wall behind him rang. He reached over and picked it up. "It's Lila, Chief."

That was when I saw the tile laced on a string hanging around his neck, one with a green dragon symbol on it. It came out of his shirt collar when he reached over to hand me the phone. I was more than a little taken aback by the surprise of seeing it, but in my state of mind at the time, I had to file it for the moment until I could get a grip on myself and had dealt with Lila. It was important to keep my wits about me, whatever wits I had left anyway, especially since I'd just lost it big time. I took the phone.

"Lila? It's me."

"Chief," she said. "I've been trying to reach you."

"Is everything alright?" I asked, expecting the worst.

"Oh, yeah, everything is under control. I just wanted to keep in touch to give you a status report." I let out a sigh of relief. "Your mother called looking for you," she said. "She's thrilled with the new stuff. She just wanted to tell you. I told her you were out on a call but I'd have you call her as soon as I could, before midnight if it was possible."

"Please call her Lila, and tell her I'm stuck over here at Martin's place. I backed the car up into a goddamn ditch and now I can't get it out," I said with embarrassment.

She giggled. "Don't worry, Chief. I'll let her know. Anyway," she continued, "things in town have been pretty quiet. The plows and the sanders have cleared the streets, so everything in town is passable for now. The snow seems to have slowed, but I'll keep up on it anyway. Town is deserted, so I let Eli come over to eat and get some…rest," she said, giggling again. "I told Joe he could go home, but he said he preferred the cot in the backroom of the station to the flea-bag motel he's been staying in, so he'll sit tight there." She went on without a breath.

"Sounds good," I managed to slip in before she was at it again.

"On that front, I had a call from Sharon Rogan. It seems she tried to call Joe at the Old Colonial and when he wasn't there she got worried, so I filled her in and told her not to worry. He was safe and warm at the station until morning. Sounds like that marriage is on the mend or will be soon…'til the next time anyway," she said snickering. "But, Chief, I just had to send Bjornstrand and a couple of tow trucks down to the exit ramp off the highway onto Route 9 a little while ago. It seems some blockhead in a Volvo wagon hit his brakes a little too hard coming down the ramp and spun out. One car skidded into him, and to avoid hitting him, two other cars went off the road behind them. One went into a tree and the other one into a ditch. Gunner got there just before I called to report in. Nothing major really, he says. No injuries or much damage either. The EMS guys were on their way there just in case, but the tow trucks are going to be busy for a while. I'm not sure if any of the cars are drivable. They may have to make two trips, and then they'll probably want to go home and get some sleep themselves. I don't know if I can get one out to ya 'til very late tonight or close to morning. Is that okay?"

I looked at my watch. It was already getting late and my head was splitting. I looked at Martin and another wave of guilt washed over me for snapping at him. "Sure, that's okay. I can stay here," I said hesitantly, "but make sure I can get out by seven or eight in the morning. I'll need to get cleaned up and be at the station by nine just in case the Mayor comes by and wants to go over how much the storm cost us...oh, and Lila. Let's keep my ditch incident just between us. It would just look bad."

"Gotcha, Chief," she said with a sigh, like I should've known that it goes without saying. "Oh, and Chief?" she said as an after thought, "please turn your cell phone on and keep it close, just in case. Okay?"

"I'll do it right now, hon," I promised her.

"Over and out," she said signing off. She loves saying that, even on the phone.

I hung up the phone and turned around. Martin was making up plates of food, left-over meatball sandwiches and some of the potato salad I'd brought, chuckling to himself as the microwave timer went off.

"You know what, Chief? This situation reminds me of that old comedy routine about the Chinese proverb that when you save someone's life, it becomes yours. The one where the guy becomes so beholden to the one who saved him that it gets on his nerves to the point where he has to fake a situation so the first guy saves his life in return and they can call it even. Who knows? I may have to get through this just so I can get on your nerves until you throw yourself on some railroad tracks and wait for me to come by and pull you off. Then we'll be even," he said and laughed again.

"I'll bring the plates. We can eat by the fire so you can dry off. Don't forget the beer and the bottle when you come in," he said as he hobbled through the swinging door to the living room, holding onto his crutch with one hand and carrying the two tenuously stacked plates with the other. He seemed to have snapped out of his 'I wanna die' mood for the time being, so maybe I did a good thing after all, but I still felt crappy about the things I'd said to him. To try and make it up to him, I grabbed the cheesy Christmas tree I'd bought and took it into the living room with me. When I plugged it in, it lit up like a Mexican carnival, and so did his eyes, bright and shiny, like a child. He nodded appreciatively and smiled. "Thank you, Chief. It was very kind of you to think of me. I love it. Thank you," he said, giving me another one of his broad toothy smiles. He was better. I was glad.

❋ ❋ ❋

We sat down in the living room, me in the rocker and he in his chair, and began to eat. When I regained myself, the first thing I thought to do was some fishing about the tile around his neck. I hadn't forgotten what Sylvia had told me about finding them in the house. I just wanted to know what he knew so I said, "I see you play Mahjong. I'm a backgammon man myself."

"Oh, this...I found a few of these on the kitchen table when I got home from the hospital," he said, pulling the tile out of his shirt. "They may have been here before. I really don't remember anything yet from the time my car broke down up the road until seeing you by the river. The doctor says it's not at all unusual with a head injury. It may come back, or it may not. You can never tell. It doesn't really matter, I guess. I'm here to stay, it seems, at least for the time being," he said, casting a glance at the crutch propped up against the side of the chair. Then he went back to the tile, his spirits still above ground.

"It's kinda funny. I got the idea from meeting Grace at the Thanksgiving dinner over at Jenny's. She had a bracelet made out of them. It was so unusual, I thought. Then I found these on the table. This one already had a hole through it, so one night when

I woke up and couldn't get back to sleep I got creative, pushed a string through it and made myself a charm. Good luck, I hope," he said and smiled again.

"It's funny what people will do to entertain themselves when sleep isn't an option." I could see the clouds roll over his eyes and his mood as he spoke.

"I don't sleep well at night," he said. "I guess I'm not used to living in an old house. Creaks and groans, sounds when the wind blows, you know. Kind of like us and our bones," he said with a faint smile. I could see he was slipping back down again. "I guess I got spoiled living in a high rise in New York. I've even taken to leaving the TV on in the other room or the radio in the kitchen at night just so it doesn't seem so isolated. Then I cat nap during the day to catch up. All in all, it probably wasn't the wisest move to make to take this place so far from town, but who knew I'd end up stuck here all winter with nothing but the sounds of an old house and my old bones to work on my nerves. I can understand now how old people can get lost in their own little worlds when they become housebound. It's a coping mechanism, when they have nothing else to occupy them."

As I sat there listening to him, I could hear Martha Portensky's voice again, "...things moved...the walls breathed," and Jonah Denton saying he was "talkin' to the man," and the hair on my arms and the back of my neck stood straight up. I've heard that there are times in people's lives when reality and unreality become so blurred that it's hard to tell which is which. My mother talked about it when I was growing up, trying to help me understand why her 'sick people' were different than other sick people. I was having one of those moments right then, allowing myself to consider that ". . . *there were more things in heaven and earth, Horatio, than are dreamt of in your philosophy.*" Martin's voice brought me back to myself.

"Chief, are you alright?"

And I was back. "Yeah, I was just thinking..."

"About what?" he asked.

"That I shouldn't drink so much and take pills at the same time ...and neither should you," I replied with a weak chuckle. "Between you, me and Betty Ford, it's not the healthiest way to live."

"I know," he said sadly, diverting his eyes away from me. By then we'd eaten as much as we were going to and sat back to relax, but my conscience started working me over again about how I'd roughed him up earlier. I had to try and make it right.

"Martin, I'm sorry for getting so over-heated with you earlier. Please forgive me. I'd never want to hurt you, really. I'm so sorry," I said, shaking my head and feeling like a heel.

"I know, Chief, but there's nothing to forgive. Everything you said was true. I guess I just needed to hear it from someone who cared enough to say it. It's the sign of a true friend. You've been that for me unfailingly ever since that night by the river. I'll never forget that. He looked directly at me as he spoke, but I couldn't look back. I changed the subject instead.

"You haven't talked much about what happened in New York yet, or why you really left," I said. "I'm here now. We've got plenty of booze and nowhere to go, so maybe it's time," and I poured us some shots. He just sat quietly and lit a cigarette, staring into the fire, then took a deep breath, letting it out with a whistle, like a steam valve.

"I can't, Chief…" he said, then hesitated. "It would change everything for me here and I don't want it to change."

"I don't understand. What does it have to do with things here?" I asked, not having the slightest beat on where this might be going.

"It has to do with you, Chief," he said softy. "If you understood who I am…who I was. It would change everything. I wasn't the kind of man you would ever respect. I know we haven't known each other for very long, but I think I know the kind of man you are and I don't ever want you to regret helping me the way you have. I don't think I could stand that," he said quietly, holding his head down covering his eyes with his hand.

"I'm not here to judge you, Martin, and I could never regret helping you," I said getting concerned about the turn this seemed to be taking. "Why don't you let me be the judge, and believe me, with my background, I can give you a very wide berth, really. I promise. I'm in no position to judge anyone," I said, trying to sound as sensitive as I could allow myself. He took a good long slug of his beer and lit another cigarette, considering what I'd said. Then, looking resigned and dejected, he began to speak.

"I wasn't just a lawyer back there, Chief. I was a Wall Street shark, a corporate 'hired gun.' It was my job to make greedy men richer by robbing the American public and keeping them out of jail while they did it. While others may have been just 'doing their job,' I knew. I knew what they were doing and didn't care. I even helped them and was proud of my cleverness at it. All that ever mattered to me back then was my own success. You couldn't respect that...not in a million years. I know that much about you." He rubbed his forehead hard as he spoke, like he was trying to erase the words from his head after they came out, like I do when I have a bad headache. He wouldn't look at me, but I could feel it coming, like a small crack in a dam, swollen and waiting to burst.

"Then when the disaster hit...it destroyed who I was as completely as anything could," he said, sounding defeated. "It took away my confidence in who I was, my security in my surroundings and within twenty-four hours, I was afraid to leave my apartment, afraid to see people...talk to them...be touched by them." He started to sway slightly as he spoke. It might have been hardly noticeable to others, but not to me. I recognized it at once. He was going side to side. The dam was about to blow.

"I sat and watched the news coverage, turning it on then off, pacing around the room in circles for hours like a nutcase in a padded cell. I had to know what it'd done, but then it made me sick when I saw it and I had to turn it off again. I couldn't leave my apartment without holding onto the walls for security. I had trouble breathing and panicked all the time. When it was over and the death toll was growing, I found out that most of the people from my office were dead, and even more from the offices around mine, nice, good people. People with families. Secretaries, couriers, people I said 'good morning' to every day. They were dead. All dead, Terry." He started rocking as the emotion rose in his voice, looking at me like he couldn't believe his own words.

"I knew so many of them. I went to lunch with them, had drinks with them. I played volleyball with them at our summer outings and had dinner at their homes. All dead." His eyes began to leak. He wiped them on his sleeve as he spoke.

"Then it occurred to me. I was alive. Why was I alive and not them? Why was Rod August dead? His office was next to mine. He was such a nice, harmless guy who handled life insurance and annuities. He had a wife and three kids. He was innocent. It doesn't make sense...or Linda McIntyre. I went on smoke breaks with her every day for three years. She was just a secretary, a single mother of two. She used to bring me soul food when she cooked because I couldn't get it anywhere else. Why was she dead and not me? I was not harmless. I was the corrupt one, not them. It should have been me, Terry, not them! They had people they loved and who loved them. That's when I realized I didn't mean anything to anyone. The things I had done out of blind ambition had made me not worth caring about. There was no one who wanted to get close to me. Sometimes, I even think they were afraid of me. My life wasn't important to anyone worth having. I was the expendable one...and yet, I was spared.

"I'm even more ashamed of that. People struggling to raise families died and I lived. There's no justice in that. I feel so guilty all the time and...so ashamed. I can still see their faces and hear their voices in my mind, smiling, laughing, making jokes about their bosses and their lives, griping about how rough city life can be, like we all did every day.

"Sometimes...sometimes I even think I can hear them calling to me...wanting me to come join them...because that's where I really belong, dead with them. The guy who had my coffee and paper ready every morning was a Lebanese guy named Dave. My secretary, Caridad, was only twenty-five. She had her whole life ahead of her. God, I'm so sorry." His whole body started trembling, like a frigid wind had just blown through him, and his chest started to heave, like a child who'd just fallen down and skinned his knee stubbornly trying not to give in to tears, almost choking on his grief. "Why them and not me?" He was looking straight at me again, small tears running out of the corners of his eyes, gliding down the sides of his face, asking me for an answer that was beyond human understanding.

"Then I come here and have the accident, maybe getting what I really deserved after all. But what I found were some of the most genuinely caring and emotionally generous people I've known since my aunt died and I feel even guiltier, not worthy of life, of living. Jenny, Jeff, Lila, your mother and you. I look at you all and feel your kindness, all the while knowing inside that only a few months ago, I was helping the corporate monsters take bites and chunks, bits and pieces out of your lives, and hundreds of thousands of others like you. Laughing all the way to the bank. I can't look at you...any of you...or myself."

He bent over in his chair, covering his face with his hands. The dam had burst. He started to sob in great heaving sighs. I poured him a shot and put it in his hand, laying my hand on his shoulder. He took it, drank and wiped his face on his sleeve again. Then he raised his head, looking at me then with an intensity I've rarely seen anywhere in my life.

"But I want you to know, Chief...I need you to know that the man I was in New York died there in the blast. I'm not the same man now. It's so very important to me that you know that," he said turning away from me, holding his trembling hands in his lap to keep them from shaking.

His honesty floored me. I never expected anything so raw and real to come out of him. He'd just laid his soul bare before me, like an ancient sinner from the Bible repentant before an altar. I felt helpless, not knowing what to say or do. I wanted to give him some peace, but I didn't know how. He was like me, suffering every day, inside and out. But I knew one thing. I couldn't let him suffer anymore, and I wasn't going to give him some half-ass, back-handed crap like the shit I got from that asshole analyst about not having any fucking answers. After all he'd told me and trusted me with, he deserved better than that, and I was going to see that he got it. Even if I had to lie. I couldn't let him suffer, and in one of those rare instances where my luck won out, I found what I needed within myself and didn't have to lie. I took a drink, lit a smoke for myself and gave it my best shot.

"Listen to me, Martin," I said, looking him straight in the eye, stirring up all the conviction I could to bring it out of myself. "I want you to follow me here. Maybe that is the reason you were spared...to become the man you are now. Maybe walking away from that disaster was your trial by fire, and the crash in the river your baptism to who you are now. I'm not going to try and justify

what you may've done before you came here, and I won't
pretend to minimize all the lives lost and the grief of those
families. But we each have our own destinies and just maybe
yours was to find your way here and be the man I see sitting
across from me right now. You may have felt unimportant in 'the
City', but you're not in 'the City' anymore. You're here in
Jennisburg, population 936, and you mean a great deal to
people...right here."

It's always been hard for me to talk about my feelings so I
leaned over, folding my hands together and looking down at the
floor as I always do when I get uncomfortable with them.
Looking at my hands that way brought me back to that first night
in the hospital men's room and the way I felt when I saw his
blood on my hands, following it as it swirled down the drain. It
took me further outside of what I knew to be myself and the
words just seemed to flow out.

"It may make me sound like a selfish son-of-a-bitch for all
you've been through, but there's something else I want you to
know," I said, taking a deep breath and letting it out slowly.
"You've been my salvation, Martin." My voice wavered as I
watched my feet shuffle nervously, keeping my focus only on
them in order to get through it.

"That night by the river made me feel like a living, breathing
human being again for the first time in years. If I could take away
your pain, believe me, I would without hesitation. But I can't be
sorry for feeling alive again. I won't. To me, you are not
expendable...so if you need something to hold on to when
things get too much for you, try and remember that your life is
not unimportant to me, or the others around you here. We all see
so much good in you and think that after you've had a chance to
heal, you'll do something wonderful with your life to make us all
so very proud of you. I can't say what that something may be
right now, but it will happen and you wanna know how I know?"
I asked, managing to raise my head back up to look him straight
in the eye again, letting him hang there for a minute. "Because I
fucking said so, and Chief Terry has been through too much in
his goddamn life to hold with any crap," I said sternly, jabbing
my finger at him. "You got me on this, Martin?" I stressed in my
deep commanding voice, the one that never leaves any room for

compromise or debate. "You are going to do something to show everyone who you really are...now."

He sat up straight. "Yes, sir, Chief Terry!" he said, giving me a salute with his hand, his damp eyes starting to shine again.

"Good!" I said definitively.

Then he surprised me. Sitting there looking at me wet eyed with a bemused smile on his face, he said, "I may not have any of the answers to the questions in my life, but there is one thing that I do know for sure, Chief."

"What's that?" I asked, expecting some profound pronouncement from the self confessed 'oh so clever' Wall Street shark.

"I know that Mrs. Chagford raised herself one hell of a son."

That one caught me way off guard and I rebounded in the only way I knew how.

"Nah. I'm just a washed up, broken down, has been," I said, waving it off and laughing at myself, but on the inside feeling satisfied that, at least for the moment, I'd succeeded in fixing him. The tension seemed to evaporate into the air after that, but it wasn't only the tension. The effect of heat from the fire on my damp clothes made it so I could almost see the steam rising off my skin.

"Well that makes two of us then, so at least I'm in good company," he said, putting out his hand for me to shake. By then it was late and I could see the drugs, booze and emotional drain of the conversation were taking their toll on him. He could hardly keep his eyes open.

"Come on old son, it's off to bed for you," I said, getting up to help him out of his chair. But as he tried to stand and steady himself with the crutch, it slid out from underneath him and he stumbled. Luckily, I was close enough to grab him before he could land hard. He was weaker than I thought. "Leave the crutch tonight. It doesn't look like you're up to it. Put your arm around my neck, I'll getcha there," I said, taking him by the waist, trying not to hurt him by holding him too tight. He was light as a feather not good sign. *Not eating.* I could feel the bones of his ribs. *We'll have to work on that, and soon,* I thought. "Where do you sleep?"

"On a folding bed that Jenny had Jeff bring over. It's in the dining room until I can manage the stairs and...it's close to the bathroom," he said bashfully.

"Doesn't it get cold back there?" I asked as we stumbled our way toward the kitchen.

"Nah, Jenny lent me an electric blanket too. No grass grows under that woman's feet. She's been a real godsend. I don't know what I'd have done without her. I'm as comfortable as I can be back there and who knows? I may even get to sleep through the night knowing there's someone else in the house. It sounds silly, I know, but I can really feel a good sleep coming on knowing that you'll be here," he said as we limped our way through the swinging door to the kitchen, then the other door opposite into the dining room. When we got there, I sat him down on the folding bed and he kicked off his slippers. There were some blankets and pillows stacked on a chair behind the door so I took the top pillow and pulled a blanket out from underneath the one that was left.

"The tow truck should be here by seven. I should be out of here by seven thirty," I said, heading back out. "Get a good night's sleep, Martin. I'll just be out there on the sofa if you need me."

"You too, Chief. Thanks for everything and...Chief..."

I stopped, turning to let him finish.

"...I'm really glad you're here," he said as he laid down. I nodded, winking at him with a smile, switched off the light and was gone.

"Yeah. Me too, pal."

※ ※ ※

I went back to the living room, choosing his big chair over the sofa. I just felt the need to be upright that night instinctively vigilant, I guess, like an animal in unfamiliar territory. I sat down, pulled up the foot stool from the side of the chair and covered myself with the blanket. I was so tired from all the day's antics I could hardly move.

The warmth of the fire felt good on my bones again as I started to unwind to the sound of the big wall clock ticking away slowly in the otherwise quiet room, soothing my nerves as I closed my eyes, feeling myself starting to drift off to its hypnotic rhythm. Tick, Tick Tick. My eyes couldn't have been closed for more than a few minutes when I heard a sound from somewhere upstairs and they shot open again. There it was again, footsteps. I sat upright with a bolt to listen more closely.

The wind, I thought. Then I heard the sound of breathing, amplified…strange…immediate, but still distant…otherworldly. I know that sounds corny or crazy but that's the way it was. It was upstairs. The hairs on my neck and arms were standing straight up again.

What do I do? I thought to myself as I stood up and went to the foot of the stairs. Then I heard what sounded like muffled sobbing…a woman sobbing.

This can't be happening! I thought, still feeling driven to find out what it was. Then I did what any self-respecting cop would have done. I got my gun from the table and went back to the foot of the stairs to listen again. It stopped for a moment, but then I heard what sounded like the squeak and the slight bang of a door closing, then another.

Somebody is up there. Somebody is up there trying to fuck with me, fucking with my head, and I started up the steps with my gun drawn. When I got to the first landing, I stopped. There it was again, more sobbing, baleful, mournful sobbing. It was unmistakable, and seemed like it was echoing, almost like it was coming from inside the walls.

This can't be happening. This cannot be real! I kept thinking. I took a few more steps, hearing for the moment only the creak of the floorboards under my feet. The sounds stopped. I waited for what I didn't know. Then I moved onto the second floor hall. God, my bladder was so full from all the drink I'd had, if I didn't get a grip, I was going to piss myself.

Then I heard movement, like furniture moving. It was coming from the room at the end of the hall. I kept going. It was dark, but I could still see. There were no curtains on the windows. The moon was shining on the snow, reflecting off of the white walls, making everything seem illuminated. The sound stopped and then started again. Then there were more sounds, furniture moving or scratching on wood.

When I got to the top of the landing, I could see that all the doors to the rooms off the hallway were open. I looked in each one as I passed. Nothing. They were empty, completely empty and...cold. No furniture. Nothing. Apparently, Martin hadn't managed to get a real bed in there before the accident. As I closed in on the room at the end of the hall, the sounds stopped.

God, I'm going to piss myself, I thought, then argued with myself in my head. *No, you will not! You're a grown man. Grown men don't piss themselves.* I walked through the door of the room at the end of the hall. There was nothing, no sound, no furniture, just more emptiness and cold. It was so cold I could see my own breath. I saw moonlight coming through the window facing the back of the house. I walked over to look out. At first there was just the cold, white bleakness of the snow. Then something moved.

What's that? What the hell was that? I thought. There it was again, a shadowy figure out back by the garden house a couple hundred feet behind the house. It looked like a man. I couldn't be sure at that distance, but I knew I couldn't move. I was frozen. I watched the figure come away from the garden house and move toward the back of the main house.

It was a man...definitely a man. He was walking through the snow toward the back of the house. I was sure of it. Just then it...he...walked into the path of a moonbeam shining through the clouds and I saw him. He had something in his hand like a hammer. He was wearing a white shirt with dark blotches over the front and on the sleeves. I thought immediately that it looked like blood. As he moved closer to the house, I saw what he had in his hand. It was a hatchet. He had a hatchet in his hand and he was moving toward the back of the house. Then he was out of the moonbeam and I couldn't see him, but I still couldn't move.

I stood there staring out of the window, transfixed. Another moonbeam struck and I could see him clearly again. It was definitely a hatchet in his hand, and it was definitely blood on his shirt. He was covered in it. Just then he looked up and saw me. I saw his face, red eyes, blazing blood red eyes looking at me and his mouth. God, his mouth was...all twisted, drawn back in a horrible, snarling grimace, almost like he was smiling at me, but he wasn't smiling. He was taunting me, daring me. Oh God! It was the man from the dream.

This cannot be real! I kept thinking to myself. He turned his head back down, continuing to walk through the snow toward the back of the house. He was almost at the back door when I thought, *Oh, my God! Martin! Martin is in the back of the house. He's going after Martin!* The danger instinct shot through me like a lightning bolt, my feet unglued from the floor and before I knew it, I was on my way out of the room. Just as I stepped outside of the room, the door came slamming shut behind me. *Boom!* I thought I'd piss myself right there, but I held it and I ran...ran down the hall, the doors of the other rooms all slamming shut as I passed them. *Boom! Boom! Boom Boom!* The sound was thunderous, deafening, and the smell, that horrible, rotting, fetid smell from the dream hit me in the face like a shovel. I thought I would vomit, but by the time I reached the stairs, the smell was gone.

I grabbed the stair rail instinctively to stop myself from falling, but still moving as fast as I could. My leg and shoulder rocked in pain with each running step. Then I was in the kitchen going toward the rear entry hall. I stopped dead as I faced the back door. Martin was sleeping just off to the left in back of the dining room. *Was the back door locked?* I didn't know.

I walked slowly to the door and looked out. Nothing. No foot prints in the snow. No sign of anyone. *Did I imagine it all?...What do I do now?...Check on Martin!* was my first thought. I pushed slowly through the swinging door and looked toward the bed, feeling for the light switch I knew was on the right and turning it on. Martin was there sleeping quietly, undisturbed.

I made a quick scanning sweep of the room. Nothing. Everything was as it had been. I switched off the light before it could wake him, letting the door swing back closed and finding myself facing the back door again. The next thing I knew, I had the doorknob in my hand, shaking it to make sure it was locked. Then in the split second that I looked up, my nuts shriveled, contracting themselves up into my guts. It was there, on the other side. A bloody hatchet raised over a blood-spattered white shirt, and that face with its nauseating corpse-like skin. Bloody masses for eyes staring back into mine, snapping at me with those awful decaying sharp teeth, lips pulled back in a sneering death grin, like it was laughing at me.

My mouth shot open, "Jesus Christ!" I reeled back, pressing myself flat against the side wall out of striking range just in case its swing came crashing through the door. I stood there for a moment panting breathlessly, winded, as if the sight of it alone had sucked the air out of my lungs. I turned into the dining room, gripping the woodwork for the strength to keep standing and flipped on the switch, shouting,

"Martin, wake up! We gotta get outta..." But before I could get the words out of my mouth, his blanket flew back and it leapt out at me, hatchet in hand, snarling and gnashing its bloody teeth as it drew back to swing at my head.

"GET...OUT...OF...MY...HOUSE!" it rampaged, bloodshot blue eyes bulging with violence as it brought the hatchet down. I closed my eyes, hearing only the sound of my own throat shredding scream as I felt the sharp edge of blade land on my forehead. My bladder exploded sending a warm stream of piss shooting down my legs. Then I realized that my eyes were open.

I was already out of the chair and on my feet, bathed in sweat and shaking, but making no sound. I hadn't screamed at all. My throat was as dry as sandpaper. I reached down and felt my crotch. I hadn't pissed myself either. *It was just a dream, Terry,* I thought to myself. It was just a dream. "Oh, thank God," I said out loud, letting myself fall back down into the chair and wiping my face on my sleeve.

I sat there for a moment, completely unhinged, unglued, still shaking and needing a drink, a cold one. It took me a minute, but I found my balls again and got up to go check on Martin and get a cold drink. Water. I needed water.

I went to the kitchen and pushed slowly through the second swinging door into the dining room. I looked toward the bed and felt for the light switch and turned it on. Martin was there sleeping just as he was in the dream. I looked around as I had before. Nothing. Everything was as it had been before and in the dream. I switched off the light and let the door swing back closed. As I faced the back door again, I held my breath, sweat dripping from my forehead. I took the door knob in my hand and turned it. *Locked.* Then I looked up, half expecting to see that face staring back at me, but there was nothing. Then, just in case,

I looked back in on Martin again only to find him sleeping peacefully. Nothing was wrong, nothing at all...and no moonlight. The night was pitch black.

I took a deep breath and went to the bathroom, my bladder aching for release. From there I went to the sink, splashed cool water on my face and drank from the tap until I was full, then dried myself off. I sat in a kitchen chair and went to put my head down on my folded arms when I saw by my watch that it was 5:30 A.M. It was Christmas Eve. I put my head down and waited for the light of true morning to rescue me. *God, let it be soon,* I prayed. The next thing I knew, I was roused by a knocking at the front door. I looked around and saw Eli smiling and waving to me through the front door window, holding up a brown paper bag which I assumed held hot coffee. I looked at my watch. It was seven thirty.

I got up to let him in and saw he had one of the tow truck guys with him. I stepped out on the porch, got my car keys out of my pocket and tossed them to the tow guy. The cold fresh air felt good in my lungs and went a long way in clearing my head.

"I brought'cha some coffee, Chief," he said smiling.

It was good to see him, breakfast or no breakfast. "Come on in for a minute and let me get my things together...but be quiet about it."

"Sure, Chief," he said, still smiling. I could tell Lila had worked him over good that night. Eli never smiles at seven thirty in the morning. He followed me into the kitchen, set down the bag and opened it, took out a Styrofoam cup and handed it to me.

"There's a couple bacon, egg and cheese sandwiches in here too, if yer hungry," he said, pleased with himself. I opened the coffee, grabbed a sandwich out of the bag and started shoving it in my face. I was starving.

"Thanks," I said with my mouth full "You are a true prince, my Eli," and nodded to him to go back into the entry hall. Before I headed after him, I picked up a pen from the table, wrote on the bag, "EAT THIS!" then put on my boots and jacket and was out the door. I slapped Eli on the back.

"Thanks, bud," I said as he got back into the tow truck. "I'll be fine from here." My car was already running, ready and facing out of the drive.

"No problem, Chief," he said, smiling again.

I yelled to him through the window, "...and don't forget to tip the tow guy. I'll getcha back later." He waved, nodding that he understood.   *Damn! She must be good,* I thought and was off.

CHAPTER 6

An Age of Grace

"Being deeply loved by someone gives you strength, while loving someone deeply gives you courage."

Lao Tzu, Chinese Philosopher-
Founder of Taoism, 6th Century BC

I went to my house first to shower and change. I could smell myself the whole ride home and it wasn't pretty. I made a plan while I scrubbed off, deciding not to take a coffee cup in with me *this time.* The last thing I needed then was for my already shaky composure to be rattled even more. Then, as I looked up, wiping the steam from the mirror, I saw my own reflection and realized I couldn't live in denial about it anymore. Martha Portensky was right. There was something definitely wrong in that house. I knew it in my heart and felt it right down to my toes.

I couldn't explain it, but it was true. It didn't matter if I could explain it. It was still true. That night's dream had convinced me beyond all reason. I couldn't deny the signs I'd had all along anymore either. Angelica tried to warn me. The hand on my wrist was her hand. She wanted me to be well enough to pull Martin out of the river. I had that idea at the time, but I really saw it in that mirror, God bless her. In the dream, she left me the tile to tell me something, to warn me. I was just too thick and blind to see it.

It had something to do with the tiles, and then I remembered the dream after the Thanksgiving party and Grace Coutraire's bracelet. It all had to do with the tiles and Martin wearing one around his neck. *What is it about those fucking tiles? And what does it have to do with Grace Coutraire?* I asked myself. I had to find out, and soon.

Then another question reared itself. *Why me? What the fuck does any of this have to do with me?* I'd never met Martin Welliver before. I'd never seen that house before. *What in hell could it have to do with me?* I was just a sad, lonely, drunken, middle-aged failure, becoming increasingly crippled both emotionally and physically in the bargain. But I kept coming back to the bracelet. What did Grace say about it? It was a gift? From someone she loved? Something like that. My mind was too disjointed and muddled to get it straight. It all just seemed like one big jumble, but for better or worse, I decided I had to speak to Grace...and it had to be that day.

❋ ❋ ❋

It was almost 9:00 A.M. by the time I'd finished dressing. I'd make it to work alright. *Let me just get past that for now,* I thought, struggling to stay focused. When I got to the station, Lila was already there.

"How's the baby?" I asked, trying to sound normal.

"Much better. Thanks, Chief...but that's more than I can say for you. You look like hell," she said, trying to make it sound funny.

"Not now, sweetheart," I grumbled. "I've got too much to get done today. You can give me all the grief you want after Christmas, but I need you to be on your toes for me today."

Sensing the stress in my voice, her expression changed. "Anything you need, Chief. I'm with ya." Her eyes spoke the rest for her.

"First, I need you to call my mother and tell her that I'm up to my ears in holiday mess and that I'll see her for dinner. Next, I need you to call over to Grace Coutraire and ask her politely if I can have an audience with her today," I said, managing a smile and a bow to go with my reference to Grace's status as local royalty, trying not to raise any unnecessary suspicion, "but tell her it's important and that I can be there by lunch time if that works for her."

Lila was like, "Huh?" I could tell she was thinking, *What business could he possibly have with the old librarian on Christmas Eve that was so important?'*

"Then call and check on Martin Welliver. Let him sleep for awhile. Make it after ten and make it nice and cheerful, a holiday 'well wishing' call. You with me?" I rattled off.

"Yes, Chief."

"And I'll need the preliminary numbers for the Mayor when he calls and he'll call before lunch if possible."

At that she handed me a manila folder with a self-satisfied smile and said, "Done!"

"Lila, you're an angel from heaven!...oh, and Lila?" I said and bent over and kissed her cheek, "Thanks. I don't know what I'd do without you," and was gone into my office.

A few minutes later, Lila came in with a cup of coffee saying, "Mayor called just now. He's on his way over."

"I'm ready."

❀ ❀ ❀

I made quick work of the Mayor who was pleased with the low cost of the numbers, at least my numbers anyway. The cost of sand, plowing and towing wouldn't be in for a few more days. I just had to give him manpower and overtime numbers.

He was gone by ten forty-five, then Lila buzzed in. "I talked to your mother. She says she'll see you at dinner. I also spoke to Grace. She can see you anytime after eleven."

"Perfect!"

"I haven't called over to Martin's yet. I'm still dealing with the labor."

"Lila," I said with a firm voice I rarely ever use with her, "you tell them your word is mine and they are not to question it."

"Gotcha, Chief. I can handle it," she said and buzzed off. Of that, I was sure. I had a feeling that by the time she was through the people of this town would be calling her 'Madame Mayor' and she'd get my vote. I just hoped I'd live to see the day.

On the way over I stopped over to Marchand's Flower Shop and picked up a dozen mixed red and white carnations to take with me for Grace. My mind was swimming with anxiety over how to even broach the subject with her. Then, at the last minute, it occurred to me that I'd forgotten my other holiday duties.

I took the time, then and there, to work it out as best as I could. I ordered large holiday bouquets to be sent to Lila and my mother, and a large box of assorted chocolates that the store had there just for the holiday to be sent to Jenny. Then as a last-minute thought, I ordered a dozen long-stemmed white roses to be sent to Jenny from Martin. It was only right. I knew he was the kind that would have if he could if he'd been well and had his full faculties about him. I had them add a card saying, "With sincere gratitude for all you've done for me. Merry Christmas. Love, Martin." Whatever else anyone might say about me, no one could ever say Charlotte and Arthur Chagford hadn't raised a gentleman for a son.

❀ ❀ ❀

I arrived at Grace Coutraire's door at eleven thirty and rang the bell. She appeared a moment later, smiling in pale green silk lounging pajamas under a deep green silk robe, looking as much a lady as ever.

"What lovely flowers," she said, not seeming in the least surprised as she opened the door to allow me to come in. "Please do come in, Chief. I rather expected I would be hearing from you...sooner or later."

Her 'expecting' me surprised me because, for some strange reason, it didn't sound like she was referring to the call from Lila. I stepped inside and followed her through her entry hall. I couldn't help but notice a number of gilt- and silver-framed photographs on an oversized telephone table and a few more on each side of the walls. They were of a striking young woman in various outfits and poses, some in black and white, others in color obviously Grace in her early twenties.

She walked ahead without turning around and said, "Yes, those were from my days in New York. I was quite a lovely girl then. Don't you think?"

One photograph on the table, in particular, was larger than the others, and in color. It was of a beautiful, young red-headed Grace in a strapless, backless, emerald green satin evening gown standing with her bare back to the camera, her head turned partially over her shoulder in semi profile, a fur, mink I assumed, draped over her far shoulder. Sumptuous imagery, stunning photography and glorious subject. 'Breathless,' is the only word I can use to describe how I felt during those few moments as I followed her into the parlor area. She turned around to face me.

"Please make yourself comfortable, Chief," she said, using her hand in a fluid manner to direct me to a chair by an elegantly set table with another chair opposite. Her 'receiving' room, I supposed. Everything in the room reflected the woman before me, refined, dignified and, above all, stylish in every way. The walls were covered in a green and gold delicately patterned silk paper. The drapes were green with gold appointments. The walls had what I assumed to be original paintings and sketches. Most were modern. There were also small sculptures artfully placed around the room, crystal and glass every where, and intricately carved pieces of cherry wood furniture that looked to be well over a hundred years old.

'Thank you so much for seeing me," I said as I took off my hat and coat and placed it as gently as I could on the chair in the far corner of the room.

"Oh, no," she said with a dismissing wave of her hand. "It's my pleasure. I should apologize for not being able to see you earlier. I haven't been sleeping well these past few nights and it seems to be taking me longer and longer to make myself presentable. The price of getting old, I guess," she said, smiling faintly as she sat down opposite me, crossing her legs as I'm sure she'd done thousands of times before when in the company of men.

"Some tea, Chief?" she asked as she reached for the steaming tea pot on the table, cups and saucers already set out in front of us.

"Yes, thank you. That would be very nice," I said, well aware by then that I was completely out of my league in her arena when it came to manners, but trying, nonetheless, to keep up.

"Or would you prefer something stronger?" she continued, maintaining a faint, sly smile. "I have some fine, old Armagnac here that I've kept for an occasion just like this. I'll be adding some to my cup if that makes it any easier for you," she said as began pouring the tea.

"Sure," I replied, feeling like the proverbial bull in a china shop.

"Lovely," she said and added some of the brandy to each cup from a tall, molded glass bottle. From there, I kind of jumped right in, bull in a china shop that I am.

"Grace, you said when I came in that you expected to see me?"

"Yes," she nodded, "since the party at the Denton's actually. You're here about the house on Randolph Road, aren't you?" she asked with a practiced sounding control in her voice.

"You know about the house?" I asked, surprised by her intuitive aim in hitting the bull's eye right off the bat. I hadn't expected such a forthright answer.

"Yes, I know about it," she said with a sigh as she looked out of the window behind the table. "I've been there, many times, long ago. It seems like a lifetime ago now." From there the conversation took on a heightened level of understanding, like a secret among old friends where some things didn't need to be said.

"And that's why you expected me? You *know?*" I asked again, stressing the fact that I wasn't merely referring it its location.

"Yes, I know," she said, maintaining her reserve and taking a sip of her tea. From then on there seemed to be a sort of electricity between us, like we were the only two people in the world, bound together by a knowledge that no one else shared.

"Why haven't you said anything to me before this?" I asked, astonished by her confirmation.

"Would you have believed me, Chief?...or would you have thought I was a rambling, senile old woman who had lost all touch with reality?" she asked with a slight, self-satisfied grin.

"Touché!" I said, nodding my head and feeling a bit embarrassed by her candidness. "But I'm here now, and believe me, I do not think you are senile or rambling far from it. I need your help, Grace. Please tell me what you know now," I asked her humbly.

She took a deep breath and said, "As you wish…but,…I see you have a pack of cigarettes in your pocket, Chief. Could I trouble you…"

"Oh, of course," and placed the pack on the table close to her. She took one and I lit it for her. She smoked for a moment, contemplating, then began.

"I've both waited for and dreaded this day for over fifty years. Most of my life actually, if you think about it. Sometimes I think I've lived as long as I have because I've held it all so tightly inside myself." I lit a cigarette for myself and took my teacup in my hand. She pushed her saucer to the middle of the table to act as an ashtray.

❋ ❋ ❋

"I guess I'd better start from the beginning and let it all out." She paused thoughtfully for a moment then began again. "I'm over eighty years old now, but as I'm sure you've noticed from the photographs in the foyer, I wasn't always old. I was young and beautiful once."

I wanted to say that she was still beautiful, but held myself to let her continue.

"I left this town just before the war. World War II, that is," she said with another faint smile. "When I was a young girl, and a poor one at that, I dreamed of being a clothing designer. I'd seen so many films and loved all those beautiful clothes so much. I wanted to make a life of it and was lucky enough to get into a design school in New York City. That was when life first opened up for me. It was a mad time to be in Manhattan then, with the war brewing in Europe and all the modern technologies coming about. I worked as a fashion model to help make ends meet. Those are some of my pictures you saw as you came in." She paused for a moment to think as she smoked.

"It was a heady time…a romantic time, and the world of Greenwich Village that I lived in was filled with new ideas, writers, actors, poets, models and painters. It was a marvelously creative time for a young girl from a small town and very bohemian, indeed," she said with a daring glint in her eye. "That was where I met my first love and only husband, Hugh Coutraire."

"Hugh was from a rather 'well to do' family in Louisiana, living in New York to get some world experience before he went home to join the family textile business. My name was Van Oakhurst before that. The first time I saw him I thought he was the most beautiful boy I had ever seen, big and strong with hair the color of wheat and bright, sparkling blue eyes. I fell in love with him almost immediately. He had the most darling southern accent...and he was kind and generous, and loving and gentle. I loved him dearly." Her eyes began to fill.

"The world was on the brink of war then and we were deeply in love, so when he asked me to marry him, of course, I readily agreed. I hadn't yet met his parents, nor he mine, when the United States entered the war." She took a deep breath, a sip of tea and lit another cigarette.

"You're a bright young man, so you must know where this is going."

"I think so," I said patiently, "but please go on."

"He got called up...drafted I think they call it these days, and so we decided...he decided that we should get married before he left. He was a very practical young man, sure footed and responsible. He wanted me to have all the benefits the wife of a serviceman would be entitled to while he was away and particularly in the event of...well...in the event he didn't come home."

She dabbed her eyes with the corner of her handkerchief, stopping for a moment to reflect. "The day he left me at the train station he was so full of life and hope for our future. His eyes were so blue in the winter sunlight and his cheeks so rosy red from the cold as he kissed me good-bye. 'I'll come home to you, Grace. Wait for me. I love you,' he said as he got on the train." She stopped for a moment, then said to the air, "I love you too, Hugh," as if he were in the room with us, then she directed her attention back to me and went on.

"Those were his last words to me. I stood there waving and crying with all the other women as the train pulled away. Most of us stayed even after it was gone holding each other and telling ourselves how we'd count the moments until they came home again." Then her voice suddenly changed, drastically, from fondness to something completely different.

"Well, he didn't come home...he was killed," she spat in a burst full of sad anger. "I was a widow at twenty-one with my heart shattered into a million pieces. Oh, there were many of us in that situation then...too many...so I can't be so selfish as to think it just happened to me. But I can't help but live with that image in my mind to this day, my beautiful young man dying in the stinking mud on some foreign beach so far away from me, his bright eyes once so full of life, empty and dim...staring lifelessly at the sky without me there to hold him and comfort him...to tell him that I'd always love him. "

Her voice broke completely as she turned her head to weep aloud, sounding like a young girl again with a knife turning in her heart as she must have so many years ago.

"Grace, please." I said. "You don't have to do this." My eyes began to fill by then, too. Her grief was so fresh and alive that I could feel her pain almost as if it was my own, and my heart broke for her. I reached over the table to put my hand on hers as she wiped her eyes delicately with the other.

"Yes. Yes, I do. It takes me where I need to be...and where you need to be. I'll be alright. I've had to be everyday for sixty years now," she said, dabbing her face delicately as she worked to regain her composure. She poured more tea and brandy for both of us, smiling sadly at me. "Please forgive an old woman her memories. When you get to be my age, memories are all one has and we tend to live in them."

I just looked at her, sharing her sadness, and said, "You don't need anyone's forgiveness, Grace."

"You're a very kind young man, Terry. Charlotte is such a lucky woman to have a son like you," she said, and took a deep breath before beginning again.

"After Hugh died, I lost my reason for living. I made it through the days until graduation, but I'd lost my desire for city life. I had no interest in other men or pursuing the career I had planned, so there was only one thing left to do...come home, and that's what I did. I packed up and came back here. It was much smaller then, and everyone really knew everyone else. My father was the local butter and egg man before he died of cancer. Everyone knew us, and there I was with the distinction of being Jennisburg's first widow of the war, so everyone accepted me back sympathetically."

"I bought this house with the insurance money I got from the government. But I must tell you, and I know you won't be surprised to learn, I grieved terribly for him, for a very long time. I still do. Sometimes I'll see an old war film on the television like *Mrs. Miniver* or *Since You Went Away* and I just fall apart all over again like it was yesterday. That's why I kept his name. I suppose I didn't have to. We were only married for a little over a year, but I wanted to keep him alive somehow. I wanted the world to remember that there once was a beautiful young man named Hugh Coutraire who had a young wife who loved him very much, Mrs. Hugh Coutraire. " Her tears were quiet now, resigned, as they streamed slowly down her face.

"It was such a waste," she said disdainfully as she dabbed her eyes. "It was the good fight, I know, and a necessary one, but so many women suffered because of it, not just American women but French, English, Italian, Russian and German women, too. Wives and mothers. Daughters and sisters…and how they tortured and murdered all those poor Jewish people…God help us all…and for what? Land? Power? Greed? Dominion over others?" she sighed, shaking her head without waiting for an answer before going on. "As much as I've loved men individually in my life, sometimes I hate them as a species for what they do to each other…and the reasons that make them do it," she said bitterly.

"There were times when I even thought I'd lose my mind over it. My mother was so worried about me. She lived here with me for a while to help me through it. Later, when the worst of it was over, she moved over to Henriston to be close to her sister. My aunt was one of those delicate ladies who never married. It was after my mother left that I started working at the library," she said and lit another cigarette.

"The library was so small then. The woman who was running it was an extremely well-educated woman, and one of the few school teachers we had over at the Bennett Street

School. I had her as a teacher myself. By the time I came back, she was already getting on in years and finding it hard to do both jobs, so it was politely suggested that since I had an education and was spending so much time alone that it might benefit everyone all around if I took over at the library and let her become principal at the school."

"It's probably hard for you to understand, but in those days farmer's children were still uneducated for the most part and there was an important movement in the rural areas to get them into the schools. The school had grown even in the short time since I had attended, from the three room schoolhouse over on Bennett Street, which isn't there anymore, to the larger building over on Hudson that they use now for the Revolutionary War Museum. The library is where it's always been. It's just been built on. That was my idea. I made it my life. I put all my efforts into it and the work helped me cope. It was my only interest and my only outlet. Not that there weren't young men who were interested and tried. There were, and many, believe me. But I had no interest. This is where it becomes important to you, Terry." She stopped and lit another cigarette, looked at me, then at the cigarette, smiled and said, "At my age, there is very little that can hurt me anymore, so please indulge an old woman her few remaining pleasures." I smiled back.

"Be my guest, Grace. Help yourself."

"Thank you, dear." I could tell that the brandy was having a mild effect. She called me "dear" with an almost flirtatious inflection that I'd heard a few times before in my life from women of a certain age.

❋ ❋ ❋

"I'd been at the library for a little over five years and had accomplished a great deal expanding its reach with my 'city ideas,' and over a great deal of...local resistance, mind you," she said, smiling wryly. "By then, I had hired an assistant and over tripled the number of volumes we owned. Then one day something out of the ordinary happened. A stranger came into the library. It was unusual because strangers never came in. There were only school children, the farm wives and the town wives...oh, and of course, the men who came in strictly to read the newspapers or gape at my high heels and tight skirts. I don't think they ever got over that," she said and laughed out loud. It was the first time I'd heard her laugh. It was so full of life. I liked it, and I laughed with her.

"In any event, this man came in. He wasn't handsome in any conventional way, but very well groomed. He was dark, black hair, dark brown eyes and he had a tan. A real tan, not just a farmer's tan, which was all anyone ever saw around here, and about thirty-eight years old. He wasn't very tall, not much taller than I was really and slightly built. He stood out because he was so very well groomed and dressed, which was rare around here at the time.

"When I met him at the front desk he told me he was a writer and that he needed some help with research for a new project he was starting. I must say that my interest was piqued and, of course, I told him that I would help him all I could. He told me his name was Norman Harper and that he'd come from California to finish the book he was working on and to begin the new project, a play about the effects of the war on small town America. I admit I was fascinated by him from the start. It reminded me of the types of things I'd experienced during my time in New York and sounded rather exciting. I showed him around the library, where he could find 'this and that' and he went about his business.

"A short time later, he came back to the front desk with a few books he wanted to take out and I registered him for a card. While he was filling out the papers, he asked me if I knew of anyone who might be interested in some work. He needed someone who could type, take shorthand, do proofreading and other types of general secretarial work. I told him that I would see what I could find out, and that if he stopped back later in the week or the next, I might have someone for him. It wasn't until after he'd left that I looked at the registration papers and I noticed that he put down his address as Randolph Road, but, of course, it didn't mean anything to me...*then*." She stopped then, wrapping her arms around herself as if she'd been overcome by a sudden chill.

"Oh, my goodness!" she said as if she'd just remembered

something important. "I've forgotten all about it. Please forgive me, Chief. I made some light sandwiches to serve with the tea and I've forgotten them in the kitchen. Please excuse me for a moment." She got up, taking the flowers I'd brought, and made her way through the door behind her before I realized what happened. I was mesmerized by her story, and she was just going to tell me about the house. Looking back, I think it was her way of balking at the subject, buying time to steady herself while she searched for the words to describe the incredible story she was about to tell me.

A moment later, she was back with the carnations in a cut glass vase and a plate of small sandwiches, no crust, setting them both on the table. "Please, help yourself," she said, "some are tuna salad, some are cucumber and some are tapénade, it's an anchovy-olive paste I took a liking to on my trips to Europe. Please try some," and retook her seat.

I took a few sandwich corners on a napkin and sat back in my seat. She took a few on her napkin and refilled the teacups, brandy and all.   "Now where was I? Oh, yes...I was just getting to the part of how I learned about the house," she said with a sharp inflection in her voice, frowning when she said 'house,' like it was a dark shit stain on a white rug.

For the first time, I could see furrows in her forehead, which was otherwise remarkably smooth for a woman her age. It made me think that the stress of addressing the subject might be too much for her, but I couldn't bring myself to stop her after she'd waited so long to talk about it.

"Well," she said, "I had decided before he even left the building that I would take the secretarial job myself. My life was empty enough. I had the time, could always use the extra money and...I guess it would be alright to say it now, I did find him strangely attractive in an exotic, California sort of way. He was so unlike my Hugh, and I was so lonely."

She began to look like she was aging before my very eyes as she spoke. "So, when Norman came back, I volunteered myself for the work. I cautioned him that this was a small town and I was a single woman who couldn't afford any talk in my position, so I would rather if he dropped off the work to me there at the library with the assurance that I would do the work in the evenings.

"He was a real darling about it. He said that since it was really just straight typing and correcting to be done to finish off the novel, my caution would not be a problem. He told me that when it came time to work on the play we could work something out then, but since he was only in the early stages of research and plotting, it would be at least six or eight weeks before he would need someone on a more regular basis.

"And that's how we began. I finished off the typing within a few weeks, realizing almost immediately what a brilliant man he was. By then I felt much more comfortable with the situation and agreed to spend Saturday and Sunday afternoons at the house to organize, read back and do the things he needed to work on the play, but at that point, it was only during daylight hours. I was still a nice girl after all," she said with a devilish glint in her eye. "And as it turned out, the hidden drive at the house really worked in my favor. No one could see my car from the road."

Hold on, old girl, I thought, feeling myself redden with embarrassment at the idea of what might be coming next.

She continued, either oblivious to my embarrassment or amused by it. "So, I started spending my weekend evenings there at the house as well, and as you may have guessed by now, within a few weeks, we became lovers."

It was official then. I was thoroughly embarrassed. I shifted in my seat nervously and must have blushed a dozen shades of red because she said, "My dear boy, we're both adults here. There's no need to be embarrassed. Love isn't something to be ashamed of love is to be celebrated, even if it's only by the two who are sharing it. It's the nature of true intimacy, my dear Chief.
"

"Yes, ma'am," I said and lit another smoke, my leg starting to bounce slightly.

"We had a lovely time together, Norman and I, drinking wine and laughing, writing and making love. It was truly a magical time in my life, one that I never thought I would have again after Hugh's death. I will never be ashamed of it, even after he began telling me the truth about himself which, by all rights, should have shocked and angered me, but for some reason it didn't," she said, waving her hand dismissively as she had a way of doing. "Maybe because by then, I knew that he loved me as much as I loved him and didn't care."

"His name wasn't really Norman Harper at all, although I'll always think of him as 'Norman.' He was married with his wife and two young children living just outside of Los Angeles, and he hadn't come to town to write a play about the effects of the war on small town America, or not just for that reason. He was hiding...from the government. Apparently, when he was a young man he'd joined the Communist Party and it had come back to haunt him after the war. He'd written a few novels and a few plays and was beginning to make a name for himself writing screenplays when he was called to testify before the House on Un-American Activities Committee. They wanted him to name the names of his friends and colleagues who were supposed to be *Reds*.

"The Red Menace was what they called it in those days, among other things, I'm sure. When he joined the party in the early thirties, they were just a bunch of regular men and women suffering terribly from 'the Great Depression' who wanted better lives for themselves and their children, a fair wage for a day's work, equality among all the different sorts people of this country and the freedom to think and feel and create as they chose without government interference. They weren't at all the monsters they've been portrayed to be since then.

"You'll notice that today we embrace all of these very same values and call it 'the American way' with labor unions, civil rights movements and social services. I've always thought it curious how things can be turned around without anyone noticing, don't you?" she said, pushing the irony of what she was saying home to me before continuing. "The real monster was that lousy muckraker, Joe McCarthy, and his bottom-feeding band of Fascist henchmen, using their dirty tricks to turn American against American, neighbor against neighbor, spreading the fear that there was a Communist 'boogeyman' hiding under every bed in the country in order to justify their jobs and their feelings of superiority and self-importance."

She stopped then and took a breath. Her color was flushed and she took another sip of her tea. "I do apologize for digressing, Terry, but when you've seen what I have seen of how

our 'so-called American civilization' can make men who should
be brothers turn on each other, and have lived long enough to
see the hypocrisy of it all over time, so much becomes clear.
Young people only seem to know about the times they live in.
It's when you get old and have seen what those with short
memories would like to forget about the horrible things they've
done under noble banners that it makes one angry and bitter.
But let me get back to Norman." Flushed with the power of
nostalgia or possibly the stress of the subject we were
approaching, she began to perspire slightly and took a moment
to dab her cheeks and brow.

"Norman decided that, rather than 'rat' on his friends, as he
called it, he would run. He and his friends arranged for someone
pretending to be him to leave the country for Europe while he
packed his things and drove out of New York to find a small,
quiet, out-of-the-way place to continue his writing without
worrying about the threat of being arrested at every turn."

"That's how he found Jennisburg, the house on Randolph
Road...and me. It was around that time that he gave me this,"
she said, pulling the bracelet made of Mahjong tiles from her
wrist and setting it on the table before me. "He told me he'd
made it with tiles he found in the house when he moved in. It
wasn't long after that the troubles began and things started going
downhill," she said with a sigh. I could see her expression go
from calm and direct to anxious and agitated, her pale green eyes
darkening with the change in her expression, becoming tense,
taut. She began to wring her hands in her lap and seemed to
become distracted by her own thoughts. She turned her gaze
back to me.

"Up until that point, about six or eight weeks since he first
came into the library, we'd been working feverishly on the play
and it seemed to be going awfully well. It was like he was in a
creative frenzy, and so pleased with what we'd accomplished. He
even told me he was basing one of the main characters on me,
but then he suddenly started to change. He began acting
strangely...not bizarrely...I don't mean that...but unusual...for
him."

"Remember, I was only with him for any length of time on
the weekends, so I didn't see him much of the time, but he

started complaining about not being able to sleep, which was not like him at all, and he was drinking a great deal, not just wine either, as we had together, but the hard liquors, scotch and whiskey . . . and he stopped washing and grooming himself. At first, I thought it was part and parcel of the artistic temperament. I had seen a great deal of that sort of thing in New York before, so I wasn't unduly alarmed at the time, but then he started to get sick. It started with a cold, just like any other, and before anyone knew it, it had moved on to pneumonia." She started wringing her hands more intensely as she spoke, her fingers turning pale, the color beginning to drain from her face. She stopped looking at me. Instead, she seemed to look above me, into the air above my head, her words became slower, more deliberate.

"I got there early one Saturday morning in the middle of November. It was raining that cold rain we get around here about then. When I pulled up, I found him wandering aimlessly in a circle out in front of the house wearing only his pajamas, no shoes, no coat. He was soaking wet and shivering mumbling incoherently to himself. I think he must have been out there all night. I was frightened out of my wits. I didn't know what to do."

She looked at me absently as if she was reliving the moment and I wasn't really there. "'Norman! Norman!' I cried, shaking him . . . but he didn't respond. He didn't seem to recognize me, so I did the only thing I could think to do. I got him back into the house and called the local doctor.

"When the doctor got there, we put him into some dry clothes and got him into bed. He was using the back bedroom at the far end of the upstairs hall. The doctor gave him a shot of something and left me with some pills and instructions. He was burning with fever, perspiring furiously. I had to change his shirt every few hours and keep a cool towel on his head. He was pale as a sheet and so terribly weak. His breathing was shallow and he had coughing spells so severe that the bed shook. I was so afraid for him. When he finally quieted and fell off to sleep sometime after midnight, I was as exhausted as I'd ever been and went downstairs to sit by the fire and get some rest. I couldn't have been asleep for more than an hour when I woke up to the sound of screaming." Her eyes got wider as she spoke.

"I was disoriented and panicked at first, but I ran up the

stairs to the end room as fast as I could. Norman was crouched down in the far corner of the room screaming, 'WHO ARE YOU? WHAT DO YOU WANT? GET OUT OF HERE!' At first I thought he was looking at me, but he wasn't. He was looking behind me and screaming, scrambling to get further into the corner. 'GET AWAY. DON'T TOUCH HER. AAAHHH GRACE! BEHIND YOU!' Oh, the terror in his voice was like nothing I've ever heard," she said looking at me blankly as if she was reliving her own disbelief.

"I turned to look behind me. There was nothing there. I thought he was delirious. I tried to go to him and comfort him. I didn't know what else to do. I was scared to death. Finally, I got close enough to get my arms around him and hold him. He was trembling with fever, burning like fire. Suddenly, he looked up at me, like I was a stranger…then down at my neck." She dabbed her forehead and cheeks again lightly.

"Before I knew it, he had grabbed the crucifix from around my neck and pulled it off," she said, putting her hand around her throat as if she could still feel the chain tugging after so many years. "and held it out against the empty room. 'GET OUT! GET AWAY!' he screamed as he struggled to get up from the floor, keeping me behind him as he moved closer to the door. It was as if he were trying to hold off a dangerous circus animal with a whip and chair.

"Then, before I realized what was happening, he was pulling me down the stairs, through the front door and off the porch onto the lawn, leaving the door open behind us. A freezing wind rushed past us. He stopped and turned as if to see if something was following us. His eyes were huge with fear as he looked back at me. Then suddenly he just collapsed, right there in front of me, like a scarecrow. I panicked and screamed, struggling to keep from getting hysterical. I had no idea what to do. The only thing I could think of was to pull my car up and drag him into it. It took all of my physical strength to push him into the backseat and all of my emotional strength to get him to the hospital in Henriston without driving into a tree. I didn't know what else to do," she said, tears slowly streaming down her face again. "I just didn't know what else to do," she repeated, as if seeking some validation of her actions. I took the bottle of brandy and poured a straight shot into the cup and went over to her.

"Here, drink this, Grace. It's okay. It's okay."

I realized that I was sweating then. My shirt collar, underarms and crotch were soaked. It was all sounding frighteningly familiar to me. The cup rattled in her shaking hand as she took it and drank. I lit a cigarette and handed it to her.

"It's okay, Grace. I'm here...maybe we shouldn't do this," I said. She looked up at me with a look of...amazement...is the only word I can think of to describe it.

"He was dead, Terry. By the time I got to the hospital, he was dead. They said at the hospital that his heart stopped. It just stopped," she said, a fresh expression of disbelief on her face, as if it had happened yesterday. I went and took my seat again. Her terror seemed to dissipate as she finished her drink and came back to me, focusing on me again.

"They said he had a heart defect, most probably from birth or a childhood illness and that the pneumonia had weakened it to the point where it just stopped." She took a moment to smoke. By that time, I had lit another one myself. She looked empty, like a deflated balloon. I could tell from the way she told the story that she'd been carrying a great deal of guilt around, blaming herself somewhere in a closely held lock box of her soul for all these years. Now that it'd finally been unleashed, she was spent. Having had my own reality shift underneath my feet, I did my best to assure her she did the only thing she could've done. She looked all of her eighty some years then, but I also could tell she wasn't finished. She still had more to tell...and it frightened me.

"I stayed at the hospital that night," she began again, sounding exhausted. "The next day, I was numb. I didn't feel anything. I was like a robot going through the motions," she said nervously...edgily, "and I think that my next move was probably my greatest mistake. I went back to that house.

"I had it fixed in my mind that I had to finish what we'd started. I had to get the play and finish it, so I went back to the house to get it. It was the only thing we had together, like our child. When I got there, I went in and began collecting his papers before his wife could come and claim everything. I knew she had to be notified, so I took the papers, his phone book and address book and put them all in a bag. I had started feeling the extremes of my loss then too, and began walking around the house...just walking...pacing...back and forth, clinging to the bag our child and crying."

"I could have been there for only a few minutes or possibly for hours, I really don't know. I had completely lost track of time when I heard a noise in the kitchen and walked over to look. That was when I saw it. God help me, I thought I was losing my mind. There were four ceramic canisters on the counter...flour, sugar, coffee and tea...and they were trembling. At first I thought it was an earthquake...but we don't have earthquakes here. Then they went from trembling to shaking, violently." Her eyes went wide again.

"I couldn't believe my eyes. The lids flew off and smashed against the walls...then the canisters began dashing themselves against the cabinets, exploding into pieces. The cabinet doors suddenly flew open and the dishes started hurling themselves out of the cabinets, flinging themselves at the walls, shattering everywhere. Then I saw the table begin to shake...and the chairs. It was like the whole room was alive, smashing and shaking, cabinet doors slamming furiously, shattered pieces of china cups and saucers flying through the air like a hail storm. The sound was deafening, and there was this smell, this sickening, indecent smell. I couldn't move. I was stuck where I was." She began to wring her hands again. I could see the astonishment she must have felt, fresh in her eyes again.

"I just stood there watching it all with my mouth hanging open, struggling with the reality of it, clinging to the bag I held. Then I heard a man's booming voice scream, 'YOU BITCH,' at me, and out of the center of it all a china cup come shooting straight for me. It struck me in the middle of my forehead before I could bring myself to move. I staggered back, stunned. It loosened my feet from the floor and I turned and ran. I ran for my life, out of the front door, down the steps and into my car. I tore out of that drive as if the devil himself were chasing me and my life depended on it, and as I sit here speaking to you now, I'm not all that sure that it didn't, and I've never spoken of it to anyone since. Not until now...to you." She paused for a breath, a deep sighing breath.

"You do believe me, don't you, Terry?" she asked, like a

frightened child awakened from a bad dream. I looked her in the eyes so she could see the truth there.

"Yes, Grace, I do. Every word of it." She took a sip from her cup and lit another cigarette, then reached behind the lamp base and pulled out a thin manila file folder.

❊ ❊ ❊

"After it was over, I had time to think. There was no doubt in my mind. No doubt," she repeated to stress her point, "that it was the house, or something unholy in it that killed Norman. I just didn't know what I could do about it. He was already gone...but then it came to me. 'Do what you've been doing for the last five years, Grace,' I told myself. 'Find out what the hell is going on there!' I was a librarian, after all, that made me a pretty good researcher, so I set myself to it. I looked into the history of the house." She dabbed off her face, which by then had registered steely determination, and she started again.

"I found out that it was built in 1901 by a man named Charles Lawson Eccleston, a doctor, English, but most recently of New York. I found that out in a community announcement in the local paper. It was called 'The Times,' if you can imagine," she said, smiling wryly to herself. "Then there was nothing again until 1924 when it was sold to a Russian woman by the name of Magda Ivanova Romanovsky, also from New York. I thought it curious at the time that they both came here by way of New York, but didn't find out more about it until later. There was nothing again until 1946 when it was sold at auction for taxes to a real estate company in Hamilton. The company apparently held it itself until Norman bought it in his wife's name in late 1949," she said, as if telling me a secret.

"It wasn't until a few years later, when I began to get restless here in town and began going back into New York to shop to revisit the places I knew from my days there, that it dawned on me to try looking these people up while I was there. I was bored and so very lonely by then I became rather obsessed with the past."

"I couldn't shake the fact that both the doctor and the Russian woman found their way up here from New York. It was just too much of a coincidence for my liking. So, I went to the New York Public Library and started reading the newspapers. I even got some of the librarians there involved as a professional courtesy, you know. Actually, it was one of them who suggested that I check the immigration records to find out when these people entered the country. She thought it might help narrow my search."

"So I did, and I found what I was looking for in the records on Ellis Island. The Russian woman, Romanovsky, had entered the country in 1898 and the doctor a year later in 1899. Armed with this new knowledge, I went back to the library and spent at least two afternoons a month there for about four months." She stopped, took another drink and lit another smoke. She was talking and acting like a real life detective then, and picked up where she left off. I couldn't help but be fascinated by this extraordinary woman, her capacity for love, her courage, and her determination.

"I found it a few months later," she went on with a burning intensity in her eyes, "in an article written in 1900 in one of the long gone papers, *The New York Gazette*. It appears there had been some sort of a melee somewhere down on the lower east side of Manhattan. You can read the article yourself for the details. It's in the folder. Three people were attacked in one of their houses. It was all there. I couldn't believe my eyes. Two of the three people I had been looking for were named in the same article, the doctor and the Russian woman. I hadn't heard of the third man, but apparently it was his house."

"The article tells of how a mob of local immigrants had battered their way into the house and dragged the three of them into the street. The third man, named Andros Kakospharmakos, was hanged by a lamp post outside of the building before the police could arrive. The other two were beaten severely, but saved and taken to the hospital. They were identified as "Dr. Charles Lawson Eccleston, prominent English physician, recently of New York, and Madame Magda Ivanova Romanovsky, world renowned Russian spiritualist, medium and author, also recently of New York."

"When I showed the article to the girl at the library who was helping me, she told me that occult studies, practices and spiritualism were more common than one might expect back then. 'All the rage,' she told me and guided me to the section where the books written about it were shelved. I spent hours reading them and found she was right. From the mid 1800s until on into the 1930s, there were groups of people all over London, Paris and Berlin involved in it. All over Western Europe, as a matter of fact. It seems they were having ceremonies, conducting rituals and having séances attempting to conjure up God only knows what. Apparently, it became so fashionable that these people were even being invited into the parlors and drawing rooms of the influential and well-heeled of all the major cities of the world, including New York.

"There were stories about other attacks, too. It seems that the less well heeled and the newly arrived immigrants took this sort of thing very seriously and felt threatened by it. There were several cases of mob violence...even murder. That was it. I had it. The article says that those arrested for the attack claimed that the three were practicing black magic and devil worship in the building, and that the neighbors on both sides had been complaining of strange occurrences. They also claimed that the three were somehow involved in the disappearance of a local child. In the end, it seems the locals got spooked and attacked them fearing for their own children."

My mouth must have been gaping by then. It all sounded so . . . unreal.

"That's when I knew," she said, her voice raised in triumph. "He was on the run, afraid for his life to stay in New York, or of being arrested for the disappearance of the child, and for some reason probably couldn't return to Europe. That's why he came to Jennisburg and built that house the next year, but something must have happened there...in that house, something special to them. That's why the Russian woman came and took it. She...they didn't want it to be out of their hands for some reason."

"I checked the local Birth and Death Records here. There was none issued for the doctor, but I did find out that the Russian woman had died in New York in 1944. You see? It all fits. It would have taken them that long to perfect a tax lien on the house and execute it so it could be auctioned off. Then of

course, the real estate company had it, and Norman bought it
from them. Then she...Norman's widow, held it until Sylvia
Hadrada bought it from her sometime in the late fifties, or early
sixties, I think. Sylvia and I have always been friends. She really
is a dear girl once you get beyond all the bluster and make up,
and she always makes me laugh with the things she says. When
she told me she had let the place to some churchman and his
family from over in Hamilton, I felt so relieved, like a great
weight had been lifted from my shoulders. It would finally be
over I thought, but apparently I was wrong...very wrong,
indeed!"

I was reading the article myself as she spoke. Grace
continued, sounding more like herself again while I read.

"It all came back to me at Jenny Denton's party when I
heard that someone was living in that...*house*. I had never really
forgotten it, but after fifty years" she shrugged, "and since I
hadn't heard of anything unusual happening out there, it all
seemed like a bad dream, but make no mistake, Terry, it's an evil
place. It was built by evil, it has lived in evil, and it brings evil to
those who are susceptible to it. I know it. I've known it most of
my life and held it inside myself all these years.

"I've been so worried about that Martin Welliver ever since.
When I met him, he seemed so sad and..." She paused and
thought a moment, "he reminded me strangely of Norman. I
knew in my heart there would be trouble, but what could I do? I
couldn't tell anyone for fear of being labeled a senile old woman.
The best I could hope for was that you would want see to me
eventually...and want to know before something terrible
happened... again. Oh, my goodness!" she stopped, putting her
hand up to her mouth. "I didn't even ask. He is alright, isn't he?
Mr. Welliver?"

"Yes," I answered. "I saw him early this morning."

"At the house?" she asked, the pitch of her voice rising in
panic.

"Yes," I said.

That's when she leaned up in her chair, looked me straight
in the eyes to drive home her point and said in a voice rising to
the edge of shrill, "You must get him out of that house, Terry.
Right now...today...before it's too late. Do not delay. Every

minute counts. Please believe me! Get him out NOW!"

As she spoke those last words, I knew I couldn't deny it any longer. I got light headed and my blood felt thin, chills ran down my arms and legs. Every belief I'd ever held within the tiny, little limits of my mind about the reaches of heaven and earth came crashing down around me. She was right. I had to move and move quickly, or risk Martin's life out of my own fear and stunted emotions. There was no way I could let that happen. Since that night at the river, he was my responsibility and I'd promised that I'd not let him die. I meant it then and nothing had changed since. I was up and out of the chair in seconds and nothing was going to get in my way. Logic, sense, reality, reputation, sanity, all of it be damned along with that monstrous place and whatever hideous thing that was lurking inside...waiting.

Before I left, I promised Grace I would call her as soon as he was out somewhere safe. She said her nerves would be on edge until she heard from me and that I must let her know. On my way out the door she called to me, "Terry...Wait!" and handed me the bracelet. "Take this with you, back where it came from and...destroy it," she said with a tone of disgust I had never expected to ever hear in her otherwise genteel voice.

"I will, Grace." I said as I headed down her front steps. "I will."

CHAPTER 7

Danse Macabre

"Courage is not the absence of fear, but rather the judgment that something else is more important than fear."
Ambrose Redmon

I was in my car and on my way over to the house with the same incendiary urgency I felt when I saw his car go into the river. When I looked at my watch, I saw that I had been at Grace's for almost two hours and hit the gas. About half way there, I heard Lila on the car radio,

"Chief?...Chief?...Do you copy?" and I picked up the receiver.

"Yeah, Lila, I'm here."

"I've been trying to reach you, Chief, but I didn't want to bother you while you were over at Grace's. I got the feeling it was important." She was fishing.

"Okay, ya got me now. What's up?"

"Well, not much really. It's Christmas Eve. Everything is pretty quiet. Mostly people doing last minute errands," she chattered on, then paused. "I called over to Martin's like you asked me."

"And...?" I asked expectantly.

"He didn't sound good, Chief. He was congested, his voice was hoarse...and he was coughing the whole time I talked to him. I asked him if there was anything I could do for him. He told me that he just had a little cold coming and not to worry. When I asked him if he had any plans for the holiday, he just said he just planned to stay warm. He didn't sound good at all, Chief. Maybe you could stop over and check on him."

My gut wrenched as she spoke and I stomped on the gas pedal.

"Is there anything else I can do, Chief?" she asked, concerned.

"No. You've done good, Lila. I'm on my way over there now. I should be there any minute. I'll take it from here. It's time you went home to your family now. Leave Bjornstrand at the station. He's single and low man on the totem pole," I said, trying to sound in control.

"No need to tell me twice. I'm out the door. But, Chief…you call me if you need me."

"I will, sweetheart. Now go and have yourself a good holiday," I said, still managing a smile at her loyalty through it all, thinking, *That's my girl!*

"Over and out," she said, signing off.

I was only a few minutes from the house by that time, and trying to form a plan in my head. I couldn't just barge in there and drag the guy out of his own house without some plan. I pulled up the drive being very careful not to go near the drop offs on the side. I'd had enough of ditches for one winter. The snow was already tamped down by then, so it was easier to maneuver. I pulled up close to the porch, put the car in neutral with the hand brake on and left it running. Not one to stand on ceremony by that point, I just opened the door and went in. The house was quiet—too quiet—deadly quiet. I didn't like it at all.

"Martin?" I shouted in. "Martin? It's me," I shouted again as I walked into the kitchen. I saw the half-eaten sandwich and half empty cup of coffee he'd left on the table then headed toward the back of the dining room where his bed was.

"Martin? Are you asleep?" I called more softly, pushing through the door into the dining room. He was there on the bed, shivering and sweating, burning alive with a high fever. I rushed over to him and knelt down by the cot.

"Martin? It's me."

His eyes were glazed as he struggled to open them. "Chief...I'm so glad to see you," he groaned, smiling faintly as he tried to push himself to sit up.

"It's okay, Martin. I'm here now. Everything will be alright," I said as I helped him sit up, pulling the blanket around his shoulders. He started coughing, a thick, congested, rattling cough. "I'm gonna take you out of here. Can you stand up and walk if I help you?"

He nodded and tried to push himself up to a standing position. I had to help him up. He was so weak he could hardly stand. I had to half carry him by the waist into the kitchen and sit him in the chair with the blanket.

"Martin, you're gonna come with me now," I said. He looked up at me, his face too weak for any real expression.

"I'm so sorry, Chief," he said, coughing. "I'm so sorry for the things I said last night. I don't want to die. I don't want to die," he said again, tears welling up in his eyes. "I'm scared, Chief."

"I know you are, Martin," I said. "It's okay. I'm not gonna let you die. Don't worry. I didn't let you die before and I'm sure not gonna now. I promise. I know it wasn't you thinking those things, saying those things." He looked up at me weakly again, not understanding.

I knelt down to his eye level and took him by the arms, looking into his eyes. "Tell me Martin, and please be honest. Tell me the truth. I mean it," I said, trying to sound as tough as I could muster without scaring him even more, like I would talk to a child. "Have strange things been going on here in the house? Have you seen things moving?" He hesitated for a moment.

"Yes," he said, sounding ashamed. "Am I losing my mind?" he asked. I got up and started pacing.

"Have you heard things, Martin? Tell me, please," I asked him, feeling my own panic welling up inside me.

"Yes," he said in the same ashamed tone.

"What kind of things?" I demanded, kneeling and taking him by the arms again.

"Please don't be angry at me," he said, like a sick child who'd messed the bed.

Dear God! He's regressing, I thought.

"I'm not angry at you, Martin, but you've gotta tell me!" I

pleaded.

"Yes," he said weakly, letting his head hang down.

"What, Martin? What have you heard?" My voice was almost a shout.

"A voice," he said, letting his head drop into his hands.

"What does it say?" I lifted his head to look at me again.

"It keeps calling my name and telling me that it's coming for me," he said with a trembling chill in his voice.

"Anything else?" I went on, "It's important. Please tell me."

"There are shadows...moving and whispering, and crying...things moving on their own and, sometimes, when I wake up in the middle of the night, the room is filled an awful, rotting smell. I am losing my mind, aren't I? Please tell me, Chief. I'm going crazy, aren't I?" he asked, falling further to pieces with each word.

"No, Martin, you're not. I'm here now. You'll be fine. I promise...but you have to help me now. Where are your things?" I asked him, my panic turning to knots in my stomach.

"Things?" he said and coughed, not understanding what I was asking him.

"Your personal things, papers, bank books, important things. Things you don't want to lose and your clothes. Where do you keep the things you've been wearing? I need you to focus now, Martin. It's important that you focus."

He started to cough again, badly. When he stopped, he said, "Most of my things are in storage. I didn't have the chance to get them out before the accident. I only have a few things here, mostly over close to the bed on the end table. My papers are in the drawer, my bank books and my check books, the house bills. I don't have many clothes, some jeans and shirts, some sweat clothes and tee shirts piled on the dining room chairs.

Perfect...of course, everything had to be close at hand, I thought.

I grabbed the trash can, emptied it on the floor and took out the liner bag. "Stay here!" I said and made for the dining room. I grabbed everything I could see, the clothes off the chairs, the bottles off the table. I took the table drawer out and just dumped it into the bag. Then I was back in the kitchen. He was there with his head still in his hands. "Okay," I said. "Come on. Let's go." Then it hit me, like a blast of hot desert sand in my face, that smell. The awful smell from the dreams. It was there with us, all around us, and it was getting cold. All of a sudden it was freezing in there. I could see my breath, just like in the dream. I snatched him up.

"Come on, Martin, we've gotta move. Now!" I shouted, feeling the fear well up from my guts into my throat. I heard it before I had the chance to turn around, the front door slamming. We'd gotten as far as the doorway to the entry hall before I saw it. The furniture was moving, skidding across the floor, piling itself up against the front door. I couldn't believe my eyes, chairs and end tables, shifting, sliding, hurling themselves against the door creating a tower of wood, blocking our way out, and that smell. It'd gotten overpowering, thick and nauseating. I started to choke. It was smothering me, just like in the dream. I thought I'd vomit. I knew I had to act, and 'pronto.' My first thought was, *The back door!* I leaned Martin against the wall, blanket and all, and went for the back door, grabbed the knob and turned. It wouldn't open, wouldn't budge. It was hot under my palm, scalding hot, scorching my fingers. I heard a loud crack and looked up.

One by one, each of the nine small panes of glass in the door began to crackle and craze before my eyes. Then, one after another, each pane shattered and blew in, showering my face with bits and shards of glass, as if in some concerted effort to blind me. I just shut my eyes and pulled as hard as I could. It still wouldn't budge, so I started kicking at the fucking thing with the blind rage of a captured gorilla caught in a net. Nothing. It was useless, and with Martin in the shape he was in, I couldn't afford to screw around with it too long. When I looked back, he'd slid down the wall and was crouching down on the floor. Then the banging started, intense, thundering sounds of banging, everywhere, like the house was coming down around me. I saw Martin put his hands up to his ears. That was when I knew. It was either it, or me, and, fuck it all, I wasn't going to give up.

I bounded through the kitchen, past Martin, into the entry hall and threw myself at the pile of furniture blocking the front door with savage abandon, grabbing whatever I could get my hands on, pulling it off and smashing it against whatever was closest, the floor, the wall, the doorframe. It seemed like it went on for hours, but when I looked up again, the door was cleared.

I grabbed the knob. It was hot too, searing. I turned and pulled no movement. *Damn!* Then I looked at it closely. The deadbolt was pulled through. I tried to pull it back no luck. *Shit!* I'd had more than enough by then and over the top I went. I couldn't stand the pounding anymore, or the stink, or the cold, or the fear. I pulled my gun, stepped back and blasted the fucker once, then twice more just to make sure. The bolt flew off, glass raining everywhere, but to my amazement, the door came open.

Then, still clinging to the bare instinct of a hunted animal, I went back, grabbed Martin and pulled him back up against the wall. But something was wrong, terribly, horribly, sickeningly wrong. He was writhing and jerking, convulsing violently...moaning in a low throaty growl. His head jerked up and I saw that strange inverted five pointed star symbol from the dream raised on his forehead like a welt, and his eyes...were no longer his, but a startling blue, glaring at me, red rimmed and bloody. His mouth was twisted, drooling and foaming like a rabid dog. The shock of what was happening right before my very eyes loosened my grip on him.

"Don't touch us! Leave us alone, you stinking, filthy pig, or I'll kill him right now!" he spat at me in a snarling, raspy, English-accented voice. My mind splintered like an old piece of rotted wood, rocking with spasms of the impossible, its vibrations rippling down to my fingertips. "You don't think I know who you are?" he sneered with a snide chuckle, shoving me away with a strength I knew Martin didn't have. I went flying back, crashing hard against the opposite wall, my mind reeling from what I was witnessing, my body stunned from the force of a blow I knew couldn't be real. Before I could shake it off, he leapt at me, his hands reaching for my throat. I came back at him like a boxer, a split second of conflict swirling in my head.

"Fuck *you!*" I raged at the thing that had been Martin just a few minutes before and hit him hard with a short, quick jab, tagging him on the chin with a momentum that sent his head snapping back. His eyes rolled up and he crumbled in my arms like a broken doll. I'd knocked him out cold. Then, holding him up under one arm, I snatched up the bag in the other and dragged them both toward the door. Only semi- conscious, he groaned in pain with his own voice, thank God. But as I saw it, our choices were limited, so as I had decided for him once already, a little pain now was worth his life later, and before I knew it, we were out on the porch. I helped him down the front steps and into the back of the car, threw the blanket on him, the bag in after that then ran around and got in myself. Thank God the engine was still running. In a second, we were down the drive and out of there.

As I pulled out of the drive onto Randolph Road, it occurred to me what Grace had said about Norman Harper wandering around out in front of the house. It must have been someplace he felt safe...then it dawned on me. Whatever it was, it seemed limited to the house itself, but not the property, or it could have fucked with the car...but it didn't.

Then another thing occurred to me from the dream, the man walking from the garden house to the main house. The garden house had something to do with it. I didn't know what, but it did. It was limited to that area. The main house, the garden house and the path linking the two, but not the front. Something must have happened to link the two buildings, but quite honestly, at that point, I didn't give a shit. We were away from there and Martin was still alive. I could hear him coughing and groaning from the back seat, and when I looked back at him through the rear view mirror, I could see his forehead. The symbol was gone. I wasn't sure what my next move would be, but then I had a simple thought. *There's no place like home.* It was decided. I headed toward my mother's.

※ ※ ※

By the time I pulled up into my mother's driveway, I was running on the last stretch on my last nerve and had no choice but to wing it, so I did what came naturally. I wiped my face with a rag that I had in the car, got out and headed toward the door convincing myself that everything was fine. I opened the door and yelled in, "Ma, it's your baby. Ho Ho Ho." I hated it when she called me 'baby' but at that moment it served my purpose, so I went with it. She came out of the kitchen wiping her hands on a dish towel.

"My baby what ?" she asked, smiling as she came toward me.

"Your baby elephant!" was the traditional response. I was almost thirteen pounds at birth and she never let me forget it.

"Merry Christmas, sweetheart," she said and hugged me.

"Merry Christmas, Ma," I said.

She pulled back, looking at me sternly and said, "And I wasn't hinting at new appliances when I said that thing about Martha Portensky's sons...but I love them all the same. Thank you so much, sweetheart."

"Nobody deserves it more than you do, Ma...for all I've put you through in my life," I said, kissing her cheek and meaning it. Then I broke into it. "How would you feel about some company for Christmas, Ma?" I asked her. She looked at me curiously. "I have Martin out in the car and he's sick," I said, sounding more ominous than I had intended.

"He's sick and you left him in the car? Terry, bring him in," she said, like I'd committed a grievous error in etiquette.

"But before I do, I gotta tell ya, Ma. He looks bad, so try not to act...alarmed. He feels bad enough already and it'd only scare him more. Just do what you do best and we'll take care of him. Okay?"

With that she got indignant. "Terrence Arthur Chagford! I raised you better than that. You go and bring him in. Right now!" she said and meant it.

I went out to the car and brought Martin out, but before we got to the door I told him, "Martin, you gotta straighten up now. Try and pull yourself together, and stand up straight. My mother doesn't know anything about this and I don't want her to. You gotta pick yourself up by the balls, boy. You got me?"

"I gotcha, Chief," he said coughing as he tried to straighten himself up the best as he could, still clutching the blanket around him, shivering. We were at the door.

"Martin, my dear!" She was all over him in a flash. "Come, in son, come in," she said, helping me bring him in.

"Thank you, Mrs. Chagford," he said politely, shivering under the blanket. "Thank you for having me over." He started coughing again.   We got him to the nearest chair.

"Oh, it's no trouble at all, Martin. We're glad to have you," she said, doing a remarkable job of hiding her growing concern. No fool is my mom.

"Terry, let's get Martin something warm to drink...in the kitchen." That was my cue to follow her in. "He looks terrible, Terry. Sounds like pneumonia to me," she said, the worry washing over her face.

"Close to it, Ma, but I think we may have just caught it in time. He hasn't been taking care of himself and I couldn't leave him alone, so I brought him here. What do we do? I don't want to take him to the hospital just yet. We can take care of him here, can't we?" I asked, finding it hard to conceal what I knew. Mothers always know.

"Well, we can try, but if there's any sign that he's getting worse, we'll have to get him to the hospital," she said, painfully aware of the potential complications.

"I know. I was just hoping to have him with us for Christmas," I said using a son's secret weapon, the kind of sad cow eyes a ten-year-old uses when he's just found a stray puppy or a kitten he wants to keep. That did it. She was on with me.

"I have some antibiotics in the medicine cabinet in the downstairs bathroom that I keep on hand for emergencies. I just hope they're still good. Let's get him started right away and see if we can nip it in the bud. I'll make him some hot tea," she said, waving me off to get them and heading over to the stove.

I went and got the bottle from the bathroom cabinet, took two capsules out and handed them to him. "Here, take these," I ordered. He did as I told him. Mom was there right behind me with a glass of water. "Now we've got to get you cleaned up," I said. My mother looked at me as if to say 'what are you going to do?'

"Ma, I need you to get some clean clothes of mine from my room, sweat clothes if there are any...and some blankets and pillows too and make up the couch down here, will ya? We're going to get cleaned up in the downstairs bathroom," I said in a commanding voice that I hardly ever used, especially with my mother.

"Are you sure that's wise, hon?" she asked, looking at me like I had gone over the edge.

"Gotta be done, Ma," I said. "We gotta scrub it off." I had to get his blood flowing again. He was in shock, she just didn't know it, but she would soon enough if I didn't deflect her. A hot shower would do the trick, for both of them.

I helped him into the bathroom, sitting him on the toilet seat while I turned on the hot water. My mother's shower seat was in the bathroom closet. I got it and put it in the tub.

"Okay," I said. "Here we go!"

"You've got to help me, Terry," he said weakly, looking like a shaggy dog just saved from drowning. I unbuttoned his shirt, took it off and bent down.

"Lift your foot," I said and pulled off his sock. "Now the other one," and did the same. "Can you stand?" I asked him.

"I think so," he said, "if I can hold on to your shoulder." I helped him stand and he pulled his sweat pants down.

"I'm so embarrassed," he said with his head down, starting to sob.

"Don't be. I'm not," I said, trying to sound as clinical I could, given my own precarious state of mind. "Now, step out of the pants," I said and put my foot in the crotch of the sweats to hold them down. He stepped out of them with some difficulty, holding onto my shoulders for support. I felt the water. It was just hot enough.

"Okay, in ya go," I said, getting him into the tub and sitting him on the tub seat. "Arrrgghh," he groaned as the water hit him.

"Too hot?"

"No. It's fine," he groaned. I shut the shower curtain, tossed in the soap, shampoo and a wash cloth.

"You got it?"

"Yes."

"Okay. I'll wait out here until you're ready to come out," I said as I sat on the toilet to rub my temples and worry. He didn't look well at all, and my head was throbbing like a fucking jackhammer.

A few minutes later I heard the water shut off.

"Terry, can I have a towel…or two," he called out to me.

"Sure…hold on, right here," I said, handing the towels in behind the shower curtain. A minute later he pulled the curtain back, standing there wrapped in a towel. He was actually standing on his own, and he had some color back in his face. I was amazed . . . and relieved.

"Better?" I asked

"Much," he said, grabbing onto the safety rail to steady himself and smiling weakly. "If you could just lend me your arm again so I can get out..."

I did and sat him back on the toilet seat. My mother knocked on the door.

"I have your things here, hon," she called in.

"Okay, Ma. Hold on," I reached outside the door and took the pile from her. Everything was there, a baggy shirt, sweat pants and socks. She'd also put in a comb, a razor, my shaving cream, a fresh toothbrush and a hand mirror from the upstairs bathroom. *Smart girl, my mom!* I thought. She knocked again. I opened the door, "Yeah, Ma."

"I though you might need this. I still have it from when I twisted my ankle," she said, handing me an aluminum cane.

"You're the best, Ma!" I said and closed the door. I set the things down on the sink counter and looked at him. "You can do this, can't you?" I asked him, more as a statement than a question.

"Yeah, I think so," he said, trying to sound confident, probably more for my sake than his own.

"I'm gonna leave the door ajar. If you need me just yell," I said and left him to it.

I was having a cup of coffee with my mother at the kitchen table, discussing the situation when, about fifteen minutes later, he appeared in the doorway. His hair was combed and he'd shaved. As he stood there swimming in my oversized clothes, leaning on the cane, I was awed at the difference a shower and a shave could make. "A new man!" I said. He smiled, still weakly but genuinely. My mother was up on her feet.

"Come sit down and make yourself comfortable. I have a cup of hot tea ready for you," she said, leading him into the living room and onto the sofa she'd made up. "Are you feeling better, dear?" she asked him like she was his very own mother.

"Yes, much better. Thank you, Mrs. Chagford," he said. He was very polite. I had to give him that.

"Please, Martin. Call me Charlotte," she said.

"Oh, I couldn't," he stammered, sounding bashful.

"Okay then, you can call me Mrs. C. All my patients do," she said looking at me and winked. I laughed nervously. She and I were the only ones to get the joke. She was a psychiatric nurse. All her patients were out of their fucking minds, for God's sake.

"Okay, Mrs. C," he said. "I can do that." I laughed out loud again. If either of them only knew how close I've been walking to that very border.

We'd just sat down in the living room when the phone rang in the kitchen. Mom got up to answer it. A moment later, she was back in the doorway.

"Terry, it's for you," she said, searching my eyes. I went in to take the call. She had her hand over the mouthpiece.

"It's Jeff Denton," she whispered. "And he sounds upset," she stressed, looking questioningly at me as I took the phone.

"Jesus H. Christ. What now?" I swore as I took the receiver.

"Terry, it's Jeff Denton." I heard through the receiver.

"Yeah, Jeff, what can I do for ya?" I asked, trying to sound calm.

"It's Jenny, Terry." He sounded rattled, way off the mark of his usual jovial demeanor. "Can you come over right away?" he asked, his voice breaking.

"What's going on, Jeff?" I asked, feeling the beginnings my own panic welling up in my guts again. I knew whatever it was it wasn't going to be good.

"It's Jenny. She came in a little while ago all…all bruised up. Her clothes and hair were all a mess. She's locked herself in the bathroom. She won't come out. I think she's been attacked." He started to cry. "She won't let me call a doctor. She won't let me in. She won't tell me what happened. She just told me to call you. She wants to see you. Please come, Terry!" he begged.

"I'll be right over," I said. God, my body was aching. The fight with the furniture was just catching up with me and I felt like I was just about to lose what was left of my few cracked marbles. I didn't know how much more I could take.

"Ma, ya got any Advil?" I yelled into her, then took four as I put my jacket back on. "I gotta go over to Jeff's," I told them. My mother and Martin both looked at me curiously.

"What's going on?" Martin asked, coughing.

"I don't know," I said, rubbing my head, "but I've got to go," and headed out the door, then stopping in my tracks said, " . . . and Ma, I need you to call over to Grace Coutraire's and tell her that Martin is going to spend Christmas over here with us. Please don't forget. She'll worry and I promised her I'd call," and I was out the door again.

She followed me to the door, calling from the doorway, "I will, sweetheart."

I stopped again, turning back up the path toward where she stood looking worried and whispered to her in a low voice. "And do me a favor, Ma. Pray over him some for me while I'm gone, will ya?" Her mouth opened, wordless with the surprise of what I'd asked her to do. I'm sure she'd given up on hearing anything like that from me a long time ago, but when I looked up at her earnestly, her eyes were shining.   "Yes, of course I will, sweetheart," she said quietly and nodded.

I kissed her on the cheek. "Thanks, Ma. I'll be back as soon as I can," and headed back down the path.

❄ ❄ ❄

Something's going to happen…and soon. I can feel it. The tension in the house is more stifling than ever, oppressive, crushing me more and more every day, every hour. When I came home from work today, I passed by the mirror in the hall. I still try to avoid looking at myself any more than I have to, and never look into my own eyes, but this time when I went by it, I caught my own eye and saw hollows in my cheeks that weren't there a few weeks ago. My eyes look like they're sinking in their sockets, and there's this pasty, green tinged look to my skin. If everyone else could see what I saw, they'd only be able to come to one conclusion. "He's dying."

I haven't been eating much. It just throws my guts into knots. The only time I actually eat is when I come home and Martin has made something. I'm still trying desperately to keep this all from him, so I have to eat when he cooks. Otherwise, I've been living on coffee and cigarettes, booze and pills, sleeping only a few hours day . . . and it shows. Lately I've been starting to worry that, at my age, my heart may just give out the way Norman Harper's did. Maybe that's its plan to get me out of the way, to wear me out so it can have at Martin. He's asleep now. It's late. I'm going to try and get through as much of this tonight as I can. My head is so heavy...

❋ ❋ ❋

"Martin!"...I just heard him cry out...*upstairs...run...* "I'm coming!"

❋ ❋ ❋

It's been over twenty-four hours since I've been able to come back to this. Things have been happening around here, bad things, things that make me think that the end is not far off...for both of us.

When I sat down to write last night, getting prepared to talk about the worst of it, I heard rumblings upstairs, like the bed was shaking, and Martin crying out, so I ran. When I got there, his door was half open and he was shouting in this horrible, distressed voice. When I pushed the door open, I was only half relieved to see he was alone, thrashing around on the bed, crying out in his sleep. "No, I won't...You can't make me...Ahhhhhh...Don't touch me...hurts...Help! ...Help! ...No! ...He won't let you...Ahhhhh... Terry! ...hurts...Help me! ...Help me!"

I stood there dazed for a moment, grasping frantically for what to do. I rushed toward the bed to wake him, but when I got to his bedside, he calmed...almost immediately. It was attacking him in his sleep, but it stopped when I got there. That gave me a strange idea, one that would have never occurred to me before. Could it be that it feared me in some way, maybe the same way I feared it? I was too tired to think about it. I knew I couldn't leave him alone, so I just covered him with the blanket and stood there watching over him for a few hours. Then, when the pain in my leg became more than I could endure, I pulled up a chair and sat by him. I must have dozed off because the next thing I knew, I could see the sun rising through the window, so I hurried back downstairs before he could find me there and I had to explain myself. I slept for a few more hours on the sofa before Martin came down to make breakfast. He didn't mention anything about his troubles during the night and neither did I. I just ate my pancakes, showered and went to work. He looked pale in the morning light, pale and tired. It worried me, overwhelming me with guilt for having failed him, and after he was doing so well. *I'm trying, Martin. I'm trying so hard. Please forgive me.*

❋ ❋ ❋

When I came home tonight, I brought dinner, not wanting him to have to cook after such a rough night, and we ate in relative peace.

"Terry, you look tired. Is everything alright? You're not letting it get to you, are you? You'd talk to me and tell me, right?" he asked somberly.

God, at that moment, I thought I'd split in two, half of me wanting to tell him, the other half wanting to protect him for as long as I could.

"Yeah. Sure. I'm fine, really. My joints have been running riot lately. The leg in particular has been giving me ten kinds of hell, so I haven't been sleeping too well. That's all."

Being so tired himself, he accepted it half-heartedly, letting it go while we watched *Now Voyager* in silence on Channel Thirteen before going to bed around nine thirty. I stayed up later to write, telling him I had some office paperwork to do, but with the hovering feeling of impending doom still creeping up my spine, twisting it, winding that old rubber band back up to the point of snapping.

I had a nice, stiff drink, took a pill and paced the house back and forth until my leg ached, waiting for them to kick in, using the time to try and collect myself. I was just about pick up where I left off last night, before I heard him cry out and had to run, the part where I took on the house in what I know now was my inevitable 'showdown' with it. It was about eleven then and I'd been working up the courage to get back to this again.

I'd only just sat down at my desk and kicked off my shoes when I heard what sounded like a thump come from upstairs, then another. I sat there paralyzed, but with my ears still cocked to listen. At first, I couldn't be sure that the thumping sound wasn't the sound of my own heart beating in my ears. After a few more, I couldn't deny it any longer. It wasn't the sound of my heartbeat at all. It was coming from upstairs.

My heart sank with the thought of what I might find when I went up. I was too tired to run, and I since I'd started dragging my leg again, running wasn't an option anyway, but still, I knew what I had to do. I took the last of my drink in one gulp, pulled myself out of my chair and headed for the stairs. I had to stop after every step, holding on to the railing to recover from the shooting pain that ran up my leg every time I lifted my foot off the floor.

When I reached the top step, my heart sank into my bowels with what I saw. It was Martin. He was standing facing the wall, taking a step, bumping into the wall, stepping back and then doing it again. The thumping noise was the sound of his head hitting the plaster with each go at it. *Oh, dear God in Heaven! He's trying to walk through the wall,* I thought as I stood there trying to get a handle on what I was seeing through the sweat that was dripping in my eyes, making me see double.

"Martin?" I called out to him softly as I approached him from behind, putting my hand on his shoulder. "Martin, are you alright?" He didn't respond. I summoned up what was left of my already bottomed out resources, terrified as much by knowing as not knowing, and turned him around slowly.

His eyes were open, staring blankly into space, but a least they were still his eyes, not the cold blue eyes I had seen when I went to take him out of the house. The rubber band inside me began to unwind. *He's just sleepwalking,* I thought, waving my hand in front of his face in an attempt to get some response.

"Martin, are you awake?" I whispered. Again, no response. He just kept staring straight ahead. Then I saw the smudges on the wall behind him, faint lines going up and across the wall to form what looked like a doorway, and there were symbols, strange symbols drawn in smudges along the outside of the false door, like the symbols I saw on the walls of the house that…last time. The rubber band inside me rewound itself again at warp speed. *He's trying to get out,* ran through my mind, *to get away.*

I saw the ashtray on the small wall-side lamp table and I looked at the fingers on his right hand. He had ashes on the tips of his index and middle fingers. *Dear God, what do I do now?* For a moment I thought I could see the faint mark of the star on his forehead again, but I can't be sure. With my eyes so weary and the light so dim, it could have been my imagination, or the light playing tricks on me, but still, it could have been real. I just couldn't be sure. Then when I looked again, it was gone, like a . . . ghost.

I took him gently by the elbow and led him quietly back to his bed, pushing lightly on his shoulders until he sat, then laid back down, curling himself into the fetal position while I covered him. I couldn't leave him alone and I needed time to think, not that it would do much good anymore. But I still had to try, so I went back downstairs, grabbed my notebook and pen and came back upstairs to stand guard outside his door until I could think of something else. That's where I am now, in a chair outside his door.

These last nights have given me something to think about. Boy, have they! Last night I got the idea that it might be afraid of me because he quieted when I came near him. Now, tonight, it tried to take him away. It wants to get him away from me, but why? Am I that much of a threat to it? That's not possible. Why doesn't it just kill me? I'm probably just that close to dying anyway...Wait! It's just hit me. I've had another idea. Could it be that it doesn't necessarily fear me at all? Or maybe it's not me that it fears, but what I'm doing. Maybe my writing this is some sort of a threat to it. I've had the sense all along that it didn't like what I was doing, although the real concept of it as a weapon hadn't crossed my mind until now...but why now?

Other than almost scaring me to death, the effect of it attacking Martin these last two nights has accomplished what? It's kept me from writing about it...it's distracted me...and the timing. I was just about to tell how I came face-to-face with it, and not just in my dreams, but actually confronted the real thing, saw it with my own two eyes. That's it. That's gotta be it. It doesn't want me to expose it. That's what it fears. Maybe as long as it stays in the shadows, it's safe, but if it's exposed to the light of day for others to understand, it won't be able to get what it wants.

I've got to give it a try. Exposure will either make it go away or force it to kill me before I can finish, but I can't worry about that now. Either way, I've got to run with it and finish. I've got to get back to where I left off, to when I saw it and learned what it's wanted to keep secret for a hundred years now. There's nothing else I can do. Where was I? *Focus Terry. You've got to focus again. It's more important now than ever.* I was on my way over to Jenny's. She was in trouble.

CHAPTER 8

Flores de los Muertos
(Flowers of the Dead)

"Stress is when you wake up screaming, and then realize that you haven't fallen asleep yet."

Unknown

I was over at the Denton's in less than ten minutes. Jeff came to the door red faced, puffy eyed and flustered, looking like he was about to have a stroke. I followed as he led me to the stairs.

"Where are the kids?" I asked, winded and trying to control my limp.

"I sent them to the neighbors," he said as I followed him up the stairs.

"I thought Jenny was in Albany with her mother."

"She came home yesterday afternoon. She wanted to be here with the kids for Christmas," he rattled nervously. "She went out this morning to do some last minute shopping. I was here with the kids. She came in less than an hour ago, like I told ya, rushed up here and locked herself in. I've been out of my mind with worry." He stopped in mid step and looked at me. "Do you think she was...?" His eyes went all squirrelly with the thought.

"Hold on, Jeff. Just hold on," I said in my most professional 'let's not panic' voice and put my hand on his shoulder to steady him. "We don't know anything for sure, but you've gotta keep cool. Stay even. You know what I mean? You can't help her if you're all freaked out. Okay? Keep it even. I'll do everything I can." We were at the bathroom door. I knocked.

"Jenny! It's me, Terry. Let me in, honey," A few seconds later I heard the lock on the door turn and saw the door open a crack. "Come on. Let me in, Jen," I said, pushing the door lightly. It gave way easily. As soon as I was in, she locked it behind me. When I looked at her, I was floored by the state she was in.

"Oh, Terry! I'm so glad you're here," she cried, throwing her arms around me. Her eyes were bloodshot and had the wild shine of hysteria behind them. Her face was wet and smeared with make up, her hair and clothes disheveled. She grabbed my hands and sat down on the toilet.

"Jenny, what happened? Please tell me!" She burst into tears, sobbing uncontrollably. I knelt down and put my arm around her. "You've gotta tell me, hon How can I help you if you don't tell me what happened?"

She heaved, struggling to hold in her sobs.

"You won't believe me. I'm not sure what happened, or even if it happened. You'll think I'm crazy." It was starting to sound all too familiar, so I had a feeling I knew where it was going. I took her firmly by the arms and looked her in the eye, much in the way I did with Grace and Martin.

"No, Jenny. I won't think you're crazy! Here, take some of this." I said and pulled a half pint of Wild Turkey out from my jacket pocket. I knew I'd need it myself on the way over and felt that she might too when I got there. She took a sip and coughed, wiping her mouth with the back of her hand.

"You have to trust me," I said. "Whatever you say to me here will stay between us. No one else needs to know anything, but Jenny, you've gotta help me here," I pleaded with her.

"Okay...okay..." she said, drying her eyes. "I wa-was out doing some last minute sh-sh-shopping this morning...and...and when I was done, I thought I'd st-stop by and see how Martin was doing," she said, hitching and halting, then took a deep breath. "When I got there, I went up to the door. It was open. Oh, Terry, please tell me you'll believe me," she broke off. I did my best to reassure her and she went on. "Okay. Okay. So, I went into the house. There was broken furniture all over, like maybe the house had been broken into and I got scared...for

Martin. I called out to him but he didn't answer." I gave her the bottle and she took another sip.

"Go on," I said. She nodded.

"Then I heard a noise upstairs. I got worried thinking that maybe Martin had gone up there to get away and fallen or something, so I went up. I heard crying, Terry. Crying! I was sure it was Martin and he was in trouble. It was coming from the room at the end of the hall." She took the bottle from me and had another sip on her own. "And then...and then...I went to the room and looked in. There was a woman there sitting in a chair, looking out the window and crying. I couldn't believe it. I couldn't believe Martin could have been keeping a woman upstairs all this time. Then I noticed her clothes and her hair. She was wearing old-fashioned petticoats and her hair was done up in an old fashioned style like I've seen in pictures of my grandmother, but it was all matted and dirty looking. I went over close to her. She looked up at me, but not at me...through me...over me... Oh, I don't know. Her face was bruised, her neck was ringed with red...like rope marks and when I looked down I saw that her feet were chained to the chair."

"At first I was overwhelmed by the scent of gardenias, then suddenly it changed and this horrible smell filled the room. The temperature dropped to freezing and I heard a strange pounding sound, like thundering footsteps on the stairs. It was so loud it felt like the whole house was shaking."

"I went to the door and looked out. There was a man on the landing coming down the hall toward me...with a hatchet. He was...he was wearing a wh-white shirt and black trousers. He had...black hair and...a long black beard and his eyes. Oh, Terry, his eyes. They were filled with blood. I was so terrified. I slammed the door shut, threw the bolt and stepped back trying to think of what to do next. I was trapped and this man was going to hurt me. I was petrified. I couldn't move. I looked behind me to the woman in the chair, but she wasn't there anymore . . . she was gone . . . disappeared.

"When I turned back to the door and the sound, I saw...I saw...the man...he walked straight through the door, Terry." She was sobbing uncontrollably again. "He...came toward me...raising the hatchet over my head," she stopped and took another drink, "and before I could scream he was on me, but not on me...through me, and I couldn't breathe. It felt like I had the wind knocked out of me."

She looked in my eyes the entire time, trying to see if I doubted anything she was saying. Satisfied that I believed her, she went on. "I heard the woman scream behind me, but before I could turn to look, I felt icy cold fingers close tightly around my neck and a low, growling voice whisper in my ear, 'Get out hag and don't ever come back or I'll eat your children.'"

I could see the hysteria rising up in her eyes again, so I took her hand.

"Oh Terry, I couldn't breathe. I was so scared. I thought I was dying. Then I felt it come through me again. The bolt on the door threw itself back right before my eyes and the door flew open. I grabbed hold of the door jamb to hold myself up and pull myself out of the room then I ran. I ran down the hallway to the stairs and...and...the doors, the doors started slamming behind me and I heard this awful laughter. It sounded like it was coming out of the walls, the blackest laughter I ever heard, vibrating and echoing in the walls as I ran. It was after me. Oh, Terry! It was after me!" she cried out loud, on the verge of breaking down again.

"Wh-when I got to the stairs, it pushed me, or I fell...I don't know which anymore. All I know is that I screamed as I tumbled down the stairs head first. Then I got up and ran to the door and out onto the porch. I looked behind me to see if it was following me. I didn't see anything, but I could still hear thundering footsteps and that insane laughter, so I just got in my car and got the hell out of there. Terry, please tell me you believe me," she begged through hiccupping sobs of her terror relived.

"I believe you, Jenny, every word," I said. "Now, I want to tell you something..." and I took a long slug out of the bottle myself. "Look at me, Jenny. I want you to look right at me."

She did, tears streaming down her face.

"You are not losing your mind. What you saw...what you felt was real...as real as you or me. It's the house, Jenny. There is something evil in that house."

She cocked her head back with an astonished gaze. "You do believe me. You know something, Terry. Tell me what you know," she begged.

"I've seen things and felt things there myself...and so has Martin, and others too," I said, making a point not to mention Grace specifically.

"But why didn't you say something...tell somebody...warn people?" she pleaded, wiping her face.

"Who would have believed me, Jen? Would you have believed it if you hadn't seen the things you saw today?"

She looked at me like she'd had a revelation and straightened up.

"You're right, I wouldn't have," she said, like it had just dawned on her.

"And I wasn't all that convinced that it wasn't all in my mind," I went on. "I didn't want to believe it anymore than you do now ...but it was threatening Martin, hurting him, so I had to do...something. I just got him outta there this afternoon," I told her, taking another slug for myself.

Suddenly, the panic came back into her eyes again and she put her hand over her mouth. "It was 'the man'...the man that Jonah was talking to upstairs. It wasn't an imaginary friend. It was...that thing! He was talking to my baby. Oh, my God! He wants to eat babies!" she said in a high pitched howl, her eyes bulging with fear. She clutched my arm and starting to cry again. "My babies!"

"No, no Jen. It was just trying to scare you. It's all over now. I promise. The kids are fine. You're fine...and Martin is fine. He's over at my mother's now...and I'm fine. We're all going to be fine. It's over. I'm going to take care of everything," I said, doing my best to comfort her.

"What are you going to do?" she asked me, looking stricken.

"That's my worry," I said, but honestly at that moment, I had no idea what I was going to do. "You have another problem," I told her. "You have a husband out there worried sick about you, thinking you were raped. You can't tell him the truth, Jen. It would cause more trouble than it's worth. You and I know the truth and that's all that matters. You have to think, would he believe you if he hadn't seen it himself?"

She thought a moment. "No, you're right," she said, thinking, then looked up at me. "What are we going to do?" she asked.

"Well, the best thing I can think to do is . . .," and I was winging it again, "stick as close to the truth as possible. You went over to Martin's. The door was open so you went in. The place was wrecked and you heard a noise upstairs. You thought it was Martin and you were concerned so you went up. When you got up there, you realized the house was being ransacked...by burglars...vandals. One of them saw you and chased you...so you ran...and fell down the stairs. You got up and got out to the car before anyone could get to you."

She nodded throughout my recitation.

"How's that?" I asked her.

"Good, that works. I can do that," she said coming back to herself, nodding.

"Are you sure, Jen?" I asked, trying to make sure, or try something else.

"Yeah, I can do that. I hate lying to Jeff, but I don't have any choice." She was more like the old Jen by then.

"Now you've got to pull yourself together for Jeff and the kids. You can't worry the guy over something he can't do anything about," I told her as firmly as I dared.

She nodded.

"And he's gonna want you to see a doctor to make sure that you weren't raped. He's got a right to know, Jen. I'll try to convince him that you weren't, but if he insists, you gotta let him have his way. You don't have anything to fear from it and it would give him peace of mind. He's a good man, Jen, and none of this is his fault. He shouldn't have to suffer unnecessarily."

She looked at me, tears of relief brimming in her eyes. "You're right, Terry. I love him. If he wants it, I'll do it. Thank you, Terry," she said wiping her eyes again.

"Good girl!" I said. "Now I've got to go out there and talk to Jeff. I'm gonna ply him with some alcohol so he'll be more likely to accept our story. You clean yourself up and come out when you're ready...Yes?"

"Yes," she smiled weakly, sitting up straight and smoothing her hair. *That's right, sweetheart, shake it off.* I was glad to see her smile again.

I went down to speak to Jeff. He was waiting for me, sitting at the foot of the stairs.

"Is everything ok?" he asked nervously.

"Yes, Jeff. Everything is going to be fine." I replied, looking him straight in the eye and putting my hand on his back, leading him into the living room.

"Are you sure, Terry?" he asked again.

This is going to take a bit of work, I thought to myself. "Yes, I'm very sure." I could already smell the alcohol on his breath and was glad of it.

"Was she...attacked?' he asked, starting to huff.

"No, not in the way you're thinking." He stopped and looked at me unsure, so I went on. "She went over to Martin's after she was done shopping...when she got there...the door was open and she went in to look for him. She didn't know that I had already brought him to my mother's for the holiday. She heard some noise upstairs and thought he might have fallen or something." He was anxious for the upshot of the thing so I got to it. "Apparently, the place was being robbed and she walked in on the burglars upstairs."

"Oh, my God!" He shouted and grabbed my arm. "Did they hurt her?" His eyes went wild.

"No, Jeff...they just scared her badly. Come sit down with me." I said, leading him by his arm to the sofa. "When she saw one of them and, I guess he saw her...she ran. She got all banged when she panicked and fell down the stairs trying to get away. No one ever laid a hand on her. It seems one of them made like he was going to chase her, but he was really only trying to scare her away so they could finish the job and get out themselves. She went into shock from the fall but she still got up and got out." *Whew!* That was a lot for me to get him to swallow.

"Are you sure, Terry?" I could tell he was going to need a lot of reassurance.

"Yes, Jeff, I'm absolutely sure," I stressed. "They were just burglars. They didn't really want to hurt anybody," I said, hoping it would sink in this time. "They were out for money, not to hurt anybody. My guess is they were just kids...probably the same ones who've been vandalizing the cemetery lately," I said and thought, *Nice touch,* to myself. "She's much better now. She'll be down any minute. She just needed some time to calm down." I could see relief easing into his face after that.

"You're sure, Terry? You're not just trying to protect me are you?" He was getting hitched up again.

"No, Jeff. I'm not. Look at me. Do you really think I would just sit here with you like this if anyone had laid a hand on 'our Jen.' You have to trust me on this...and even if you don't trust me, you have got to trust your wife. She'll be down any minute and she's agreed to get checked by a doctor if that's what it takes to convince you. She loves you very much, man, and she'll do whatever you want to give you some peace of mind." He seemed satisfied with that.

"Oh, thank God!" he sighed with relief. Just then Jenny appeared on the stairs, still looking uncertain, but much better. He jumped up and was over to her in seconds, putting his arms around her.

"It's okay, sweetheart," she said to him, returning his embrace. "Really, I'm okay." It just...scared me, that's all." she said and winked at me behind his back. He brought her over to the sofa and they sat down.

"Really?" He asked her, needing to hear it from her.

"Yes . . . really." She looked at him convincingly.

Good girl!

Confident now that she could pull it off, I stood up and said to Jeff, "I've gotta go now and check the place out." That was when the fire burning in their fireplace caught my eye and heard Pierra's voice ring in my head. "Follow your destiny and meet it with the fire I've seen burning inside you," she'd said to me. There it was, I had my answer, but it meant I had to make up a quick lie, so I took it and ran with it.

"But Jeff, before I go I need a little favor from you," I said to him, trying to sound 'business as usual' and hoping he wouldn't catch the shift to the lie I was about to lay on him.

"Anything, Terry, anything," he said gratefully.

"In all the excitement, I forgot. Lila called me on the radio just as I got here. She had a call about an auto breakdown a few miles from here over by Marvin Petrovic's horse farm and she wants me to go over and see what I can do...it being Christmas Eve and all. She says they got lost somewhere over there and ran out of gas on they're way to some family gathering or other."

He looked at me expectantly.

"So, I was wondering...it would make my life just a little easier if maybe you had a gas can around here with some gas in it." In his hypersensitive state, he bought it all—hook, line and sinker. Jenny looked straight at me, the knowledge of my plan shining in her eyes.

"Uh," he thought for a moment. "I think so," he said and got up. "I should have a can out in the potting shed from last season. I use it all the time for the mower and weed whacker. I don't know how much is in it, but sure, you're welcome to it. Let's go see." I followed him out the back door into the potting shed. Once inside, he bent over and pulled out a red five-gallon plastic gas can with a yellow spout, weighing it as he lifted it. "Almost full," he said, looking satisfied. I took it from him and thanked him.

"I'm gonna go now, Jeff. I really shouldn't let it wait too long. It's gonna to get dark soon and the last thing I need is a couple of frozen city people on my hands," I said smiling. Jeff put his hand out to shake mine.

"Thanks so much for coming over, Terry," he said shaking my hand firmly, looking much relieved. Jenny came out the back door over to where we were standing.

"Yes. Thank you, Terry," she said, hugging me tightly and whispering in my ear, "Please be careful."

"I will, honey. I promise."

On her way back over to her husband she said, "Jeff, I'm gonna go over and get the kids from next door, then go upstairs and have a nice, long, hot bath to relax. If you give the kids something to eat, maybe you can come up and scrub my back for me," and kissed him lovingly on the cheek.

Very good girl, I thought as she walked toward the neighbors on the right. I walked around the left to my car in the driveway and put the gas can on the passenger seat. I was on my way.

❈ ❈ ❈

The drive over to the house was nothing less than...hellish. Before I even saw the house, I could feel the sweat building on my forehead and the palms of my hands. That old feeling squeezing in my stomach was back, too. When I was with others,

I could forget my fear for a while, but when I was alone, it overwhelmed me, bringing home to me how truly insignificant I was...a small, scared, shell of a man, helpless in the face of God only knows what.

It was just starting to get dark by the time I arrived and I was already soaked with sweat, again. I sat motionless in my car as the sun slowly went down, watching as that malevolent funhouse look appeared again out of what should have been just an old white house, the one I'd seen that first time, except the character of it seemed to be changing. This time, the bareness of the ice-covered trees set against the backdrop of the snow gave it the impression of a dead thing, but one that you couldn't be quite sure would stay that way. This time it carried with it all of the menace of a giant white spider, lying in wait, salivating as it watched the fly venture into its sticky white web, ready to pounce, aching to savor the life it was about to suck out of it as it gobbled up the poor helpless creature in its bottomless black hole of a maw.

The squeezing in my stomach intensified to the point of agony, my head swam with it, like a drowning man going down for the third time. I doubted my legs had strength enough to hold themselves up if I tried to move them to stand. I didn't know if I could go back in there...alone. The pressure on my bladder was immense, like in the dream, making me think I might piss myself if I had to go back in there...in the dark. I sat there for a while just looking at it, dazed by the unfathomable threat of it. *You've got to hurry, Terry,* my inner voice told me. *It's going to be dark soon,* and somehow I started to move.

I reached into the glove box and got out a couple packs of matches, shoving them into the pocket of my jacket. I couldn't risk leaving my lighter behind as evidence. I turned off the car, got out with the gas can and went around to the trunk. There were three cans of motor oil in a box with my other 'might need' things. I shoved them in my jacket, zipping it up to hold them in. Then I had a thought, *Fool me once, shame on you. Fool me twice, shame on me,* and pulled a hammer and screwdriver out of the box, shoving them in the pockets of my pants.

I turned back to look at it. My heart felt like it was going to pound itself right out of my chest. My belly felt like it was being squeezed by a steel claw as I stood there like some pathetic, frightened scarecrow. I couldn't do it. I couldn't go back in there.

Gripped by the most paralyzing fear I'd ever experienced or was ever likely to, I was frozen with it, beaten by my own cowardice, tortured by my own shame. Then, as I stood there in the freezing cold, I was struck by an odd thought from somewhere out of the haze of my subconscious, reminding me of another time, a time when I stood before a burning temple of God, running in, unafraid, to try and save a life that was lost. And, here I was now, all these years later, standing in front of a temple of evil intending to torch it, afraid to go in, wondering if the life to be lost this time would be my own, and the simplest of concepts washed over me in a wave.

It may not be profound to others, but to me, where I was and what I was contemplating, it was the most powerful thought I'd ever had. I thought that, there I was, the product of all the love two people could muster for each other, and for me. I was in a moment that gave me the chance, for the first time in my life, not only to be the man I wanted to be, but more than that, to be the man I should be to make them both proud. I drew on the strength those two people had given me all their lives, and it came to me. *What would my father have done? What would he want me to do?* and suddenly my feet started to move, shaking themselves free from the grip that had held them motionless.

Then I thought about my mother. *What would she want me to say?* and suddenly my lips began to move. This time without the childish trembling that'd possessed them until that very moment. "The Lord is my shepherd; I shall not want…" and for one brief shining moment in my life, no matter what was to follow, as I faced the fear of crossing back over the threshold into the darkest depths of the unknown, I was the man I should have been all along and, before I realized it, I was in.

"He maketh me to lie down in green pastures…" I mumbled to myself as I smashed both panes of glass in the storm door then went around to the big door.

"He leadeth me beside the still water…" I took the hammer and screwdriver and pounded out the bolts that held the door on its hinges, letting it fall to one side. "I'm not gonna to go through that again," I said to myself out loud, then went on with my chant.

"He restoreth my soul; He leadeth me in the paths of righteousness for his name's sake…" I mumbled as I picked up the gas can and headed upstairs. I started with the room at the end of the hall, opening a can of oil with the screwdriver.

"Yea, thought I walk through the valley of the shadow of death, I will fear no evil; for thou art with me…" I poured oil all around the room, then some gas for good measure. The smell of gas was strong, but somehow I was struck by the fact that it was suddenly overpowered, replaced by another smell, floral…Lily of the Valley. I recognized it from my mother's garden. Then I heard a sound. It was the sound of a girl's voice, giggling behind me. I thought of Lila, but it wasn't girlish and lively like Lila's. It was demented, insane giggling, then words…faint, whispered words.

"Burn it…set us free, Terrence. Burn it."

I turned around toward the voice and in a flash of an image I saw a young, dark-haired woman dressed in old fashioned petticoats, tied to a chair. Her breasts were exposed and scarred, her hair dirty, hanging and mangled. She was pale and bruised, starved looking with a haunted stare in her eyes that seemed at the same time, somehow eager. Underneath her chair, a five pointed star was scrawled in white chalk on the hardwood floor. There were eerie symbols too, and scribbling all over the walls in what looked like charcoal, some in Latin, some in Greek and some in a language that reminded me of maybe, Hebrew? Then it was gone. A few seconds later there was another voice.

"Burn it…help us…" it said.

This time it was a different voice, higher and fuller. I looked around, another flash, another woman and another scent, Camellias. She was blonde, taller and dressed similarly to the other, shackled by her wrists, hanging from a hook. Her breasts exposed too, and bleeding from small, round sores, dozens of them, looking infected. Her wrists were bloody from the chains that bound them, and she had the same haunted, eager look in her eyes. There was a chalk star beneath her as well, and more symbols, and more scribbling on the walls.

Oh, dear God! I thought. *I've lost my mind. This has got to be a nightmare. It can't be real. It's gotta be a dream.* And as in a dream, I was driven by an irresistible compulsion from somewhere outside of myself to go on to the next room, pushing me, urging me on. In the core of my being a sense of knowledge grew, *You must destroy this place at all costs, no matter what the consequences, even if you die in the process.*

"Thy rod and thy staff they comfort me..." I continued my chant as I got to the next room. It happened again.

As I was pouring the gas, I heard choking sounds, then more words, in a different voice, "Set us free. Please...Burn it," it said in between desperate gasps for breath.

This time I closed my eyes and kept pouring. I didn't want to see, but I couldn't help myself. When I opened my eyes, there was another flash image and the room was suddenly filled with the scent of stale Jasmine. There was more writing on the walls and two women this time, older and worn with dark hair tied in big knots at the tops of their heads, roped together back to back in chairs above another chalk star with a thick leather belt binding their necks together. One's head was slumped down. She had been beaten badly, professionally it looked to me. The other was staring at me with that same haunted look in her eyes. I had the impression that they might be sisters, twins maybe, then they were gone.

As I stood in the hallway before the next room, I doubted if I had what it took to go on, physically or emotionally. My body hurt so badly...and my poor mind. This had to be hell. *Was I really here or was I already locked away in some mental hospital with these tortured souls as my companions for eternity?* My head was spinning and my eyes were beginning to blur from the fumes of the gas.

I stood in the hallway, my mind careening in all directions with what I was seeing, my body about to lose all control, convulsing in spasms from what I was doing when the door to the next room opened wide right before my eyes, inviting me in. It wanted me to come in, fear made me hesitate, but whatever was pushing me, drawing me in, was stronger than I was, and I went. Automatically, I started pouring gas on the floor and it started all over again. This time it was sobbing, girlish, hopeless sobbing, anguished and tormented.

"Help us, Terrence...we need you," it said in a faint, young voice, barely more than a whisper. "He hurts us so bad, Terrence.

Please, burn it," she begged through her sobs. "Burn it. Burn it, Terrence…I'll help you if I can. We all will."

I finished pouring gas around the room, keeping my eyes closed. The smell of the gas vanished again, replaced by the scent of roses, strong and sweet. "My name is Rose," the voice said, seeming to force me to open my eyes. God, I wish I hadn't. There was another flash, a young girl with small, delicate features, no more than sixteen, with strawberry blonde hair and freckles, crucified on the wall in front of me, her wrists extended, attached to hooks above both sides of her head. Her ankles were on hooks too, her legs spread wide, hanging there over a large charcoal star on the wall behind her. She had the same haunted look in her eyes…staring at me. When I saw the large blood stain on her petticoat between her legs, I thought I'd faint. I bounded out of the room just to keep moving, and started my chant again, "Thou preparest a table before me in the presence of mine enemies…" throwing the empty oil can in behind me.

There were still two more rooms to do as I headed toward the front stairs. I could still hear the demented giggling, the choking and gasping, and the tortured sobbing behind me, the words still echoing in my head, "Burn it! …Set us free…Burn it!"

I moved on, limping, and stood in the doorway of the fourth room slinging gas into it, splashing it everywhere. I stopped for a moment and bent over, gagging. A voice whispered in my ear, "Hurry, Terrence, please!" and I felt the slight nudge of tiny hands push me from behind. Before I could react, I was in. The smell of the gas disappeared again. It was Honeysuckle now. *Oh, my God. No more, please. I can't bear it.* Then, just as I thought my mind was bent to its limit, I heard the most awful moaning and saw another flash, another woman. She was young and brunette, probably pretty once, bound in a chair over yet another star, and more symbols. Her breasts were exposed and there were marks carved into her arms, neck and torso. Her mouth gaped open before me, blood dripping thickly from her lips and chin. I knew what that meant. "Oh, sweet Jesus!" Her tongue had been cut out. *Do not look anymore,* I thought to myself. *Just don't look!* I ran from the room, stumbling back into the hallway and vomited. "Thou annointest my head with oil; my cup runneth over…"

The last room upstairs was on the left. I didn't want to go in, but knew I had to. I knew they wouldn't let me leave, or leave my head, unless I did. I heard another voice whisper in my ear, "Please, Terrence, please!" it begged me in a voice so lost and lonely it broke my heart in ways I could've never envisioned. Suddenly, 'the protector' in me surged up through my body again, like a sword from the depths of my soul, and I opened another can of oil. They wanted me to know what happened to them in that place before I destroyed it, and I would at least give them that satisfaction. I had to. I stood before the doorway with the open oil can in one hand and the gas can in the other.

"Surely goodness and mercy shall follow me all the days of my life..." I mumbled under my breath, stepping forward to drizzle oil around the floor.

"Burn it all, Terrence...please. We want to go home," I heard a voice call to me from the corner of the room, an Irish accent, soft and lilting, and the scent of Lilacs. I diverted my eyes at first, but then forced myself to look of my own free will. There was another flash, another girl. She was bound, shackled and hanging upside down above another chalk star, her feet suspended from a hook in the ceiling. Her long, curly, black hair dangled down to the floor. Her eyes looked up at me with the same haunted look as the others. There were small puddles of water under her head where her tears had fallen. I ran out, struggling to breathe, desperate to hold onto what was left my sanity, if there was anything left to hold onto. There was no way I could be sure anymore...the only thing I could be sure of was that it was done.

As I headed toward the stairs, I could hear them behind me, all of them calling to me all at once.

"My name is Daisy. My name is Adelaide," they called out to me. "My name is Molly...My name is Lizzie. My name is...Pansy...Deirdre ...Lily...Cora . . . J'em appelle Camille. Burn it! Set us free. Please Terrence, save us," they whispered in haunting, heart-rending pleas.

By the time I reached the top of the stairs, I couldn't breathe, my lungs seized in my chest. The smell of the gas and oil was smothering me, the power of the shocking tableaus of intentional human misery and torture that I'd been shown had blown the ends off of my poor little brain cells. I looked down the stairs. My head throbbed, spinning out of all control, my eyes grew gray and my vision narrowed. I was going to pass out. I grabbed onto the rail, but knew it was too late. I was going down.

My knees buckled underneath me and I lost all sense of time or place, falling . . . falling. Then, just as I thought I was about to hit the floor, I smelled the strong scent of roses again, and felt something like a soft wind blow through my body. I heard that young crucified girl's voice whisper in my ear. "It's Rose, Terrence. I'm here," and suddenly, my eyes cleared. I was up again and turning around, working my way backward carefully down the stairs, splashing gas as I went. When I got to the bottom of the stairs, the voices were gone, and the scents. It was quiet again, and I was alone.

I did the same thing on the first floor working clockwise, the sofa and the living room, the kitchen and the dining room. Finally, I worked around to the TV room and I was back in the entry hall. "And I will dwell in the house of the Lord forever."

I was just about to set it off when heard a low creaking. I turned slowly toward the sound in time to see the door to the basement swing open, inch by inch. Every muscle and bone, fiber and cell in my body screamed. *Set it, Terry! Set it NOW!* but I couldn't...not yet. Something was pulling me, drawing me, to the basement door.

I took a few steps closer. I had to know. It wanted me to go down there. I had to find out. Against all logic, sense, reason and fear, I had to know what it was that had done this and what the whole thing was about. I took the hammer and screwdriver from my pocket again and pounded out the bolts of the basement door, then began again.

"The earth is the Lord's and the fullness thereof..."

I felt around the walls to the left and right for a light switch, finding it on the right. I turned it on. Stairs descended to a floor that I could see was dirt. I picked up the gas can and crept down slowly, my animal senses keenly aware of any movement around me. I continued my prayer to help me summon all the strength and protection I could to face whatever it was that wanted me to see it. Fear griped my guts, sweat poured off me. My bladder felt so distended that I thought it would burst inside me.

When I got down to the floor, I looked around. The walls were rough, cave-like, and whitewashed. There was a boiler or furnace, whichever, and some packing crates scattered around, older and dusty, not Martin's. I scanned around carefully. Nothing. I opened the third can of oil and began to drizzle it around the floor. That was when I smelled it, that awful, decaying, rancid smell again. "The world and they that dwell within..." It was there, with me. I looked up and around. That's when I saw it, on the big wall in front of me, bleeding through the whitewash.

I stood staring at it in stark amazement, my mouth gaping open as the black letters appeared dripping on the wall, written like some maniacal child's finger painting, using God only knows what for paint. "*I STOOD AT THE EDGE OF THE ABYSS...THE CROSSROAD BETWEEN REALITY AND MADNESS...A CHOICE TO BE MADE...FALL IN AND SURRENDER BLINDLY...TO THE DARKNESS AROUND ME...*" line after line it went down the wall.

I followed it with my eyes as it continued, "*...OR LEAP IN FEARLESS, UNAFRAID...SO I CHOSE, AND I LEAPT...AND WAS CONSUMED BY THE DARKNESS...OUT OF THE VOID CAME A WHISPER...'COME FLY WITH ME...BE A MONSTER AMONG MEN...AND I WILL MAKE YOU THE FINEST OF YOUR KIND'...SO I FLEW...I BECAME...AND I WILL ALWAYS BE...FEAR ME! GIVE HIM BACK...OR WE WILL EAT YOUR SOUL!*"

Each line disappeared from the walls not long after I had the chance to read it. Then, out of the corner of my eye, a shadow moved. I heard a rustling noise somewhere behind me to the left and was suddenly engulfed by the scent of...Mimosa.

I turned slowly, not really wanting to see what it was, the compulsion to know and fear of knowing battling inside me, but I kept my promise to the girls upstairs and myself, and I looked. What materialized before my eyes was the most gruesome scene I could have ever imagined. Appearing slowly like a holograph in three dimensions was a makeshift surgical set-up with some sort of operating table. There was a girl on it, tawny skinned, her wavy, matted, raven-colored hair hanging over the side. Her breasts were exposed, the rest of her covered by only a dirty, blood stained sheet. She was gagged but her eyes were open, and she was breathing.

My eyes were immediately drawn to what seemed to be a tourniquet around her upper arm. Everything looked like some weird colorized silent film. What I saw next ripped to shreds every concept I ever had about the nature of humanity, and revealed to me the very depths of the darkest realm of human depravity because, as she turned her head to face me with the same haunted, eager look as the others, I saw her severed arm leaning hand up in a rusty, old tin bucket on the floor below her.

Then I looked up and saw a trickle of blood ooze from under the sheet where her arm must have been and her severed leg propped up on the wall few feet behind her. My soul splintered like delicate glass slammed cruelly on concrete when I realized what'd happened to her. It was dismembering her while she was still alive, still conscious. Numb with revulsion, disgust and...fear, I couldn't move. *No more, no more. I don't want to know anymore...see any more...Please,* and the scene with the girl on the table began to fade until it was little more than a shadow. But before it was completely gone, I heard a woman's voice whisper in my ear. "Mi nombre es Iris. El esta detras de usted. My name is Iris. He's behind you."

In the time it took me to understand what she'd said and turn around, the temperature had dropped to below freezing. I could see my breath again and heard a low, confident, chuckle come from behind me.

"For he hath founded it upon the seas..." I closed my eyes and chanted, the intense pressure on my bladder pressing even harder. "Get out of here, Terry," I heard myself say. "Get out of here. NOW!" but my feet refused the command. "...and established it upon floods..."

The laughter got louder, hateful, seething laughter. When I opened my eyes again to turn around and finally see it, I was pelted in the face by that smell, the most rancid, rotting, decaying smell my feeble mind could imagine. My stomach heaved in rebellion against it. Then I saw him, the man from the dreams, standing in the shadows in the far corner of the room, creeping slowly toward me.

The first thing I could see clearly were those blue eyes, deep set in that pallid, corpse-like flesh that was somehow not solid. He was coming closer, still in half shadow. I could see he was smiling at me, moving in slow, jerky, sepia-toned, silent film movements that made me think of tin typed, time lapse photography, solidifying more and more with each step he took toward me. About thirty feet away, he stopped. Completely out of the shadows by then, I could see his mouth was smeared with blood. "Give...him...back...to...me!" he said, in a low growl through clenched teeth, glaring at me, his icy blue eyes beginning to bulge.

"No! ...No! I won't...Not ever!" I heard myself bark at him, not quite knowing where I found the strength to speak to him directly. He glared at me menacingly, sneering and snickering malevolently, streams of drool running down the sides his mouth. He raised his hands, palms upward toward the ceiling. His eyes rolled up in his head and he began to mutter to himself in some unintelligible language, his drool turning to foam, cascading down his chin like an over-boiled pot. He started swaying strangely, like a serpent caught in the thralls of a snake charmer's trance, his head lolling backward, his tongue darting and licking hungrily at the air in-between verses.

His chant and movements had a hypnotic effect on me and I felt myself begin to sway with him. I shook my head to throw it off and started backing away slowly, step by step, until I felt my back flat against the wall behind me, trapped. All I could do was stand there, my fingers gripping the wall, a gormless lump of quivering inertia, watching, waiting for God only knows what to happen next. Then it did.

His head suddenly snapped forward, his mouth opening wider than any human being should be capable, exposing a great gaping, frothing chasm of razor sharp, jagged teeth. Its tongue blotched in shades of pink and red, twisting and twirling as it wagged and darted defiantly at me. No longer a him but a thing, it hissed at me ferociously like a grotesque medieval gargoyle unleashed from its granite casing after hundreds of years of captivity and finally allowed to come to life, fueled by a pipeline drawn right from the very bowels of hell itself.

My stomach flew into open revolt. My heart rate soared almost to the point of spontaneous combustion. I jumped toward the stairs so violently it felt like I'd left my skin where I'd stood. Soaked with sweat and trembling with the endless night of mortal fear, I was as close to shitting my own pants as any grown man should ever get when it started to move again, coming closer, closer...closer.

That was it! My blood raced through my veins like raging river. My nerves flew into unrestrained twitches of feral electricity, like a deer being stalked, hunted for prey. "Who shall ascend into the hill of the Lord or who shall stand in this holy place."

It's coming for me! Oh, my God. ! It's coming for me, now! raced through my brain. My lips began to move faster. "He that hath clean hands and a pure heart; who hath not lifted up his soul in vanity nor sworn deceitfully..." I don't know if it was my deepest primal instincts or my prayers being heard, but I found my balls again somehow managing to get my feet moving, scrambling back up the stairs with the gas can still in my hand, unconsciously splashing a trail of gas behind me.

The next thing I knew, I was in the entry hall again. I threw the gas can out through the front doorway and reached for the matches in my pocket. My fingers fumbled clumsily. I wasn't sure how much longer I could hold my bowels or how long I had before it reached me. The pressure of both was so excruciating I thought my whole body would detonate at the slightest shift in the atmosphere. Then, working purely on autopilot, my heart nearly pounding through my chest, my guts eaten alive by indescribable terror, I lit a match and tossed it into the basement hearing myself scream, "BURN IN HELL MOTHER FUCKER!" and the "Whhoooossshh" of the fire as it ignited.

Pumped with the adrenaline of my narrow escape, I went over to the stairs and tossed another match. The flames flew up the stairs in a ribbon into the second floor, then another one onto the gas soaked sofa, another burst of flames. The thing was laughing again, louder and louder, and the walls began banging again. The entire house shook with it. Flames were trailing everywhere as I turned for the door, ready to run out. I'd paused only for a split second when I felt it, the iron grip of two bony hands on my shoulders, icy fingers digging into my flesh...pulling me back, hot, putrid breath on the back of my neck and that voice, that awful, miserable, groaning voice, "My move!" it said in my ear, followed by the hysterical, ear splitting laugh of a madman triumphant.

Screaming at the top of my lungs, my bladder let loose sending a spray of piss down my leg as I felt myself being dragged back into the blackness and flames of the house. Then, just as my mind was fading and I'd resigned myself to a death in flames, clinging only to the knowledge that, at least, I was taking it with me, it happened. My nostrils and my lungs were suddenly filled by the smothering scent of a floral bouquet, Lilacs and Roses, Lily of the Valley and Hyacinth, Jasmine and Lavender mixed with so many others I couldn't identify them, and I felt dozens of tiny delicate hands yank me forward, pulling and pushing, flinging me out the door. The next thing I knew, I was out front, stumbling and falling down the steps with a force I couldn't reckon.

I landed flat on my chest on the snowy ground, the wind knocked completely out of me. I scrambled away breathless, crawling on my hands and knees until I was safely holding onto the car, gagging and dry heaving, but safe. I knew it. I could feel it. From there, it only took me a moment to regain some control. I used the car to pull myself up and turned back to look at the house. The fire was doing its job. The inside had become a raging inferno.

I stood for a moment to catch my breath when another thought struck me *the garden house!* I could hardly walk by then, or lift my arms. My whole body was shrieking and howling in a chaos of pain, my mind swimming with gas fumes, smoke and all I'd just witnessed.

I found the gas can and dragged myself around back to the garden house, that hideous reproduction of the monstrous original. It had to go, too. Hesitating only for a second, I flung the door open. What happened then almost finished me. I heard its voice scream at me ". . . EAT YOUR SOUL!" and felt an immense rush of hot air filled with a staggering stench slam me in the face with a force so powerful that it took my legs out from underneath me, knocking me off my feet and sending me flying helplessly backward to land hard on my ass at least twenty feet from where I'd stood.

I struggled to my feet, shaky at first, but then a compartment somewhere inside myself that had always remained closed seemed to open its own door to unleash a feeling I can only describe as how a mother tiger wounded in battle must feel when defending it's young, my girls, my flowers, from a predator. I opened my mouth and roared back ferociously into the portal of that unwholesome place, stomping back at it barbarously like a caveman, oblivious of any pain, and wildly splattered the last of the gas in it, on it and over it. I lit another match and tossed it in standing there for a moment to make sure it took. When I was sure, I took the gas can and stomped back around to the front, my mother tiger slowly retreating back to its lair, the pain in my leg returning me to my human state.

By then I could see flames licking at every part of the house. As I leaned against the car to take the pressure off my leg, I felt the shape of my bottle pressing against my flesh from my back pocket, took it out and drank what was left in one long swallow. Then Grace Coutraire's words came into my head. "Take this with you, back where it came from and destroy it," and I felt for the lump in my pocket. The bracelet was still there. I took it out, examined it closely one last time, then picked up the gas can, walked back up to the porch, flung the bracelet through the open door followed by the empty gas can, and just backed away to watch.

Watching the flames shoot up throughout the house made my heart soar, and then the most incredible thing happened. I heard the women's voices from upstairs sigh in a resounding outpouring of sound. "Frreeee. Frrreeee. We're free," they cried in long, joyous sighs. "Free going home," they echoed, "...home..."

I just stood there in awe, eyes wide, mouth open, watching and listening. For a moment I thought I could see tiny shimmering points of light in pastel colors of pinks and blues, yellows and purples, rise from the flames like shooting stars into the sky as the house turned into a blazing mass. I guess it could have just been the effects of the fumes, but I know my heart felt laid open with the feeling of their freedom. It was inside me, too. I could feel their song vibrate through me like heavenly chorus, a lightness in their laughter and sighs, their cries of release and of relief. "We're freeee...no more pain...Free..."

Then the voices started to fade away, but before they were

completely gone, I smelled the faintest scent of roses curl in my
nose and felt the light touch of lips on my forehead. It was the
girl who called herself 'Rose.' They were her hands, and the
hands of the others, that had pulled and pushed me out of that
door. I knew it then. I looked up to the sky as her scent faded.
"Thank you, Rose. You'll be alright now. You all will, I promise,"
I told her, and they were gone. I was alone with the sounds of
crackling fire, shattering glass, and the creaking and crashing of
the house beginning to cave in on itself.

    As I watched, I was struck by a thought out of the blue,
whether it was put there from somewhere outside me or came
from within, I don't know. The son-of-a-bitch liked girls who
smelled of flowers, or were named after them, or both, like my
poor Rose. That must have made her a 'particularly special' treat
for him, the sick son-of-a-bitch, but that's how he chose them.
I'm sure of it and for the second time in my life, I felt the burning
sensation of hatred in the pit of my stomach, welling up through
my throat into my mouth. I spat on the ground as violently as my
aching head would allow to rid myself of the taste of it until it
passed. "I love you, Rose."

                              ❋ ❋ ❋

    I watched the blazing mass of flames burn for more than an
hour while I waited by the radio for any call that might come in
that someone had seen something. None came. It was only when
I started feeling the chill from the natural cold of New York in
December that I realized I was soaked in my own piss and
reeking of gas, vomit and sweat. I looked back up at the house
and watched as the second story collapsed, completely caving
into the first floor to create a conflagration that reminded me of
the black churches. I stayed just long enough to see that it didn't
spread to the surrounding trees, but there wasn't much chance of
that. Everything was still pretty much covered in snow and ice,
leaving me confident that the fire would stay contained as I
drove off. I still had live people to contend with who I knew
were probably worrying about me, and it was Christmas Eve.

    It wasn't until I was halfway into town that I realized that
tears were streaming down my face. There I was, stewing in my

own stinking sweat, vomit and piss, crying like a baby. I don't think I had ever felt so degraded in my entire life, and in my life, that was going a long way. I thought about the way Martin sounded when I had to help undress him. "I'm so embarrassed," he'd said. The smell of gas and smoke, alcohol and piss pervaded the car almost making me sick again. If he could've only seen me and know I understood.

I got back to my house some fifteen minutes later. Once in, I dispensed with my half-and-half pill combo and took a full dose with another half dose for good measure. I got myself a beer and sucked it down, took another then hit the shower. Nothing has ever felt as good as that hot water pouring over me. I let it run over me for a while then scrubbed off roughly, head to toe.

I was just coming back to myself when the practicalities of 'the real world' hit me. I had to report the fire to the Fire Department and make out an incident report of my own. If no one called in to report it before the next morning, the only way to work it was for me to 'discover' the burned out building myself, after the fact. The Fire Department would have to investigate it as an arson and send samples for analysis to the State Police, which meant I had to investigate it as well. No problem there. No one would ever retrieve my fingerprints off of the gas or oil cans after that blaze. I was confident that it'd be listed as unsolved in the end. I just hoped Martin had managed to get insurance on the place before the accident because I'm sure he wouldn't have had the presence of mind to do it afterwards. I also had to deal with the clothes I'd worn and air the car out. That pretty much covered it.

I got out of the shower and dressed in fresh things, then collected the clothes I'd worn, tossed them in the wash on hot with a ton of detergent. There was nothing else that could link me to the fire. I wasn't too worried about it. No one would ever suspect me, of all people, not with my background in arson. The only loose end would be what Jeff Denton might think when he learned that the house had burned. Would he make the connection between me taking the gas and the fire? I'd have to get Jenny to tell him it that the burglars had set it. I was sure she could handle it like a pro, so I didn't concern myself over it too much.

I was back out of the house within an hour heading toward my mother's, squeaky clean and much relieved, thanks in large part, to my increasingly polished knack for self-medicating.

CHAPTER 9

A Christmas Carol

"I heard an angel singing,
When the day was springing
Mercy, Pity, Peace,
Is the world's release."

William Blake, 18th Century English
Visionary, Poet & Artist

When I got back to my mother's, the only lights going were the twinkle of the blinking Christmas tree lights and the light from the fireplace. My mother came to the kitchen doorway and made the 'shhh' sound signaling me to be quiet and pointing to Martin asleep on the sofa.

I went straight into the kitchen with her. She had the Yule log burning on the small kitchen TV I'd gotten her the year before last and was just sitting down to a cup of coffee.

"Well?" she said. "What's going on over at the Denton's? Is everything alright?" She sounded concerned, more than a little nervous, and she wasn't the nervous type.

"Yeah, Ma. Everything is okay. Jenny slipped and fell down the stairs and hit her head. She was out for a few minutes and Jeff panicked. That's when he called me," I said in the most convincing voice I could muster, but it wasn't easy.

"Did she go to the hospital?" she asked, alarmed.

"Jeff was on the phone with one of the doctors from the

hospital when I left, but she seemed fine, honestly. She was a little scraped up and bruised, but by the time I left she was back to her old self. I think Jeff was more scared than anything else," I said, somehow managing to miraculously come back to myself, leaving the rest behind for the moment.

"Oh, the poor thing. On Christmas Eve, of all times. I'll have to call her tomorrow and see if she's alright," she said sympathetically. I sighed with relief. She'd bought it.

"You go ahead and do that, Ma, I'm sure she'd love to hear from you."

"It hasn't been an easy day for you either, has it?" she asked, coming over to hug me.

"No, Ma. You can say that again...and I gotta tell ya, I won't be sorry to see it go," I said as she set a cup of coffee in front of me. I took a good slug of it and changed the subject. "So how's 'our patient' been?"

"Well," she said, "he fell off to sleep not long after you left, but it's been a rough sleep. I've been watching him closely. He's been burning off the fever ...and talking in his sleep saying, 'Hot...hot...hot,' over and over. He was soaking wet an hour ago. I had to wake him up and help him change into a dry shirt. He fell back to sleep after that, but he's been quiet and dry since. I think we might have just caught it in time, but he hasn't had anything to eat and by the looks of it, neither have you. I wish you wouldn't drink so much, Terry," she said, on the verge of a nag and could tell she was about to lay a guilt trip on me.

"For God's sake, Ma. Not now, please. Tomorrow maybe, but please, not now. I've had such an unbelievably rough day and I'm so tired I can't even see straight." I must have sounded like my nerves were as shredded as they truly were because she backed off and started over.

"I've made some of that chicken salad that you like so much and I had a nice pot of vegetable soup going when you brought Martin in this afternoon. Let's let him sleep for a while more. I'll make up some sandwiches and we can all have a bite when I'm done. I want to make sure both of you get some food into you tonight. Humor your mother once in a while, will you?" she said, in the 'listen to your mother!' voice she always uses when she's determined to get her way...the one that always works.

"Sure, Ma. Go ahead and make up some plates. We'll have a nice quiet Christmas Eve, and to tell you the truth, I am starved!" She seemed pleased with that and went to the counter to feed her child.

I sat there for a moment hanging my head and feeling guilty for being so off-handed with her. I was just so tired and my mind so preoccupied, still whirling with all that had gone on in those last few hours. I knew I had to smooth it over for both of us, so I got up and went over to the counter where she was busy making sandwiches and put my arms around her.

"Did I ever tell you that you were the best mother a guy could ever have? I love you very much, Ma." I felt her arms cross over mine and hug them.

"I know you do, sweetheart. I love you too, more than anything in this world. I just worry about you so much," she said, starting to sniffle.

"I know you do, Ma," I said and kissed her cheek.

She tapped my arms and said, "Go have your coffee. I'll give you a yell when the food is ready."

I took my coffee and went and sat in my chair by the Christmas tree, trying to remember what it was like to be a child again…in the days before it was possible to know how ugly the world was, how unabashedly evil the human creature could be and, for the first time in more years than I have fingers, I felt eternally grateful for all the love I'd had the good fortune to know in my life, appreciating it more than I ever had reason to before.

A few minutes later, the smell of Mom's soup warming came wafting into the living room. It was wonderful. Not long after that, she came in and turned on the small light on the end table behind Martin's head. Putting her hand gently on his shoulder she said softly, "Martin, wake up, dear. Come and eat something."

He roused easily and, in a moment, was sitting up rubbing his face. "Sure, thanks, Mrs. C," he said, sounding groggy. He got himself up carefully using the cane, and followed her into the kitchen. I followed behind him just in case he started to fall. The table was already set with a plate of huge chicken salad sandwiches and steaming bowls of soup.

"Okay, dig in boys," Mom said, taking her spot over on the counter at the end of the table and lighting a cigarette.

I helped myself at once. It wasn't until I smelled the soup that I realized how hungry I actually was. Martin was slower to move. Mom had to come over and take a sandwich and put it on his plate. He took a small, tenuous bite, wincing and going a little pale before taking another. I guess he was feeling the effects of my little tap on the jaw, but at least I could see some color come into his face. Then he was on it, large bites. He seemed not to be able to get it in his mouth fast enough, like he was starving too but hadn't known it. Then he was on to the soup. My mother makes delicious vegetable soup. His bowl was empty before mine.

"So you like that huh, Martin?" I said, managing a smile, but aching so badly by then that even that hurt me, pills or no pills.

"Yeah," he said through a mouth full. "Great soup, Mrs. C."

"Would you like some more, Martin?" she asked, suppressing a small laugh. She saw it, too. He was coming back.

"Yes, please," he said, still chewing and handing her his bowl. Mom took her time eating and didn't mind taking a break to dish out more soup to both of us. She'd taken care of my father and me like that for years.

"How about a glass of cold milk to go with that, Martin?" she asked. He nodded eagerly, his mouth full again. She was working him. I could tell. I'd seen it all my life. She was pushing just hard enough, but not too hard. He downed the glass of milk. I was done, so I pushed back from the table and lit a cigarette. Martin looked at me expectantly, so I handed the pack and my lighter over to him. He lit one and asked about what went on over at Jenny's. I gave him the same old song and dance that I'd given Mom earlier. Then she was on it again.

"How about a nice, big piece of homemade chocolate cake and a cup of hot tea, Martin?"

"Yes, please. That would be great. Thanks Mrs. C," he said sounding insatiable and nodding his head.

"I'm so glad you're feeling better, dear," she said in that tone I'd come to know so well. She was working up to something. When she came back with the tea, I knew what it was.

"Here we go," she said, and plunked down a pile of pills in

front of each of us. "There are three vitamin Cs, two B-12s and two Advil for each of you. Martin, you have your antibiotic there in your pile," she said, smiling at him much like I imagine she had thousands of times at her patients on her ward at work. "Take your time," and she set down two gorgeous, large pieces of cake, one in front of each of us.

Ooooh, you're a sly one, Charlotte Chagford, I thought, shrugged at him and took my medicine. There was no way I was passing up that cake. He took my lead and followed suit.

Having been amply fed and feeling secure in our surroundings for the first time in what seemed like ages we retired to the living room to watch the black and white version of *A Christmas Carol* on the new TV. Martin went over to his sofa and Mom and I to our favorite chairs. The multi-colored lights on the Christmas tree blinking in harmony were tranquilizing. Martin fell asleep in the first half hour and my eyes got leaden after about an hour.

"Why don't you go up to bed, sweetheart? It's been a long, hard day for you," she said to me.

"I think I will. I don't think I could keep my eyes open another minute."

"I'm going to finish the movie then I'll be off to bed myself," she said. I got up and kissed her on the cheek.

"Merry Christmas, Ma. I love you."

"Merry Christmas to you too, sweetheart. I love you, too...and thank you for those beautiful new appliances," she replied as I headed up the stairs to my old room. I knew what that meant and let loose a huge sigh when I got to the top of the stairs.

You don't love someone all your life and not know them. She was going to finish the movie to make sure we were both asleep. Then she'd go to her room and get ready for bed. She'd take my father's picture and talk to him, telling him how much she missed him, how worried she was about me...and cry.

My heart broke for her, her loneliness and her grief . . . and my own. Through all of it, all the anger and guilt I'd felt over his death for so many years, and for all I had been through in those long past weeks... and especially that night, I missed him and needed him, too. I could only imagine the enormity of her loss compared to mine.

In the end, I was helpless. There was nothing I could do to comfort her. I just sat on my bed and cried until I was dry. The last thing I remember before sleep over took me was seeing his face, the strength in his eyes and in his smile as he waved to me from his car the last time I saw him, wishing I'd had one last chance to tell him how I really felt about him.

❊ ❊ ❊

I slept the sound, blissful, undisturbed sleep of a child that night, waking around ten to the smell of bacon frying downstairs, but it was a fool's sleep. The kind one has when they're completely unaware that the other shoe is about to fall. So, in the end, I guess I should have been more than a little at home there, but just didn't know it. I got up, washed, dressed and went downstairs. Martin was already up and sitting at the kitchen table talking to my mother while she cooked at the stove.

"Good morning, Chief," he said, as cheerfully as I had ever heard him.

"Good morning, sweetheart." I heard from around the corner by the stove.

"Ho, Ho, Ho," I said, taking a seat. Martin poured me a cup of coffee from a pot on the table. I lit myself a smoke to go with it.

"It's a lovely day out," Mom said. "So what are we going to do with it?"

"I don't know, Ma. What would you like to do?" I asked, already aware that there was something brewing.

"Now that you mention it, I was wondering if you wouldn't mind driving me over to church for the noon service. All my friends will be there and I'd love to be able to tell them all about my new things. They'll be just green with envy," she said, knowing she could have whatever she wanted that morning.

"Sure, Ma, no problem," I said.

"I could always get a ride home from one of the girls, so you won't have to pick me up," she said, not wanting to sound demanding.

"If that's what you want, Ma, it's fine with me. If you wanna call me, I'll be here and I'll come get ya. Whatever you want is fine by me."

She turned around smiling from the stove with a large plate full of scrambled eggs and bacon in one hand and a plate full of toast and hash browns in the other, and set them on the table.

"You boys go ahead and eat. I've got to start getting ready, and at my age that may take a while," she said, beginning to sound rushed.

"Aren't you going to eat?" I asked.

"Oh, I'm not very hungry this morning. You go ahead and help yourselves. We can open the presents when I come down," she said as she went out. I looked at Martin and was going to say, "Dig in," but he was already way ahead of me so I went about the business of stuffing my own face.

We didn't talk while we ate. It'd been the first time we'd been alone since the afternoon before and I think we were both more than a little uncomfortable. Neither of us had had a chance to say a word about what happened at the house. He pushed back from the table, lit a cigarette and looked at me questioningly. The spark of life was back in his eyes, but there was still a darkness lurking behind them.

"What did you do, Terry?" he asked. I sat back, took a cigarette for myself, flicked the lighter and held it for a minute. He looked at it.

"It's over," I said.

He was silent for a moment then asked, "You burned it?" to confirm what he was thinking.

"To the ground, son," I said and took a drag of my smoke. The darkness went out of his eyes, replaced by relief and...anger.

"Good!" he said defiantly.

I went on, "But I have to go out this afternoon and take care of things. I'm gonna do it after I drop my mother off at church. If she calls here looking for me later, you'll have to stall her and call me on my cell phone." He nodded in agreement. We talked a little while about having to report it to the fire department and I asked him whether he had it insured. He did. We'd just finished off the pot of coffee when my mother came down dressed for church in her new Christmas outfit with matching Christmas tree brooch and earrings.

"Okay boys, let's get to the presents. I don't want to be late for church," she said in her usual cheerful voice.

We sat around the tree and she picked up a small box and read the tag, "For my Terry, from Santa Ma," and handed it to me.

I took it and kissed her on the cheek. "Thanks, Ma," I said and opened it. It was a gold cross on a chain, plain, simple and large enough to suit my chest. "It's beautiful, Ma. I love it," I said, hugging her and kissing her on the cheek again. It was her way of telling me that she was worried about me again. I took it like a man and put it on, having recently found a new respect for her beliefs.

"It makes me feel so much better," she said, smiling contentedly. I smiled back, genuinely touched for reasons she couldn't know, much less understand. Then she said, "Oh look," and took another small box from under the tree and read the tag, "To Martin, from Santa Ma," she said, putting her hand to her chest and looking at him in an expression of feigned surprise.

"Oh, Mrs. C, You shouldn't have," he said with real surprise, struggling to stand and take the box from her.

"Oh, yes I should have…and I did," she smiled triumphantly, feeling very pleased with herself. "Go ahead and open it." It was another cross, smaller and made in delicate gold filigree.

"Oh, it's beautiful!" he said and stood back up to hug her, kiss her on the cheek and receive hers. He was genuinely touched. They both were.

"Wear it in good health," she said. "After all you've been through lately, a boy like you could use some special protection," she said, looking him deeply in the eyes and touching his cheek.

"I love it," he said. "I'll wear it always. I promise."

She was very pleased with that and I was pleased with her. She's a remarkable woman, my mom. After dealing with the pain and suffering of others all her life, the ones no one else wants to deal with, damaged castoffs and broken spirits…surviving my father's death when others of less substance would have crumbled…loving a son whom she had to know was crippled in so many ways…she still had love in her heart to spare and give away. She's a woman of true substance, my mom. I'll always be very proud of everything she's done in her life.

"But I haven't had a chance to get anything for you..." Martin said, sounding embarrassed.

I jumped in then. "Don't worry, Martin. Before you know it, she'll have you out there sweating your ass off in the hot sun working in her garden out back. My mom likes to call in her markers when she needs 'em," I said and laughed, knowing it to be a totally true statement. *Like mother, like son!* I thought and smiled to myself. "She'll getcha!"

"As a matter of fact," she said, "I do know of a certain Police Chief who's been too busy to plant a summer garden for his dear old mother for the last few years, so maybe that wouldn't be a bad idea." She said, probably thinking that a little sun would go a long way in ridding Martin of his 'City' paleness.

Martin smiled brightly, nodded his consent to the contract and said, "It'll be my pleasure, Mrs. C. I'm from New Jersey, remember? They don't call it the Garden State for nothing and it's been a long time since I've gotten my hands dirty," and we all laughed.

Good boy!

Then it was off to church. From there, I had to go back...to the house. God knows, I didn't want to have to go back there but I had no choice because, as skilled a liar as I had become lately, I had to make sure that when I called the Fire Chief that I knew what I was talking about. I couldn't afford any screw ups, so after I dropped my mother off at church, I headed for Randolph Road dreading every second that brought me closer to it.

I was there a few minutes later, pulling into the drive and holding my breath that nothing had gone wrong. When I saw the spot where the house should have been, I was more relieved than I had ever remembered being in my life. It was gone. There was nothing left but a great pile of burned rubble, no smoke, no burning embers. It was complete, with most of it collapsing into the basement hole. It was almost poetic in its completeness . . . and the garden house, too. Gone.

I stopped just as I reached the end of the drive, took out my trusty cell phone and made the call. My end went something like this.

"Hello, Ed. Terry Chagford here. I don't mean to spoil your holiday, Ed, but it seems we've had a fire...over here on

Randolph Road...Yeah...the house at the end just before you hit
the Hamilton line...Yeah, I'm there now...No, no, no... It's over.
Must have burned itself out during the night...No, no one was
hurt...the owner? Martin Welliver... you know, the guy who
crashed into the river a few months ago...Yeah, him...no...he
was over at my mother's spending the holiday with us...No, no,
Ed. He can barely walk. I picked him up to bring him my
mother's myself yesterday afternoon...my guess would be
burglars or vandals...maybe the same bunch that's been hittin'
the cemetery ...yeah, it's completely out..."

"No, we didn't get any calls. Did you? ...No, no smoking, no
smoldering embers. Nothing. It's cold, and there doesn't seem to
be any surrounding damage because of all the snow...yeah, I
was bringing him back home when we came on it...yeah...he's
here with me now...Nah, I wouldn't say there was a need to
come out today, but if you want to, help yourself...yeah...I'll
canvass the perimeter for about fifty or a hundred feet and see if
I can find anything. I'll send some of my men over tomorrow to
do a wider search..."

"Yeah...I'm going to take him back to my mother's in a little
while. He's kinda shook up about it...Yeah, I'm sure you can
imagine...Yeah, it's fine...if you want, you might send one of
your guys over here tomorrow morning to inspect it and collect
some samples to send to Albany for analysis...yeah, it'd be my
guess something was used...no, not a stick standing...must have
gone up like a tinderbox...yeah, an all wood structure."

"It was old...nah, there's no danger, but just to be sure I'll
put up some police tape to close off the driveway, more to
preserve any evidence and keep sightseers out than anything
else...yeah, it's set back about three hundred feet or so from the
road... yeah, just tell your guys to look for the police tape on
the left side of the road about a half mile from the Hamilton line
when they come out tomorrow...okay, Ed, yeah...I'll talk to you
tomorrow. Yeah...I will... yeah. Merry Christmas to you, too. Kiss
Nancy for me," and I hung up. *Okay, that's done.*

I took a quick walk around the edge of the burned hole just
so I could say that I did and mean it when fate took a turn in my
favor. Maybe a sign that my luck was changing. As I scuffed at
the ashes and dirt with my foot around the area where the front

door had been, I saw one of the bullets I used to blow the door open. *Damn!* I'd completely forgotten about them. Bullets from my gun left at the scene would definitely have been the last nail in my coffin. There'd have been no way I could've explained those away, so I scuffed around the area some more until I found the other two and put them safely in my pocket. Now it was perfect. *Whew!*

When I got back to my mother's, I went in and looked for Martin on the sofa. He wasn't there, but I heard the clinking and clanging sound of pots and dishes from the kitchen. "Martin?" I called out.

"In here, Chief!" his voice came out from the kitchen.

"Hey, whatcha doin'?" I asked and headed in that direction.

"I was feeling much better, so I thought I'd clean up the breakfast dishes and do some other things so your mother wouldn't have to work so hard when she comes home," he said with his back to me, his hands moving in the sink.

"Well, that's very thoughtful of you, Martin. I'm sure she'll appreciate that," I said, finding myself increasingly more impressed with 'my newest stray.'

"Lila called to thank you for the Christmas bouquet you sent. She's really a sweet girl and a real giggler too, isn't she?" he asked, laughing.

"That she is," I agreed.

"And your mother called. She said to tell you that she was over at Hannah's. She's going to stay for lunch over there. She said Hannah would bring her home on her way over to her daughter's for the holiday. She'll be home in about an hour or so."

"Sounds great to me," I said pouring myself a cup of coffee from the steaming pot he'd obviously just made and sitting myself down at the kitchen table.

There was a brief silence, then with his back still turned away from me he said, "With all that's gone on, I haven't had a chance to think...or think clearly anyway," and paused. "Now that the house is gone, I don't have anywhere to go," he stopped.

So that was what was on his mind, I thought. Time for another one of my quick fixes. "Don't worry, Martin...you can come and stay at my place until we sort things out. You know I wouldn't let you fall on your face, now don'tcha?" I asked him sincerely.

"I know you wouldn't, Chief…but I have plenty of money," he said as if he was trying to show me he wasn't completely helpless.

"Good…then you can buy us a pizza this week…sausage, peppers and mushrooms…and make it a large. Now that you mention it, make it two if that makes you feel better," I said, trying to lighten him up a little. I could tell he was starting to feel displaced again, never a good place to be. He went on washing and drying then changed the subject.

"Oh! and Jenny called. She said to thank you for the large box of chocolates you sent for Christmas, and she emphasized 'large.' She said to tell you that the boys were thrilled with it, particularly since she doesn't allow them to eat much candy and never keeps any in the house. She said for you to remind her to add another big pinch to the one she already owes you the next time she sees you, and she laughed," he told me.

"That's my girl," I said, relieved that she was feeling back to herself enough to threaten me with another pinch.

"And she thanked me for the beautiful bouquet of long-stemmed white roses I sent her. She said with all I had going on, she was touched that I would remember her that way."

I stopped and I swallowed hard. *Damn!* With all that I had swirling around in my poor addled brain, I'd completely forgotten to tell him what I'd done. "Martin, I'm sorry. I meant to tell you…I hope she didn't catch you too much by surprise and spoil it."

"No. Actually, there'd be very little you could do that could ever surprise me anymore, Chief," he said, still without turning around. "And I'm a lawyer, remember? I'm quick on the upswing, but I need you to do one other little thing for me. I need you to take your coffee in the other room and occupy yourself there while I finish up in here. I need the table space to peel potatoes and carrots for dinner," he said letting out a small chuckle and wiping his nose on his sleeve, still not turning to face me.

"No sooner said than done." I picked up my coffee and stood up.

"Oh…and your mother left you your vitamins there on the

table by the salt and pepper. I had mine this morning before you got up. Good luck!" he said, chuckling again. I was glad he didn't see the face I made at that. It probably would have scared him. I just picked up the pile and left.

"Gotcha."

When I got to the sofa and sat down, I picked up the TV Guide and saw that the old sword and sandal flick *Jason and the Argonauts* was the afternoon holiday movie and just about to start. *Perfect!* I thought, *two hours of completely harmless magical nonsense.* I've always loved that stuff. I could take my boots off, put my feet up and be in 'hog heaven' for a little while. About an hour later Martin limped in with a plate of lettuce, sliced tomatoes, red onion and thinly sliced pieces of steak and set it down on the coffee table in front of me.

"Lunch!" he said proudly. "Cold steak salad with mustard vinaigrette." I looked up at him and smiled, trying desperately to contain the mirth welling in my throat.

"Thanks," I said and thought *Cold steak salad with mustard vinaigrette, huh? That's a New Yorker for ya.* I devoured it, nonetheless, as I watched the great god Neptune rise out of the sea to save the Argonauts from the crumbling cliffs. It was a damn good salad, too. My mother came in just as the film was ending, looking tired.

"So how are my boys getting on this afternoon?" she said as she saw me stretched out on the sofa. "Where's Martin?" I just pointed to the kitchen. She went in. "Oh, I can see you boys have been busy while I was out," she said, impressed that anyone had done anything while she was gone. I hate it when she calls me a boy but whaddaya gonna do? By then, I was standing behind her in the kitchen doorway.

"Wasn't me," I said. "I've been too busy in there struggling to get down those horse vitamins you left me." Then I put on my best hill folk accent and said, "But Maw, Martin o'er thar did fix me up one of them fancee salads them hah toned folks down in Noo Yawk eat. It was deelisheeeus!" She looked at me as if I'd completely cracked. Martin gave a great guffaw from across the room. It was hearty and loud and sounded good. He was getting better.

"Isn't he the silliest thing, Martin? I don't know where he gets that from. It sure wasn't me," she said, laughing herself. She was right. I was feeling silly and it felt good, damn good. I was getting better, too. I hadn't had a pain pill or a drink all day.

"I've already peeled the potatoes and carrots, Mrs. C. They're in cold water in the fridge," he said to her.

"Oh, thank you so much, Martin. That was very thoughtful of you," she said, giving me a sly sideways glance clearly meaning that I should have done it. "I must admit, I am feeling a bit tired today. I don't think I slept too well last night, so if you boys don't mind, I think I'll take a short nap before I start dinner...and Terry, if you could chop me a large onion and fry it up with some bacon and mushrooms for the stuffing, I'd appreciate it. You know how I do it," she said, putting her hand gently on my arm as she went out to go upstairs.

"No problem, Ma. I'll take care of it. No problem."

"Thank you, sweetheart," she said and was gone. No...I don't imagine she slept well that night at all.

"Okay, Hazel," I said to Martin with a smug laugh. "Why don't you go take a load off and have a cup of coffee or something while I get this done."

He poured himself a cup, went and sat at the kitchen table, lighting a cigarette. A second later, trying to imitate my hill folk accent, he said, "Don't mahnd if ah doo, ah always woahnted to see how you cuntree folk go about yur down home cookin."

"Ha!" I laughed out loud. "Touché!"

After I got going with the frying, I decided I'd give Mom a break and just go ahead and finish the dinner. I figured if I got the bird in the oven then, it would be well on its way to being done before she got up and there'd be only a few things left to do to get dinner ready after that. It was about three thirty by then and I'd found I'd spoken too soon. I had to take two Advil and give Martin two with his antibiotic. That set us right about cocktail hour, so I cracked us a few beers and we went and watched the last hour or so of *The 7th Voyage of Sinbad* in peace.

Just as the film was finishing, I was surprised by a knock at the door. I sure wasn't expecting anyone, particularly since, in my experience, it usually meant trouble. I was even more surprised when I opened it to find Grace Coutraire standing there wearing a mink coat and matching hat like the kind Jackie

Kennedy used to wear when she was First Lady.

"Grace!" I said, the surprise at seeing her still in my voice.

"Merry Christmas, Terry," she said smiling. I opened the door to let her in and kissed her on the cheek. "I take it Charlotte didn't tell you I'd be coming over," she said, taking off her coat, hat and scarf, her perfume wafting under my nose.

"No, I'm afraid she didn't, but that's no matter. I'm always pleased to see you," I said, then, "Especially lately," under my breath.

"Thank you, Terry. Charlotte said you'd asked her to call me. I was so pleased to hear from her, as I'm sure you can appreciate," she said with a wink. "Then when she asked if I had plans for the holidays and invited me over to join you all for Christmas dinner...well, what could I say? To be surrounded by two such handsome young men and such a charming hostess...It just sounded too lovely," she said as I led her in and offered her a seat.

"You remember Martin Welliver" I said, feeling the need to make the gesture of reintroducing him. Martin didn't know about my meeting with Grace, or anything she'd told me.

"Yes, of course. Good to see you again, Martin. How are you?" she asked him as he struggled to raise himself up to greet her like a gentleman before she sat down.

"Much better, ma'am. Thank you," he said, taking her hand and bowing slightly.

"Yes, I see. Your recovery seems to be coming along nicely," she said, giving me a short glance and smile of approval as they took their seats. When I offered her a drink, she replied, "Some tea might be nice...oh, and by the way Chief, I would have felt so embarrassed to have come to dinner empty handed, but on such short notice, the best I could do was to bring you this..." and her eyes twinkled as she pulled a plastic carrier bag from the beside her chair. It was the tall slender bottle of Armagnac from the afternoon before. I hadn't noticed it when she came in.

She looked at Martin and said, "It's very old brandy. Just the thing to warm up a cold Christmas night," then smiled and winked at me again.

You're a good old girl, I thought, smiling back as I put the bottle on the table.

"Let me put the water on and get some cups set up," I told them and went to the kitchen to try my hand at making a proper tea.

When I returned, Grace was just saying to Martin, "The turkey smells wonderful. I've always heard that Charlotte was a brilliant cook. I hope she hasn't gone to too much trouble just for me."

Then it was my turn. "Yes, she is a terrific cook, but I'm afraid I have to take responsibility for this bird. Mom is still taking a nap upstairs, so I took the liberty..."

"Oh, I hope I'm not intruding. Is Charlotte not feeling well?" she asked, genuinely concerned.

"I'm sure she'll be fine," I assured her. "She was just up early this morning then it was off to church, then over to Hannah's for brunch. She's just a little tired, that's all."

"Brunch?" Martin mouthed to me silently with a silly grin. I glared at him and turned my attention back to Grace.

"I'm sure she'll be down in an hour or so. In the meantime, it gives us some time to have a drink and to talk. I've been meaning to hear the end of your story." I went back into the kitchen and came back with her tea. "I'm not much of a tea drinker, Grace, so I don't know how well it came out. I hope you don't mind," I said, probably sounding as inept as I felt.

"Of course not, dear boy...after all, I just use it to hold the brandy. Ladies in my day always did it that way," she said, giving me another sly wink as I added some to her tea before pouring drinks for Martin and myself.

✻ ✻ ✻

Once we were settled, I looked at Martin and said, "Grace was just telling me the story of her life the other day. It was fascinating." I cast my attention toward Grace then. "You were just telling me that your author friend had just passed and you still had his last play." My caginess in avoiding specifics wasn't wasted on her, and as we sat by the warmth of the fireplace with the Christmas tree lights blinking, she began where she'd left off the day before.

"Oh, yes, Terry, I did want you to know that there was a

happy ending to the story. It wasn't all so sad, not for me anyway." She looked at Martin and spoke. "I had an author friend once, Martin. He died unexpectedly, here in Jennisburg, just as he was about to finish a play I was helping him work on. Well, anyway, a few weeks after he...passed, a young man from New York called on me. Apparently, he was Norman's literary agent and a close friend as well. It seems he had found some notes of the play Norman and I were working on over at the..." She paused, thinking for a moment, then said, "...that Norman had left lying around. As it turns out Norman had discussed our...relationship... with this man, Abraham Levi was his name, and after a little while, he found me."

She was looking at me then, smiling. "I can't imagine that it was too difficult in a town the size it was then. He asked me if I knew of anything Norman might have been working on at the time of...his passing."

"I was concerned at first, hesitating to be too truthful with him until he pulled a document out from his jacket pocket. 'There's no need to worry, Mrs. Coutraire,' he said. 'I've been Norman's friend since his early days in New York and have never been particularly fond of his...widow. I'm not here to hurt you. That piece of paper is his Will...and you're in it,' he said to me."

"Well, I was stunned, to say the least. Norman must have made it just before he died. He must have known. Somewhere inside him he must have known he was going to die," she said, looking directly at me like she still couldn't believe it all happened. "Then, when I recovered myself and looked it over, I discovered it was a Will, and it was signed with Norman's signature, so I took the chance to trust this man for the moment and sat down to read it. It turned out that Norman had left me all the rights to his last novel, '*Nowhere But Here.*' He'd also left me all the rights to our play. '*A Town Like Time,*' it was called." She took a moment for a sip of tea then asked if I minded if she had a cigarette. I handed her one of mine and lit it for her. She went on.

"The young man told me that when the actual play wasn't found in any of Norman's effects, he began to wonder if I had any idea where it might be. He was very delicate about it, but it was clear he knew to come to me for a reason, which is to say,

Martin, that he knew I was Norman's mistress," she said in a tone I think she used to intentionally try and shock him. I looked at Martin, watching him struggle valiantly not to blush at Grace's frankness, but I could see it in his face as he turned his head, smiling to himself. After all, he hadn't had the benefit of seeing Grace's photographs to know what a desirable young woman she'd been and appreciate her the way I could.

Grace went on without skipping a beat. By then she was glancing alternately between both of us as she spoke. We were a rapt audience and she knew it. "It seems that, with Norman's growing reputation and all of the publicity surrounding his 'problem' with the government, along with the fact that it was his last work, there was significant interest in producing the play on Broadway, so with the Will in my hand, I got up, went to my coat closet and brought down the bag with the folder. The young man punched the air with excitement when I turned my back. He thought I didn't see, silly boy. He must have guessed all along that I had it."

"Well, not to drag things out too much, the play ended up being produced a year or so later and turned out to be very successful. They did some editing, but for the most part, they kept it intact. I even went to the Opening Night. It was a marvelous experience. For the first time, I saw what Norman must have seen in me. At the time he was writing it, I hadn't thought the character he said he'd created after me bore much resemblance on paper, but when I saw it performed, I could see exactly what he saw and realized, probably for the first time, how he deeply he must have loved me. It made me feel that I'd actually given him something worthwhile of myself before he died, something valuable that he saw in me that inspired his creativity, and I fell in love with him all over again. Later on, both the novel and the play were made into successful films and I've never had to think about money since."

Martin looked at Grace engrossed and said, "I saw that play. It was in revival a few years ago at the Roundabout Theater in New York. It was intense. I loved it...and the character of 'Faith'...that was you?"

"Yes, Martin. That was me. When I was young and in love...at a time when the world, and this country, had been torn apart, not only by the war, but by itself afterward...a lifetime ago."

Martin nodded as if he were thinking, "Yes, I can see it now." Grace's face glowed with pride in the firelight. As for me, I don't know the first thing about theater. I just wanted to hear more of her story, "But you said there was a happy ending," I broke in.

"Yes, there was. Only I wasn't to know it for another six years after Norman," she replied, clearly endeared by our interest. She looked back to me...deeply, into my eyes.

"I've learned in my life that there are many kinds of love in these, our lives, and that one doesn't necessarily have to be eighteen years old, or twenty-two years old, or even forty years old to find a love that can be unique to them, for them. I was close to the far side of thirty-five and had lost all hope in the possibility of love...for the second time after Norman died. After all, with my track record...well, the writing seemed to be on the wall, so after Norman, I gave up."

I shuddered at being forced to recall the concept. *If you only knew, Grace. If you only knew.* I thought at that moment, but then she was speaking again.

"Then I met Lance Jamison while I was shopping one day over at Hamilton Common. I was just standing there admiring a dress in a store window and when I turned around, there he was, standing there staring at me, a big, strong, well-built man of forty-five, dressed very smartly in tweeds. It was like magic, all over again. As it turned out, he was a very prosperous gentleman farmer from the far side of Hamilton. He had big strong hands, a broad chest and a rugged handsomeness to him. Oh, and he had such a glorious sparkle in his eyes. So unlike Hugh." She turned then to Martin. "That was my husband, Martin. He was killed in the war," she said, skipping over it quickly to keep herself together on the subject.

"And he was so unlike Norman, too. He was what they called in my day 'a man's man,' gruff in manner, but gentle in nature," she said and looked at me, "Very much like our Chief here. I've often thought recently how much you remind me of him," she said reaching over to pat my hand, smiling. It was my turn to blush. She had the strangest way of doing that to me. She took another cigarette from the table and I lit it.

"Lance and I spent over twenty-five years loving each other... discreetly, of course," she said looking at Martin to make sure he got her point. "He was a widowed father of three young children at the time. His wife had died a number of years before giving birth to their last child, Julia, named after her." It was Martin's turn to flinch then pass it off.

"We never married because he didn't want them to think he was bringing in another woman to replace their mother, and by the time we realized that we never wanted to be apart, I was almost forty. In those days for a woman of that age to have children was still dangerous for both the woman and the child, not like today, so any reason for us to marry was gone with the wind as they say," she said, waving her hand dismissingly as was her habit.

"But I was satisfied. As a matter of fact, Lance gave me the emerald set I wore on Thanksgiving. He gave me that particular set after we'd decided it was best not to marry. He told me that he didn't want me to think that his love for me was in any way cheap because we didn't marry, and that our time together meant everything to him. He was always very generous with me, both during his life...and after his death. I think he wanted to make up for what we didn't have...a home together and children of our own." she said. Her eyes got teary and vacant for a few seconds, as if she could hear a voice somewhere off in the distance calling her name and was reaching to catch it. Then she was back again.

"Lance was the only one who ever called me Gracie," she said, shaking her head as she smiled in fond remembrance. 'Come on, Gracie,' he would say to me, 'it looks like yer just about out of that fancee perfume of yours. Let's go to Paris for a week and git ya some more. Whaddaya say, darlin'?' Then we'd go and he'd take me to the Louvre and spend hours showing me his favorite paintings and sculptures. I've never felt as secure in my life as I did while holding onto Lance's arm as we walked together." Her expression spoke volumes as she tried to imitate his voice. She still loved him deeply and must have missed him almost beyond endurance in the twenty odd years that had passed since his death.

"I had the most complete love I'd ever had in my life with

Lance and never regretted a moment of it. When he died, it was quietly in his sleep...of a stroke. Of course, by then he was just over seventy, so it had a sense of naturalness to it, but I grieved as much as I ever thought I would again. There were times I even thought I would die from sheer loneliness at the thought of having to go on without him."

She paused then, took a deep breath, sighed and said, "And soon it will be my time, and I want you two youngsters to know something. When one lives their life fully and completely, as I have, and have loved with all their might, and lived their lives the best that they could, when you reach my age...or anywhere near it," she said waving her hand again with a laugh, "and everyone you've ever loved is gone, the end can be a blessing, a relief...a release." As she finished, I could see Martin's eyes well up. I don't know how I did because mine were full, too. On that note, I poured us all another drink and we stood and toasted.

"To life and to love!" Grace said, with Martin and me raising our glasses to follow her. "To life and to love, Grace."

That was when we heard from the end of the stairwell, "To life and to love, Grace. Merry Christmas to us all and thank you, I couldn't have said it better myself." It was my mother standing there smiling, looking well rested, and ready for her company.

From there, Mom came and joined us for a few drinks and reminisced with Grace about women's things...clothes fads and hair styles. Then it was on to favorite movie stars. They debated who was the more handsome, Clark Gable or James Dean. I think at last they decided it was neither Gable nor Dean, but settled on Gregory Peck.

They talked of things long past but not forgotten by those who lived through them, about how in 1962, the world's most famous blonde movie star bombshell could traipse herself on stage at Madison Square Garden, clearly wrecked out of her gourd and wearing little more than a few well placed sequins to sing "Happy Birthday, Mr. President" while an innocent country cheered. Then forty odd years later having to watch the same type of President go on national television and debase himself by denying that he ever had, "sexual relations with *that* woman" and a week later being forced to do it again. This time to confess that he did, indeed, have improper relations with "that woman" while a hypocritical country booed.

They both got misty eyed talking about how the most popular woman in the world, "the People's Princess," could put aside her own unhappiness and unselfishly use her influence to benefit the unfortunates of world, and then be murdered, in one form or another, by the very world she tried to help, with no one being held accountable.

By then, there was no doubt that the old girls were getting tipsy together. Martin and I just listened quietly, not having nearly the experience to offer insightful comment on the things they were discussing. Luckily for Martin, just as they were moving on to the touchy subject of World Trade Center attacks, the timer on the oven went off announcing that the turkey was done.

Mom was certainly well rested and a few cocktails made her lighthearted at what would have otherwise been a lonely time for her. As the evening wore on, it looked like we were going to have two rollicking old broads on their way to being a couple of handfuls by the end of dinner, but by then I was sure that we'd all be. So to get a jump on things before it started to snowball, I took Mom by the arm and we excused ourselves to the kitchen for the hour it took to finish dinner, leaving Martin and Grace to their own devices…to talk about…who knows…'tapénade' and 'revivals' or 'cold steak salads with mustard vinaigrette,' I suppose.

But when I went back to tell them dinner was ready, Martin was leaning over with his head in his hands. Grace had her hand on his arm and was leaning over into him, whispering quietly in his ear. When he looked up as I came though the door, I got the feeling he was riding the crest of an emotion I couldn't place. Maybe it was just the firelight or the blinking of the Christmas lights reflecting in his eyes, but it troubled me, and before I could say anything Grace looked up at me. "Thank you, Terry. We'll be right in. Martin will escort me, won't you, dear?" she said in a tone that left no room for doubt. She wanted me to leave them alone, so I went back in and got things ready, but I couldn't shake the feeling that they were talking about…me.

Dinner was a great success. Everyone, either in truth, out of politeness or inspired by the drinks, praised my turkey and stuffing, and a sense of good fellowship raised up the evening for all of us, a feeling that was sorely needed all the way around. After dinner, we had coffee and cake around the tree before I went to take Grace home. By then it was late, close to eleven.

The car ride on the way over was the first time Grace and I had to be alone since the conversation at her house the afternoon before. She filled it by telling me how pleased she was that Mom was looking so well, how lovely she kept the house, and that she was much relieved to see Martin looking well on his way to recovery.

I pulled into her drive and got out to open her door and help her out. As I stood with her on her doorstep for the moment while she opened her front door, she looked at me with water in her earnest, pale green eyes and said, "And by the way, Sylvia Hadrada stopped by late this afternoon to wish me happy holidays and invite me over to spend it with her and Harry but, of course, I had already accepted Charlotte's invitation. She mentioned that she'd heard through the grapevine that there was a house fire somewhere over on Randolph Road and was wondering if it was the place she sold to that nice young man from New York." I heard a sharpness come into her voice and the same bitterness I had seen the day before return to her face.

"You burned it. Didn't you?"

"To the ground, Grace," I said. "To...the...ground."

"And the bracelet?"

"Right along with it," I said, watching a look of relief come into her face.

"You're a good man, Terrence Chagford. God bless you," she said in a tone that made me, for that moment, believe it.

"Thank you, Grace," I said. "That means a great deal coming from a woman like you."

At that she stepped over the threshold, turned to me with a sparkle in her eye and a mischievous smile on her lips and said, "And you're such a damned handsome devil, too." Then she kissed her fingertips and touched my lips with them before shutting the door. I stood there for a moment feeling the color rise up in my face all the way from my toes. That old woman had the strangest affect on me and, although I wasn't to know it for close to a week afterwards, it would be the last time she would ever touch me, but her voice, and her words, there would be more of those still to come.

By the time I got home, Martin and Mom had the kitchen cleaned up, the leftovers were put away and they were pretty much ready for bed. I walked with Mom up the stairs figuring it was as good a time as any to tell her the news, some truth, some lie. I couldn't risk her hearing it somewhere else first and becoming suspicious. After all, I was the Police Chief.

"Ma, can we talk for a minute," I asked quietly.

"Sure, sweetheart," she said.

"I had some 'not so great' news this afternoon." I could see the look of concern coming over her face.

"Okay . . . ?"

"Martin's house burned to the ground last night."

"Oh, my God!" she said putting her hand to her mouth.

"I went over there this afternoon to pick up some things for him and found it."

"Oh, the poor boy! Does he know?" she asked, moving her hand to the side of her face, trying to absorb what I'd just told her.

"Yes...I told him before you got home this afternoon," I said, struggling not to sound like I was lying.

"How did he take it? Oh, that poor boy!"

"He was pretty shaken up for a while, but I promised him that I would make sure that his insurance would cover it. It looked like burglars or vandals to me. I've already reported it to Ed Ward and he's going to take some samples over to Albany to find out the exact cause...and I told Martin that he could come stay with me at my place until we could get him settled somewhere else, so he's okay," I said, finding it increasingly hard to keep lying to her.

"But why didn't you say anything sooner?"

"There was nothing you could do Ma, and Martin and I decided that the last thing either of us wanted was to upset your holiday. Actually, it was Martin who insisted that we wait until later to tell you and I just agreed." It made me feel better to lay a little of it on him.

"Oh that poor boy," she said again, "and after all he's been through."

"Please don't worry, Ma. I'll take care of everything. You know I've never been able to turn away a stray," I said, forcing a crooked smile for her.

"I know you will, dear. I raised a good boy. Martin is lucky to have someone like you to look after him," she said and kissed me on the cheek. "It's no wonder you were so edgy today."

Praise twice in one night, lies and all, I thought to myself on the way to my old room. *I must be on a roll.* Of course, I didn't know then that what I was rolling toward was the edge of yet another kind of hell.

※ ※ ※

The next day after work, I gathered up Martin and we went back to my place. Things went on as normal for the next few days. I met Ed Ward out at...where the house 'used' to be. "Well, whaddaya know?" was pretty much all he kept saying while one of his men collected samples. I had to remind Martin to contact his insurance company, give them his new contact information and leave them with the promise that we would forward the police and fire reports as soon as they were available. Martin settled in nicely, feeling stronger and more confident in his ability to get around, so I let him take an upstairs room. My life seemed to be getting back to its usual grind, but it wasn't for long. When I came in from lunch one day a few weeks ago, I found Lila looking glum, very unlike her smiling, giggling, girlish self. As I came closer to her, I saw that her eyes were...sad, red and...moist. She tried to avoid looking directly at me.

"Chief, can I speak to you in your office?" she said in a very unusual tone for her, flat, colorless. It instantly put my sensors on alert.

"Sure Lila, come on in." She came in and shut the door behind her. I went and sat at my desk. "What is it?" I asked, getting increasingly concerned. My original thought was that she'd heard or had a visit from her ex.

"I had a call a little while ago, Chief...from Sheila Woolf. You know, from over at the library." I knew then, in my heart. I knew.

Lila spoke softly. "Grace didn't show up for the weekly staff meeting this afternoon...and Sheila got concerned. She told me that Grace had never missed a meeting before so she went over to the house," pausing for a moment before she could say it. "Grace passed away last night, Chief." I jumped to my feet feeling like I'd been kicked in the stomach. "Quietly in her sleep," she said, trying to make it easier. I had no words. I just headed around my desk to go out. Lila stepped in my way.

"I know you were close recently, Chief, so I sent Gunner over. He's the newest and he didn't know her. I though it was best. Her doctor is there and Sheila's already contacted her lawyer. He told her he'll begin making the arrangements as soon as he can get here."

I felt like I had nothing left inside, so I did what came naturally. I went back to my desk and pulled my spare bottle out of the drawer and took a nice, long slug.

Lila came over and put her hand on my back and hugged me. "I'm so sorry, Chief...is there anything I can do?" I sat down again, putting my head in my hands.

Just as my eyes filled and I thought I would let go, Grace's voice and her words from Christmas came to my mind. "When you reach my age...or anywhere near it and everyone you've ever loved is gone, the end can be a blessing, a relief...a release." Then I felt it, in my heart. It was...a release. Her release had come. Her blessed, long deserved release had finally come, and wherever she was now, she was loved and at peace.

"I need you to call over to Jenny Denton and please be gentle with her, Lila. She had a...fall...over the holidays and I'm sure she's still not feeling too well. I don't want this to be too much for her. Then I need you to go over to my mother's house and see her...take whatever time you need... We had Grace over for Christmas, you know."

"Yes, I know Chief...is there anything else?" she asked, downcast.

"I need you to call over to the Mayor's office and let them know over there. I'm going over to Kendall's and wait for her there. I want someone to be there when she gets there. Tell the Mayor he can meet me there if he wants. We can discuss what needs to be done with the lawyer when he arrives."

"Yes, Chief," she said and was gone, closing the door behind her.

I took another slug and went to my bathroom to wash my face. I took my half-and-half combo and washed it down with another long slug before leaving to go over to Kendall's. I had to try and keep it together as long as I could, and it was clear that it wasn't going to be getting any easier. Chemicals would definitely be required.

Having sufficiently sedated myself, I met with the lawyer, a man named James Gibb, and Mike Kendall, the funeral director. The Mayor arrived shortly after I did. There was no question that Grace was much loved and well respected by generations of the people in town. Her passing and funeral would be an event with everyone but the transplants and the last crop of school kids participating in paying their respects. It was a Tuesday then. It was decided that there would be one day of viewing with the burial on Friday. It was her request that there be a closed casket, and that she be buried in a plot she had purchased years ago...opposite Lance Jamison.

※ ※ ※

Knowing Grace the way I'd come to recently, it made perfect sense. I thought then about Hugh Coutraire. He was probably taken back to his family in Louisiana, and Norman Harper taken back to California to his wife. Lance Jamison was the only man that Grace could really call her own, even though Jamison's late wife would be on one side and Grace the other. She could be happy with that. Her words and voice rang in my ears again, "I had the most complete love I'd ever had in my life with Lance and never regretted a minute of it." I knew it was right. That having been taken care of, I went home to talk to Martin.

When I got there, he was already on the phone with my mother. When he saw me, he just stopped and stared at me. His eyes were red and he looked pale again. I thought to myself, *That Grace was a woman who loved men and was sure loved in return by them.* Even Martin, who had only known her for a brief time, had been affected by her, and he knew nothing of what I knew. The next few days weren't going to be easy on anyone. I took Mom and Martin out to dinner that night. No one wanted to do much of anything really, especially cook.

The next morning when Martin came down, he asked me to take him into town with me. He wanted me to drop him off at the local men's shop to get some real clothes and he wanted to get a hair cut. When I asked him if he was sure that he could manage it alone and offered to lend one of my suits which, of course, would have been much too big, he looked at me with a determination in his eyes that I had never seen in him before and said,

"There is no way I'm going to that lady's funeral to pay my last respects looking like a cross between Raggedy Andy and Charles Manson. I'll manage...I'll take the cane." The image that conjured made me want to laugh, but I was proud of him and did what he asked. I brought in the bag from my car with what was left of his belongings in it so he could have his bank card or checkbook or whatever he needed. The more we talked, the more he began sounding like the man I'm sure he had been before life spun him out of control.

Later that afternoon he showed up at the station all cleaned up with a bag in one hand and the cane in the other. "I brought lunch," he said, smiling and holding up the bag, then took the nearest seat he could find with a wince and a groan. Since it was only Lila and me there, ate at her desk and somberly discussed the plans for the next few days. We ate Italian subs and tuna sandwiches from the shop around the corner, trying not to show how we were really feeling, as people do at times like that.

Then Martin announced sincerely but 'matter of factly,' "By the way, I've taken the liberty of ordering flowers to be sent over to Kendall's, a blanket of long-stemmed red roses from you, Chief, and a spray of two dozen long-stemmed whites from me." he paused and looked at Lila. "It's a trademark of mine...white roses," he said to her with a sly smile, which I took to be a veiled reference to Jenny and the Christmas flower thing meant exclusively for my benefit. He took a bite and went on, "And a large, bright multicolored assorted arrangement from Mrs. C, so if you could tell her that I've already taken care of it." Then he looked at me and, sounding very much the lawyer asked, "Can we assume you'll be saying a few words at the service, Chief?"

"Yes, I think it would be fair to say that we can assume that, Counselor," I said with a smirk of my own. That was when I first started to think that there was a lot more to our Mr. Martin Welliver, Esquire, than I'd previously thought, or was conveyed in the hospital, at the house, or at my mother's. He really must have been a force to be reckoned with back in his New York days. I could see it at that moment, and was . . . impressed. *Touché! Counselor!*

After we'd eaten, Martin struggled to get out his chair as Lila began to clean up. I went in to my desk and pulled out my local bottle of Advil, handed him three and said, "Big day, huh?"

He took them and swallowed them with the last sip in his glass. "Thanks," he said.

"No problem." I winked at him then I called out to Lila

"Lila, can you call whoever's on duty to give Martin a ride home?"

"Sure, Chief," she called back in. He frowned at me then, frustrated.

"But I have to pick my new clothes up by the end of the day. The suit needed some tailoring," he said, sounding high strung.

"Don't worry...I'll grab them on my way home. You've done enough for one day, Champ," I said, smiling and winking at him again. Once he was gone, Lila came back in and shut the door behind her.

"Why didn't you tell me his house burned down on Christmas Eve? I had to hear about it just now from that witch, Sylvia Hadrada. She just called to talk to you about it. I'm sure she keeps a broom in the trunk of that barge of hers instead of a spare tire. I told her you were 'in conference,'" she said, sounding miffed. "And here I thought working here that I had my hand on the pulse of things in this town," she spouted, regaining her good humor.

"I'm sorry, honey. I've just had my hands full these days...it just seems to be one thing after another," I said sincerely, rubbing my temples. I'd meant to lay better groundwork, but I really did have my hands full lately...to say the least.

"Oh, my poor Chief," she said, sounding kittenish again. "I'll bet you have. Is there anything I can do to help?" she asked, practically purring.

"Nah. Thanks, hon. You already do more than your share around here." With that she left, seemingly satisfied for the moment, but undoubtedly off to find out the details elsewhere. The fire must've been the second most talked about subject in town next to Grace's passing. That was three weeks ago.

CHAPTER 10

Expedio - (Latin: To Release)

"...courage is not the absence of despair, it is, rather, the capacity to move ahead in spite of despair."

-Rollo May,
- 20th Century Existentialist Philosopher

I picked up Martin's things on my way home that night. When I got there, my mother was in the kitchen cooking dinner. I could smell it, the wonderful Hungarian goulash dish she'd been making since I was a kid. God only knows where she got the recipe from. There probably wasn't a real Hungarian for two hundred miles, but it was always a treat for me. I hung Martin's stuff in the closet along with the bag of shoes, socks, and who knows what else, then went and kissed her, grabbing myself a beer from the fridge as soon as my hands were free.

"Ah! Mother of mine," I said with histrionics, "you know how much I love that stuff. Where's Martin?"

"He's upstairs having a lie down to recover from his first day out...by himself. It really drained him, Terry. You really shouldn't have let him go out on his own yet. What if he'd fallen or something?" Now *she* was sounding miffed. I hoped this wasn't going to be a trend.

"He's a big boy, Ma...and besides, he insisted...and I have a job, remember? Next to the Mayor, I'm the guy that runs this place," I said, beginning to feel a little put upon.

"I know, sweetheart. I'm just a worrier, you know," she said, mildly apologetic.

"I know, Ma. I am too. At least you know that's where I get it from…and that's more than I know about your Goo- lahhhh-shhh recipe," I said with a fake naughty laugh.

"That just goes to show you, even your dear old Mom has secrets," she said and laughed, sounding young again for a moment. I'm sure she got it from Family Circle Magazine or the Betty Crocker Cookbook or something like that. She'd never been farther than nursing school in Albany or Niagara Falls on her honeymoon, and no farther than Henriston since my father died. A real hometown girl she is, my mom.   Martin came down a little while later, obviously drawn to the kitchen by the smell of my mother's concoction. "Ummm…smells, wonderful Mrs. C. What's cookin'? I'm starved," he said, sitting down at the table.

"Hungarian goulash…one of my specialties," she said proudly. "It's one of Terry's favorites. It'll be ready in just a few minutes," she said as she set out my mismatched plates and silverware. "So, did you get some nice things to wear on your day out today, Martin?" she asked lighting a cigarette and watching the sauce pot, waiting for it to come to a simmer.

"Yes, I got a nice suit, shirt, tie, shoes…all of it. I didn't have a single thing suitable…under the circumstances."

"And you look so handsome with your new haircut," she told him then looked at me, "and what are you going to wear, sweetheart?"

"I'm just going to wear my old gray Hugo Boss-London suit," I said.

"Oh, that's got to be six or seven years old. Are you sure it still fits?" she asked with a slight nudge, referring to my weight.

"I haven't gained an ounce since I bought it, Ma. I've only worn it three or four times since then. It's practically new. I still wear a lot of the things I've had from back then," I said, pinched by her comment.

"Yes, I know," she said with a distinct air of disapproval as she dished the food into a serving bowl. She wasn't going to let go of this one. "Still, you know you're not a young boy anymore and weight distributes itself differently after a certain age. Just look at me. I used to have a real hourglass figure when I was young. I just want to be sure you look nice, honey. After all, you'll be standing up before the whole town to speak." She had her hands on her hips.

"I will, Ma. You gotta trust me on this one," I said. Martin looked at me, grinning like a Cheshire cat.

"Hugo Boss-London, huh?" he said, raising his eyebrows.

Now *I* was getting miffed, and went into my routine. "Don't be fooled for a minute, my friend," I said, tight lipped. "I wasn't always the beat down wreck of a small town cop you see sitting before you. Believe it or not, there was a time so maybe it was a life time ago when I thought, probably with the help of a few shots of Remy, that I just might rebound and actually become someone in the world," I huffed.

Before I knew it, Mom was on it. "But you are someone," she said indignantly, putting the food on the table. "First of all, you are my son, and secondly, you may not hear the things people around here say about you, but I do, and my friends do and you are, without a doubt, the most respected man in this town...and don't you ever forget that."

"Oh, Ma!" I said in as close to a whine I as could ever manage.

Martin looked at me with a flash of sincerity in his eyes, then made a comical face and shook an exaggerated finger at me saying, "Listen to your mother!" and we both looked at her.

"So there!" she said vindicated, and we all laughed.

"Yes, Mother," I said and began to dig in. Suddenly, there was a crash somewhere upstairs and I jumped up, my nerves jangling like a string of bells as they ran down the length my body. I looked at Martin and could see his startled look, fear returning to his eyes. I collected myself the best I could for my mother's sake and excused myself to go upstairs and see what the hell was going on up there. When I got there, I felt the greatest sense of relief discovering that Martin had apparently left a window open in the hallway and the strong January wind had blown through the curtains knocking over the lamp on the table under the window and sending it crashing to the floor. "Whew!" I sighed wiping my forehead and returning the lamp to its rightful spot, closing the window with a slam before heading back down.

When I got back to the kitchen table, I could tell by the

looks on their faces that I'd interrupted them in mid conversation. "It was nothing. Just a lamp blown over by the wind from the window Martin left open," I said, glaring at him accusingly for being so foolish when we were all so tense.

Sensing my ire, but completely unaware of its implications, my mother spoke first. "Come sit down, sweetheart. I was just starting to tell Martin the story of how I met your father," she said, touching his arm across the table.

"Oh Jeeze, Ma, I'm sure Martin doesn't want to hear old family tales," I said, still irritated from having the piss almost scared out of me...again.

"Actually, I'd love to hear it," Martin said to my mother then looking at me said, "if you don't mind, Chief." Now *he* was miffed at me. *Jesus H. Christ, there must be a fucking epidemic of 'miffing' at me going on around here,* I thought to myself, throwing up my hands in surrender.

"Go ahead, Mrs. C. I'd love to hear your story," he said to her, clearly having won that battle. So she began.

"Well, I was only sixteen and just going into my third year of high school when we met," she said girlishly, directing all her attention toward him and away from me. "It was the first week of school and Zona Budley and I had gone around the school building to have our lunch on the athletic field on the sunny side of the building. The weather was beautiful that day, warm and bright. We were best friends, Zona and I. We were what they called 'bobby soxers' back then. We had pony tails, floppy skirts and saddle shoes. We went to sock hops together, the soda shop and that sort of thing. It must sound so corny by today's standards," she said, the shine of youthful romanticism seeming to wash away the years as she spoke.

"Well, anyway...Zona and I were having our lunch on the field talking 'girl talk', you know, movie stars and school gossip, when Zona gave me a good shot with her elbow. 'Look Charlotte, there's something going on over there,' and pointed over my shoulder over into the field, so I turned my head to look. There was a pile of bodies moving around over in the middle of the field, all arms and legs, punching and kicking, dust flying everywhere. We watched as the security guard and a few of the male teachers ran out there to break the fight up. The teachers pulled out two boys in the leather jackets they used to wear back then, and sent them out away from the school. They were very Marlon Brando in *The Wild One* types. We knew who they were but didn't mix with them. They had their own type of girls. Then the security guard pulled up a third boy and sent him walking in our direction, back toward the school." She took a break then, got up, refilled her coffee cup and lit a cigarette. When she sat back down, she picked up where she left off. Martin ate quietly as he listened.

"Anyway...as the boy the guard sent in our direction came toward us, I could see he was a big, strapping boy in a plaid flannel shirt and blue jeans with his hair all askew. He had dark red hair...auburn really...just like that," she said and turned, pointing to my head.

Martin smiled, nodding his head that he understood. I just looked back down at my plate as Mom went on.

"Well, as he got closer, I could see a cuff mark was already swelling under his eye, and his lip was swollen and bleeding from where he'd been hit. He had a face like the boxers my father used to watch on Saturday night on our little black and white TV. A few minutes later, he walked right past us, then stopped and turned to looked at me. I felt like a bolt of electricity went through me...from my head right down to my toes," she said and flushed. "He had the most beautiful eyes I've ever seen, deep, sea green with thick, feathery lashes, but they were angry and hurt," she said, getting teary and pointing to my face as she had at my hair.

"Jesus H. Christ, Ma," I said, feeling my nerves twinge with embarrassment. I got up to get myself a real drink.

"Will you please let your mother finish?" Martin said to my back, sounding fed up with me. "Go ahead, Mrs. C. I'm listening." My mother just ignored me and went on.

"After he passed us, Zona gave me another sharp elbow. 'Did you see the way he looked at you, Charlotte?' she said grinning. 'Oh Zona, go on,' I said blushing, and gave her a playful push on the shoulder. I was a nice girl and had never had a boyfriend before, but I must admit I couldn't think about anything else the rest of that day. Then after school, while I was waiting on the bus for Zona, she rushed up into the bus and sat down with me. 'So, Charlotte, do you want to know his name?' she asked, toying with me. 'Not particularly,' I said, playing coy, 'but if you want to tell me, I'll listen,' and we both laughed. 'His name is Arthur Chagford and his family just moved here from Philadelphia,' she said, going out of her way to sound like a know-it-all. 'He's a senior in my sister Karen's homeroom. Whattaya think of that?' and she pinched my leg, giggling."

"I couldn't get my mind off the angry, hurt look in his eyes all that evening. By the next morning, I'd decided that if I ran into him that day, I'd gather up the courage to speak to him, and I did. When I walked into the cafeteria that day for lunch, he was there sitting all by himself at an empty table over in the corner of the room with his head down. Well, I gathered up all my courage and went over to him with my tray. 'I'm Charlotte Gilbert. Do you mind if I sit here?' I asked him, hoping I sounded as confident as I'd planned. 'Why would you want to?' he asked, looking up at me with that dark brooding look in his eyes."

"The question caught me off-guard. I searched as quickly as I could for something to say then found it. 'Because I think it was a very brave thing you did yesterday. Coming to a new town and a new school, then having to stand up for yourself like that can't be easy. It says a lot about you, Arthur, good things.' All of a sudden his eyes changed. They weren't angry, or hurt, or brooding anymore. They were gentle and kind...and accepting. Please forgive an old woman her romantic fantasies, Martin, but at that moment, I thought I could see the whole world in his eyes. Doesn't that sound crazy?" she asked, directing the question to Martin alone.

"Not at all, Mrs. C. I know exactly what you mean," he said, not taking his eyes from her. I was about to put up another protest when Martin looked over at me as if to say 'don't even think about it,' so I held my tongue and let her go on with it.

"Then he did something no one had ever done for me before. He stood up and held his hand out to offer me a seat. It was the first time anyone had ever treated me like a real lady. I'm sure I blushed, but he didn't let on that he noticed. I sat down opposite him and we spent the rest of the time talking about different things. He told me that he was from Philadelphia. His father was in the military police in the war and they'd just moved to Jennisburg so his father could take a job at the glass factory over on the other side of Henriston. Then when the bell rang and I got up to go, he stood up again. I'll tell you, I couldn't have been more impressed if the President of the United States himself had walked into the room. He touched my arm to stop me, 'I ride my bike to school, but if you'd like, I can meet you at your bus stop and walk you home,' he said, looking down at his shuffling feet. 'I'd like that very much, Arthur,' I said, hardly able to contain myself, then rushed off to tell Zona everything."

"We saw each other every day after that. My mother just loved Arthur. She couldn't get over what a perfect gentleman he was. My father liked him too, but for different reasons. He thought Arthur was a prize because he came over to mow our lawn every weekend," she said, smiling and shaking her head fondly, "and because he finally had a buddy to watch the Saturday night fights with. Well, that next year, after he graduated, he came to see me…and the fights…as he always did on Saturday nights when he wasn't working over at the gas station on Main Street, and he proposed to me, right out of the blue. He got right down on his knee, held my hand and asked me to marry him. Of course, I accepted, but there was a catch to it. Right after I'd accepted, he told me that he'd also gotten accepted by the State Police Academy. I was so proud of him. We'd talked so often about his wanting to do it, but I was just a girl then. I didn't have a full realization of the risks." Her eyes started to fill again then, and I got another 'don't speak' look from Martin.

"That will always be the greatest regret of my life, Martin. I should have said 'no.' I should have said, 'No, Arthur. Please don't. I'll be worried sick every day.' If I had, I know he would have listened to me. We were so much in love. He would have listened to me and he'd still be here with us now, but I didn't have the wisdom, or the courage, or the strength. I was just a young, small town girl in love. I didn't have any experience with the real world to know how truly dangerous it was," she said, touching her eyes with the corner of her dinner napkin. She looked directly at Martin then. "It was a hard lesson learned, Martin, the hardest of my life. Sometimes, no matter how much you love someone, for their own good, you have to say no." He took her hand then and held it.

"No...please...Mrs. C. There was no way you could have known," he said with his own eyes misting up, clearly in touch with what she was feeling. I could see the resignation of it all return to my mother's eyes as she shifted the subject in another direction.

"And there is something you don't know about your father, Terry. Something he would never have wanted you to know. I don't think he even knew that I did. It's the real reason the Chagfords came to Jennisburg, but I guess it can't hurt now. Who knows? It may even help." She was talking directly to me then.

"The job in the glass factory wasn't the real reason they came here. I found out the real reason one Saturday afternoon when I was over at their house and Meggy was teaching me how to bake a peach pie. Meggy was my mother-in-law, Martin. Arthur was out mowing lawns. I think she wasn't feeling too well that day. Maybe she even had an idea of how sick she would become later. She turned to me without warning and said, 'Thank you so much, Charlotte, for coming into our lives,' and hugged me. 'I don't understand,' I said to her and smiled, returning her hug. She took my hand and we sat down at the kitchen table. 'I can't thank you enough for caring about my boy the way you do. It's made all the difference in the world to his father and me...and to him. He's just not the same boy anymore,' she said with tears in her eyes. As it turns out, the real reason they came here was because Arthur was in trouble. They were living in what Meggy called 'a rough neighborhood' in Philadelphia, and Arthur had gotten involved in a street gang. She told me that the year before they came here, she'd gotten a call to come to the hospital because Arthur had been stabbed in a gang fight and needed a relative to donate blood in a hurry to save him." Mom took my hand then, and squeezed it hard.

"She told me that after he recovered, she and your grandfather decided that, rather than to sacrifice their Arthur to drugs or jail...or death, they would try to bring him somewhere safe so he could have a chance...to grow up right and become something. She said Arthur didn't want to move, but they forced him, and they were afraid that he might run away back to Philly to look for revenge. She said he could be such a 'wild, willful and headstrong boy,' that they didn't know if they could keep him here. Well, after what I'd seen on that first day at the athletic field, her description was not only accurate, but not news to me...but that's why she was thanking me. She said I gave Arthur a reason to stay and that they'd always be grateful to me for that."

I guess I must have jumped up a little abruptly then because the next thing I knew, I was at the kitchen cabinet with my pill bottles in my hand and heard Martin say, "Whoa!"

"I'm so sorry, sweetheart, maybe I should have said something sooner. I guess you've always had a right to know where your wild streak came from, just like you get your penchant for strays from me...but you come by it honestly, sweetheart, and being Arthur Chagford's son is never anything to be ashamed of. He grew up to be the most loving man I could have ever hoped to meet and marry...and he gave me you," she said without turning around to face me at the cabinet.

As I turned around, I saw Martin take her hand with one of his, nod to her, and motion his other hand forward to her as if to say silently, 'He'll be alright.' She took his lead and moved the conversation in a lighter direction then, but no matter what, it was becoming clear that it was going to be her night to vent, one she richly deserved, no matter what effect it had on me. I realized that.

"Well, of course, we got married a few years later, after he graduated from the Academy and I graduated from nursing school, then it wasn't long before our little 'bundle of joy' arrived," she said, reaching over and giving my cheek an exaggerated pinch. She was smiling again. "Arthur was a wonderful father and Terry was the true apple of his eye. No one would ever have believed that such a big, tough guy like Arthur could be as gentle as a lamb when he wanted to be. I used to let him baby sit for Terry when I worked the night shift and never had to lift a finger after coming home from a night's work."

My legs had started bouncing with tension under the table by then. I'd already had three drinks and my pills. I just couldn't stand it anymore. It was time to put a stop to it, so I tried a different approach.

"So...Ma...did Martin tell you that he made arrangements to

send flowers for all of us today while he was out? And nice ones, too. I hear you spent a small fortune," I said taking my chance to turn things around.

"Why…no, he didn't. I just thought you would take care of it. Oh, Martin," she said sweetly. "That was so very kind of you. Thank you," and touched his hand. Martin looked at me as if to say 'how the hell do you know how much I spent?' It had worked.

"Barbara from the flower shop called me today to see if there was anything special I wanted on the blanket sash from me," I said with an awkward, guilty chuckle. "It's a small town, Martin. You'd better get used to it."

After my mother left, I was exhausted. The strain of the last few weeks really started to catch up with me, and with the next few days promising no relief, I went to bed early. That's when it started again. I smelled it, or I think I did. That smell from the house. That rancid, black smell. When I woke up, it was two thirty in the morning and I could have sworn I smelled it, but then it was gone. I couldn't be sure if I dreamed it or if it was real, but I know that my nerves were screaming in my flesh. It couldn't be. It just couldn't be. I'd destroyed it. I was sure of it. I couldn't get back to sleep, so I took another full dose of my pills to help me.

After awhile, I had the strange sensation of not being myself, but then again, still being myself. I opened my eyes, but they were heavy…sleepy…all I could see when I lifted my head was a big pair of feet in gray and red hunting socks, and then I realized I was small. The feet were my father's and I was tucked behind his legs on our old sofa. I felt a hand on the back of my head and heard a voice. 'You there, sport?' it asked me. It was his voice. 'I think it's time we got you into bed. Your mother will have a fit if she comes home and finds I've let you stay out here with me so late,' and I felt a huge pair of hands pick me up and a strong pair of arms hold me to his chest. I laid my head on his shoulder, comforted by the smell of his aftershave. *Old Spice.*

The next thing I knew, he was carrying me to my room and

tucking me into my bed. I could see the circus elephant and bear appliqués on the light blue walls of my old room through my half opened eyes and could feel his hand on my head, stroking my hair as he hummed in his deep, familiar voice an old tune I haven't heard since, until I fell back to sleep. I was feeling so safe and secure when the alarm went off, but I woke up feeling...wrenched, gutted, like a jagged knife had ripped me from navel to Adam's apple. I sat on the edge of my bed and cried for what seemed like hours. "Don't leave me. Please, don't leave me!" I cried out loud into the empty air, shaken to the core, grasping to hold onto the scent of his aftershave. I could've sworn I could still smell it on my shaking hands as I cried into them that morning.

After a night like that, I felt so beaten down I wasn't sure I could make it to work, so I went and sat downstairs in my chair, waiting for that feeling to go away...but it didn't. I was never going to make it without help, so I did something I'd never done before. I went to the kitchen cabinet and got out an old bottle of Jack Daniels, not my favorite, filled half the cup and the rest with coffee and downed it, then did it again. It wasn't until I saw the first rays of the sun come up that any feeling remotely resembling security returned to me. When it did, it was like a warm, safe, comfortable womb of alcohol that allowed the knife in my guts to come out and let me breathe a sigh of relief. I made breakfast, left some for Martin and got ready for work. When I got to the station, Lila was there waiting for me with a smile as usual.

"Good morning, Chief." she chirped

"Bad morning, sweetheart," I said, sounding as glum as I felt. I didn't even have the energy to put on a front for her.

"Gotcha. No sweat, Chief. I'll take care of everything," she said as I went into my office and shut the door behind me.

By midday, I still hadn't thrown the thing off. I had Lila call over to Martin to tell him that my mother was going to the early viewing with Hannah and that I'd pick him up when I came home to get changed so we could meet Mom over at Kendall's at seven. Then I went out to the pharmacy down the street from the station and bought a bottle of my father's aftershave. God, I'd forgotten how much I love the smell of that Old Spice. I put it on my hands and neck immediately, just to have it near me. It made me feel better. I did my walk around town after that and went back to the station feeling a little more like my old self, managing, miraculously, to make it through the rest of the day.

When I got home, Martin was already dressed. He was sitting smoking a cigarette, and for the first time, I could see it. I could see him for the Wall Streeter he had been, blue suit, white shirt, deep red, grey and blue striped tie, black shoes, hair slicked back, black overcoat thrown over the arm of the sofa. That was it. That was the uniform. He looked like a real 'pro,' and I guess I can confess it now, I was intimidated.

This guy was the real thing. He was a success...and I was...well...I didn't know quite what the hell I was anymore then I got the signal. *All lies and jest, still a man hears what he wants to hear and disregards the rest.* The depression was coming on again ready to whack me the way it did on Randolph Road just before I saw his car go off the road. *Not now. Oh, God. Please, not now! Not another tidal wave!* I prayed. "Come on, Chief," I heard him say. "We gotta get ready to go. Come on, you've got get showered and changed."

❋ ❋ ❋

While I was in the shower, my mind became overcrowded with thoughts and memories. I was overwhelmed again, my father, my mother, Angelica, Martin, Lila, the 'monster', Rose and the others. I thought of Grace and my mother and all they'd gone through in their lives, the grief, the loss and all those years alone, surviving it all on their own. Then it happened. It was like a miracle. I smelled her. It was Grace. It was her scent. It was in the room with me, unmistakable. She was in the room with me.

"Grace?" I said out loud to the empty room, starting to sob. "I can't do it again, Grace. I can't do it all by myself!" I cried, crouching down in the shower like a frightened child alone at night in a storm. Then suddenly, a bright light went off like a star burst in my head, and I heard her voice...there in my head...saying some of the last words she had said to me "You're a good man, Terrence Chagford. God bless you." Then it was gone, the light, the scent, and her voice. It was all gone and I was alone again. I was losing my mind, still...again...I didn't know anymore. I couldn't tell. Was it all just a product of my own sick mind chasing me further out on that already cracked and shaking limb? The old fissure widening yet further into a crevice?

A few minutes later, I heard a knock at the door. It was Martin. "Terry, are you alright in there? It's a quarter after six. Come on, Chief. You gotta hurry," he yelled in.

"Yeah, I'm okay. I'll be out in a little while. I still gotta shave." I don't know where the words came from or the strength it took me to get back up, maybe it was the strength of the defeated, when you just don't have what it takes to care anymore, but I did it nonetheless.

The next thing I knew, I was shaving. I looked at myself in that dreaded mirror. My eyes were red and swollen and I realized that I couldn't go anywhere looking that way, so I took a few minutes to soak my face in cold water and use the eye drops I had in the medicine cabinet before I got dressed and went downstairs.

Martin was waiting with a bottle of Wild Turkey and glasses on the table. "Come on, Chief...it's okay. I gotcha covered," he said and poured us a couple of doubles, then two more. Just as we were about to leave he smiled kindly at me and said, "You scrub up nice there, Chief."

I felt some relief once we were outside. The cold felt good on my face, reviving me, so I drove with the window open. We were at Kendall's in what seemed like only a few seconds. Just before we got to the door, my feet hesitated. I couldn't get them to move. Martin stopped with me. I felt him take my arm and say, "It's alright, Chief. You'll be alright. Jenny will be there...and your mother...and Lila...and me. I won't let you down. I promise. None of us will." I had to trust him. I did trust him, and we went in.

CHAPTER 11

Grace's Heart

"To fear love is to fear life, and those who fear life are already three parts dead."

-Bertrand Russell 20th Century
-English philosopher & Social critic

Kendall's is a small place, as are most things in town. The room was jammed with people milling around, speaking in quiet voices to each other. I knew all of them and they knew me. As we moved through the crowd, I managed to shake the hands of the people who greeted me. They all shook their heads and said things like "So sad..." and "She was a wonderful woman..." All sentiments I could heartily agree to without reservation.

The next thing I knew, Martin was guiding me over to where Jenny and Jeff were sitting. My mother was next to them and Sylvia Hadrada beside her. Martin took a seat next to Jenny. I saw the Mayor wave his hand to me and point to the seat next to him that he'd saved for me. On my way past, I kissed Jenny on the cheek and shook Jeff's hand. I went to my mother and kissed her, heard her sniff and knew she smelled the Old Spice on my neck. "Do you mind?" I asked her.

"Not at all, sweetheart. You look very handsome and you were right, the suit still fits perfectly," she said with a sad smile. I even kissed Sylvia, knowing how close she had been to Grace saying, "She spoke very highly of you to me, Sylvia...about how close you two were." She cried and thanked me for my words. Then I took my seat next to the Mayor.

After about an hour or so, the Mayor got up to speak. I remember he made a few opening comments, then said that, "...for over fifty-five years, Grace Coutraire has been a beacon of light for the minds of generations of people in this town, with her kindness, her knowledge and her generosity. She was a testament to small town America, a monument to the town she loved while she lived, who has now, at her death, passed into the realm of legend, never be forgotten. To ensure that fact, the town council and I have agreed that the Jennisburg Library will, from this day forward, be known as 'The Grace Coutraire Memorial Library,' to preserve forever the memory of a woman who feared no art and through whose strength and perseverance, we have become a richer community."

I don't really remember much more of it. I think I drifted off somewhere again, but I do remember that I was never more impressed with anything he'd ever said and was touched by his sentiments. It wasn't a particularly political speech at all, but the words of someone who truly seemed to have an appreciation for the woman herself. I liked the "woman who feared no art" part because I knew it to be so true. He was right. That was Grace.

Out of the rolling fog swirling around in my head, I heard him introduce me saying that he was proud to tell those assembled that I had asked to be able to say a few words, then he called me up. I found my balls again, walked up to the podium sluggishly, like a zombie, and began to speak. It was slow going at first. I wasn't used to speaking in public and was feeling so terribly unwell on top of that. My head was throbbing, my leg hurt and my eyes burned, but I gave it my best shot...for Grace.

"I wholeheartedly agree with everything you've said, Mr. Mayor, about how much Grace meant to this community over so many years, and I congratulate you for capturing so eloquently what she's meant to all of us assembled here this evening to remember her. But I'd like to take a different approach to remembering Grace. I'd like to take a moment to talk about Grace's heart." The words just seemed to come flowing out of me then. "Grace Coutraire was nothing if not a woman of heart. As we all know, she was widowed by World War II and never remarried...but life didn't stop for her there. I know because she and I had occasion to spend a great deal of time together in recent weeks."

I shifted back and forth on my feet, holding tightly to the podium to take some of the pressure off of my leg, then continued, white knuckled from the strain of holding myself up. "It started out as business, but it wasn't long before I realized she was telling me the story of her life. We, here, may tend to think that, because she was a widow and childless, Grace's life may somehow have lacked the love of a family, but I know that isn't true. I saw the love in her eyes when she told me about her brief marriage to Hugh Coutraire. I also saw the sadness and grief there when she spoke about losing him so young. It was real and human, and poignant. Losing him broke her young heart, leaving her only her grief and his name to cling to, but it didn't end there."

I had to pause for a moment to catch my breath and shift my legs again before going on.

"A few years later, Grace's heart went on to love and be loved again by the famous novelist and playwright, Norman Harper (I used his real name). Norman Harper came to Jennisburg to find a story and people to write about, but along with it he found love...in Grace's heart. He died shortly after coming here, but not before memorializing her forever in his last play, '*A Town Like Time*,' to express the depth of his feelings for her.

"When she told me her story, and his, she bloomed with love all over again...and again she suffered terrible grief at his loss. She told me that after Norman died, with the flower of her youth gone, she had given up on love. But to her surprise she found that love had not given up on her when she met a man named Lance Jamison shopping one day in Hamilton Common. I smiled to myself at the simplicity of it as she spoke of it. Out of the clear blue sky, Lance Jamison found love in Grace's heart and she in his. They loved each other dearly and completely for over twenty-five years until he was taken from her as they came into what most people consider to be their golden years...and again, as she told me their story, her face was filled with love, happiness...and loss. She shined like the diamond in the sun as she spoke of each of them Hugh, Norman and Lance sparkling with the knowledge that she had, indeed, had a life filled with love."

I paused to wipe my face with my handkerchief. It was so hot in there with all those people, and with the alcohol and my nerves, I felt like I was melting, but I went on.

"What I didn't realize at the time she was telling me her story, was that she was trying to teach me a lesson...a most valuable lesson about life...and the meaning of love...from someone who knew it well. To love and be loved doesn't mean a life of perfection without loss, bliss without pain or grief, happiness without toil or strife, but the opening of the heart in the face of all that, and in spite of all that, to be grateful that God has allowed us the ability to feel that love. ...and for that lesson, I will hold her in my heart forever."

"When she told me her story, she was giving me her heart...her wisdom, and her courage, which I have a feeling she secretly knew I needed so desperately. I understand now, Grace," I said looking toward the sky. "I understand. So for all of us assembled here, please don't leave here believing that Grace lived a life unfulfilled. We can grieve for the loss of a life that meant so much to us all, but not for Grace herself, for her remarkable life was not an empty or wasted one and her release from it not an unwelcome one for her." I shifted gears then.

"Now, I'd like to take a moment to talk about family. As I said earlier, we all know Grace spent most of her life without family as we tend to define it in terms of biology or certificates. But I ask all of you now to open your hearts and know that there is more that Grace had to teach me."

"She taught me that there is a wider definition of the word 'family,' one not bound by biology or certificates, but by love. For not only did Grace have the love of men in her life, she had the love of all of us here tonight. She had Sheila Woolf, whom she described to me once as being 'her arms and legs when hers didn't work so well.' She had Sylvia Hadrada for the companionship she valued so highly, and who she told me made her laugh unlike anyone else. She had Jenny Denton, whose life and whose family's lives she was so pleased to be included in."

"She had our Mayor, who clearly understood and shared Grace's love of art and knowledge. She had Charlotte Chagford, who understood her pain and shared her knowledge of life and loss as a widow…and as I stand here before all of you assembled here tonight, I am honored, pleased and proud to say that, in her last weeks, Grace had me…to hear her story of strength and endurance so that I could so greatly benefit by it. She had my love too."

"She had us all, and that's why we are all here tonight. *We* were Grace's family, and from looking around at the faces here tonight and seeing this room overflowing with flowers to honor her, it was a large family. So, as we all leave here tonight, I would like each and everyone in attendance here to look around, see each other and know what Grace knew. Redefine what the word 'family' means to us all and know there are no limitations to the meaning of the word 'love.' Her personal legacy to us is to live our lives as best as we can, give and accept love, and feel content in the knowledge that we have each other. So let us celebrate her life for the incredible journey that it was, take to our hearts all that she had to offer us during her lifetime and remember the legacy of love she has left us as we go forward."

Then I took out the flask I'd filled with what was left of Grace's Armagnac and raised it to the sky in salute.

"To life and to love, Grace!" I said and drank, but before I'd finished I saw Martin and my mother standing and saying, "To life and to love, Grace." Then Jenny and Jeff were standing…and Sheila Woolf…and Sylvia and Harry…and Lila and Eli and the Mayor. Everyone. The whole room…the whole town was standing. I had made it through…for Grace.

As we walked out together, Martin put his hand on my back and squeezed my good shoulder. "You were brilliant, Chief. Really, I mean it." he said. "I had no idea you could communicate so powerfully. You really sent a message she would have been very proud of…and I am too. I'm proud of you."

We stood outside for a while smoking when my mother came out and hugged me saying, "Oh, sweetheart. You were wonderful. Grace would have been so pleased." Soon our little group was standing there smoking and talking, but I was drained to the core. I could hardly stand and I wanted to be alone for a while, so I sent Martin with the group to eat over at the Tavern House Grill. Someone...Jeff or Eli, said they would make sure he got back alright and I left. That was when I came home to find the coffee can turned upside down and the chairs moved.

What was I going to do? I didn't know. Was it happening again or was it in my mind? Had I disintegrated that far? And after we'd gone through so much? It wasn't until I saw the writing on the mirror that I knew for sure. It was not over and I was wrung out of...everything, a dried out husk of a human being.

I've been going on trying as hard as I can to keep things seeming as normal as possible while I think things out. The house has been quiet and there haven't been any more signs for a few days. Maybe my vigilance has counted for something...kept it at bay because it doesn't have the benefit of surprise anymore.

Grace was buried the next morning with only a short sermon by the minister. The turnout was huge and we all left quietly afterward. I didn't go to the reception Jenny gave for Grace's closest friends. I had other things on my mind. It caused a bit of a stir that I wasn't there but Martin and my mother made my apologies. I was 'over tired,' they said.

❄ ❄ ❄

The following Monday after New Year's I got a letter in the mail from Grace's lawyer requesting that I attend the reading of her Will that Thursday at his office in Henriston. Martin got one, too. It came to my house in care of me. Jenny got one as well. She called and told me. Lila's came to the station. When we arrived that morning, Jenny and Jeff were already there, so were Sylvia and Sheila, the Mayor...and Lila.

After the lawyer's secretary was sure that all who had been invited were in attendance, she buzzed into the inner office. James Gibb came out and invited us into his conference room. It was a quiet, comfortable room, very old fashioned in its furnishings with dark wood everywhere, the walls all lined with old books, the very epitome of staid lawyer's digs. We all waited solemnly for him to speak. He started out by saying he was going to dispense with a formal reading and just get on with it.

The first announcement he made was that he was named executor of Grace's estate, then went on with the specific bequests. Her first bequest was to the library. She left the library $75,000 and her paintings and sculptures with the stipulation that the money be used to build an addition to be named "The Lance Jamison Art Appreciation Room," to house her artworks and serve as a reading room surrounded solely by books relating to art.

Her next bequest was another $75,000 to build another addition to be named "The Norman Harper Reading Room" (his real name was used), to house a display of his works and papers still in her possession at the time of her death and be surrounded exclusively by 20th century novels and plays. Included in this bequest were all rights vested in her to the novel '*Nowhere but Here*' and the play '*A Town Like Time.*'

Her third bequest was another $75,000 for "The Hugh Coutraire Garden," to be created behind the library on an adjacent piece of land owned by Grace and donated to the library by way of her Will for that purpose. Attached to the bequest for the garden was the additional requirement that there be a plaque placed near the back door leading to the garden dedicated to all the soldiers sacrificed in World War II with the additional stipulation that the entire back wall be used to house books on the subject of war to teach young people that the realities and casualties mean more than toy guns and waving flags.

Next were the personal bequests. "To Sheila Woolf, the sum of $75,000 to be held in a trust created and administered by James J. Gibb, Esq., the income to be distributed to Miss Woolf until her retirement. Upon her retirement, the body of the trust to be distributed to her in full. Along with this trust, Miss Woolf is to receive Grace's three-strand pearl choker necklace with the diamond clasp."

Sheila just cried as he handed her a large velvet box and read a note. "Live long, Sheila. I hope you find someone to care for you the way you've always cared for me. You are a kind and gentle spirit and I hope you've always known that I would never leave you unprotected. Love, Grace." Obviously overwrought with grief and overwhelmed by Grace's generosity, Sheila took the box, but said nothing. Mr. Gibb continued.

"Sylvia Hadrada,...Grace left you her white gold, pearl and diamond cocktail ring." There was also a note for Sylvia which he read. "To Sylvia, You're a real pistol! You really should have been on the stage, dear. You've made me laugh more than anyone I've ever known and for that you have my love, many thanks, and the ring that you have admired so much over the years. It's now yours. Wear it and be wonderful as you are, darling. But no money. You already have more than God! Love, Grace."

Sylvia laughed and cried at the same time. "Thank you, Grace," she said as Mr. Gibb handed her a velvet ring box.

"To Mrs. Jennifer Denton...Grace has left you her emerald, diamond and pearl necklace with matching earrings and bracelet, with a note. "My sweet Jenny, these were given to me as an expression of deepest love, a love I've seen again in you and your husband. I now pass them onto you in honor of that love. Wear them long and well, dear. I'm sure they will suit you as much as they did me. Love, Grace." Mr. Gibb handed her a large velvet box.

"I will, Grace. I will," Jenny said as she took the box, tears quietly streaming down her face.

Then he moved onto her personal effects. "The proceeds from the sale of all her clothes, shoes, hats, remaining jewelry and car are to go to the Children's Health Foundation attached to the Henriston General Hospital, for which I have already made arrangements." He paused and took a sip of water before going on.

"To Lila Horn or Beauchamps, whichever name she holds at the time of my death, I leave my gold and sapphire lion's head earrings and brooch set." Mr. Gibb cleared his throat a moment then read the accompanying note. "I leave you my lions for a reason, child, to always remind you to dare to be the woman I know you are inside. Wear them to remember all of the confidence I have in you and my thanks for being sensitive and caring to an old woman you hardly knew, out of the pure goodness of your heart, expecting nothing in return...and don't be afraid to wear more black, dear. With your eyes and hair, you can't go wrong. Love, Grace," and Mr. Gibb passed another velvet box to Jenny who handed it to Lila, but before he went on, he reached into his briefcase and came up with a small white box with black trim. "Miss Horn, Grace asked me to see that you got this in the event that she didn't survive to see your marriage," he said and handed the box to Jenny who looked at it, raised her eyes to the sky and, shaking her head and smiling, passed it onto Lila. When Lila saw what it was she burst into tears and ran out of the room. Jenny followed her. It was the bottle of 'My Sin, Lanvin-Paris.' Grace had kept the promise she made the night of the Thanksgiving dinner.

"To Mr. Martin Welliver…" surprise etched itself all over the faces of everyone in the room. "Mr. Welliver, Grace has left you her house and all the furniture, including antiques, and appliance contents."

Martin's face just went blank, the color draining out of it like a plummeting thermometer. His eyes filled with humility as he looked down at his hands, fumbling with his fingers as is his way, but said nothing.

Mr. Gibb added, "…and I'd like you to know, young man, that Grace had me come specially to her home the day after Christmas to make that particular arrangement…with one other. I'll also have you know that there is no other client of mine that I would have dropped everything to do that for. It appears she felt you were in need of a home, Mr. Welliver. Use it well. Grace was a special woman and she must have thought a great deal of you to give you hers." I knew then that something more than 'tapénade' or 'cold steak salad with mustard vinaigrette' had passed between Martin and Grace on Christmas Day, but I also knew it would never be my place to ask.

James Gibb cleared his throat, took another drink and began to speak again. "The rest, residue and remainder of her estate of whatever kind and wherever situated goes to Mr. Terrence Chagford."

I was stunned. Everyone looked at me, astonishment rippling across their faces. "…which I estimate, Chief, to be in the neighborhood of $200,000 to $250,000 after liquidation."

My jaw dropped. "Was…was…there a note…for me?" I stammered once I'd had a chance to absorb the shock of it.

"No, there was no note, but I don't mind telling you that I

gathered from my meeting with Grace that day that she cared for you very, very much. She just said to 'tell him not to worry, he'll be alright,' and that you would know what that meant," and he closed the meeting.

❄ ❄ ❄

That was a week ago and the house has been quiet since. I dreamed about the tiles again last night. I was just standing there, naked again, as they fell from above my head. Not on me, but around me in a circle, piling up, penning me in like a brick wall, trapping me. I looked up to see where they were coming from, but it was dark...black, fathomless, a darkness without end. They kept falling around me, surrounding me, a wall of them rising higher and higher. I couldn't move. I felt like I was being smothered as they kept piling up endlessly around my feet, my knees, my waist . . .

When I woke up, I was soaked again. It was waiting. I knew it then. It was lying in wait for us. That's why there hadn't been anything since Martin's trying to sleepwalk through the false door. It's watching and waiting for its chance, but to do what? Drive me insane so I would be carted off and leave Martin alone?

I can't figure it out, but I know one thing for sure. I'm as afraid as I've ever been since I torched the house, tipping the scales of anything I think I can endure. I live every moment excruciatingly afraid, paralyzed with it. I've been so weakened by it that I've taken to sitting for long periods of time when I'm alone, or in the middle of the night while Martin is asleep upstairs. I just sit and wring my hands or rub my face, rocking back and forth. I'm doing it right now. I can't stop.

I've decided tonight that I can't take it anymore. I have to tell Martin what's been going on. It's not fair to keep it from him. I'm sure it's back now. He has a right to know what's happening, and that there isn't anything I can do about it. I can't just let him go on...like a lamb to slaughter. I have to warn him. I'm going to tell him tonight. He's out with Lila and Eli now at a movie, but he should be home soon. It's killing me inside to have to tell him, to let him know that I've failed him, failed us both.

I hear a car now. It must be them. *Oh please, Martin, don't bring them in. I don't want them to see me this way.* I've just heard the car door slam. His footfalls are on the front porch steps. His key's rattling in the lock. He's home. *Martin, I'm so sorry.*

※ ※ ※

He's just come in and said, "Hello." He's telling me how good it was to go to a movie again. He's just grabbed a soda from the kitchen, chattering as he goes, telling me that he is going upstairs to change into his sweats and he'll be right down to tell me about it. I dread seeing the look on his face when I tell him...that he'll have to leave here to survive...and never come back...if he wants to live.

※ ※ ※

He's just come down again. He's sitting across from me. "What's up?" he's just asked me. "What are you writing, Chief?" I have to stop now and tell him. I don't know if I'll be able to come back to this. Either I'll come back to finish it or...I'll die. There can be no in-between this time. I don't know what's going to happen, but I have to tell him that it's back, and I have to tell him now.

※ ※ ※

Well...I'm back, so I guess that means I'm not dead. I'm in too much pain to be dead. I've survived to come back and finish the tale, to tell the last of it. I can hardly breathe. My nose is broken and packed with cotton. My head feels like it's been hammered by a log splitter. I've bled out quite a bit. At least it's stopped now. My left eye is swollen shut, but I have to finish it and I have to finish it now, bleed myself of it once and for all, so here goes.

When Martin came down, he sat across from me. I looked up at him and he saw me. I mean he really saw me, not the me I'd been pretending to be for the last few weeks. He knew something was wrong, terribly wrong...again. I'd managed to cover it for as long as I could, but he could see it then. I must have looked like a madman to him, deranged with fear.

"Chief, are you alright?" he asked, wearing his concern in his words. I had to force mine out of me.

"No, I'm not alright." I said putting my hand to my mouth, feeling myself start to tremble. "I'm not alright...I'm afraid...you may not be alright, either."

"What is it, Terry...please?" He asked, the pitch of his voice rising with alarm.

"It's back Martin. It's come back for us...It's not over...It's here...It's been waiting for us. It's been here for weeks." The words came spilling out of me. "I've smelled it. I've heard it, and so have you. It's made you do things at night while you're asleep, and things are moving by themselves again. I haven't seen it yet, but it won't be long..."

I was panicking...losing it...I could see the spittle flying from my lips as I spoke. The color drained from his face. "I've failed, Martin...I thought I could beat it. I thought I'd destroyed it, but I didn't. I gave all I had...but it's back for us...and I don't know what else I can do. It wants you, it's always wanted you. You've got to leave, Martin. Now! Tonight! You've got to get out before it can kill you! I'll stay here and fight it until I die, but I don't want it to have you. I can't live with that."

He just sat there staring at me, his eyes huge and sad, dark and...defeated. Somewhere inside him he had known all along. He felt I was telling the truth. Then the phone rang. I didn't want to answer it, but if I didn't and it was my mother or Lila, they'd know something was wrong. I couldn't risk that yet, so I got up and went to the kitchen phone leaving Martin to absorb what I'd just told him.

It was Jenny. She started rattling on about what a lovely time they had out with Martin last week, and what a shame it was that I couldn't have joined them. Did I like the curry that she chose for Martin to bring home for me? I carried on with the conversation the best I could, but the voice I heard when I spoke was voice of a dead man. Then she said something that made my knees buckle. I broke out in another cold, drenching sweat, fighting to keep from passing out.

"I think it's such a lovely gesture for Martin to wear a

Mahjong tile around his neck in memory of Grace," she said. "He must have gotten the idea from her bracelet. It's such a beautiful piece and the boys think it's too cool."

I dropped the phone and turned back to the living room. *That's it!* My brain screamed in my ears. *It's the tile! Martin has the tile. Oh, my God, he doesn't know. I never told him.* I looked down for a second too numb to move, grasping to hold on to consciousness. *Dear God! What had I done by not telling him?*

I heard a crash from the other room then choking, struggling, smashing sounds. I looked up and around the corner. It sounded like all hell was breaking loose in there. I dashed into the other room and saw Martin suspended in the air, kicking furiously, his hands clutching at his throat like he was hanging from some invisible rope. My blood pressure went off the charts, the top of my head feeling like would blow off at any second.

"Teeeerrrryy!" he gasped as he struggled, his feet dangling above the ground like some nightmarish marionette. I tried to run to him, bellowing at the top of my lungs. "I WILL NOT LET YOU FUCKING HURT HIIIIIMMMM AGAIN..." but as I launched, the dining room chairs suddenly flew in my way, taking my feet out from under me. I hit the floor with a thud, smashing my face against the hardwood planks, warm blood spurting out like a fountain all over my cold skin.

Before I knew it, I was on my hands and knees trying to launch myself up again. A voice hissed in my ear, "My Game!" and I felt a dizzying bolt of pain as something sharp and heavy struck the side of my head, blood gushing down the side of my face. I went down, floating somewhere between conscious and unconscious, every second falling deeper into blackness. The room had become a maelstrom of smashing, spinning, whirling things, flying around the room, off of the walls...papers...pens... books...lamps...ashtrays...everything hurling itself randomly around me. Blood sputtered from my lips as I heard myself saying, "Help me! Please, help me!"

Then I smelled it. Through the blood, through my broken face, it was Grace's scent again. I felt a burst of light and energy in the pit of my stomach and, propelled with strength that was not my own, I was up and moving again.

I grabbed Martin by the legs, trying to hoist him up to stop his awful choking. He was already turning blue, just like I saw him in the first dream about the tiles. It was happening and it was happening now! Then I saw it, the tile with the dragon symbol on it. It was hanging out of his shirt. Without thinking I reached up and grabbed it. It seared my hand with scorching heat, but I was already beyond pain. I looked up at his face, trying to speak to him.

The mark of the star was on his forehead, his eyes shot open, startling, icy blue surrounded by masses of bulging redness. "I win!" he growled at me through sharp clenched teeth, foam spewing from his mouth.

A blast of hot energy slammed against my body, an immovable force flinging itself at me. I flew backward, arms and legs flailing helplessly in the air as I went careening across the room, landing against the far wall with an impact that almost shot my eyes out of my head. I couldn't move. I just crumpled down feeling an enormous weight pinning me down, like a massive boulder had landed on me. All I could do was watch Martin slowly giving up his struggle for breath, hanging helplessly in the air...dying right there in front of me.

Suddenly, it was there again, the smell, Grace's scent and I felt my head being turned by gentle hands to look over to my left. I heard her voice whisper in my ear, "Destroy it." I saw I still had the tile. It must have come off in my hand with the blast. That was when I saw the paperweight out of the corner of my eye, the Italian paperweight I'd brought back from Europe, shaped like a squat bowling pin, rolling on the floor toward me. It was at the tips of my fingers. A few seconds later I had it in my right hand. I could still smell Grace around me, but my eyes were graying, black spots floating before my eyes.

I wasn't sure if I was in or out, but I sensed that she was still there...with me, and as I took one last look at the paperweight in my hand, I could swear I saw Grace's youthful face reflected in the dark glass. Somehow I managed to reach deeper inside myself than I ever thought I could for everything I had left, all my might and all the strength that she could give me, and I fought back against the force holding me down.

I brought my left hand around, holding the tile by the string, laying it on the floor before me. Then, in that last split second before I raised the paperweight, I saw it, the dragon symbol on the tile. It was changing, coming to life. The eyes got large and red. It turned its head toward me, opening its mouth wide, grinning and baring its sharp teeth. Its long, black tongue snaking out of its mouth, darting off the tile at me.

Animal! Animal! Animal! pounded in my brain as I took that paperweight with every ounce of my being and brought that fucking ugly chunk of glass crashing down on its hissing head as it lurched off the tile at me, shattering into a thousand splinters, scattered pieces spraying across the floor, screaming at the top of my lungs.

"No, mother fucker. I WIN!"

There was a cry, an earsplitting, echoing shriek of tormented pain, and suddenly the character of the atmosphere in the room changed. Everything that was randomly flying through the air had formed itself into a whirling vortex of household items, like the eye of a tornado in my living room.

As the cry began to fade away, there was a thunderous crack, like the house was struck by something so immense it would split it in half, then four rapidly paced explosions of shattering glass as the windows blew out of the front of my house. The whirling objects dropped in mid air.

For a few seconds there was nothing—dead silence—but by then I had become like a wild beast that'd been cornered too long, striking out beyond all reason. I kept smashing and smashing, even though what had been splinters before were, by then, reduced almost to dust, I couldn't stop.

In the background, I heard Grace laughing, that light, charming, ladylike laugh I'd heard only that once during our afternoon. The room was filled with her scent and triumphant laughter. She'd won after all. I'd won. We'd both won, together. Then, somewhere in what was left of the human portion of my mind, I heard a crashing thud from across the room and my brute rage slipped away. *Martin!* My mind screamed at me. *Save Martin!*

I got up and dragged myself, half crawling, over to where he lay crumpled on the floor and tried to help him up. He was limp. I picked him up with what little strength I had left and put him on the sofa. "Martin! Martin!" I yelled. Nothing. I slapped him lightly on the face to try and revive him. "Martin, please...come on. Wake up. You can't leave me now!"

Then harder...Nothing. He just laid there lifeless, but I could not, would not, give up. I hadn't come that fucking far to give up then. I grabbed him by the arms and shook him hard, roaring like a savage jungle creature again, shaking him furiously "I WILL NOT LET YOU DIE!" Suddenly there was a gasp, then a cough. His eyes shot open, his own dark brown eyes. Kicking and shouting, he struggled against my grip. "Martin! Martin! It's me! It's Terry! Thank God! It's over. It's finally over."

He stopped struggling and looked at me, coughing and shaking. His eyes were still bulging, insane with fear, but the color was coming back into his face. Then I saw the huge reddish purple welt ring coming up around his neck. I got up and went to the kitchen for some water and a cool towel. When I got back, he was sitting up, coughing again... still struggling to catch his breath.

"Martin...can you breathe?" I asked him. He nodded. "Here, drink this. It's cold," I said, as I wrapped the cool towel around his neck.

"My cross! Where's my cross?" he asked with a croak, straining to speak and panicking as he felt around his neck. I looked around and saw it on the floor under where he'd been hanging, grabbed it and put it in his hand. It seemed to calm him. "Is it really over?" he pleaded hoarsely.

"Yeah, it is," I said in the most confident voice I could muster.

"How do you know? How do you know it's really over this time?" he wailed, still not finding his own voice. I thought he was going to go off the deep end. His voice was thready, his eyes still aflame with terror.

"It was the tile," I said, trying to reassure him. "The tile on the string, it was the last link... but it's gone. I destroyed it. That's when it all stopped. I can feel it, can't you? "

He looked up at me, panic leaving his face gradually in stages, but I could see something replacing it, sadness. His eyes filled with water.

"What happened to your face?" he asked quietly. I must have looked like a crash test dummy.

※ ※ ※

A few minutes later there was banging at the door.

"Terry! Terry! Are you in there?" It was Jeff Denton. He was yelling and banging, then I heard Jenny's voice.

"Terry? It's Jenny. Are you in there? Let us in." I got up half crippled and opened the door.

"Oh...my...God!" was all Jeff could say when he saw me. From the look of him, I thought he'd be ill. Jenny rushed through the door.

"Oh, my God, Terry! We were so worried," she said, throwing her arms around me. "Where's Martin...is he alright?" I just pointed to the sofa.

Jeff came in and looked around "What the hell happened here?" he asked, the expression on his face shifting from alarmed to mystified. Jenny went over to Martin on the sofa, looking at his neck.

"What the fuck happened here?" Jeff asked him. Martin looked to me to answer.

"Burglars." I said, and Jenny knew.

"Burglars?" Jeff asked, sounding like he didn't comprehend what I'd said. "Burglars..." he repeated. "...this place is fucking trashed." His color flushed as his voice climbed to a shout. "Did you call the police?" he asked, but Jenny was on it.

"He *is* the police, Jeff!" she said, trying to pull me down on the on the chair next to her. "Honey, just calm down for a minute and help me. I need you to go in the kitchen and bring out a bowl of warm water and towels so I can try and stop this bleeding," she pleaded with him. I got my bottle of Hennessy and pack of cigarettes from the desk before coming back and sitting down to do what she told me. I was going to let her handle this one.

After she cleaned up my face, I pushed my nose back into place before I let Jenny pack it. You should've seen the way the color drained from Jeff's face. He looked like he'd faint when he heard it crack. Then she cut a home-made butterfly band aid for the gash in my head, but what she really wanted was to take us to the hospital.

"Jenny, really. That's not necessary. I'm much better now. It's not as bad as it looks. How about you?" I asked Martin.

"No, I'm okay, Jen. Really, I am," he croaked, following my lead.

"You're not going to stay here tonight are you? What if they...come back?" she asked, the pitch of her voice rising.

"They won't come back, Jen," I said, starting to slur.

"But how can you be sure?" she asked, giving me a loaded, knowing look.

"Let's just say I gave 'em a good thrashing on the way out, but you're right. I would feel better staying somewhere else. We'll go to my mother's."

Jeff just paced around the floor in a state of abject confusion. "I just don't understand what the fuck is going on around here anymore," he said, scratching his head and looking around the room at all the shattered pieces lying scattered around the room.

"Jeff, honey, it's freezing in here. Isn't there something you can do to block up those windows?" she asked in her 'sweetheart' voice, trying to throw him off the track by changing the subject.

"Yes, of course. Terry, you got anything around here I can use on those windows?" he asked, giving into his bewilderment, shaking his head and throwing up his hands.

"Boards...plywood...nails...hammer...basement..." I slurred and pointed to the back of the house. He came back a few minutes later with my tool belt over his shoulder, arms filled with old boards, cut pieces of plywood and went to work. I began thinking I'd rather be dead than have to listen to another skull thumping whack of that hammer. Each whack felt like the nails were being driven straight into my brain instead of the window frames. Mercifully, there were only four windows blown and it didn't take him long to finish in his efficient, workman-like manner. *Thanks, Jeff!*

❋ ❋ ❋

That's where I am now. Jenny and Jeff have just left. Martin is upstairs grabbing some things for me to change into while I write this. I can't let Mom see me covered in blood. It would scare the life out of her and I can't have that. I've just had to open the front door for some air. It's so hot in here, and my chest hurts. I can feel the pain now with the cold blowing in on my face. I just hope Mom has plenty of Advil at the house, because I don't have any left. I don't think I can get up again to get any of my other pills. It's all on me now, my leg, my ankle and my hip...my arm, my back...my head and face. I don't think I can walk anymore... not sure I can even stand...maybe I should ask Martin to get my pills when he comes down. I can hardly hold the pen now...or keep my head up. I think he'll have to help me...change...I think he'll have to...drive...but at least . . . we're alive. Thank God...we're still alive.

BOOK TWO

A Book of Revelations

"If you could read my mind, love
What a tale my thoughts could tell
Just like an old time movie
'Bout a ghost from a wishing well
In a castle dark, or a fortress strong
With chains upon my feet
You'll know that ghost is me
And I will never be set free
As long as I'm a ghost that you can't see."

If You Could Read My Mind
Gordon Lightfoot

"They've got catfish on the table
They've got gospel in the air
And Reverend Green be glad to see you
When you haven't got a prayer
But, boy, you've got a prayer in Memphis."

Walking in Memphis
Marc Cohn

CHAPTER 12

Charlotte's Turn

"Thou art thy mother's glass, and she in thee calls back the lovely April of her prime."

-William Shakespeare
-16th Century Playwright.
-From Sonnet #3

It's been six months and I'm writing again. So much has happened since that night that I feel I have to return to it, one last time. It was the only outlet for my desperation for so long that it's become like a part of me, part of my heart and...soul.

In the end, I believe it's been the key to my sanity and survival, the therapy that's led me to both, so I'm going to finish it here and now. I'm going to write about the tremendous 'burn off' it all had for me and the lives of the people around me. It's time to end the story with the knowledge that it has overwhelmed me for the last time. I'm going to go back, back to the night we were saved, and bring it forward to today...then let it go, forever...if I can.

✳ ✳ ✳

After we left the house that night, Martin drove for the first time since he'd gone off the bridge into the river. He was really very shaky, so was I, but we rallied. It was necessary, and since I had the security of the knowledge that it was all over to shore me up, we managed it, pain and all. On the way, we made a plan about what we would tell my mother about my face. Martin had the presence of mind to put on one of my old turtle neck sweaters to cover the marks on his neck, but I couldn't very well put a bag over my head. We couldn't tell her the real truth, that was obvious, and we couldn't tell her the lie about burglars either. That would have scared her too much.

In the end, we decided on a second set of lies, one where I took the fall…literally. We agreed that, once we got in the house, Martin would take her into the kitchen and tell her that I'd fallen from the top of my stairs in a drunken stupor. I knew she'd believe that, and although I also knew that it would hurt us both, it was the lesser of all evils, so to speak. I could take whatever she'd toss at me and it went pretty much as planned.

She had tears in her eyes when she saw my face, but didn't criticize me for it. The emotional blackmail would come later, when she knew I was strong enough to take it. She just made me a bowl of clear broth with some tea and toast and let me go to sleep on the sofa. Martin had brought my pills and gave me a full dose, one of each, then went to sleep in my old bed. There was no way I could ever have managed the stairs that night. *An ironic switch of roles,* I thought. I slept for a few hours five or six maybe, before I was awakened by a pain-filled shake to find Martin standing over me with a wild expression on his face.

"Wake up, Terry. Wake up!" he said in a whispered shout.

"Martin, what the hell is it? Jesus H. Christ, I feel like shit. Just let me sleep," I groaned, sounding cranky but feeling much worse.

"I remember! I remember now, Terry. It just…like…came to me while I was sleeping and I remembered." He was getting emotional.

"Remembered what?" I asked hazily.

"What happened…at the house…that led me to the bridge," he said, sounding like an excited child, and not the kind who'd just got a pony, but the kind who had just seen a three car pile up. I couldn't help staring at the huge purple bruises on his neck. I guess he saw me because he put his hand up to his throat, covering it.

"Here, drink this," he said and handed me a cup of tea as he pulled up a chair and sat next to me so he could look at me. He started talking in a low voice while I hiked myself up as high as I could without actually sitting up. "I remember being upstairs...in the end bedroom. There were mud stains on the window over looking the back yard, red mud, splattered on the inside of the window. I remember thinking that some kids must have gotten in and raised hell up there. I got a bucket with some warm, soapy water and a scrub brush to clean it." I motioned to him with my fingers for a cigarette. He got up mechanically and got me one without stopping.

"I was scrubbing the window and the mud was coming off, but it was strange. It got very 'red' as it dripped all down the wall, like the way red clay gets in the rain, but deeper. I didn't pay much attention to it. By the time I finished cleaning it up, it had gotten dark outside and started to rain again, the way it had been on and off for days. I stood there for a while admiring my excellent cleaning handiwork when I saw a shadow moving outside, down below on the ground. I remember thinking at first that it was a shadow of a tree swaying in the wind. Then I saw a flash of white. It wasn't a shadow of a tree. It was a man. A man was walking through my back yard. I remember it as clearly now as if it were yesterday." He stopped and lit a cigarette for himself, his hand trembling.

"He was dressed in a black suit and tie with a white shirt. He was balding, and had a long black beard," he said getting agitated, beads of perspiration forming on his forehead as he spoke. 'Who the fuck would be out walking around my house...in the rain?' I thought to myself. Who knows? Maybe I had a trespasser or burglar, so I grabbed a closet pole out of the closet and went downstairs to handle it New York style, but by the time I got there...he was gone. I walked around the house to make sure and when I didn't find anything I went back inside, soaked." Sweat was dripping down the side of his face. He wiped it with his sleeve but didn't stop.

"When I got back inside, I headed for the living room and noticed an awful odor in the house...like...I don't know, something dead, decomposing and felt a blast of freezing cold air hit me as I went through the living room doorway. He was in there!" His voice went up several pitches.

"It was the man from the back yard, but he wasn't facing me. He was sitting in a chair facing the rear window of the living room. 'Who the fuck are you...and what the fuck are you doing in my house?' I shouted at him, strengthening my grip on the pole in case I had to use it on the fly. He laughed a low, guttural, echoing laugh. 'I am you, Martin...and soon, very soon, indeed...you will be me,' he said, his voice a growling hiss with an English accent.

'Get the fuck outta my house before I call the cops.!' I shouted. I already had the phone in my hand, but it was dead. That was when I started to get afraid. The man spoke to me again.

'I need you, Martin...and you need me,' he said in the same flat, hissing voice, still not moving. I stood there, stunned. I felt...I don't know...like I was going into some sort of a trance, then he spoke to me again.

"'I need you to die for me, Martin...so I can live.'" Martin had gone into full tremors by then, his face glaring with intensity as he spoke. "His voice terrified me, Terry. I tried to go after him with the pole. 'You fucking freak!' I heard myself shout, but I was hypnotized by his voice and couldn't move. It sounded like slow steam escaping from a water heater. 'I know you want to die, Martin, and I want to help you...you don't have to be afraid...you'll never have to be afraid again...I'm here to help you,' he hissed."

"I started gagging from the smell and shaking from the cold. It was like all my strength, my life, was being zapped out of me." Martin's voice began to take on a frenzied, manic quality. He stood up and started to pace back and in front of me, limp and all, waving his hands around, gesturing wildly as he spoke.

"'Who...who are you?' I asked him again. 'I'm the good Doctor, Martin...and I've come for you,' he said, laughing with that same dirty sounding laugh, moving to stand up, but still not facing me. That's what did it for me. I knew somewhere deep inside me that if I had to look at his face, it would be the face of death and I would die right there on the spot."

"Then, just as I saw he was beginning to turn to face me, I heard a loud crash from somewhere below me. It seemed to come from the basement, metallic, like a big box of kitchen utensils dumped on the floor. Whatever it was, it startled me. I jumped and turned to look toward the basement door. I started to turn back to look back at the man in the chair, but something stopped me. I could swear I heard a small, faint voice whisper in my ear, 'Run, Martin. Now!' and felt something like…a strange rose-scented breeze flow through me. It brought me out of whatever trance I was in, and when I looked back over to the chair by the window, he was gone."

"I turned and ran as fast as I could. The next thing I knew, I was out in front of the house with my car keys in my hand. I jumped in the car and headed down the road to town. I didn't know where I was going, but I knew I had to get away from there."

As he spoke, I couldn't help but think about the poor, pretty face of the strawberry blonde girl at the house named Rose. What a brave child she must have been in life, how fiercely she must have fought to survive the unspeakable acts she was forced to endure at the hands of that monster and yet, even after death, she managed the strength do what she could to save Martin…and me. Those words…her words…swept through my mind again in that plaintive little voice, "I'll help you if I can." And, as I sat there listening to Martin, I found myself wondering whether she'd found her way to that same field of wildflowers that Angelica had, and prayed silently for the deliverance of her courageous little soul to somewhere peaceful and safe…at last.

Martin went on talking and pacing, turning occasionally to look at me. His eyes were full of fear, tears steaming down the sides of his face. I'd managed to sit up by then, but my head began to swim. His pacing was making me dizzy. "Martin, come sit down…please. You're making me dizzy… and my head hurts." He stopped pacing and came to sit down close to me again. I put my hand on his arm.

"Martin, it's okay. It's over now, remember? It's finished," I said, trying to sound supportive, while at the same time working through the pain caterwauling its way through me.

"But, Terry…I believed him. That's what scares me. He knew what was in my mind, in my heart. He knew my fears. He knew me!" he cried, putting his face in his hands.

"No, Martin, no...that's not it. Like I told you, you've been suffering from Post Traumatic Stress Syndrome. It was playing on your fears, but they weren't real. You didn't really want to die. You just needed help." He looked up at me, trembling all over as if he were reliving the terror of the entire episode right in front of me. I already knew where it would lead and, although the effect might be cathartic for him in the end, right at that moment it was leading into trauma and didn't look good.

"I remember now. I was driving too fast. I was so scared and still wasn't used to driving yet, not in the rain. I must've hit a puddle. I remember my windshield suddenly being showered with water and I couldn't see." His body was shaking violently by then, well out of control. His voice had changed from thready panic to shocky calm.

"I felt the car go off the road and I hit my head. I don't remember anything after that, until I saw your face and heard your voice. After that, I woke up in the hospital and Jenny was there." He took a deep breath and let it out.

"That's good," I said, "good you remember...it helps...but you don't have to be afraid anymore...of anything. Tell me that you understand that now." He was rocking back and forth. I recognized that, boy, did I ever!

"Stop! Stop now, Martin. It's okay." I said firmly, still holding his arms and searching for his eyes. "You're here and safe now, at my mother's house...with me!" I said, trying to ward off another episode of shock like the one we had when we left the house. *Jeez, this guy needs a drink!* I thought. I needed one too. "Come on, go get the bottle from the cabinet and let's have a nice, long slug." He did what I told him and we each took a long draw of Wild Turkey, him first, then me. I didn't know it then, and wouldn't for a few days yet, but that long, sweet slug of Wild Turkey was to be my last.

I let the drink sink into him for a minute then I took him by the arms again and said, "Look at me! Look me in the eyes! Tell me that you know that you don't have to be afraid anymore." He nodded, like a child who'd just had a near miss from drowning. "I promise you, Martin...and I always keep my promises. Don't I?"

"Yes, Chief . . . You always do."

"Good! Now help me up and let's go in the kitchen. We can

make breakfast for Mom and surprise her before she gets up. God knows, we owe it to her after scaring her out of her wits last night." I saw the sun was peeking over the horizon and knew there was no way either of us would be able to get back to sleep after that scene and, even more, that I'd have keep my eye on him for a while. He helped me up, putting me, crippled, into a kitchen chair. "The neck, the neck..." I said pointing, and he went upstairs to put the turtle neck back on. He gave me two more of my pills without me having to ask when he came back down and, boy, was I ever grateful. *Blessed be the codeine.*

He went over to the counter. "So, what'll it be? Bacon? Sausage? Eggs? Toast?" he asked, taking out a frying pan from the cupboard above his head with his good arm, sounding more like himself again, but still chockfull of nervous energy.

"All of it, if you don't mind. I'm starving, aren't you?" I said, more to keep him busy than anything else. I was trying hard to hold my swollen watermelon head up realizing I probably couldn't open my mouth too far without grinding pain.

"Yeah, I am, kinda, now that you mention it," he said as he put the coffee pot on. I don't think he realized his throat was going to give him holy hell too, but it didn't matter as long as it kept him busy.

While he was cooking, I went off into a daze with the warm, comfortable feeling the pills gave me, but something was still nagging at me, hovering somewhere in the back of my mind. Then it came to me, like a puzzle coming together in my head.

I heard Grace's voice in my memory as she spoke about Dr. Eccleston, "He was on the run. Afraid for his life to stay in New York or of being arrested for the disappearance of the child and for some reason probably couldn't return to Europe," and again about Norman Harper, "He was hiding. Hiding from the government." Then I thought about what Martin had said to me the night I gave him a good what for. "I'm a lost cause Terry. A sad, weak son-of-a-bitch trying to hide away from the world." A lightbulb went off in my head. *That's it!* That's what they all had in common. They were men on the run...and hiding. That's what had made Norman Harper his target...and what made Martin his target. He used his own insight against them. It's what made them vulnerable to his attacks on them. It's why he identified with them, and then I thought...*and with me, too.* That's how he got to me...I was running and hiding too, from my guilt over Angelica's death, running to Europe to drink and then coming here to hide...from my failure. It seemed I was just beginning to understand it all when I heard my mother's voice from the kitchen doorway behind me, ever the early riser.

"Well, look at this! My two boys making breakfast for me. Thank you, Martin," she said, smiling at him as she went to pour herself a cup of coffee. "How are you this morning, sweetheart?" she asked me, tight lipped, as she lit a cigarette.

"Much better. Thanks, Ma," I answered. She turned around, exhaled and, looking at the turtle neck, said to Martin.

"Is it chilly in here? I can turn the heat up."

"No, really, Mrs. C. It's me. I'm still on the mend and just get cold easily."

Quick save, and a beauty, I thought. Then she turned to me.

"Well, Terrence Arthur...you and I are going to have ourselves a little mother-and-son talk about this tomorrow when you're feeling better," she said to me trying, but sounding none too cheerful.

"Yes, Ma," I said, feeling the undercurrent of tension she was sending me. She looked tired. I'm sure she hadn't slept too well that night either, on my account. She just went to the counter and picked up some silverware to help Martin set the table.

"Please don't be too hard on him, Mrs. C." I heard him say to her in little more than a whisper as she reached for the dishes in the other overhead cupboard. "I'm as much to blame for this as he is. I encouraged it and I'm really very sorry."

"Well, I guess you and I will have to have a little mother-and-son talk of our own then, won't we?" she said back to him just as quietly, extending the range of her undercurrent.

"Yes, ma'am," he said humbly.

"Good!" and she turned around, her hands full of dishes. Things went on from there as if nothing had happened throughout breakfast. Martin and I ate, taking only very small bites. My jaw howled. Hunger or no hunger, it just wasn't worth the pain at that moment. Mom just picked as usual, preferring her morning coffee and cigarettes to any real food before 10:00 A.M.

When we were done, Mom said, "Why don't you boys go

and get some more sleep while I clean up in here. I'll call Lila and tell her you won't be in today. I'll say that you aren't feeling well and ask her to call here if something happens that she or Eli can't handle."

"Thanks, Ma. Sounds great to me," I said, and we were off.

We slept most of that day. I got up just in time to answer the phone when it rang. It was Jenny calling to see if I was alright. Mom had already left for work on the three-to-eleven shift again. I hated her working nights, but she preferred it. She said it gave her time to be her best before she went in, but it wasn't going to be long before I exacted a promise of my own from her on that score, once I was back in her good graces.

Jenny said she'd expected to hear from me about going over and cleaning up my place, but I told her I just wasn't up to it yet…maybe not for a while. She understood completely, telling me she'd have Jeff send some of his workmen over to my place to repair the windows before "word could spread around town about strange events going on over there." I told her how I'd explained the whole mess to my mother and asked her to try to explain it to Jeff so that he wouldn't slip and let it out to find its way back to my mother. Quick on the uptake, she said she'd handle it. Good girl, that Jen. Jeff is a luckier man than he knows. Sharp as a tack, she is. I also told her that was the story I was going to give Lila and everyone else so we were all on the same page. She agreed it was best and told me she would do what she could to help keep it down.

Dinner was take out, pizza and antipasto. I ordered a special sausage, pepper and mushroom for Mom to be delivered just before they closed. I felt horrible about the way I'd worried her all my life, and especially that night. I had to try to make it up to her as best as I could and prepare myself to take whatever I had to the next day when we "talked."

Lila called about ten to check on me. I gave her 'the' story. Knowing me the way she did, she believed it, no questions. She said she was just relieved that it wasn't more serious. That part was only because she hadn't had a look at me yet. I realized after speaking to her that I was going to be in for at least a week of non-stop ribbing from my men and 'oh, the poor dear' looks from the women in town. More for my mother's sake than my own, I just hoped it hadn't gotten to the point where it was followed by, 'I hear he drinks a bit.' I'm sure she'd already suffered more embarrassment over my less than conventional behavior than any mother should comfortably have to bear.

By the time Mom got home, Martin had gone upstairs to sleep and I'd taken another dose of my pills, so I was pretty much out of it. I heard her come in and turn on her kitchen TV. I knew she got my note about the pizza in the over when I heard the oven door squeak, then I was out of it for the night.

I got up a little late the next day. Martin was already up and having breakfast when I came into the kitchen. Mom was standing in her usual spot with a cigarette and coffee cup in hand. It was clear from the expression on their faces that I had come in unexpectedly and interrupted something.

Mom handed me a cup of coffee and three Advil with my vitamins. "Sweetheart, why don't you take your coffee into the shower with you. I'm sure the hot water will go a long way to loosening your muscles." she said with a push in her voice. I took that to be my cue to leave them alone, so I just refilled my cup and did what she asked…and to tell the truth, by that point, I'd had enough of the sickening smell of my own dried blood. "I already called Lila and told her you still weren't up to coming in again today. She asked if you could give her a call later…" her voice trailed behind me as I headed toward the stairs.

"Okay, Ma, I will when I come down."

I was finally up to making the stairs to my own bathroom without too much trouble, as long as I held tightly to the handrail. When I came back down awhile later, I was clean, shaven and feeling much better for it, but still with a God-awful splitting headache. Martin met me as I came down the stairs. I heard my mother's voice call from the kitchen.

"Terry, I've asked Martin to run to the store and pick up a few things for me. He says he's up to the drive…and it's only a few blocks away, so he should be alright." I knew what that meant. I was really in for it now…big time.

"Come on in, dear, and sit down. I've just made a fresh pot of coffee." she called out as Martin limped passed me on the way out, making the silent 'lock and key' gesture over his mouth and tossing the imaginary 'key' over his shoulder on his way to the front door. I lit a cigarette as I went into the kitchen and took my seat, preparing myself for what was coming. Mom put a fresh cup of coffee down in front of me and went back to her spot leaning against the counter to light a cigarette of her own. I didn't notice her big bathroom hand mirror on the table until she pointed to it.

"Go ahead," she said, "pick it up."

"I know what I look like, Ma," I said, feeling all of fifteen again.

"Do it for me," she insisted, her voice still calm.

So I did. I held it up to my face to look. "What do you see there, Terry?" she asked me, the tension breaking slightly through the restraint in her voice.

"Little better than hamburger, Ma," I answered, embarrassed.

"Now, I want to ask you. Where is my beautiful boy? ...my handsome son?" she asked, winding into an upset. I could hear it in her voice. I didn't say anything. "Well I'm going to tell you. He's hiding behind that beaten up, swollen, alcohol-soaked mess...Look at me!" she said, on the verge of shouting.

So I did.

"I'm only going to say this to you once, and I want you to hear me. Almost twenty-five years ago I lost your father, the only man I've ever loved...or ever will, and I live with that knowledge every day of my life. I sacrificed my life so he could have the life he wanted because I loved him. I gave up any control I may have had over that the day I married him and have paid dearly for it ever since, but I will not...*will not*...stand by and watch my only son destroy himself right before my very eyes. Do you understand me? I will not sacrifice you to whatever demons that are making you drink yourself to death." A single tear came streaming down her cheek. She pushed it away angrily.

"Ma, please don't hurt yourself this way. You don't have to..." She stopped me before I could go on.

"I'm not hurting myself, Terry!" she shouted, pointing at me, "You are hurting me, and I never thought I would ever say anything like that to you in my life." There were more tears now, angry and hurt. She was on a roll like the kind I have. I knew at that moment where I had gotten that quality from and knew that I had to let it run its course.

"First, I've got to bring you home half dead from a Spanish

hospital after you fall over drunk in some filthy bar. Now, I have to watch you walk in the door looking beaten to a pulp so I almost can't recognize you anymore…and in-between, I've got to look at the face of the beautiful child I gave birth to swell more and more every day with liquor until you look like some kind of a monster…and the pills? You think I don't know about the pills? Do you think I'm a fool? Do you know that I hold my breath…*hold my breath!*…every time the phone rings and you're not in the house…waiting to hear that you've wrapped yourself around some pole and are…dead? It would kill me, Terry…absolutely kill me! I would just lay down and die." The tears were streaming now, furious and out of control. Her hand trembled as she wiped them away with a dish towel.

"I know what losing your father meant to you. It broke my heart, too…more than you could ever know, and I know that losing that little girl took away what little self esteem you may have had left after he died, and all the guilt you've been feeling since…but where is it going to end, Terry? I thought that pulling Martin out of that car would have given you some peace.

"Then I have to ask myself. 'What about me?' I've thought, in the last few years, that maybe I should've been more strict with you when you were growing up, maybe if I'd instilled more of a sense of discipline in you, you wouldn't have become so…self-indulgent. Maybe that's my fault. Okay, I'll take full responsibility for that, but you are my only child, all that he left me…all I have of him, and I will not stand by and watch you take that away from me…from him…or from yourself. Do you hear me? I'm not a young woman anymore, Terry…and I can't take…I just can't take it anymore, so I'm going to do now what I should have done a long time ago."

My head was hanging low by then, puddles of tears forming on the linoleum floor between my feet. She was right…about all of it and I knew it. Notwithstanding the fact that she didn't have the right accident this time, she was right about all the rest.

"Look at me!" she shouted again, as close to hysterical as I'd seen her since the two officers came to the door to tell her my father was dead. I looked up. "I want you to promise me…promise me now, Terry! No more liquor! …and if you can't do it yourself, I'll get you some help, but you must do this for me. *Promise me now, Terry! Promise me!"*

As I looked at her, a waterfall of tears came streaming down my face, stinging my wounds and I was slapped hard in the face with the realization of a lifetime. Growing up we tend to see our parents in their prime, young and strong. Then, as we grow older, the strangest thing happens, or doesn't happen. We continue to see them as they were when we were young, without change, until some crisis happens. Then, suddenly, in a flash, we see them as they truly are, old and frail...and afraid. That day in the kitchen was that moment for me, and my heart broke out of love for her, and shame for myself, dreadful shame for all I'd put her through.

"I promise, Ma. No more. No more alcohol. Not another drop. I swear. I'm so sorry for worrying you so much...and for being such a disappointment to you...I'll do better, I promise!"

She looked up at the ceiling with her hands on her hips and let out a long sigh of relief, because whatever else I may have been in my life, or may have become, as I sat there, she knew that I was never one to break my promises.

"Okay, then..."she said and wiped her face, slowly regaining her composure and lighting another cigarette. "We don't need to speak of it again . . . unless you think you need help. Promise me that if you can't do it by yourself, you'll come to me."

"Yes. I promise, Ma."

"Okay then . . ." she said, slowly regaining her usual calm, light, voice and setting a plate of scrambled eggs with pork roll and toast in front of me, "eat your breakfast." Then as she went to leave the room to go straighten herself up, she stopped in the doorway without turning, "...and you have never once, ever in your life, been a disappointment to me. As a matter of fact, you've surpassed the greatest hopes I had for you as a man from the day you were born, and having that in my life gives me the strength and reason I need to get up every morning. No mother could ever ask for more than that." Then she was gone.

When she came back, I picked up the thrust of the conversation while I finished eating, still wincing with every bite. "There's something else I'd like to tell you, Ma."

She picked up her coffee looking at me, mild apprehension in her eyes, waiting.

"I've decided to sell my house," I said, hoping it would make her feel a little better.

"What?" she said almost shouting, blindsided.

"I've decided to sell my house and move into town," I repeated.

"But why?"

"Well, it's too big for me for one thing, and you know I'm not much of a housekeeper. It's a shithouse in distress more often than not." I went on without stopping. "and...I'd really like to be within walking distance of work and here. I think it would just be better all around for both of us."

"Are you sure?" she asked, testing my resolve, probably thinking that the knock on the head had affected my thinking.

"Yeah, Ma. I'm sure. I'm so sure that, if you want, you can call Sylvia today and tell her what I want to do. You can tell her I'll sell my place to her if she wants it...or she can find a buyer for it, it doesn't matter to me, and ask her to see if she can find something for me close...you know...maybe one of those small A-frame cottages on the other side of town from the station, or maybe a full floor apartment over one of the store fronts in town. I can use the sale price or some of the money Grace left me to renovate it, and even put in an elevator so I don't have to deal with stairs...and I'm sure Sylvia could use someone to talk to now that Grace is gone. She's probably feeling a little lonely these days."

Mom looked like she couldn't quite absorb what I'd just told her.   "So, can I go in and finish eating in the other room and watch Jerry Springer? I could really do with a good trashy laugh right now," I asked her, wanting to be done with it.

"Yes, of course, dear," she said as I picked up my coffee and was gone.

I hadn't but sat down and started to get comfortable when I heard her pick up the phone and say, "Hello Sylvia...Charlotte Chagford here. How are you, dear? I've been meaning to give you a call since Grace's funeral..." and her voice trailed off. She must have turned and faced the sink. I guess she wasn't about to wait to give me a chance to change my mind. Of course, I wasn't going to.

Martin came in a few minutes later toting a bag full of Diet

Pepsi bottles. *Nice touch, Ma!* I thought to myself, then said to Martin, "What? Did you have to make that shit yourself? You could have in the time it took you to get it." He smiled at me nervously and went to the kitchen where I heard the new refrigerator door open and close.

After Mom went to work, Martin finally had a chance to take off the turtle neck he had been wearing since that night. He came out after showering in an open collared shirt and sweats. The marks on his neck had turned that nauseating mixture of colors...purple...some red and yellow, all with the greenish tint that symbolized healing. The sight of it made me cringe, so I tried not to look. I figured it would still be a week or ten days before they were completely gone.

"Jeez, I'm glad not to have that collar around my neck for a while," he said with a sigh of relief.

"Come on in and sit down for a while and breathe," I said, already bored with being housebound. "The 'Judge' shows are almost on."

Just after the news started, about five fifteen, there was a knock at the door. Martin jumped up and limped up the stairs so as not to have his neck seen by whoever was there. I could see his feet through the spindles of the stair rail before I got up to get the door. He was sitting on the top step out of sight, but still within hearing distance. By the time I got to the door, there was more knocking.

"Chief, it's me. Are you there?" It was Lila. I should have known. There was nothing left to do but open the door. When I did, she just stared at me with her mouth hanging open, startled apparently, by my appearance.

"Come on in, Lila," I said. "It's cold out." She came in without saying a word. I went and sat back down to wait for her reaction. I didn't have to wait long. In a second, she was sitting close next to me on the sofa...her eyes filling. Then without saying anything she put her hand up to touch my face. I let her. It hurt like hell, but her hand was so cool and soothing I didn't mind.

"What happened?" she asked in the quietest voice I've ever heard her use, stroking my face.

"I fell. I was drunk and I fell from the top of the stairs at my house. It was stupid, Lila, and I'm so embarrassed."

"Oh, Chief..." she said with a mixture of relief and sympathy. "I was so worried...even when you're not feeling well, you always still come in, even if it's only for a little while. I knew it must have been something bad."

"Nah, it's not that bad. It looks worse than it is. I was just stupid and careless, that's all." She looked around.

"Charlotte working?" she asked.

I nodded.

"...and Martin?"

"He's upstairs sleeping. He's always either sleeping or eating these days, but at least it's a sign he's getting better. My mother is pleased so it must be okay."

She took a deep breath and let it out. "What am I ever going to do with you, Chief?" she asked sympathetically.

"I don't know, Lila," I said, and shook my head looking down, "but for what its worth, my mother made me promise her that I would never take another drop of alcohol again, so it's all over but the cryin'."

She touched my cheek again. "I'm glad," she said, sounding even more relieved. "It's the right thing."

"I know," I said, content at that moment just to feel the coolness of her hand on my face again. Eli is a very lucky man. Then she picked up a bag I hadn't seen her come in with and set it on the coffee table.

"I brought you some cheese steaks," she said, giving me one of her girlish smiles. It was my turn to be relieved. Lila is so important to me. I never want to upset her again like I did that day.

"Thanks," I said, "and for the record, for whoever asks, I slipped and fell down the stairs...wet floor...okay?"

"Sure, Chief. You know I'll always have your back...always," she said, kissing my forehead as she got up. "But I'd better go now. Eli's waiting for me. He's been worried sick about you. He cares about you very much too, you know. He looks to you like a big brother more than he does his own. You only have to see his face when that stuck-up asshole of a brother of his comes home for a visit and calls him 'retard boy' because he only graduated high school, then see his face when you tell him that he's 'a true prince' to understand how he feels about you. When he's not in bed with me, his sun rises and sets on 'what Chief says and what Chief does.' He'd be lost without you. We both would, so try and take care of yourself, will ya? As much for us, as for yourself.

"Anyway...I really gotta run and let him know that you're alright and...I gotta tell him the truth, Chief. He'll think it anyway, and I want to tell him that you're off it, too. It'll stay between me and him. I have my, ways you know," she said, giving me a naughty, little smile.

I'm sure you do, sweetheart...I'm sure you do, I thought, but decided to keep it to myself, content to just look at her. "Thanks for everything, Lila. You're my right arm and half my left, too." She kissed me again, lightly on the cheek then rushed out the door.

Martin came down the stairs after he was sure she was gone and put his hand on my shoulder. "It's almost over...in a week or two it'll all be a memory. We've just got to hang in there a little while longer...then we can forget it and move on," he said optimistically.

I took a deep breath, exhaling loudly in a long sigh. "I know. You're right. Now, come on. Let's dig into these cheese steaks. I know you're dying to. Could smell 'em from the stairs couldn't ya?" I said with my crooked smile. He had his hand on the bag before I could finish. *Damn! Can that guy eat? If he doesn't watch out, he'll get as big as a house,* I thought, then again, *Nah. Probably not his nature.* But it sure was mine, and promised myself I would get back to exercising again as soon as I could, maybe in the spring. My exercise coach was probably thinking I'd dropped off the face of the earth, and she wouldn't be too far off the mark on that one.

Then Martin, not to be daunted by the cheese steaks, asked me later on that evening if there were any fried chicken places around that we could call out to for a delivery and, being the enabler 'til the end that I am, I got it done.

CHAPTER 13

Forced Recovery

"The greatness of a man's power is the measure of his surrender."

-William Booth
-19th Century Spiritualist
and founder of the Salvation Army

The next day caught me by surprise. Martin asked if I could take him over to Grace's to have a look around. He'd never even seen the place, and since we had had the keys from the lawyer the day of the Will reading, it seemed like a good idea. It was a real experience and spoke volumes about him. The photos of Grace as a young woman in the entry hall left him as breathless as they did me when I first saw them. He said she reminded him of the red-haired film stars of her day Greer Garson, Rhonda Fleming, Rita Hayworth and Eleanor Parker.

As we did a walkthrough, he was awed by the paintings and sculptures. His mouth looked like it was actually set for catching flies. He recognized a number of them, naming some of the artists on sight, something that sounded like 'Kaminsky' and something by...Scott Davis or Stuart Davis. I don't really remember. All I know is that they were modern and abstract. That was about the extent of my knowledge. He was impressed by her, now his, antique furniture as well. He used words like Art

Deco and Art Nouveau, Depression Glass and Eames. He fell
particularly in love with her writing desk, saying he would put it
in the room where he'd greet his clients when he finally got
himself together again.

By the time we got home, it was after lunch. I knew
something was up when we got in. My mother was setting out
large plates of sandwiches and chips. There had to have been
enough for a small army.

"What gives, Ma? Not even Martin can eat that much," I
asked, laughing stupidly at my own joke.

"It's my day off today, so I've invited some of your friends
over for a late lunch," she said, avoiding my glance.

I don't know why I hadn't seen it coming. I should have. I
guess I just can't shift gears as fast as I used to. A little while later
Jenny and Jeff showed up, Lila and Eli not long after that.
Everyone made themselves comfortable in the kitchen eating,
drinking, talking, some sitting, some standing. When Lila came
and sat across from me and I saw the look in her eyes, it finally
dawned on me. This was going to be some sort of a fucking
'intervention.' They were going to gang up on me. Immediately
the room seemed filled with static electricity, especially hovering
around my head.

"We'd like to talk to you, Chief," Lila started hesitantly, a
nervous twitter in her voice, eyes wide with apprehension. I
waited for the other shoe to fall. "I've been...so worried about
you lately." They all followed suit.

"Me, too, Chief," Eli said, putting his hand on her shoulder
for support, his eyes more grown up than I was used to seeing.

"Us too, Terry." Jenny and Jeff said in unison.

"...and me." Martin chimed in, with his mouth still full,
avoiding my glance. I looked at my mother.

"You know I have been, sweetheart."

I drew back and said with bullishly stubborn defiance,   I
know where this is going, and as much as I love and care for you
all...I AM NOT GOING INTO SOME GODDAMN REHAB!"

"It's not a rehab, Chief." Eli said hurriedly.

"It's a vacation," Jenny jumped in. "You've been so tired
lately and under so much stress." She was looking me directly in
the eyes so that I knew she was referring to 'the house.'

"We just think a rest would do you good, Terry...you know we're all on your side," Jeff said, his usually humorous look changing to real concern. "You do so much for all of us...including me." He went on, referring to the bathroom episode with Jenny. "And we want to do this for you, to help *you* for a change." Then he looked at Martin and said, "Martin, you're on!" Martin finished his drink as he reached into the waistband of his sweats and pulled out some papers.

"It's not a rehab, Chief. I swear. It's Mexico and it's only a week. I took this exact tour myself a few years ago. It's a resort called Excaret, lots of sun, sand and food, all inclusive. You won't have to lift a finger if you don't want to. You just have to relax." I wasn't sure if I was angry, flattered, patronized or what. I didn't know how to react. Martin continued.

"I took the liberty of booking a few side trips for you...just in case you get bored lying around the beach...to the ancient Mayan ruins, Chichén Itzá and Tulum. They really are amazing, Chief, and you can walk around at your own pace. You'll love it!" he said pulling a paperback book from on the floor beside the table. "I got you a book to help you relax, too. It's historical fiction called *Maya* but it captures their civilization in a personalized way. I read it myself when I was there. It'll take your mind off things around here for a while." I looked at my mother.

"You won't have to worry about me here, sweetheart. Martin will stay here with me until you get back. We'll look after each other. Everything will be fine," she said.

"We want you to do this for us, Chief...and for yourself," It was Lila again feeling more confident now that the possibility of my exploding like a time bomb had passed.

"Please, Terry...for me." Jenny said.

"...and me, too." It was Eli

"...and me." It was Jeff.

"...and me, too." Martin said, his mouth full again and nodding, still avoiding my glance.

Then it was Mom's turn again, "For all of us, Terry, and especially for yourself. Please take a rest."

I pushed myself away from the table, looked up to the ceiling then down again, let out a deep breath and threw up my hands. I was clearly outnumbered. "Grrrrrrrrrr, fine!"

There was a general sigh of relief in various tones around the room "That's it?" Lila asked with a small smile of accomplishment, like she couldn't believe that I'd allowed a big bully like myself to be railroaded so easily. Then, before I had the chance to say anything else, she was on it again, probably thinking she'd better get to it before I had a chance to change my mind.

"It's all set. Eli will take you to the airport in Albany tomorrow morning. It'll be early, so you'd better get a good night's sleep. I've already arranged for all shifts to be covered for the week and notified the Mayor that you were going to take some of your piled-up vacation time. He was fine with it, and you have plenty stored up."

She was speed talking now, sounding like her usual self again. From there the women hugged me and the men shook my hand and we finished the lunch. Lila dismissed the band. "The Chief has got so much to do before tomorrow morning, we'd better leave him to it," she said, and they all started filing out. She was right. If I was going to do this, I still had to go back to my house to pick up the things I took to Florida and pack up. They didn't leave me much of a choice.

The window repairs Jeff's men had done left no trace of previous events from the outside, and even though the house felt clean when I went in, it still gave me the creeps. I wasn't sorry I'd decided to get rid of it. While I was there, I took the opportunity to pick up most of the larger broken pieces from my last night there. So much was ruined I just threw it all out. I cleaned up the dried blood on the floor where my face was smashed, too.

While I was at it, I found out that it was an old cut glass lighter that struck me on the side of head that night. It must have rolled under the table in the corner of the room afterward. The blood and skin still on it was sufficient identification to make my stomach lurch and my head throb. It wasn't broken, but I threw it out anyway. It hurt me just to look at it.

When I got home, Martin filled me in on the details of the trip over dinner. After seeing my place again, I could admit to myself that I needed the rest to recover from what had happened that night, but what I didn't know then was that I would need it just as much to steel myself for what was yet to come…when I got back. *Boy, would I!*

The next morning came as early as Lila had predicted. I was up by five. My mother got up with me to make sure I got off alright. Talk was slow at that hour, but by her second cup of coffee and cigarette she was ready to relay to me what Sylvia had to say.

Apparently, Sylvia wasn't interested in buying my place herself, claiming that she was getting too old and such, the same speech I got when she first took me to the house on Randolph Road, so it wasn't all that unexpected.

What she did tell my mother was that she'd had a couple of clients in the area not too long ago looking for a place to open a bed and breakfast, a married couple who'd retired early from some high powered corporate jobs in Boston. She thought of them as soon as she heard about what I wanted to do and called to see if they'd found anything yet. Apparently they hadn't, so she made an appointment with them to look at the house in the coming week. Mom needed to know if I minded if they looked at it while I was away. So, it was a good thing that Jeff had replaced the windows when he did and I managed to pick up around the place.

I told Mom I didn't mind as long as she went over there with them to keep them from snooping too much. Not that I had anything in particular to hide, it was just the principle, really. Mom said she didn't mind going over with them at all, and since she was on the three-to-eleven shift again, she'd be free all day to do it. That three-to-eleven shift stuck me again like a thorn in my side. I decided then that I would deal with her on that issue when I got back and had a couple weeks of sobriety behind me for leverage.

Eli was at the door by six fifteen. On the way out, I hugged and kissed Mom, restating my promise to her. "Not a drop, Ma," I said.

She put her hand gently to my face. "I know, sweetheart. It'll be alright."

❋ ❋ ❋

The ride to the airport seemed slow. I could hardly keep my eyes open, snoozing most of the way. In-between dozes I listened to Eli talk about his being nervous about the wedding and being an instant father, although he'd basically been doing it all anyway for close to a year now and seemed to be loving it. I think it was the formality of the thing that scared him. I knew he'd be fine. He was just the kind of guy who was made for that sort of thing.

He asked me to bring back all the brochures and pamphlets I could find while I was down there for him to look at. It seems he and Lila hadn't even begun discussing honeymoon plans yet, and he thought it would be an 'awesome' surprise for Lila if he took her somewhere 'exotic' since neither of them had ever been outside of the northeast in their lives, and with a ready-made family, it might be years before they would ever get the opportunity again.

When we got to the security checkpoint before heading to the gate, Eli seemed jumpy, nervous. He stood there shuffling his feet and looking down. When I put my hand out for him to shake, he looked up at me with what seemed to be a mixture of sadness and worry in his eyes that I'd never seen there, pushed my hand aside and threw his arms around me, hugging me awkwardly and tightly.

"Be good, and come back safe, Chief. I'll be back here to get ya next Sunday," he said in my ear, then turned quickly and walked away. I turned at the same time, put off kilter not only by the physical impact of it, but also the emotional one, and walked through the security checkpoint knowing something of what it must be like to be a man on suicide watch. Although I knew he felt things deeply sometimes, Eli had never been the touchy feely type.

Mexico was glorious, bright, sunny, warm and...dry. The hotel was inside a jungle resort like nothing I'd ever seen. *Those Wall Steeters really know how to live. Go figure, huh?* I thought. Once I saw the place, I decided to take all of Martin's advice and follow his itinerary A to Z. *Why mess with success?* I asked myself. The guy clearly knew what he was talking about. I spent the rest of first day on the beach stretched out, lolling around, wiggling my toes in the sand and letting the warm sun and cool breezes wash away my aches and pains little by little.

That first afternoon I had my first craving for a drink. It was mild, only a twinge and I fought it by letting myself get engrossed in the book Martin had given me. It wasn't long before a little Mexican man with a big, floppy, straw hat approached me. He was a peddler with a bunch of silver, big colorful conch shells, blankets and hats. He had all kinds of things, but I wasn't into beach shopping, so I tried to wave him off.

He was insistent at first, but I made it clear that I had just gotten there and wasn't interested in buying any tourist goods at that moment. That was when he pulled out a small plastic bag full of the 'green leafy substance.' It was very bright, very green and very tempting, so I thought to myself, *Well... it might have to be a dry trip, but it doesn't have to be a boring one.* I asked how much? "Fifty American Dollars," he said smiling and put it inside a large conch shell he took out of his bag. *Oh, what the hell!* I thought and pulled a fifty out of my wallet, folding it between my fingers. He reached in and took it from my hand, dropped the shell next to me and went on his merry way.

That night I was ravenous. The young Mexican waiters at the outdoor Tiki restaurant seemed fascinated by the big American with the black eyes and broken face. At first they stared at me from across the outdoor dining area like I was some big, exotic, jungle animal they'd never seem before. Finally, while I was being served and they were convinced that I wasn't going to bite them, one spoke to me politely in Spanish. When it became clear to him that my Spanish was limited to basic conversational, he smiled at me making boxing gestures with his fists, seeming to ask me if I'd been in a fight. I smiled back, shaking my head and making a gesture with my two hands turning a steering wheel. "Errrrrttt!" Then clapped my hands and went "BANG!" and laughed. He laughed with me, nodding. It just seemed simpler that way.

In the end, I think they treated me so well, more because they felt sorry for me than for my tips. Even though I'd gotten used to looking at myself by then, I must still have looked an awful sight to them. Both my eyes were still very black and blue, among other colors. The entire upper right side of my forehead was colored in various shades, like a sad rainbow. I had a big new scar above my left temple where the gash was half healed, and my nose, as well as everything above it, was still very swollen.

I spent the next day hazily on the beach reading and drinking Diet Pepsi. Then it was poolside for the evening, dinner and an early bed. The climate, the kindness of the people and the beauty of the tranquil surroundings were decidedly having their effect on me. I was up early the next day for my first tour to the place called Chichén Itzá. It was a long bus trip, so I took my book and was halfway through it by the time we arrived.

The ancient Mayan ruins were astonishing. Martin was right. I kept finding myself thinking out loud, "How did they do that?" The book gave it all an additional perspective to ponder while I was examining the carvings of human skulls that seemed to be everywhere, reminding me of the first time I saw...the house and sending wave after wave of icy chills over my sunburned flesh that would normally be impossible in ninety-eight degree heat. I couldn't help but grimace and groan audibly as the tour guide described the Mayan penchant for human sacrifice, cutting out of hearts and using warrior heads in a game similar to our basketball. It took me back to the gorier aspects of my own recent experiences but, as usual, little did I know that it would pale in comparison to what I'd have waiting for me when I returned, but I'll get to that later...as it comes up...as it came to me.

After the site at Chichén Itzá, we went underground, descending a steep, stone staircase into a small valley-like area where my fellow tourists and I were faced with a large cave entrance and steps trailing deeply into it. Once inside, I could see in the center of the cave floor, a large clear pool surrounded by huge vines hanging from a small opening to the sky.

The 'younger' amongst us dove straight in, splashing around wildly and having a ball for themselves. The 'not so young' of us took our circumspect time about it. I lowered myself in, clinging to a short, jutting rock by the edge, folding my arms on it with my head down to let the quiet motion of the water have its way against my body, completely oblivious to the splashing circus surrounding me. It was a wonderful, sensuous feeling, the cool water siphoning off what few aches and pains I had left. "Thank you, Martin," I said under my breath to myself as I hung there peacefully suspended, weightless in the water.

When I came up out of the cave, I found an enormous rock in the sun to dry off on not far from the entrance. I'll never forget how good, safe and well it made me feel, both inside and out. I was so relaxed afterwards I could hardly keep my eyes open on the drive back. Once at the hotel, I smoked one, showered and changed for dinner. The same waiters I had before were as smiling and attentive as usual. By then, even they were able to tell I'd made some headway on the road back to myself and told me so by motioning around their faces with their hands, nodding and smiling.

The next day was more beach and more book. The other guests seemed to keep their distance from me, with the one exception of a pretty young blonde girl of about eighteen who seemed to like to take my picture. She probably thought I was a 'somebody.' I can't imagine who they thought I might be, or what they thought had happened to me, but it didn't matter. I wasn't into mingling anyway. I was just enjoying my solitude while I had the chance.

Then, having had such an exceptional time on the first excursion, I made it a point not to miss the second one Martin had planned . . . to Tulum. The ruins at Tulum were crude in their structure compared to Chichén Itzá, but I gathered that the real draw there was the view from the cliffs overlooking the Gulf of Mexico. It was nothing less than spectacular, mystical even. It was easy to see why the Mayans chose that spot to pay homage to their gods. For them, I imagine it was almost like touching the hand of God. From there, it was a visit to a jungle park called Xel-Ha. It was touristy, but I have to admit, I did take more than a little childish delight in scampering around after the big lizards who were around at every turn...and I laughed...hearty, healthy laughs, the kind I hadn't had in years. Then it was back to the hotel, exhausted.

I finished Martin's book that next day, but as much as it opened my eyes to the lives of the ancient Indians of the region, I couldn't help but come away from it with a hovering sense of inevitable dread, brought on, I thought, by the graphic depictions of the death rituals and blood sports that had thrived for thousands of years there as part of their everyday lives. In the end, as I'm sure so many travelers are, I was torn between missing home and my desire to get there and a sense of regret at ever having to leave the tropical paradise and return to my own particularly skewed version of reality.

At Martin's suggestion, I hadn't called home and he promised not to contact me unless he had to. He thought it was best that I try to leave it all behind for once in my life, and allow my mind to be free of all that had come before in order to get the most out of what I needed from the trip. I trusted him and never doubted that he would take good care of my mother while I was gone, so I just did what he said and let it all go. After all, I would be back in the thick of things in only the few short days it took to make up a week...and what could happen in a week? You can believe I was about to find out.

❋ ❋ ❋

When I came down the arrival ramp at the airport, I saw Eli standing there, jumping and waving...like I could ever 'not' see him. "Chief...over here, Chief!" he shouted, waving. I put down my bags as I got near him and put my hand out to shake. He took it, shaking it excitedly like a big, smiling kid. "Oh, Chief. You look great. Great tan. Did ya have a good time? Everybody can't wait to see ya." he said, nodding and grinning enthusiastically.

"I had a great time, Eli. I can't wait to see them either. Let's get outta here," I said as we each took a bag and headed to the parking lot. The ride back to town from the airport was more animated than the ride there. I told Eli that I'd remembered to bring brochures for him but, of course, by that time I'd already decided that, as part of my tropical rehabilitation, I'd make the same trip my wedding gift to him and Lila, so the exercise of the brochures would only be purely academic on his part without him knowing it. I'd still need Martin's help to set it up, but with Grace's legacy, I'd have more money than I'd ever need in my life and planned to use some of it to treat the people closest to me to a little happiness.

"Everyone is fine, Chief. I saw your mother the other day at the Cupboard. She was great and I know Lila stopped over there at least once…and Martin was over to see Lila during the week to tell her that he would be over at Grace's for the day if anyone needed him. He told her that he'd bought a few things and was having them delivered…new mattresses for the bed, I think she said." He'd clearly gone to the "Lila Horn School of Rapid News Delivery" lately. *It's only natural*, I thought, listening as he rattled on.

"We did have some sad news this week though, Chief." I held my breath.

God, please don't let it be one of my people, I prayed.

"Sam Woodville passed right after you left," he said. I let out a guilty sigh of relief. Sam Woodville was one of our older citizens, not as old as Grace, or as revered, but still a staple of town and a Councilman. Eli continued to rattle on after I said how sorry I was to hear about Sam.

"Yeah, I know. Me, too." he said, "I heard he was sick for a long time, but didn't want anyone to know about it. They had his funeral yesterday. It was nice, quiet…not as crowded as Grace's. Mostly family I guess, but then he was related to about half the folks in town in some way or another anyway." That was true. Small towns can be like that. "The Mayor spoke and the other members of the Council too," he rambled.

I changed the subject by telling him the plans for his bachelor party were almost done. I knew it should've been a surprise, but because we had an unusual situation on our hands, I thought I should let him in on it. Most of his closest friends were the other officers in town. We all couldn't very well all take off and go to Henriston for a good time and leave the town on its own. Even though nothing would probably happen, it just wouldn't look good. I'd decided to have it at my house so we would only be little more than five minutes from anything that might possibly need our attention. I told him I'd planned for food and a keg or two, and that since I wasn't going to be drinking and Warren rarely drank, we'd take any calls that came in. I didn't tell him that I had Joe Rogan looking into getting a few go-go dancers to come over and give out lap dances to the younger guys. That would be my surprise. I could see Eli's face in my mind as I thought of it. He'd turn fifteen shades of red when some big-boobed, G-string wearing hoochie mama started writhing and gyrating on his lap. *My poor Eli!*

From there it was just catching up. I told him that I was selling my house and looking to move into town. I asked if there were any more big storms expected. Was there anything that went on in town along the lines of police work that I needed to know? He surprised me a little then.

"Nah, not much, Chief...but I did have something of a 'happening' on Friday. I was doing my patrol and I went over to The Old Settler's Cemetery, like we've been doing because of the vandalism...like you said...and guess what I come across?"

"Do tell Eli, do tell," I said, egging him on.

"Well, I found Dean Simon's boy, Drew...he's just turned seventeen...and Brian Scott's girl, Janine...not even seventeen, parked and steamin' up the windshield of his old man's car. So I crept up on 'em real quiet like...you know...and knocked on the window. I thought they'd crap themselves," he said laughing with a mischievous a gleam in his eye.

"And guess what else I found? A half pint of blackberry brandy and a half empty six-pack on the floor," and he laughed more, sounding like more of a boy than a man. By then, I was laughing with him.

"So, whaddya do?" I asked, having a ball with it.

"Well, Chief...I did what I thought you'd do," he said proudly. "I had 'em lock up the car and took 'em in mine. I took the girl home first, gave her some gum and dropped her off a block from her house. I told her if I ever caught her doing anything like that again, I'd walk her right up to the door personally and tell Brian what she was up to. I thought she'd cry right then and there, but she promised me she wouldn't do it again and thanked me for bringing her home. She seemed like a nice girl, really."

"Then I took the Simon kid home...and I did take him up to the door. I told Dean what he was up to and where he could go get his car. It was funny as hell, Chief. You shoulda seen that kid's face when Dean grabbed him up by the back of the hair and took him in the house. A minute later Dean came back, shook my hand and thanked me for looking out for his boy, telling me he'd make sure it didn't happen again. I kinda felt bad for the kid then. He's just a skinny kid doing what kids do. Did I do the right thing, Chief?" he asked. I was so very proud of him.

"You did exactly the right thing, Eli. They'll all respect you for it. Even the skinny kid will respect you when Dean explains to him that you could have given him any number of expensive tickets, taken his license and made sure that Brian never let him see the girl again. Dean's a good 'Joe.' I knew him back in school, don't worry. He'll explain it to the kid, and Brian would respect you too, if he knew, for helping to keep 'the Baby Daddy' ratio down around town. You did good, Grasshopper," I said, laughing like I used to, then thought of what Lila had said before I left. "You are a true prince, Eli," I said and watched his face. She was right. He lit up like a hundred watt bulb. By then, we were at the house.

As I got out of the car, I told him to "...tell Lila that I'll be at the station bright and early tomorrow and see her then." It wasn't until I turned to go into the house that I realized something about Eli I'd probably known somewhere in the back of my mind all along. It was the way he told me about his 'happening' that brought it home to me. He really was an innocent, looking at the world through untainted eyes. I found myself envying him with the best of my nature. He was a lucky man to be that way, and he'd make a wonderful husband for Lila because of it. He was just the kind of man she needed, kind, gentle and sincere, simple in the best use of the word. I'm glad they've found each other. *Atta boy!*

✳ ✳ ✳

When I got in the house, I bellowed triumphantly "I'm hooooommmme!" as soon as I was through the door. "Terry!" I heard my mother's voice as she rushed into the living room to meet me, Martin right behind her. She hugged me tightly from one side and Martin from the other. It was a group hug thing and I returned it with renewed vigor.

"We've missed you so much, sweetheart!" she said and stepped back "Oh, let me look at you!" Martin took a step back to the side, putting his hands in his pockets and looking down at his feet. "You look wonderful," she said and touched my face, turning it from left to right, examining it closely. "The swelling is all gone...just the faintest signs of bruising left. You look just like my handsome son again," she said, hugging me again.

I hugged her back saying softly in her ear, "Not a drop, Ma," and put my hand out to Martin standing behind her. He took it and I gave it a good squeeze.

"Welcome home, Chief," he said with the widest, nodding smile I'd seen on him yet. Then Mom remembered she had dinner on the stove and ran into the kitchen. It was the unmistakable smell of her Hungarian goulash.

"Come in, sweetheart, and sit down for a while. I was just making dinner. Come have a nice cold drink and tell us all about it." After I sat down, she brought over a big glass of Diet Pepsi on ice in one hand and set down three vitamin Cs and two B-12s with the other. "You didn't take any with you, did you?" she asked with the mildest chastisement.

I just shook my head and made some remark about having to pack in a hurry when I caught Martin looking at me curiously from across the table, like he had never seen me before. The truth be told, he probably hadn't. I don't think there was a time since he'd come to town that I wasn't swollen, puffy or beaten up by one thing or another. As a matter of fact, I was feeling it myself. I wasn't sure what it was. Either I felt like 'a new man,' as they say, or I felt like the man I used to be once, but had forgotten long ago. Either way, it was better than where I'd been. Then Mom was back and on again.

"Why don't you boys take your drinks in the other room and let me finish dinner. It won't be long. I'll come in and get you when it's done and you can tell us all about it over dinner." So we went in, I set my cases on the sofa and began to unpack some things, gifts mostly. Now that I was back in the cold again, I wouldn't need the summer clothes and could just dump them next to the washer and dryer and deal with them later or more likely, let Mom do it. I got five big bottles of Kahlua in bottles shaped like ancient Mayan idols, one for Jenny and Jeff, one for Lila and Eli, one for the Mayor, one for Martin, and one for Mom to use in her coffee. I also got Mom one of those multicolored Mayan-style woven blankets from another guy on the beach for her to put over the big chair in her bedroom. It was kind of cheesy, I guess, but I knew she'd like it anyway.

When I looked at Martin again, I noticed that he was still wearing that ratty old turtle neck of mine. "That's not over yet?" I asked quietly, pointing to his neck. "Mostly...just a little yellow still," he said and pulled the collar down so I could see the large ring of yellow tint around his neck. "Your mother is starting to think that it's grown attached to me," he said laughing under his hand. I handed Martin his bottle.

"Thanks, Chief," he said, "but, to tell you the truth, I'm not drinking anymore...for a while anyway."

"So, she got to you too, did she?" I asked, grinning.

He smiled back and nodded, putting up his hands in an 'I give up' motion. "...but I'll take it anyway. I can always use it for guests," he said, probably thinking I'd be offended if he didn't. Then I pulled out an oversized, bright orange tee shirt and threw it to him. He caught it and opened it up. It read "My Friend went to CANCUN... and all I got was this lousy tee shirt." He laughed out loud as he read it, like I was sure he used to...before. We both did. I shook his hand again, squeezing it hard.

"Thank you, Martin,...so much. This trip has made a world of difference," I said, with as much feeling I could bring out of my blockhead.

"My pleasure, Chief," he said with one of his increasingly frequent broad smiles. By then, Mom had come in. I handed her a bottle, hugged her again saying softly in her ear, "Just because I can't doesn't mean that you can't." Then aloud, "It'll warm up your coffee on these cold nights we've still got coming." She took it with her into the kitchen and called us in.

"Come on, boys...dinner is ready."

I let Martin go first while I grabbed the envelopes full of the pictures I took with a disposable camera I got at the hotel and had developed before I left. While Martin and I ate, Mom stood in her usual spot over by the counter with her cigarette.

"I'll eat in a few minutes," she said. Then I saw her turn the cap on the Kahlua bottle and add a good shot to her coffee. She looked at me and asked, "You don't mind, do you, sweetheart?"

"Not at all, Ma. That's why I got it...and besides...that sweet, low-proof stuff has never been my style," I said and we all laughed.

I gave Mom the pack of photos from the first day trip to look at while we ate. As she thumbed through them, she said, "Terry...they're beautiful," then stopped. "Terrence Arthur Chagford!" she said, feigning indignance. "Look at you!" Then I knew. I had forgotten to take that picture out, the one taken of me on the day trip by the young blonde girl who was staying at my hotel, the one she took when I was drying off on the big rock in my shorts just after coming out of the swimming hole. She came up to me at dinner one night afterwards and gave it to me. 'I took this on the trip. I just couldn't resist. I had an extra print made. I thought you might like to take it home with you,' she'd said, turning pink and smiling, then went back to her party.

"My son the centerfold," Mom said, shaking her head as she looked at it, smiling proudly.

"Ma , please..." was all I could get out before she went on.

"And at your age, too." she said, giving me a slight, kidding push on my shoulder. I could feel all the color come up in my face under my tan. I was so embarrassed.

"So, who took it?" she asked, handing the pictures over to Martin who began thumbing through them as I explained.

"Well...you look wonderful, sweetheart, I guess you really haven't put on any weight after all," she said and winked at me, moving on to the second envelope. Then she was at it again.

"Oh...and look at this one...you look just like the Crocodile Hunter or Bwana Bill, sweetheart." That one, at least, was planned. I had an Australian couple take it in front of the Great Pyramid of Chichén Itzá in my khaki shorts, boots, tank shirt, jungle hat and sun glasses just to prove I had actually been there and...done that.

"Who in the world is Bwana Bill, Ma?" I asked, trying to take the subject elsewhere.

"Oh! He was a B matinee idol when I was a girl. He ran around the jungle chopping up vines and wrestling lions and things like that in the wilds of Africa," she said, revealing another glimmer of her former girlishness. I've always hated pictures of myself. That's why there are so few around. I always come out looking like a potato...with shoulders.

When she finally decided to come sit down and eat, we

spent the rest of dinner talking about the ruins, the heat, the food and the lizards. Before dinner was over, I could tell Martin was pleased that I followed his plan to the letter...and really did read the book. He was quiet, but seemed content and at ease.

Just as we finished our coffee, the phone rang. Mom was up to get it before I could move. I held my breath, having long gotten into the habit of expecting bad news, so I guess I've developed an automatic delay in responding. A minute later, Mom was in the doorway with her hand over the receiver.

"It's Sylvia for you, Terry," she said excitedly.

"Whew!" I exhaled and got up to take the call.

"Hello, Sylvia."

"Hello, Chief. I hope you don't mind me calling. I heard that you got back from your vacation this afternoon and wanted to let you know where I've gotten on your business. I'm not interrupting anything, am I?" she asked, not really caring one way or the other, I'm sure.

"Not at all, Sylvia. It's good to hear from you. Go ahead, tell me," I said, taking a seat and preparing myself for a lengthy conversation.

"Well, I met the couple from Boston while you were gone. I picked your mother up and we went over. You really should've had a girl in, Terry. You don't mind if I call you Terry...do you?" she asked, also not really caring one way or the other.

"Not at all, Sylvia," I said patiently.

"I mean, you men are all alike...really...Anyway, they seemed to like the place. At least she did, and we know that that's the most important factor, don't we?" I just let her go on and get it out. "I hope you don't mind, Terry, but I quoted them a price of more than twice what you paid for it when you bought it. After all, it was six or seven years ago, and values have gone way up around here with the new wave of urban flight and all...and you didn't tell Charlotte what you were looking for on it."

"That's fine, Sylvia. You're the expert. I trust your judgment," I said, not really wanting to contradict her. Besides, she was a damned good businesswoman.

"Oh, thank you, Terry. That means a lot," she said, sounding thrilled. Actually, it was a lot more than I would have expected, so I let her have her way.

"They called me back on Friday and said they wanted to come by again this week to take another look. It seems they're staying somewhere between here and Albany to look after his father for a few days, so it wouldn't be a problem for them. That's how they found us in the first place. The fact that they want to see it again is a good sign, in my experience. It means at least one of them has made up their mind, but I'm sure they'll want to negotiate on the price. They always do, so I need to know what you'll take for it, bottom line.

"Charlotte indicated that you were kind of in a hurry to get rid of it and move into town, so that's a consideration too, but I wouldn't take off more than ten thousand. Other than for the time consideration, you really can't be hurt by waiting and holding out for what you want."

"You're right, Sylvia," I said, trying not to sound as anxious as I really was to unload the place. "Time is an important factor for me, but I thought I'd just leave it up to you to make your best deal. You're the best businesswoman I know. I know you'll make the best deal that you can for me."

"Oh, Chief...Terry...I'm so flattered." She paused. I think she was really moved by the fact that I trusted her. "Of course, I'll do the best I can for you...like I said, they're due to come back again on Friday for their second look, so I'll let you know." There was a brief pause. I guess she needed a drink or something.

"Oh, there's something else. You must have heard that we lost Sam Woodville last week," she said with a strange mixture of sadness and excitement.

"Yes, I did. I was sorry to hear it," I replied.

"I was, too..." she cut in, "but I've known he'd been ill for some time. He was a stubborn, old buzzard and wouldn't give in 'til the bitter end, God rest his soul...Anyway, Charlotte told me that you wanted one of those old A-frame jobs over on the east side, and it just so happens that Sam's place was one of those over on McAdams Street. Do you remember it?" she asked, her voice rising to an excited pitch.

"I'm afraid I don't, off hand. I know there are a couple of them over there, but I don't remember which one was Sam's...but Sylvia...the man isn't even cold yet. Don't you think…" I said trying not to offend. She cut me off again.

"Oh, I know, Terry, but I saw his daughter, Isabelle, at the funeral, and I didn't ask her. She came to me and asked me to list it. She was really very self-possessed about it too. She told me that they'd all known he'd been sick for a long time and had a chance to get used to the idea, so when it happened they were prepared."

"She was all very 'matter of fact' about it. I told her that I already had someone in mind who might be interested. She said that she'd look for generally the same amount you paid for your house originally which makes sense, really, since it's half the size of yours. I think it's a good deal, so you might want to think about it."

God, this woman was like a cyclone, I thought to myself, and held the receiver out from my ear for a few seconds, then brought it back.

"Isabelle also told me that she was going to spend the week clearing the place out so I could start showing it as soon as possible. It seems old Sam hadn't taken very good care of the place since Marina died and there was a bunch of old junk to be hauled out, so I was thinking that if you were free on Friday afternoon, I could call you after I've finished with the Boston people and we could go over and take a look at it," she said, finally taking breath.

Absolutely no grass grows under this woman's feet. She must have a network of invisible hot lines leading directly to her brain from all over town, I thought to myself, covering the receiver with my hand when I couldn't control my urge to chuckle.

"That sounds fine, Sylvia. I'd love to look at it."

"Well, Terry, I really have to run now…Harry is going to be looking for his late feeding soon, but there is just one more thing. Isabelle said that she wanted to sell off some of the furniture in the house as well. She mentioned a big mahogany bedroom set with a four-poster bed upstairs and a dining room set she wanted to let go, and that the washer and dryer were only about five years old and she'd let them go too, for a song, so if you needed any of that stuff, keep an eye out when we go over and let me know. I'll make a deal for it. Anyway, I've got to run. I can hear Harry barking upstairs now." she said and we both laughed. "I'll call you at the station on Friday afternoon. Oh and Terry...please thank Charlotte for reaching out to me lately. It's meant so much to me to have someone familiar to talk to now that Grace is gone."

"I will, Sylvia...and thanks for everything. You really are a miracle," I said appreciatively.

"Don't mention it, Chief...and thank you, too."

When I went back in the living room, two sets of expectant eyes were fixed on me.

"Well?" Mom was first.

"Sylvia thinks she may have someone for my old place, and she wants me to take a look at Sam Woodville's house." Both Martin and Mom gave mildly pleased expressions to each other and said, "Good!" for different reasons, Martin because he was probably relieved that I wouldn't have to live in a house that had been touched by evil, even though it was clean now, and Mom because I would be living back in town again.

For the rest of that evening all seemed to be right with the world, but by the same time the next day, I definitely would not be able to say the same thing. The other shoe was about to come crashing down.

❋ ❋ ❋

I was up early the next day, and dressed in a nice, newly cleaned uniform. I really needed to get back to the business of...well...appearing to be in control. When I got into the station, Lila was already there. I hugged her lightly over her desk and handed her the bottle I'd brought for her and Eli.

"Oh, Chief! You look great. I'm so glad you're back," she said with a delighted squeal.

"Me too, hon, and as beautiful as it was down there, there really is no place like home. Thank you," I said giving her my best, healthiest smile.

"No problem, Chief. That's what I'm here for...but, listen, I gotta send you on the hoof right away. The Mayor called on Friday and asked me to send you over as soon as you came in this morning."

"Yes, ma'am!" I said with a salute and a smile.

Lila got up to make me a big coffee in a styrofoam cup, indicating that I should take it with me. I picked up the bottle I'd brought for him in one hand and my 'to go' coffee in the other and was out the door.

As usual, I expected the worst and was surprised to find him smiling when I walked into his office. I handed him his bottle first. "Why, thank you, Terry. That was very thoughtful. I'm sure Abby will love it. It's so good to see you. You look well rested and relaxed...great tan, too," he said, sounding every inch the politician.

"Thanks, Don," I said, still waiting for the punch line behind every politician's smile.

"I'm glad you came right in. There is something I want to talk to you about," he said, motioning for me to sit down in front of his desk.

"Go ahead...Shoot." I said as I sat and sipped my coffee, waiting to hear it.

"Well, I'm sure you've heard by now that we lost Sam Woodville while you were away last week."

I nodded saying things like "sorry to hear it," and all that blah, blah, blah for the tenth time in twenty-four hours.

"Well, that leaves me with a seat on the Council to fill for the remainder of his term and, of course, I thought of you first." That was quite an eye-opener for me, and it must have shown on my face because he didn't give me time to comment. He just put his stubby hands out in the 'slow down' motion. "You wouldn't have to give up being Police Chief, you know. It's only part time. You just wouldn't be able to vote on raises for yourself, your men or anything concerning police expenditures."

So that was it. The punch line had landed. I felt like I was being asked to jump in Sam's grave. First the house and now this, but the truth of the matter was that I knew Don was afraid I might run against him in the next election, and that I would win. I could see it in his eyes, and although I had no interest in being Mayor, I knew that if I wanted it, I could have had it by that point. There wasn't anyone in this town who didn't owe me some allegiance or other, from drunken kids, to pot growing woodsmen, to the secrets I knew about who was sleeping with whom...including him and the girl at the beauty shop. I took a deep breath and looked up in the air for a moment. I was going to find some way to use this to my advantage. You'd better believe it.

"Wow, Don. I really appreciate the offer, but I don't think I'm really cut out for politics…but there is something you could do for me." His eyes got round and wary, but still good natured. Small town or not, he was no fool and could tell I was going to make a game of it.

"Go ahead, Terry. You've got my ear," he said, sitting back in his big leather chair scratching his balding pink head.

"I'd like you to give the Council job to my girl, Lila Horn." The surprise registered on his face as soon as I said it.

"Lila? … But she's just a girl."

"She's a whole lot more than 'just a girl' Don, and I want this for her." I made my voice sound firm, "…and I want your promise that you'll support her re-election after this term is up, as well."

He let out a big belly laugh. "You're sure you want this, Terry?" he asked, testing my resolve.

"Yes, Don, I'm very sure and I'd be…ever so grateful if you would do this for me." I knew I had him and so did he. "And there's something else I'd like," I said. He threw up his hands with a sigh.

"Go ahead. Shoot," he said, mimicking my words with winded exasperation.

"I'd like for you to appoint Martin Welliver to the director spot at the library that Grace left." I saw the lines in his forehead come up on this one, and I knew why. Go figure!

"You mean the guy who had the accident? The one whose house just burned down?"

"Yep, that's the one." I nodded.

"But why him?" he asked, genuinely wanting to know, but more than a little afraid to find out.

"Well, I'm sure that you don't know this but he's a former Wall Street lawyer and I can't think of anyone more qualified to handle the contracts and supervise the construction of the additions Grace requested. He could really make 'The Coutraire Library' the pride of the county,…hell…the whole area.

"Would he accept it? If he's such a big shot and all…and not really one of us?" he asked shrugging and pulling a face, but I could see the calculator running behind his eyes telling him it would mean that there would be no cronyism going on by giving the contracts to his friends at the expense of the work, weighing it against the possibility that I would beat him at the next election.

"Yes, he'll accept it. It'll make him one of us," I said, more confident about it than I really was. I had no idea what Martin would think about it, and worried that I may have overshot myself on this one. When his eyes were through blinking and the calculations were done, he spoke.

"And if I do this for you, I have your word that you won't run against me in the next election?"

Bingo! I had him tilted. "Not that election or any other while you're alive," I said. He liked that, I could tell.

"I have your word on this, Terry?" he asked, seriousness coming into his eyes, searching mine.

"You have my word, Don," I said, equally as serious. He put out his hand and smiled. I could see the relief in his face as the muscles around his jowls relaxed. He was satisfied and so was I.

"Then it looks like we have a deal," he said, holding out his big fleshy hand to shake, sealing the deal. "I'll have Ruth get the Letters of Appointment out today," he said, his eyes shining again. "I'm glad we could work this out, Terry. You're alright in my book, and by the way, welcome back." As I walked out of his office, I heard him call out of the door, "Ruth! Could you come in for moment?"

It was done... and a beauty. When I hit the street, I punched the air like a speedbag with my own excitement for what I'd accomplished without a plan going in, but I still had to break the news to Lila and Martin of what I'd done and...hope for the best.

I took some time to walk around town and smoke on my way back to the station. The cold air felt good on my suntanned skin. It also gave me the opportunity to let the shopkeepers and other folks on the street that morning see that I was back and in good face and humor. An important part of my job was really just being seen and making people feel secure. It fosters one of the best things about small town life, a sense of community, reliability and familiarity. They like to see me, and for the first time in a long while, I liked seeing them, too.

It also gave me the opportunity to ponder what I had just done in the Mayor's office. It really was just so off-the-cuff...but it seemed right...it felt right. I didn't want his job, never did and never will, so it was no loss for me, but it gave me the chance to do something meaningful for the town as well as for Lila and Martin. They'd bring to it the thing every small country town needs every now and again, new thoughts, new ideas, new energy and...new life. Everyone would benefit from it.

CHAPTER 14

Bad Medicine

"Nature soaks every evil with either fear or shame."

-Tertullian, Early Roman Church Father

It was about ten thirty by the time I made it back to the station. I walked in clear, cool and confident. "Lila...my office," I said. She was behind me in a flash.

"Shut the door will ya, hon?" She looked worried. I stood behind my desk motioning for her to sit down, just like the Mayor had done with me. I smiled and put out my hand to shake hers. "Congratulations, Ms. Town Councilwoman!" I said proudly. She blinked a few times and looked around like I was talking to someone else.

"Me?" she asked incredulously.

"Yeah, you! I got old Sam Woodville's spot for you...just now." Her eyes got wide, her jaw dropping in disbelief. "You're kidding, right, Chief?"

"Nope!" Giving her my most heartfelt smile of accomplishment I came around the desk.

"Oh, my God!" she squealed and came to hug me. "How did you do that?"

"I have my ways," I said, giving her my comical cold war spy expression, then explained that it didn't mean that she was leaving the station because it was only part time, which I'm sure she already knew. She sat back down again for a minute to let it sink in, or so I thought. Her eyes were misting up.

"This is so wonderful. Eli has been worrying so much about money lately...with a new baby coming and all," she said, looking at me sheepishly. I guess it was her turn to surprise me then.

"Baby? ...Really?" I was stunned dumb by the announcement. It'd never occurred to me, stupid me. "Oh, Lila...oh, honey...are you happy, baby?" I said, gushing over the news. She came over and hugged me tight again.

"I'm very happy, Chief. Happier than I've ever been...and you've just made it perfect." Her eyes were leaking then and she went on as only she could. "...and Eli and I have discussed it, and whatever it is, we want you to be its godfather," she started crying. "...and if it's a boy...we want...we want to call him Terrence Arthur Beauchamps." Then she threw her arms around me again. "Please, say that it's okay. I've been so worried about what you'd think." she said, trembling.

"Lila, of course it's okay. I'd be honored." My eyes were beginning to leak too, by then.

She held me tightly, saying softly in my ear, "I'd never have had any of it if it weren't for you, Chief," and cried on my shoulder. "You'll always be part of our family...always." Then pulled back saying, "Oh! I've got to tell Eli. He'll be so relieved. Can I go call him and tell him now?"

"Sure...but wait. What if it's a girl?" I asked, trying to make light of the whole thing. She stopped and thought a moment. "Terrencia Arturiana?" she shrugged, giggling.

"Oh, for God's sake, Lila. You don't want to saddle the poor child with a moniker like that for her whole life, do ya?" I asked and started to laugh out loud when it came to me, a warm sensation spreading through me from head to toe. "How about Angelica? ...Angelica Rose." I asked uncertainly.

A light of understanding came into her face, a glimmer of knowledge in her eyes. She knew. Whether it was from my mother or my files she knew at least about the Angelica part. She came up to me and kissed me on the cheek again.

"That sounds beautiful, Chief. If it's a girl, Angelica Rose she'll be."

I choked with emotion when she touched me. "Go, go, go!" I said before I could break, and for a moment, it seemed like an old, long broken clock lodged somewhere deep inside me had begun to tick again, its hands just beginning to find their natural place in the universe. *Tick!*

❀ ❀ ❀

Once she was gone, I got that old feeling again. The one that told me I still had a bottle in my desk drawer. I took it out and set it on the desk in front of me, staring at it for awhile, pondering my fate. I opened it and smelled it. My head swam with want of it. Then I got up, went to my bathroom and dumped it down the toilet.

Another small battle won, I washed my face, went back to my desk to finish the incident reports from the week. I was done by noon, so I went out to the front. Lila was just getting off the phone. It was her mother, I could tell.

"Lila, I'm gonna pick up some sandwiches and go have lunch with the new Library Director." She stopped and thought for a few seconds using her knowledge of me to consider the possibilities.

"Martin?" she asked.

"Yep" I smiled.

"Does he know yet?" she asked with an approving giggle.

"Nope...I'm gonna go tell him now," I said.

She laughed out loud, clapping her hands with delight. "That must have been some meeting. What did you have to do? ...wrestle the chubby thing to the ground?" she asked, punctuating the question with a mischievous giggle.

"Nah, just an arm wrestle...and guess who won?"

"You did, of course!" she answered making it sound nonchalant, but beaming with pride underneath.

"You betcha." I said, and was out the door.

❀ ❀ ❀

I picked up some sandwiches and headed over to Grace's...well, Martin's place. I decided to walk, cold and all. I didn't mind it though. It was a dry, cold day and I was feeling okay. When I got there, Martin answered the door. He looked surprised to see me during the day, and even more pleased that I brought food. I wasn't sure how I was going to approach the job with him so we just ate and talked for a while about my plans for Eli's bachelor party.

I felt the situation out delicately, or as delicately as I knew how. I asked him what he thought about taking Grace's pictures from her modeling days and putting them behind glass in the entry hall of the library. He thought it was a good idea, but I made sure he knew I wanted to keep the original of the big one in the green dress for my remembrance and put a copy in the library. He liked that idea, too, and said he'd like to pick his favorite, keep the original for the house and put a copy in the library as well.

I told him about my feeling uneasy about Grace leaving me all that money, and of the other idea I'd gotten while in Mexico about spending some of it on a special dedication to her. I told him I wanted to commission a sculptor to make a bronze of her as I remembered her from my high school days, sitting on a marble bench reading a book in one hand and resting her other hand on a stack of books, nothing garish or too obvious, but something classy and...graceful...to be placed on the front lawn under the trees next to the sidewalk leading up to the door of the library.

He thought it was a wonderful idea. I was glad because I had to ask him to help me find a sculptor, from New York preferably, and thought he might have some connections. He told me that he'd known some gallery owners socially from his days there and that he'd do his best to find someone suitable. Then I eased into it by adding that it would all depend on the approval of the Library Director, of course. When he asked who that was, I told him that it used to be Grace herself, but that a new one had been appointed that morning.

"Anybody I know?" he said absently, sounding doubtful. He hardly knew anyone from town then.

"Well, now that you mention it...that's why I came here to ask you what you thought about my ideas, to get your approval." He didn't get it at first...then it hit him.

"Me?" he asked, his voice squeaking, sounding like Lila had earlier that morning.

"Yep," I said again, grinning like a proud papa.

"How can that be? I'm nobody around here. Nobody knows me."

"Yeah, well I *am* somebody around here and everyone knows *me*," I said, sounding more than a little full of myself, I'm sure.

"You did this?" he asked, disbelief still working its way through him.

"Yep." I smiled with self satisfaction

"But why?" he asked, and began fumbling with his fingers.

"For a couple of reasons, really." I was winging it again. He just looked at me, wide eyed, waiting. "Well, first, you're the most qualified person in the area for the job. Being a lawyer, and a damn good one I suspect, and a relative stranger around here, you could handle the business end to make sure that the money doesn't end up in some political hack's pocket. You don't owe anyone anything around here and as much as I know you, I know that you'd see the job got done right. You'd do justice to Grace's legacy and make something wonderful of it. It only seems right, and it's clear that Grace left you her house for a reason. She cared for you, trusted you and you're not the kind of guy to betray that." I could see the color beginning to come up in his face. He sat back looking stupefied with his hand on his face, one finger along the side, the others curled under his chin as he leaned on them, his mouth open.

"And the money wouldn't hurt either." I went on. "There is a salary involved, and since it may take some time for people around here to get to know you and trust you before they bring their business to you, it'll help keep you afloat and busy at the same time...and there is one other reason." I was feeling along the outer edges of my communication skills by then. I leaned over looked down at my feet as I do, feeling a little embarrassed.

"Everyone needs a place to belong, Martin. I want you to have the chance to feel connected to something, something you could belong to and that could belong to you...something you could build on and be proud of, so you won't be alone and adrift in the world anymore. It's like I told you that night by the fireplace about doing 'something wonderful,' this is your 'something wonderful.' You can have roots here, build a life here, create something for yourself and never have to run again. You'll be safe and secure here...and I very much want that for you," I said humbly and looked up. The color was full in his face, flushed.

"I don't know what to say, Terry," he said in a barely audible voice with his head still leaning on his hand.

"Just say you'll stay, and do it."

Then without hesitation he lifted the fingers from in front of his mouth, looked up to the ceiling, then back to me. "Yes, I'll do it," he said with a choke of emotion in his voice. "I'll do it!"

I exhaled a huge sigh of relief. It was the best I could muster. It'd taken more out of me than I'd have thought, to do what I'd just done, and I felt I could use some more of that cold air. *Whew!*

"Well, now that we've got that settled, I still have a town to protect so I'd better get back to it," I said, grinning because we both knew what an enormous job that was.

Then, as I got up and went to the door, I turned and said, "Spaghetti and meatballs tonight at Mom's, about seven. She's switched with another nurse this week so she's on the eight-to-four shift all week. If you want to walk over to the station around five, you can go over with me and drive my personal car back here when you're ready. You can keep it until you find yourself another one. I'll just use my patrol car. It's not a problem, I hardly use it anyway. Oh! and by the way, I'm gonna have the guys over at the shop scrap your old one. It's totaled, so you might think about putting in another insurance claim. They're holding it for me without charge as a favor. Once the insurance claim is approved, I'll let 'em have it." He looked at me, shaking his head and smiling.

"Will there ever come a time when you won't be there to keep me from falling on my face, Chief?" he said through his own relieved laughter.

"Nah! There wouldn't be much fun in that, now would there?" I shrugged, laughing. He laughed right out loud at that, still shaking his head.

"Good! I'm glad"

"Me, too," I said and left to walk back toward the station, still high on my own sense of accomplishment, but relieved that it was done. *Tick!*

❋ ❋ ❋

I'd done good that morning, but what I didn't know was that, with every step I took back towards the station, I came one step closer to something horrible…truly unequivocal…unspeakable. When I walked through the door of the station, Lila was at her desk. She had a strange, apprehensive look on her face. I saw her eyes shift over to the side of the room.

"There are some men here to see you, Chief," she said, pointing over to the side of the room. I looked over and saw two men sitting there. Then and there, I knew something was about to land on me. I just hoped it wasn't going around my neck or squeeze too hard. A cool head would have to be the order of the day, cool, calm and confident, if I was going to come through it unscathed. The first man wore a state police uniform, not just a patrolman either. I recognized it on the spot. The other wore a dark business suit. I walked over and put my hand out to the trooper first.

"Chief Chagford?" he asked me, standing with his hat under his arm.

"Yes" I answered. He was a big guy, taller than me, broader and a little older with big, blue, honest looking eyes, and a crewcut on what was left of his blonde hair making his already big ears look even bigger.

"Captain Owen St. George, Chief," he introduced himself in an intentionally deep official voice that I knew all too well. I shook his hand firmly.

"Terrence Chagford," I said, a resonance in my own voice coming out in my response to match his.

He looked toward the man next to him. "This is Mr. Kittridge…of the Union Fidelity Property and Casualty Insurance Company." I looked to the other man with my hand outstretched.

"Mr. Kittridge, my pleasure." He was smaller man, medium sized but wiry looking, I guess you might call it, and pale with dark hair, a pinched face and small dark eyes that darted back and forth. *The nervous type,* I thought.

"Chief Chagford, so nice to meet you," he said, pumping my hand.

"What can I do for you gentlemen?" I asked, keeping as professional a tone as I knew how.

"We're here to talk about the fire at the Welliver property," St. George said, discretely lowering his voice.

"Sure. Please, let's step into my office," I said without skipping a beat, motioning for them to go into my office first as I followed. On my way in, I looked to Lila and gave her a nod. She knew what to do and was behind me in an instant.

"Please sit down, gentlemen," I said, motioning with my hand to the two chairs in front of my desk. I went around and took my seat. Lila came around to my side of my desk, standing next to me.

"Can I get you gentlemen something to drink...coffee, water...a cold soda?"

"I'd really like a nice, cold water, if you don't mind, little lady...if it's not too much trouble," St. George said, nodding and smiling rakishly at Lila. "It's been a long drive and I'm a little parched," he said, putting his hand to his throat.

"No trouble at all, Captain," she said, smiling back politely.

"Just black coffee will be fine for me," Kittridge said, following the Captains lead, "if it's not too much trouble."

"Not at all, Mr. Kittridge," she said. As she stepped back behind them, I saw her mouth move silently to me with a little sneer, "Little Lady?"

I just smiled and told her, "I'll have my usual Lila, thanks."

"No problem, Chief. I'll be back in a flash," she said, shutting the door behind her.

I figured the Captain didn't want to begin until Lila had come and gone with the drinks, so we just made small talk until she came back.

"I hear from Mr. Kittridge that you were away on vacation when he called last week. That's some tan you got there," he said, keeping it light.

"Mexico," I answered, content to play his game for the moment. He took out a pencil and began to tap it slowly, eraser end down, making a barely audible sound on the arm of the chair. Tap...tap...tap. It was the oldest trick in the book, trying to see if my nerves were steady, but I wasn't about to chew on that old bone. After what I'd just been through, it would take a whole lot more than a tapping pencil to rattle my cage.

"It must have been nice to get out of this cold for a while," he said, obviously stalling. Tap...tap.

"Yes it was...and very relaxing...but I didn't get a message that Mr. Kittridge had called. I'll have to speak to Lila about it when she comes back in."

Kittridge spoke up quickly, "I didn't leave a message, Chief. I just asked for you and when she told me you were away for the week, I just said I'd call back. No big deal, really," he said, thinking it might make trouble for Lila. *As if!*

By then Lila had come back with the drinks on a tray. "Much appreciated, little lady," St. George said to her as she handed him his water. I got the feeling then that he knew he was getting under her skin, but that it wasn't mean spirited. He was just having some fun with the 'generation gap' thing.

"Thank you so much," Kittridge said.

"Thanks, Lila. Hold my calls for awhile, will you? Nothing unless it's an absolute emergency, okay?"

"Sure, Chief. I'll handle everything," she said in a tone intended to let the Captain know she wasn't just a coffee girl around there, and she was gone. Then the Captain was on.

"Let me start, Chief, by saying that I'm here for two reasons really, but why don't we start with Mr. Kittridge's business first. Mr. Kittridge, you have the floor," he said with a wave of his hand to the insurance man. Tap...tap...tap.

"I'm here, Chief, because we're investigating the claim on the Welliver property, and if you don't mind, I'd like to ask you a few questions to fill in your report and the report of the Fire Chief," he said, pulling out a pad and pen from the briefcase at his side.

"Not at all. Go ahead. Shoot," I said, chanting, *cool, cool, cool,* to myself in my head as I prepared to begin the routine I'd practiced in anticipation of a situation just like this cropping up.

"Well, I'm sure it won't surprise you to know that in cases such as this, we often look to the policyholder first. After all, the reports confirm that it was arson, without a doubt. I'm sure you understand," he said, looking me straight in the eye.

"Yes, of course. I understand completely. It'd be where I'd start," I said with a dismissive wave of my hand á la Grace, and let him go on.

"What can you tell us about Mr. Welliver?" he asked then didn't give me time to answer, continuing with a statement. "The records reflect that he purchased the house in mid October of last year, obtaining coverage concurrent with the closing."

"Okay," I said indifferently. "I didn't meet him until late October, close to Halloween, but this is a very small town, Mr. Kittridge, so I'm sure I could tell you what you would need to know about Mr. Welliver, if you'd care to hear it," I said, taking control of the discussion from the guy.

"Yes, absolutely, Chief... sorry I interrupted you." I just waved it off with my hand again. *Cool. Cool. Cool.*

"Well, I first met him when I was on my way home from work one night. We'd had a great deal of rain in the prior few days and there was substantial attendant flooding. I saw him before I met him though, when his car skidded off a bridge ramp and went into the river."

"You mean he crashed off the bridge?" Kittridge asked, twitching nervously, but by then I was sure it was just his nature.

"Yes." I said, simply.

"What did you do?" he asked, leaning over in his chair like I was about to tell him a campfire story.

"Well, I did my job and I pulled him out," I replied matter of factly. St. George smiled at that one, breaking his tapping rhythm for the first time since he'd started it.

I went on without skipping a beat. "He was pretty broken up. I found out later at the hospital that he had a good number of broken bones, an arm and a leg…and a pretty severe head injury and some internal bleeding too, if I remember correctly.

"I'm pretty sure he was unconscious for a while after that, but you might want to check the details with the hospital. I'm sure you could get Jennifer Denton to talk to you without violating any privileges, at least about the basic facts of it. She was the nurse who took care of him most of that time.

"I know he was there until sometime after Thanksgiving.

That was the next time I saw him, at the Dentons' Thanksgiving party. Mrs. Denton had him transported over to her home for the party. She's that kind...our Jen. I know it may sound strange to you, but you have to remember, Mr. Kittridge, this is a very small town and pretty much everybody knows everything that goes on around here. It's a very close community."

It was pretty clear to me that since I'd become quite the accomplished liar recently, I'd have no trouble holding Kittridge's undivided attention with my story-telling skills. I could tell by the way he furiously jotted things down on his pad as I spoke, so I ran with it.

"I actually met Martin conscious for the first time at Mrs. Denton's Thanksgiving Party. He had casts from knee to foot on one side and from shoulder to hand on the other. After that, the next time I saw him was at the housewarming party Mrs. Denton gave for him at his place. That was on December twenty-first, I think, but you can check with my girl, Lila, if you like," and I pointed out toward my door. "She was there with her fiancé. I was there with my mother. The Dentons were there too, with their kids.

"Mr. Welliver had just had his casts removed the day before, I believe. He could hardly move. I only saw him walk once that day, and that was with great difficulty. Actually, my mother and Mrs. Denton had to help him to the table. My mother's also a nurse, by the way. I saw him again a few days later. It had to be on the twenty-third. I took over some firewood and supplies for him. We were expecting a big snow and I didn't want to leave him stranded. He was very unwell, and in great deal of pain, couldn't move much and seemed like he had a cold coming on. My conscience got the better of me and I went back over to check on him the next day. I'm sure of date because it was Christmas Eve."

I could feel St. George's eyes on me as I spoke, and he was tapping again. I didn't look at him, just kept my focus on the insurance man and continued on with my story. Tap...tap...tap.

"He was very sick by then. He hadn't even been out of bed when I arrived. I got concerned that he was going over into pneumonia, so I brought him back to my mother's house so she could look after him and he could spend the holiday in a warm house with people around. You can check this with my mother, if you like. Her name is Charlotte Chagford. She lives just a few blocks away from here. Anyway, I'd guess it was about three or four in the afternoon when I picked him up. I had to help him up, practically carried him down the front steps to my car."

Kittridge interrupted, "Let me ask you, Chief. Did you smell any gasoline or anything when you were there?" he asked, like he was Sherlock Holmes or something and I was some kind of a fucking dullard.

"No, there was nothing. If there was, I'd have known. I've had some experience with arson early in my career, Mr. Kittridge. If there was anything there, I'd have picked up on it," I said, trying to keep my growing dislike of this guy to myself. Then it was St. George's turn to interrupt, directing his comment toward Kittridge.

"Chief Chagford used to work for...a federal task force assigned to investigate a string of arson attacks in the southern churches back in the late eighties and early nineties. It was a big deal back then, Mr. Kittridge, you might remember it. Based on that, I'd say his experience would count for a great deal in these matters." I looked at St. George, hoping my surprise didn't register on my face. I hadn't thought that I might be checked out. St. George just nodded to me, smiling...and tapping.

"Oh! Pardon me, Chief. I didn't know," Kittridge said apologetically.

"No problem, Mr. Kittridge, but you can be sure that I'd have known if there was even a whiff of an active accelerant around the place, and if not by smell, then by intuition. After a while, you develop a sixth sense about these things, and I'm telling you there was nothing." I said commandingly then went into my finish. "Anyway, when I took him out of the house, he only had the coat on his back and a blanket around him. He wore my stuff until he was well enough to pick up some new things for himself later on."

Kittridge interrupted again. *Officious little shit,* I thought, but let him have his way. *Cool. Cool. Cool.*

"The report says that you discovered the remains of the fire the next day?"

"Yes, the next day...Christmas Day. By then my mother had

given him practically every cold remedy she had in the house, so even though he still wasn't well, his symptoms were under control and he seemed better. My mother insisted that he stay for at least a few more days to be sure that there was no risk of pneumonia. He agreed, but asked me to bring him home to pick up some fresh clothes. That's when we found it, burned to the ground."

"So Mr. Welliver was with you at the time?" he asked.

"Yes."

"...and how did he react?"

"Well, he didn't even get out of the car when we saw it. He was still very weak. I thought he might pass out, so I told him to stay in the car while I got out and did a quick walk around to make sure the fire was completely extinguished before I called Ed Ward, our Fire Chief. After I called Ed, I walked the perimeter for about fifty feet in each direction to look for evidence of arson, but to be honest with you, I could smell it. It was still pretty strong around the place, gasoline. I didn't find anything concrete, though, no fuel cans or any other debris that I could link to it. I went back again the next day and looked around for about a hundred foot perimeter and still didn't find anything." I shrugged.

Then Kittridge pulled out my report. "I see here, Chief, you put down the cause as 'Arson by person or persons unknown.' Can I ask for more a specific explanation for your conclusion? Just a formality, you understand, Chief. I really need more for my report," he said politely. I knew I had them eating out of the palm of my hand then, at least Kittridge anyway.

Tap...tap...tap.

"Sure, no problem, Mr. Kittridge," I replied, going into my routine with a calm, almost amused voice. "Well, there are only six real kinds of arson, Mr. Kittridge. The first is the one we've been discussing, where the home owner torches it himself, and as I've said, I'm confident that Martin Welliver didn't physically do it himself. I'd personally vouch for that. The next is arson for hire, which I suppose Welliver could have arranged to be done, if he was strapped for cash. I didn't get that feeling from him, but you might know better about that than I would if you've had him checked out. Was he strapped, Mr. Kittridge?"

He stuttered a moment, shuffling papers in his lap. "Our investigation shows that Mr. Welliver was rather comfortable with large savings and checking accounts, a significant portfolio of stocks and bonds, and with the pending sale of his New York apartment for close to $350,000 after the mortgage payoff, we've concluded that the need for money would have been an unlikely motive to burn a house generally valued at no more than $85,000, excluding the value of property itself."

"Okay, then," I went on, confident that I still had him where I wanted him. I let him catch up with his notes before I continued. "The third reason for arson would be what the psychiatrists might call psycho-sexual obsession. That's where the arsonist had been stunted in some way during adolescence and finds that starting fires is the only thing that gives him any sexual gratification. On that one, I would say Mr. Welliver is close to forty years old. There would have been some traceable history of fires in his background by now if he were a psycho-sexual fire starter. I found him an unlikely candidate there, not only because of his education and successful business history, but also because of his physical condition at the time. Fire starters like to be on the scene to watch. It's what gets them off, so I'm completely confident that Welliver isn't one of those. He just doesn't fit that kind of profile. On the other hand, if I had that kind of fire starter on my hands here locally, I'd have had some history of small fires around here...you know, barns, sheds...things like that...and I haven't. These things rarely just pop up out of the blue.

"Next would be burning for revenge or what I call 'hillbilly justice.' You know...the 'you killed my cow so I'm gonna burn down your house' sort of thing. On that one, Welliver was only here for a few weeks before his accident. It's just too unlikely that he'd have the time to make an enemy that severe, so I dismissed that one out of hand. There was no one around here who wanted to hurt him. Hate crimes, like the black churches, fall into that category, too.

"Next would be arson to cover up another crime, burglary... murder...anything that would require getting rid of evidence." I saw St. George's eyes flicker out of the corner of my eye, the pace of his tapping picking up momentum. He was onto something and gave himself away, but I couldn't understand how it could involve me, so I went on unaffected. "On that score, as far as I know, Welliver has no family or any connections here, so I think that would be a weak theory. Plus, I'd been over to the house several times and there was no sign of anyone else ever being there.

"Then there is the last possibility, which I call 'blind, hateful malicious' burnings. The 'just because I can' sort of thing. Just for the hell of it...you know. So for your record, Mr. Kittridge, I concluded that it was most likely a combination of two motives...and there is something else you should know as well.

"We've had several incidents of vandalism and desecrations over at The Old Settler's Cemetery in the last six weeks, turning over headstones, attempts at digging up graves and the like, so I combined that with the likelihood of a possible burglary over at the house. I mean, like I said, this is a small, close community. It was no secret that a guy from the city had bought the house. I think the thugs that've been tearing up the cemetery might've figured that he'd gone away for the holidays, back to the city or to be with his family, and decided to rob the place. What they didn't know was that, because Welliver was in the accident, he hadn't had a chance to take his things out of storage, so the house was practically empty. Then, when they broke in and found there was nothing there worth stealing, they got angry and torched it. It also hadn't escaped my notice that it happened on Christmas Eve, and with the desecrations at the cemetery, I thought it might have some ritualistic meaning, but it'd be really difficult to be certain of that connection...and that, Mr. Kittridge, is how I came to the conclusion I did." I said with a certain amount of 'Ta Da!' bravado in my voice.

I looked at St. George then and could see him turn his face away from Kittridge, smiling to himself. The tapping had stopped. From there it looked like it would be smooth sailing. I took a sip of my coffee and waited until the insurance man finished writing down his notes. Just as he seemed to be finishing, the Captain spoke.

"There was one other small matter I wanted to raise with you, Chief. If that's okay?" he asked politely.

"Sure, Captain. That's what I'm here for," I said. Kittridge seemed to get nervous...again, and twitch, actively. More than I expect was usual...for him.

"Well, Chief..." St. George began, looking straight at me. "...you see how Mr. Kittridge here is a rather thorough fellow." I could tell he was being sarcastic, but it went right over Kittridge's head. I just nodded. "Well, it seems that when he was investigating the site for himself, he came across something a little out of the ordinary." The Captain then waved his hand at Kittridge as if to say 'go ahead and take it from here.'

"Well, Chief...when I was doing my usual walk-through of the site, I was out back by the tool shed or whatever it was, and I saw what I thought was an odd looking board sticking up out of the ground about six inches or so." He had my rapt attention with that. "So I got closer, and saw that it had a rounded end and...well...it wasn't a board, Chief,"

St. George cut in. "It was a bone," he said.

I thought my head would split in two. "A bone?" I asked incredulously. That one I didn't expect. The word "bone" caught me sharp, like a back-handed bitch slap.

"Yes, Chief." It was Kittridge again. "So I went over and tried to pull it out, but it was frozen in the ground and broke off in my hand."

The shock of it must have registered in my face and I thought to myself, *Keep your head, Terry. Keep it cool. Cool. Cool.*

"With all due respect, Chief..." It was St. George again. "Mr. Kittridge did try to contact you first, but when he was told you were away, he came to us."

I looked at St. George. "Are you telling me that someone died in that fire?" I asked, knowing it was impossible. That garden house was completely empty when I splashed it with the gasoline.

"No, not at all, Chief. I apologize. I didn't mean to give that impression," St. George said sincerely. I started to feel sweat building under my arms and between my legs. My stomach wound itself into a knotted spasm. It crossed my mind that he may have been baiting me, but I kept it cool on the outside until I could hear him out.

"My forensic people say the bone is old, very old, maybe a hundred years old...and a woman." My mind leapt backward, thinking of Rose, the woman Jenny saw, and all the names and faces I'd seen when I torched the place. "They're pretty sure it's of Native American ancestry," St. George said.

"Huh?" I said, sounding dumb, but not caring anymore. St. George went on.

"We were thinking that the house might have been built on an old Indian burial ground...something like that, or maybe an old town cemetery. Do you know of anything existing out there like that?"

"No, it'd be news to me, and I grew up here...but I guess it's possible." I said, shrugging.

"The only reason I brought it up to you, Chief, is I'd like to get your permission to bring a few men out here tomorrow and see if we can find the rest of 'our Indian maiden.' I thought it might be important to the town to preserve it as a historical site." Notwithstanding his words, I was not relieved. Whatever was out there, I knew it was no 'Indian maiden' but, of course, I couldn't let on about it, and I was still...curious.

"Yes, of course, but I'm sure you don't need my permission, Captain," I said, retreating back into my dumb, small town cop routine, like I was Andy Griffith and this was Mayberry.

"I respect your jurisdiction, Chief," he said. "I wouldn't have it any other way."

Nice guy! I thought. His eyes hadn't betrayed him after all. Then he spoke to the insurance man.

"Mr. Kittridge, is there anything else you need from Chief Chagford?"

"No. I think that covers it, but I could use those phone numbers, if you don't mind, Chief."

Without speaking to him, I buzzed Lila and said, "Lila, Mr. Kittridge will be coming out in a moment. Please give him the information he needs on how to reach my mother and Jenny Denton, if you would,...and give him a phone line if he needs one."

"Will do, Chief."

"Thank you, Lila." Then I turned to Kittridge.

"You're all set. If I can be of any further assistance to you, please don't hesitate to ask," I said, trying to be as professional as possible. After all, as far as the fire went, he had nothing. I could afford to be beneficent.

"Thank you, Chief. You've been very helpful," he said, turning to go.

"Just a minute, Mr. Kittridge." It was St George. "Can I assume that you're going to stay in town tonight to complete you inquiries?"

"Yes," he said. "I've got a room here for the night."

"Well then, if you would be so kind as to maybe stop by the Welliver property tomorrow morning...say around eight...to point out the exact spot where you found the bone so we can set up a grid around it."

"Sure," Kittridge said. "No problem."

"Thank you, Mr. Kittridge. I'm going to stay here with Chief Chagford and talk shop for a while, but I'll see you tomorrow morning." Kittridge nodded and went out the door, closing it behind him.

❀ ❀ ❀

As soon as the door was shut, St. George pulled his chair closer to my desk and leaned over, creating an air of confidentiality, his eyes sparking as he spoke in a low tone.

"I waited until he left to keep this just between us for now. I don't like insurance people anyway," he smiled, "but that was no 'Indian maiden' out there. My people tell me she was Caucasian...late teens to early twenties. Please forgive my subterfuge, Chief, but I'm from a small town very much like this one out by Syracuse, and I know how things can get. Anyway...like I said...my people tell me the bone is close to a hundred years old...give or take...the house was built in 1901 and we both know there is no way a small town would allow a house to be built over an existing cemetery, Indian or otherwise. The body and the house are almost contemporaneous...you get me?"

I just looked at him, listening, trying to absorb what he was telling me. All the emotions that must have registered in my face were real. I was stunned. I don't know why I should have been. After all I'd seen and felt out there, I really should have seen it coming, but I was actively trying hard not to think of those things and said the only thing that still let me keep some credibility.

"Are you telling me that someone killed a girl out there and buried her in the garden house...a hundred years ago?" I had to work to create the air of disbelief because, by that point, disbelief had been eliminated from my vocabulary.

"Under the floor is what I think," he said, emphasizing his point by widening his eyes. "That's why I want to have a few of my men come out here with some ground heaters to soften the soil, so we can find the rest of her, and anything else that may be out there. I know that, because of the time that's passed, it's not a great active case, but I'd still like to do my job...you understand." This guy was a good cop, and was going to be on this like a fucking bloodhound.

"Yes, of course. I'm with you," I said, letting out a huge sigh. *Whew!*

"I knew you would be, Chief," he said, sounding confident of my cooperation, but then I hadn't forgotten that he'd had me checked out before he came. "...and I'd like you to be out there with me tomorrow morning, if you could," he said, still looking straight at me, intently.

"I wouldn't miss it for the world, Captain. I'll even bring coffee and doughnuts," I said, brimming with the cooperation he was looking for, and why not? He was past the fire and into the flames, so to speak, and whatever we might find out there might be ugly, but it couldn't hurt me anymore.

"Good man!" he said, putting his hand out to be shaken. I shook it as he got up to leave. "I'll see you tomorrow then, around eight. I've got to get back and organize the men to come back out tomorrow morning. The first two should arrive around six tomorrow morning with the ground heaters. I'll get there about seven thirty, just so you know," he said as he got close to the door. I gave him a salute and he was gone.

After that little episode, I had to get out for some air to think. Just as I was heading out, Lila was in the doorway blocking it.

"What gives, Chief?" she asked curiously. I told her half of the truth, that they were just doing a routine investigation of the fire at Martin's, but eventually I was going to have to think of something. I thought I'd better hold on to the 'Indian remains' thing to toss around later on if I needed it. I did have to tell her I would be out of the office the next day, but still on duty. I fudged it by saying I was meeting the insurance investigator over at the property so he could examine it.

Martin came by the station a little after five as we agreed and we went over to my mother's for dinner. It was certainly a lively table that evening. Martin was like an excited child over his new appointment, talking about his ideas for the new additions, the possibility of bringing in some traveling exhibitions and having a vintage film night out in the garden in good weather. Of course, by the time we'd gotten there, Mom had already been plugged into Lila's appointment, so we all talked about that for awhile.

Martin kept looking at me like I could move heaven and earth in this town. I liked that. Then Mom dropped the bomb that she'd had a call 'from a Mr. Kittridge, asking about Martin's whereabouts and health condition on Christmas Eve.' He looked at me, worry coming into his eyes, so when Mom was putting the dishes in the sink, I mouthed to him the silent words, "Don't worry!" and motioned my hands forward, indicating he should 'let it be.'

Jenny called right after dinner wanting to speak to me. Kittridge had stopped by the hospital to see her. She said he just asked questions about Martin's admission and discharge dates, and some general questions about his condition upon discharge. She told him what she could, but told me that she felt uncomfortable about violating any privileges, while still wanting to steer any suspicion away from him. She kept her answers short and direct, and that at no time did he ever ask about me other than to relate what I had told him for her confirmation.

"I knew what he was after, Terry, but don't worry. It'll be alright. I wasn't born yesterday, although I still try look like it," she said with a loud, confident laugh.

That's my girl! I thought.

After dinner, I walked Martin out to the car. I could read his thoughts. "Don't worry!" I said. "It's just routine. You have to expect this sort of thing with insurance companies and fires. I expected it...and I handled it," I said confidently, but was still grateful that neither he nor my mother noticed how distracted I

was all evening. I thanked the fact that they were both too
excited about the recent political developments to really pay me
any real attention. I didn't sleep well that night...no surprise
there. I knew whatever we'd find out there the next day wasn't
going to be good, but just the opposite...it was going to be bad,
very bad. I just didn't know how bad.

That night I dreamed I was being carried through a black
tunnel, flat on my back on some sort of board. I couldn't move. I
was paralyzed, drugged into submission, unable to feel anything,
no pain, no fear, nothing. As I was carried out of the tunnel, I
could see the star-strewn sky above me and felt a warm breeze
waft over my naked body. When I looked down, I saw I wasn't
completely naked, but covered below by loin cloth made from
animal skin. Wanting to be afraid but unable to stir up any
emotion, I cast my eyes from side to side and saw that I was
being carried, high in the air, by eight small, dark men with
painted faces and plumes in their long black hair, a strong, acrid
mixture of smells I didn't recognize burning in the atmosphere
around me.

I was part of a procession, the bearers carrying me through a
sea of onlookers, chanting in low monotone voices as they
parted to give us a path. Before long, I felt my body incline.
They seemed to be carrying me up steps, dozens of them, high
into the air above the crowd. The altitude made it hard for me to
breathe. My heartbeat increased, pounding rapidly in my chest. I
cast my eyes around again and saw that I was on the top of some
sort of peak in the center of a brightly colored mud brick city,
flags billowing peacefully in the warm winds. The bearers
stopped and put me down on a table. The chanting stopped, too,
but was replaced by the sound of a non-rhythmic drumming,
"Thud...thud...thud."

I felt a presence near me and looked up. A man was
standing next to me, small and dark, with sharp hatchet-like
features covered in paint making him look like...a skull. His head
was covered with brightly colored feathers of all kinds and sizes,
rising up dramatically into the air. Dazed by the beauty of it all, I
saw him raise his hand high above me holding a crude flint knife.
I knew what that meant, but before I could scream, he brought
the knife swiftly down and I felt a 'thump' on my chest. The next

thing I knew I was looking up him as he held my still pumping heart in his hand above me, mumbling a prayer in a language I couldn't understand, moving quickly to my feet where a fanged stone god with horrifying, ferocious, bloodthirsty eyes waited for him...and me.

Just as my eyes began to fade, I saw him feed my heart to the god, it's bulging stone eyes changing from voracious to satisfied as I faded away, finally realizing I was an ancient Mayan warrior dying bravely on a ritual altar, peacefully watching as my life drained away into the black sky for thousands to cheer. I woke up shuddering violently, clutching at my heart as it seized in my chest, unable to breathe until I saw my old boxing poster on the wall and realized I was still at my mother's, 'Home Sweet Home.'

Damn that book!

❋ ❋ ❋

I was up early the next morning...about five thirty, showered and got dressed, dreading every minute. My feet felt like lead mired in tar. I picked up enough doughnuts and coffee for a small army at the diner at seven fifteen. I only had coffee myself while I waited for Margie to get it all ready. I couldn't risk losing my breakfast later on. When I got to the property at seven forty-five, it was freezing, still dark...and overcast. There were two men with glowing machines over by where the garden house had been. Captain St. George met me at the end of the path where the house had been and helped me bring out the food.

"Thanks, Chief. Glad you could make it," he said. *Like there was any chance I wouldn't,* I thought, because as much as I dreaded what was to come, the whole thing had become like an ugly part of me...and I had to know. The Captain and I talked while the two men worked with the machines. There were two other men there drinking coffee while they waited for the machines to soften up ground.

As we stood by trying to keep warm, St. George said, "I don't mean to intrude, Chief, but I know your father was one of us and I just wanted to tell you how sorry I am." It was like he'd struck me in my gut with a two by four.

"My father's a veteran trooper too, but he managed to get through it. He's retired now," he said, justifying his remarks to me. He really had done his homework.

I didn't know whether to be flattered or offended, but his eyes told me he meant no harm and probably just thought he was helping, so I let it go with a, "Thank you, that's very kind." Kittridge arrived promptly at eight and pointed out the spot where he'd found the bone. It was to the center of the burned spot that used to be the garden house, closer to the back of it than where the door had been.

Once Kittridge was gone, the men began to measure, making a grid with spikes and string. By eight thirty, they'd begun to dig methodically in the muck and mud with their tools. Although it would be physically impossible, I felt like I was holding my breath the entire time. No more than five minutes later, one of the men called up.

"I've got something, Captain." The voice came from a smallish, black haired man in a quilted, green khaki jumper.

"What is it, McCraw?" St. George called from some feet away as we walked toward the spot.

"It's a skull, sir," McCraw replied.

"Okay, carry on, son. You know what to do," St. George ordered as we watched from the edge of the plot. A few minutes later there was a voice from the other end of the grid.

"I got another one over here, Captain." This voice came from a tall, slim, Asian man in jeans and hooded camouflage jacket.

"Another what, Wu?" St. George barked, sounding increasingly more official and in command than in my office the day before.

"Another skull, sir," Wu replied. We both looked at each other, wordless, the surprise evident in both our faces.

"Okay, carry on, Wu," St. George ordered. Then it was the man called McCraw again.

"I've got something else here too, Captain…it's weird."

"What is it McCraw?"

"I don't know. It looks like…some kind of small block," McCraw said as he stood up and came toward us. When I saw him hand the thing to St. George, my knees got weak and I broke out in cold sweat, my eyes swimming in my head. It was a tile, a Mahjong tile.

"Where'd you find this?" St. George asked the man called McCraw.

"It was directly below the skull...under the jaw section, Sir," McCraw replied.

I turned away and took a deep breath. I had to keep it together. I had to. Weakness was not an option. Then another voice came from the other end of the plot. It was the man called Wu again.

"I got another one here, Captain," he called out.

"Another what, Wu?" he asked.

"A Mahjong tile, Captain." At that, St. George called the man, Wu, over to where we were standing.

"You know what this is, Kenny?" St. George asked him.

"Sure, Captain. It's a Mahjong tile, part of an old Chinese game. My mother and grandmother have been playing for years...as long as I can remember," Wu said, eager to add his specific knowledge. St. George looked puzzled but didn't have time to think about it because before long there was another voice.

"I've got more bones here, Captain," was the call from a well built, dark haired young man.

"What do you have, Burgess?" St. George asked. He was starting to sweat then, and so was I.

"Looks like an arm...a leg...pelvic region...and another skull... and, Captain...it looks like another one of those blocks is under the pelvic region."

"Carry on men. Chart everything. Code everything. You know what to do!" St. George ordered as he took me by the arm and walked me away from the plot. We looked at each other silently for a moment, neither of us feeling the cold anymore.

"You know what this is, dont'cha Chief?" he asked pensively. I nodded.

"These are definitely not legitimate burials. They're shallow graves. This is a killing field," he said as he wiped the sweat from his forehead with a handkerchief then looked at me saying, "Boy, you look like you could use a drink."

"I've been out of the field for a while, Captain and there haven't been many random bodies turning up in Jennisburg lately," I said wiping my head on my jacket sleeve and trying to work up a smile to cover the underlying agitation.

"Don't let it get to you," he said, putting his hand on my shoulder. "I could use a drink myself."

I spent the rest of that morning thinking of Rose and the others. "My name is Deirdre. My name is Molly. My name is Adelaide." Their names came back to me in a flood. "My name is Pansy. My name is Lizzie..." What in God's holy name had gone on here? Even though I knew, I guess the stark reality of it didn't hit me until I saw their remains.

By three, they'd uncovered ten full body skeletons...and ten tiles either under the skulls or in the pelvic regions before calling it a day. While the men were loading up the bones, St. George and I walked around the area. I felt he had something he wanted to say and was looking for a way to say it.

"Chief, you know this is bad,..." he said, stating the obvious and working to keep his emotion down.

"Yeah, real bad," I said, rubbing my head. I'd developed another head-splitter by then.

"...but my real fear is that it may even be worse," he said with a tremor in his voice, sweat beading up on his brow again. His color had gone up too, flushed to the top of his big ears. "I'd like to come back tomorrow with my men and extend the search at least another fifteen feet around the outside of the existing plot, Chief...where there's smoke there's usually fire, and I'm afraid there may be more." He was deadly serious and completely unaware of his pun. I didn't find it humorous, either. I was having trouble comprehending what had gone on that day myself, and what might go on during the next, but I agreed to whatever he suggested.

"...and there's another thing, Chief. You know I have to call in the FBI on this eventually."

I nodded. I knew it was coming.

"...but between two small town boys like us, I'm going to wait until we know the full extent of this thing. Whatever it is, it's old and there's no urgent need for immediate action, so I'm going to wait until we have everything out there and can take it back to Albany. I'll call them then. Nobody can understand better than I do what this kind of crime can do to a small town...old or not.

296 Inside A Haunted Mind/Malone

I'm going to do my best to keep the fuss to a minimum. If I have all the bodies in Albany when I call them, the worst that can happen here is that they may send one or two investigators out with some machines to x-ray the ground to make sure we got it all, but at least it won't be a circus with vans and units and the rest. I'll catch hell for not calling it in sooner, but trust me, Chief, I'm very well connected. That'll be the end of it. I can't be hurt…and small town guys like us have got to stick together," he said with an intimate tone of camaraderie. I just nodded to him respectfully and agreed to meet the next day at the same time to continue. Then I got the fuck outta there.

I didn't want to go back to the station just yet, so I drove around my old patrol route, wasting time, trying to get a handle on what the day had brought to my doorstep. By the time I got back to the station, Lila was already on her way out. I was grateful for that. I didn't want to spend any time explaining myself. It was just, "Hey Chief, how'd it go?"

"Okay," I said. "Routine…but Lila, I gotta go to Albany tomorrow to give a formal statement and finish it off, so I'll be gone all day."

"Okay, Chief. I gotta run to pick up Tyler now. Don't worry. I'll take care of everything."

That was easy. I just washed my face and hands before I locked up to go home. It was on the ride home that I felt the first trembling in my hands. Whether it was the shock of the discovery that day, or the fact that it had been close to three weeks since I'd had a drink, I don't know, probably a combination of both, but it was more than I needed to contend with right then, and it worried me.

Dinner was quiet. I guess Mom could tell I was exhausted, but I could also tell that she'd noticed the trembling in my hands when I lifted my glass. She didn't say anything, but I knew she saw it. I didn't sleep at all that night. I just tossed and turned, trying to get my head around all those bodies and the unthinkable prospect of more the next day. I kept hearing Rose's voice in my head, "…he hurts us so badly…"

Would it ever end? Would it ever be over? I kept asking myself. I had the shakes a few times that night, and the sweats too. I showered once during the night and then again in the morning. I just couldn't get myself clean enough no matter how hard I scrubbed, first with hot water, then with cool...and particularly the area on my shoulders where that filthy creature had touched me before I got out of the house. I couldn't seem to get it off me.

By the time morning came, I'd managed to get some control back. Strong coffee and all the strength I could gather in myself got me out the door and around to the diner for more coffee and doughnuts. I couldn't let anyone see how it was getting to me. It reminded me of the old deodorant commercial. "Never let 'em see you sweat." It was the only laugh I had that day, and a sad one.

❄ ❄ ❄

When I arrived back on the site, it was as it had been the day before, but this time St. George had brought two more men with him. One was a young blonde kid named Kerrick with a scruffy beard and dressed in digging clothes like the others. The other man was named Sculthorpe. He was older than the others, balding with a mustache and glasses in civilian clothes. Sculthorpe was a forensic anthropologist on loan from the State University and a friend of St. George's, I gathered. He was there in an unofficial capacity, at least at that point, but he began to dig, getting dirty with the rest. It wasn't long before the voices began again.

"I got one here, Captain," It was McCraw again, then more.

"Over here too, Captain." It was Wu.

Then a few minutes later. "Looks like two over here, Captain. I've got two skulls a little over a foot apart," called the new blonde man, Kerrick, from the far side of the pit. St. George and I looked at each other with queasy disbelief. There was very little left to say. We just sweated and wiped our faces for most of the day. The man Sculthorpe walked around excitedly.

"This is amazing!" He kept saying as he uncovered bodies himself. "This is amazing!" There were more tiles too. For each body, there was a tile either under the skull or under the pelvic area.

"It looks like he was shoving the things in their mouths or in their...privates, tagging them with his signature," St. George said to me.

"Or a talisman or a charm, maybe part of some sort of ritual," I said.

"Good thinking, Chief! Could be," he replied.

By the end of the second day, the body count had risen to twenty-seven and I had a rage inside me stronger than I'd never thought I was capable. It was hate again, but a kind like I never thought I could feel. Around four thirty McCraw, Burgess and Sculthorpe came to tell us that they'd searched an area thirty-five feet from center in all directions away from the original plot. They hadn't found anything in the area that would have been in front of the garden house, around what must have been the door area.

It was Sculthorpe's idea that, other than under the floor, he, 'the mortician' as they were calling him by then, had only buried on three sides, in back toward the wooded area, from the far side and the front facing the back of the main house. He said he'd also found an old hand fork and spade buried in that section, so one might assume that he planted his garden over those bodies. That way, Sculthorpe assumed, if anyone were to look, no one would see any disturbed ground but for the 'garden' area. He was relatively certain that they'd found it all because nothing was found for ten feet behind, or on the sides, of the new grid where the last bodies were found.

When I heard his thoughts about the garden area, I was overwhelmed by the sinking feeling of aching sadness, not unlike the grief which I'd come to know so well in my life. I had to struggle to hold back my tears. I knew in my heart that the bastard had planted flowers over the bodies to match their names and scents like bizarre headstones, daisies over Daisy, lilies over Lily and...roses over my Rose.

"Okay, men, let's pack 'em up and take 'em back," St. George ordered, and the men set once again to work. While they did, St. George and I walked and talked.

"I have never...in my whole life...ever seen anything like this...and I hope I never have to again. It's monstrous," he said to me, rubbing his head. "You got a cigarette, Chief? I quit a few years ago... but I really need one now." I gave him one and lit one myself.

"So what happens now?" I asked him.

"Well, after we get them back and complete the cataloging, I'm going to call Washington and see what they want to do...then I'm going to try and get the good night's sleep I haven't had since this thing began," he said and laughed a sad, tired laugh.

As we walked and smoked, he said, "I want you to know before I go, Chief, how much I respect what you tried to do when you were in the south... with the churches and all. I hope you weren't offended that I looked you up."

I was taken aback for a few seconds. *Is there anything this guy doesn't know about me?* I thought to myself, suddenly realizing that he'd been trying to reach out to me since we'd met.

"Not at all, Captain. I can respect your thoroughness, and I can't thank you enough for all you've done to keep this quiet," I said to him. His eyes were tired and bloodshot. "Is there anything I can do for you?" I asked as I shook his hand. He smiled a big, honest smile.

"As strange as it may sound, I'm starving. I haven't had much of an appetite in the last few days, but I sure could use a good meal now. Any good places a guy can get fed around here?" he asked, working to lighten up.

"Sure, there's a place called Federonico's in Hamilton Common only about two miles down that road," I told him, pointing down the other end of Randolph Road. It brings you straight into the Common. You can't miss it. They make the best pizza and pasta in the County."

"Sounds great. As soon as we're done here, I'll send the men home and head over there...and, Chief...I will be in touch as soon as I know about any activity on this, no matter what," he said, wiping his head again as we walked back to the cars. I left first.

On the way home I called Federonico's on another of those rare occasions when I actually used my cell phone. I spoke to Papa Federonico himself. I've known him since I was a teenager and he threw me out for trying to buy beer while under age. I told Papa that he could expect a big trooper named St. George to come in soon, that he was a personal friend and colleague of mine, and asked him to give St. George the best of whatever he wanted and plenty of it, then to send me the bill. It was good to hear Papa's voice. I hadn't been over there since before the river accident and promised him it wouldn't be long before I got over there again. It gave me a long past memory of normalcy to speak to him. Then I headed back to the station hoping I'd missed Lila. The last thing I needed right then was the third degree.

CHAPTER 15

Shake, Rattle and Roll

"Fear, if allowed free rein, would reduce us all to shadows of trembling men, for whom death could only bring release."

-John M. Wilson

I showered again when I got home, scrubbing myself down...hard. I felt so...contaminated by it, all of it, that it touched me...that it knew me...and I knew it. It seemed like I couldn't get away from it, or get it off me, no matter how hard I scrubbed, no matter how hot the water, no matter how strong the soap.

I wasn't afraid of it anymore. I was...disgusted by it...enraged by it...sickened by it for what it had done, and depressed by it because it'd degraded my already sorry life beyond anything I thought could endure. It'd tainted my body, infected my mind. I was consumed by it, losing track of time as the hot water poured over me. I had to struggle to pull myself together in time to go down for dinner, praying that there wasn't another tidal wave of it out there waiting for me again.

Dinner was quiet again, just small talk about my moving. Martin had invited Mom over for a visit to see his 'new' place that afternoon and have lunch with him. She said he was doing well, seemed happy, that he'd asked after me and she'd invited him over for dinner again on Friday night. I had the feeling she was watching me to see if I would get the tremors again. After all, she'd spent years seeing the DTs over at the hospital, so I knew she was going to keep a close eye on me, which meant that I'd have to keep a close eye on myself.

I didn't sleep well at all that night either, no surprise there. Twenty-seven bodies, twenty-seven lives…twenty-seven deaths, terrible, fear-filled, tortured, pain riddled bloody deaths…and for what? To feed some sick sexual appetite?…worship some evil pagan deity?…a thrill from some sadistic parlor game?

I had more tremors and more sweats that night, washing every two or three hours. I couldn't stand feeling so…unclean. It felt like it was eating me alive inside…and the fact that I desperately wanted a drink didn't help. The drink kept calling to me with the promise of some semblance of peace and sorely needed sleep, but I knew I couldn't. It would be unforgivable, not just by my mother for breaking my promise to her, but by myself for the guilt and the weakness I would feel for giving in to it. I'd just have to tough it out, no matter what it took, no matter how long it took, no matter how much I had to suffer…and I was suffering…God, I was suffering badly.

When morning came, the one thing I had to be grateful for was that I didn't have to go back to that…'killing field.' If push came to shove, I could just go into the station, shut the door, put my head down for a few hours, and hope the world would leave me alone for a while. Like the "Friends of Bill" say, "…one day at a time."

I washed my hands and face almost every half hour that day. Lila was an angel, as usual. She knew I was tired. I told her I wasn't sleeping because I was stressed out about selling my place, buying a new one and all that was involved. She started making the coffee stronger then. I gotta love that girl because, inside, I'm sure she knew what was happening and was trying to help me in the only way she knew how.

I had the evening to myself that night. When I got home there was a note from my mother saying that she was going to play cards with Sylvia and her bridge ladies and that dinner was in the oven, pasta bake.

What I really think is that she wanted to let me have some time alone…to tremble in private if I needed to…and I did. I scrubbed, and trembled, and sweated more that night, but I did sleep some, only waking up every few hours, startled out of nightmares I didn't remember. Thank God for that! But I vomited that morning and knew that the next few days would be the real test... and the worst. I just went into the station, closed my door and put my head down. The next thing I knew, Lila had her hand on my shoulder, shaking me gently.

"Chief, Sylvia is on the phone. She says you're supposed to meet her over at Sam's place to do a walk-through. You want me to put her off?" she asked delicately, caringly.

"No, it's okay. Just get the house number for me and tell her I'll be there in ten. I'll wash up and head over," I said, still half asleep. On my way out, Lila handed me a hot cup of coffee 'to go.' "Don't worry, hon, really. I'm just having some sleeping problems lately. I'm probably still jet lagged too. I'll be better after I get in the new house."

I met Sylvia over at the house, and it was one of those A-frames I've always loved. We met Isabelle at the door and did the walk-through. It had a large living room with a beautiful fireplace and a pitched ceiling, a smaller dining room opposite with a surprisingly well kept dining room set. The kitchen was smaller than I was used to, but in good shape otherwise. The laundry room behind it was very small, but functional. It had a door leading to the large, overgrown back yard with real potential from a gardening perspective. I had a thought then that I might have a go at gardening myself, recreating the lives there that I owed my life to...lilies, pansies, daisies and...roses.

Upstairs there were two medium-sized bedrooms where I could see taking down the dividing wall and making it one large loft bedroom. The mahogany bedroom set was beautiful and old. It looked soft, warm, inviting and secure. I would definitely have that. The bathroom was old, but in great shape. It still had the original fixtures from the '20s...claw-foot bathtub, pedestal sink and all. The floor was covered with small black and white tiles and the walls were covered half way up with similar, larger ones. It all needed a good cleaning and paint job, but other than that, it was perfect...and I was going to have it. As Sylvia and I walked out down the sidewalk, we stopped to talk.

"So, what you think?" she said, hopefully.

"I'll take it Sylvia. Go ahead and make the deal. I'll take the dining room and bedroom sets too, and the washer and dryer," I told her. I could tell by her eyes that she was thrilled.

"Don't you want to think about it for a while?"

"Nope. Go ahead and make the deal. You can give her the price she wants for the house and make whatever deal you can for the rest."

"Oh, Chief!...Terry. I'm so pleased." Her eyes twinkled.

"I'm pleased too. I think I may even take a stab at being happy here," I said, struggling, daring to feel hopeful for myself for the first time in a long while.

"Well, I'm sure I can set it up to close in a few weeks. How do you want to pay for it?"

"Cash," I said confidently. I knew I'd have Grace's legacy cleared by then, so it would work out until I could sell my place and put the money back. Then the most unexpected thing happened. Sylvia took my hand. She was wearing Grace's ring and looking at me purposefully.

"Chief...Terry...I want you to know that I'm going to waive my commission on this. Like Grace said in her note to me, I do have more money than...God," and she laughed a small laugh. "And there are some things more important in life." I could see her eyes misting as she went on.

"I can't tell you how much your words at the memorial meant to me...and Charlotte being so kind to reach out to be my friend. I believed what you said then. We are like a family...I'd like to think we are...and I want to do this for you," she sniffled, moist eyed. I took her hand with both of mine then and kissed her cheek. It surprised her.

"Thank you, Sylvia. That's very kind." I was moved myself.

She flustered, waved her hand at me and said, "...besides, I'll make it up on those Boston people when I sell them your house," and we laughed out loud together, genuinely.

"By the way, the second walk-through of your place went well. The wife really wants it. I can tell. They asked for two weeks to think about it. That means they'll have it. Mark my words!" she said, pointing her finger at me. Then she took out her compact to look at herself in the mirror, dabbing her eyes and fussing with her hair. "Now let me go back in there and deal with Isabelle. I'll call you next week." I waved as she went back in and went on my way. *Tick!*

※ ※ ※

I got home that night just in time to shower and scrub off again before Martin got there. I could tell Mom had heard me get sick that morning because she made mashed potatoes and baked chicken with steamed vegetables for dinner hoping that the blandness might prevent a repeat. When Martin arrived he was excited to sit down with me and show me the photographic samples his gallery owner friend had sent him. The sculptor's name was Evan Killough McNeill and he seemed to specialize in marble, but also did bronze casting. The pictures were of some marbles of both mythical and modern figures, as well as some abstract. The photos of his bronze works had "a style that was both firm yet smooth and fluid." Martin's words not mine.

I must confess that looking at them did take my mind off of other things and I did find that his bronzes had a humanistic look, not stiff or false. My words, not Martin's. There was a note with the photos from the gallery owner saying that he had spoken to McNeill, that he would be interested in the commission and would be available to come up to discuss it on a week's notice. I asked Martin if he wouldn't mind inviting him up for the weekend. He agreed, adding that he'd ask him to bring some miniatures of his bronze work so we could see them in three dimension...good ol' Martin. I could tell he would be a big help to me in dealing with this...and I was glad. I was going to need help. Then the dinner bell that's Mom's voice called us to the table.

The table was set and Mom was in her usual position, leaning on the counter with her coffee and cigarette, waiting for us to begin eating before she sat down. The food was good, but I took it slow. Martin was at it like a house afire. Halfway through, I felt it coming on.

When I went to pick up my drinking glass, they were on me,

the tremors, but more like full blown shakes by then. I tried as hard as I could to control it, but I know Martin saw it. I could see the glances pass between him and Mom. I just put the glass down and put my hands in my lap, waiting for it to pass. I was so embarrassed for them to see me like that. I remembered again helping Martin take off his clothes on Christmas Eve, his voice saying to me, "I'm so embarrassed," and I wanted to cry.

When it passed, I went on as though nothing had happened and finished my meal. Martin and I took our coffee to the living room by the fire. I could see in his eyes that he felt sorry for me. I didn't want that and hated myself for it...for being sick and weak, but as usual with my life, it was going to get worse...much worse.

After Martin left, I went to bed tired and ashamed. I slept some, but woke up in a sweat after dreaming that I'd watched myself build my own coffin. Standing in shadows, I watched as I cut the wood with my own saw and put it together with my own hammer and nails from my own tool belt. At first I thought the "watcher" was the real me and the "worker" was an illusion. Then as I watched as I shut myself up in the coffin to suffocate, I realized that the "watcher" me was really the ghost and the "worker" me was my mortal self. I jumped out of bed and ran to the shower to scrub myself off again. It was all I could do to keep from scrubbing my skin off, but at least it gave me the peace I needed to get a few more hours of sleep before the sun came up.

When I got up on Saturday, I was glad I had to go into work. I spent most of the day trying to tire myself out, walking around town, smiling, nodding and shaking hands, but really worrying about the insurance man, the state police, the FBI, and 'the mortician' a.k.a. Dr. Charles Lawson Eccleston, the monster no one knew anything about but me. That night was worse than the past few. I had chills and tremors most of the night. My head ached terribly and I was dying for a drink. I showered twice and was forced to take a muscle relaxer to take the edge off. I slept only slightly, the kind of sleep where you're not quite sure if you are awake or not...a limbo. Something had to give. Something had to break and soon, before I did. It came the next day.

❋ ❋ ❋

I was off duty that day. I had my coffee but couldn't eat much, just some scrambled eggs and toast. I could hardly get myself off of the sofa for fear that my knees would give out. I just laid there wrapped in my blanket, working hard to take the edge of my internal chills. I could tell my mother was worried. She spent a lot of time on the phone in the kitchen. Just before she left for work...that goddamn three-to-eleven shift again...she came in with some toast and tea and told me that Martin was going to come over to spend the afternoon with me.

"I'm sorry, sweetheart. If I'd have known, I would have called out, but now it's too late to get any coverage. You'll be alright. Martin will be here with you. He knows how to reach me if you need me," she said, misty eyed. I got the feeling she was ready to give me a drink herself by that point. *I can't seem to do anything right. I'm screwed up when I drink, and more screwed up when I don't. Ain't that a killer!* I thought to myself. As she went out the front door, I heard voices out in the yard then Martin came in.

"Hey, Chief!" he said, working to sound cheerful for my benefit. He went straight into the kitchen and started a pot of coffee. I followed him in and sat down. "I spoke to McNeill," he said, "he'll be here next Friday afternoon to see the site, look at the pictures of Grace, and make us a sketch. He sounds competent and together...not flaky, like some of them can be," he said. A few minutes later he poured me a cup of coffee. When I went to pick it up, my hand were trembling...badly. I couldn't hold the cup without spilling it. My mouth went dry and my ears were burning. Martin reached across the table and took my hand firmly, holding it tight.

"I'm here, Chief. It'll be alright. I know you're suffering. I've known it all along, but you don't have to do this alone. I'm here with you. I won't leave you." he said, squeezing my hand. "After all you've done for me, looked after me, don't you think for one minute I would ever let you go through this alone. I promise," he said reassuringly, his voice almost a hum. Suddenly I couldn't breathe. My chest seized up, I broke out in another sweat and started shaking uncontrollably, not just my hands but my whole body, the last vestiges of my already broken manhood falling apart like a fragile brick wall in an earthquake... disgraced. When I looked at Martin, my eyes must have looked like they'd come jumping out of my head.

"I can't breathe!" I gasped, hardly able to speak.

"Oh, my God!" He jumped up and was at my side. "Does your chest hurt? Your arm?" I shook my head.

"No pain...just tight." I gasped, rocking back and forth, clasping my chest.

"Jesus Christ!" I heard him say. The next thing I knew, he was pushing a paper bag over my mouth and shouting, "Breathe into the bag, Chief! Breathe into the bag! It's okay. It's just panic. I've got ya!."

A few minutes later, I could breathe again, but my stomach was squeezing and churning like a row boat in a hurricane. I jumped up, making it up to the sink just before it all came up. My head gave over to the spinning and my knees buckled. Martin put one hand on my arm and the other on my shoulder as I retched into the sink. He kept saying, "I'm here, Chief. It's okay. I'm here," as I stood there gripping the edge of the sink, heaving my guts up and wishing I could just crawl down the drain with it. I lost time for a few minutes. When I came back, Martin was still there, the entire weight of his body holding me up. When I raised my head a wave of relief came over me, but along with it was the realization that my embarrassment was complete. I had nothing left.

I washed my face and hands, managing to make it to the sofa to sit down, my head in my hands. It hurt so badly, pounding and spinning. *Death has to be better than this agony*, I thought. Martin came in with a cold towel and put it on the back of my neck.

"Martin, I'm so embarrassed. Please don't look at me. I can't bear it." I said with my head down, the pattern in the carpet whirling before my eyes, and started to cry.

"You never have to be embarrassed in front of me, Chief...not ever." He put his hand on my shoulder again. "Come on now, lie down for a while. See if you can sleep some. I'll stay here with you," he said and he pulled up a chair to sit by me, holding the cool towel on my forehead and eyes. Then, just as I found myself in that limbo of half sleep again, I could swear I felt a gentle hand stroke my hair and a soft voice say, "I won't leave you." *Dad?* ...and was out.

The next thing I knew, Martin was shaking me gently. "It's time to get up for a while, Chief. It's after seven. Maybe you should try to eat something. I made you something light...and they're showing *Quo Vadis* on Turner Classic Movies at eight. I think you'll like that," he said, then went into the kitchen. I sat up and leaned over. I felt better, solid, like I had my feet firmly on the ground for a change, not wobbly at all. I was feeling better and I was hungry, famished really.

I yelled into him, "Hey, what did ya make?...more cold steak salad and mustard vinaigrette?" I heard him laugh out loud from the kitchen, appearing in the doorway a few seconds later holding a tray and smiling.

"You must be feeling better to make fun of my cooking. Actually, it's just a BLT on rye toast with some Campbell's chicken and rice soup, but I can take it back if you don't want it," he said, moving back into the kitchen.

"Nooooo...that'll be just fine!" I said, laughing weakly. "Bring it here. I'm starved...and by the way, did anyone ever tell you you're 'a real good 'Joe,' Martin."

"Eh, I've been called worse," he said, smiling to himself as he handed me the tray.

I had some time before the movie so I went up and took a shower, but I didn't scrub this time. My skin had been scrubbed raw in the last few days. I fought the urge to make it worse, deciding to use one of my mother's soft cloths instead of the rough natural sponge I was used to. We watched the movie quietly, and Martin was right. I did enjoy it...very much. It was sword and sandals with heart, and soul, and moral...and faith and, for some reason made me feel 'full' inside.

By the time my mother got home, I felt pretty well recovered, but it seemed that Martin wanted a guarantee. While my mother was changing out of her uniform, he handed me two pills. "Valium...I had them in New York. Take them both so you can get a good night's sleep. Trust me," he said, more as a command than a request, so I took them and I did get a good night's sleep, no tremors, no sweats...no nightmares. The next morning I was like a rock, a little groggy, but after I showered, I still felt solid. *Tick!*

✳ ✳ ✳

That week went pretty smooth. I only had light tremors. Compared to what I'd just gone through, I figured I could handle that well enough. I got a funny note in the mail, a paper menu from Federonico's. Written on it by hand with black marker was, "Small town boys…Thanks…St. George." I laughed to myself. *Nice going, Captain,* I thought. Sylvia dropped off the Contract of Sale papers on the Woodville place while I was out of the station. I signed them when I got back and had Lila drop them off to Sylvia on her way home that night.

Martin and I met Evan Killough McNeill that Friday at the Tavern Grill. He was a smallish man, about my age, with short, wavy red hair, green eyes, freckles and almost elfin features, a real text book redhead. His hands were hard worked and rough. He wore a plaid flannel shirt with jeans and work boots. The only thing that belied his size was his voice. It was deep and resonant, gruff even. I liked him immediately. I'd half expected someone with all black clothes, dyed black hair and a world full of irritating affectations. I was glad I was wrong.

We took a table big enough for six so we could spread out and take stock of what we were going to do. I told him what I wanted as he looked at the pictures of Grace. I wanted him to age her to about fifty, wearing the clothes she wore when I was young, with the hair and the position I wanted. He seemed interested and receptive as we talked and ate. He told me he would watch some old films from the sixties to work out the clothes I wanted. He was good. I could tell. He told us that he was a night owl and would stay up to see if he could get a sketch going for us to look at before he left. I liked that about him, no nonsense.

After we'd agreed on a price and he'd had a couple glasses of wine, he started to talk more…personally. He said he was glad for the commission, telling us that from the minute he'd gotten the call from Martin that he'd felt a certain 'synchronicity' about it all. When I asked him stupidly what that meant, he said it was "when things that seemed to have no real connection turn out to be significantly related." Knowing so much more about life than I ever had before gave me pause to think about the concept. He went on to tell us that he wasn't like most New York artists in that his real aim was to be remembered for the body of his work and not to be just a 'flash in the pan' or 'hot flavor of the month.' He said it appealed to him to have his work spread throughout the country, giving him a sense of broad interest…and that a little national publicity wouldn't hurt him either. He laughed at himself as he said it, but I took the idea and ran with it.

I wanted him on my side to do what I needed to get done, the way I wanted it done. I told him that if he sent me some biographical material and some publishable photos, I would see what I could do about getting an article written about him in the local paper in town, tying it in with Grace's statue, and that I'd try and pull a few strings to get one in the regional paper as well. A few clippings of that sort couldn't hurt in his scrapbook. He liked the idea, so I made a note to myself to get it accomplished. Then when Martin went to the restroom, I got the break I needed to speak to McNeill alone, getting to the second heartbeat of the matter. I told him in confidence that I had another job for him too, a smaller piece, of a little girl to go in front of a church outside of Memphis. I told him it was personal and that I would stop by to see him at the Inn the next afternoon with a photo and the details of what I wanted, and that I needed both of them as soon as possible. His eyes twinkled and we toasted. Mine was Diet Pepsi.

The next afternoon, I went over to the Inn and brought the picture of Angelica. I told McNeill that I wanted that face on a little girl to be sitting on a marble bench, like Grace, but with her hands propping her up on each side and her feet dangling over the edge because they couldn't touch the ground. I wanted her face looking up to the sky, like she was trying to catch the rays of the afternoon sun, and smiling, like she was in the picture. It was going to be a face toward heaven for Angelica.

Because I liked him, I told McNeill her name and that it was for a memorial at the church where she was lost in a fire. I'll never forget the way he watched my face carefully as I spoke, like he was tuning into me. It made me a little uncomfortable at first, to be scrutinized that way when I was feeling so vulnerable, but I needed what he could do for me, so I let him. It was important for him to know what I wanted and that I meant business. I'm sure I hit the mark with him too, particularly when I handed him a check for five thousand dollars as a deposit and told him I had already taken care of his tab at the inn.

On his way out the next day, he came by the station with the sketches. They were exactly what I wanted. He seemed excited about the project, and more so by the fact that I was pleased with him. Then he was on his way saying he'd send the models as soon as he could. I felt a sense of relief then, another tick in the clock of my life trying to set itself right. It made me feel like I was finally on the road to where I needed to be…but still without knowing if I'd ever get there, or where that 'somewhere' might be. *Tick!*

❋ ❋ ❋

It seemed things were happening every day after that. Martin came by the station on Monday. He just walked into my office, wearing my old turtleneck, and shut the door. When he turned around, his eyes were shining and he was smiling brightly with one of the broadest smiles I'd ever seen on him.

"We did it, Chief! *You* did it!" He was beaming.

"What now?" I asked as he handed me a letter from his back pocket. It was from Kittridge. The insurance company had approved his claim, in full. He was to expect a check within two weeks. I raised my head to the sky and let out and enormous sigh of relief. *Thank God!* I felt like a ton of weight had been lifted from my chest. We were in the clear. I was in the clear. Martin sat down and started talking. *Tick!*

"It's only for the value of the house, and what little I had in it…but I still own the land. What do I do with it, Chief?…the land, I mean." he asked me. I could see the wheels turning behind his eyes. I had to think for a minute, but he didn't give me a chance to create an answer I could live with. "Do I sell it? Do I keep it?" he asked, rushing me.

"I don't think you should sell it, Martin. If anything were to happen, just think of how we'd feel knowing what we know. I know the guilt Grace felt when you moved in and I don't want that for me, or for you." He sure was a lawyer. He was on my slip of the tongue in a flash.

"What about Grace? What did Grace have to feel guilty about? What did she know?" His eyes took on an intense sheen as he began to cross examine me.

Damn! I'd let it out before I had a chance to think. I hadn't told him about Grace and Norman Harper, so I had to then. The cat was out of the bag, so I told him of my afternoon with Grace and the story she told me that day. He seemed to get paler with every word. "How did you know to go to Grace? Why didn't you tell me, Terry?" he asked, sounding hurt.

"I knew to go to Grace because of the tiles. They came to me...in my dreams first...then I saw her bracelet, and when I saw the one you were wearing with the dragon symbol the night I got stuck there at the house, I knew there had to be a link. I just didn't know what it was. I knew what I thought, but I didn't want to believe it." He just looked at me, astonished. "I didn't tell you because I was fighting to save your life and my sanity at the same time. It was because of Grace that I knew I had to go and get you out of there on Christmas Eve. She made me believe it. I thought you might be dying, Martin. I was trying to protect you and I had no choice but to carry it by myself. Then things got out of hand and I didn't want you to know how bad it really was."

His eyes got wide, sad, downcast. "Oh, Terry!" he sighed. "God, I had no idea...Does anyone else know?" he asked, shifting nervously in his chair. I felt I had to come clean then.

"Only Jenny."

He raised his head. "Jenny?" He though for a minute and the light came on in his head. "Oh, my God! She didn't fall down the stairs on Christmas Eve, did she?" his eyes got wide and his voice went high with alarm.

"Kind of...but not really." I said sheepishly.

"Please tell me, Terry!" he pleaded, so I told him what happened... and that after what happened to Jenny, I knew I had to burn it. She was the only other one who knew about me and the house. It was the only way. He started rubbing his head, trying to take it all in.

"Please don't worry, Martin. Jen is a real trooper. You saw

her at the reading of the Will. She's fine," I said, and told him about the story we'd made up for Jeff's benefit, begged him not to say anything to either of them about it.

"I got the gas from Jeff, Martin. He doesn't know what I did with it. Please let it be...for my sake. Jenny is okay, you're okay. Grace is at peace and I'm as okay as I can be under the circumstances. No one else can be hurt. Please just let it be!"

"Yes, I know you're right." he nodded sullenly.

I went on, "...and if it weren't for Jenny calling me after you'd been out with her, telling me that you still had the tile...and was wearing it...we'd both probably be dead now. I don't want her to have any more grief over this than she's already had." He shook his head in agreement.

"Terry, I just...feel... What you and she and Grace must have gone through...for me..."

"Don't do this to yourself, Martin," I said. "We did what we did because you mattered to us...and we wanted to protect you. None of it is your fault. You can't blame yourself for what went on in that house before you were born...and somebody had to put a stop to it...it just turned out to be me. I never thought I'd say this but...I'm glad it was me."

At that moment, my eyes must have been as deep with intent as they'd ever been. I needed him to believe that none of it was his fault. Lila buzzed in then, telling me that Bjornstrand was having some trouble over a traffic accident and needed assistance. It seems that the two guys wanted to duke it out and he had his hands full.

"I've gotta run, Martin...just hold onto the property and let it grow over and forget it." I grabbed my jacket and was out the door.

I didn't hear from Martin for almost three days after that. I think he still had to get his head around what I'd told him. I hadn't wanted to tell him, it just came out. I guess it was for the best in the end. He had a right to know.

When he did show up next, it was as if it had never happened. *Way to go, Martin! Walk it off!* I thought. He just showed up for dinner at my mother's and began going on and on about his plans for the library. Mom was so pleased to see him. She kissed him and hugged him like a long lost son.

We had Eli's bachelor party later that week, lots of beer, booze and Joe Rogan's babes from Henriston…and I was right. You should have seen Eli's face when it came time for his lap dance. I thought he'd fall over in a swoon of bashful, blushing embarrassment. But, in the end, he took it like a champ, making us all promise never to breathe a word of it to Lila, which, of course, no one would. It reminded me of when I was young and didn't have a care in the world. Martin took it in his stride, but I think he was more than a little shocked by all the shenanigans that went on. I never took him for the go-go dancer type anyway. He's way too cultured for that.

Sylvia called at the end of the week and told me that Mr. and Mrs. Boston had made an offer on my house. It was fifteen thousand less than what she'd asked for and said to me, "Between you, me and the wall, Chief…it's still a great offer. I'll pitch 'em for thirteen and a half and see if they bite. Either way, take it. I know I said not to knock off more than ten, but I always shoot higher than I think I can get. It's part of the game. It's a great deal and the timing couldn't be better."

I was pleased as hell, too. I told her to do what she could, then take it and run. When she called me back to tell me that they'd agreed to the thirteen and a half, the glee in her voice as she screeched through the phone could have shook the walls. She told me they'd have a bank check for the twenty thousand deposit by the end of the month and were going to finance the rest. She would send out the papers the next week. In the meantime, she thought it was a good idea that when the deposit check came, I take ten thousand of it and give it to Isabelle as my deposit on the Woodville place and pocket the rest. *Tick!*

Lila and Eli's wedding was the following week. Lila looked beautiful in her gown, low cut and snug in ivory with little pearls all sewn in a pattern. She wore a short veil and all. Eli looked very handsome too, all scrubbed up. I don't think I'd ever seen him so nervous, but you could tell he was happy. We were all there, Mom, Martin, Jenny and Jeff with Jared and Jordan dressed like perfect young gentlemen in suits like their father. Jenny looked 'goddess like,' resplendent in the emerald jewelry Grace had left her. Even Tyler and Jonah were there, looking like they'd just walked off the front of a greeting card, almost too adorable to be real.

All my men attended with their wives or girlfriends as did Eli's father, mother and brother with his wife and kids, Lila's mother and her sister with her husband and kids. Her sister, Sara, was Matron of Honor and Joe Rogan was Best Man. Ever the budding politician, Lila had sent last minute invitations to the Mayor and his wife along with the members of the Town Council and their respective husbands and wives, so the place was pretty well crammed. *That's my girl!*

Wearing my dress uniform for only the third time since I've owned it because Lila said she thought it made me look so dashing, I hung back from the crowd to keep an eye out on the off chance that her ex might show and try to make trouble, but I guess that's just the cop gene in me. It wasn't very realistic…just knee jerk.

The ceremony was mercifully short and sweet, and Lila looked so happy as she walked, teary eyed, down the aisle with her step-father. Watching them take their vows really tugged at my heartstrings, jabbing me with a twinge of selfish regret for having let yet another chance at life pass me by. But in the end, it's always been what's best for her that was important to me, well more than for myself, and marrying Eli was for the best, for everyone. *I'll always love you, Lila,* I said to myself as they left the church. From there I resolved to content myself with the knowledge that she'd never go very far away from me, or for very long, neither of them would, and I could live with that. *Tick!*

Jenny gave the reception at her place, a catered affair, of course. That Jenny does love to give parties and Jeff is always so very proud of her with his own 'Lord the Manor' approach to party giving. It wasn't long before he had the bartender making Cosmopolitans and called me over to join in the toast. I was prepared with cranberry juice on ice and faked it. When it seemed appropriate, I took Eli out onto the porch and told him what I'd done. I told him Niagara Falls could wait until they were old and gave them the packet Martin had put together for me.

Martin was a real sport about it, too. He made special

honeymoon arrangements for the week, got special rooms and rates with the same side trips I'd taken. It was worth the cost just to see Eli's face. He was thrilled to the teeth, but when I went to go back in, he suddenly turned serious and said something . . . remarkable.

"Wait, Chief. There's something I wanna say to you," he said, fumbling and pacing. I stopped and walked back to him.

"Go ahead, shoot."

"I know what people think and say about me around here, Chief, that I'm 'not the sharpest tool in the shed,' that I'm 'dumb as a stump,' and maybe they're right. I may not be the smartest guy in the world, but that doesn't mean that I don't know how to love, and I love Lila and Tyler with all my heart, Chief, and I'll do my best to make them happy. I promise. I want you to know that." He said, his eyes shining with a depth of manhood I had never seen there before.

"I know you will, Eli. I've never doubted it for a minute...and you know why?" He just shrugged, fumbling with his hands in his pockets. "Because I've watched you grow into a very fine young man and to me, you'll always be...a true prince," I said, tapping the part of his chest above his heart with my fingers. That was it. His face flushed to red and he threw his arms around me so hard I had to take a step back from the force of it.

"I love you, Chief."

"I love you too, Eli," I said giving him a good slap on the back. "Now, go back in there and tell that beautiful bride of yours that she needs to repack for a hot climate...and make sure you tell her I said to speak to Martin before you leave. Oh, and Eli,...as far as what other people think and say about how smart you are..." He stopped, hanging on my words.

"Fuck them!" I said, shaking my hand in the 'jerk me off' gesture, thumb and index finger making the requisite circle.

"Yes, Sir!" he said, standing at attention, grinning from ear to ear and saluting.

"Good man!"

I'm so very proud of Eli. He's a real man now. He proved it to me beyond any possible doubt that day on the porch. I just hope, deep inside, that in some small way I've helped to get him there. *Bravo, Eli! Tick!*

❀ ❀ ❀

Since the happy couple were off to sunny Mexico for a while, it meant I had to do double duty, both Lila's job and mine, or more correctly, do my job without her, which meant I had to actually work. I decided in my mind that when they got back, I was going to get her to go on 'unofficial' part-time, which meant she would only come in for half days and then take what she could home if she wanted. It would be too great a stress on her to do full time at the station with a toddler, a pregnancy, a new husband and the Council job. We can't take any chances with our "little prospect" now can we? It was about time Bjornstrand took on some additional duties anyway.

At the end of the week that Lila and Eli were away...it was a Thursday. I got the call. "Jennisburg Police," I answered the phone.

"Chief Chagford, please." It was a young woman's voice.

"Speaking," I replied.

"Please hold for Captain St. George." Then a click.

"Chief! How are you?" It was St. George.

"Yes, Captain. I'm fine. How are you?"

"Oh, I'm just a working stiff!" he said and laughed. "I'm always working and I'm always stiff!" and laughed again. "Did you get my note?" he asked in a much better humor than the last time I'd seen him.

"Sure did. That was very kind of you," I said, sounding like my old self as well.

"Nah. It was very kind of you, Chief. It was a wonderful meal. I enjoyed it thoroughly. Thank you."

"No problem, Captain. It was my pleasure."

"Well, the reason I'm calling, Chief, is I've got some news for you." His voice changed to serious. "After I got back, I contacted Washington about our little...situation. They sent a few agents who specialize in that sort of thing a few days later." I listened intently. "They did some work up here, then had all the...stuff...shipped down there for further analysis."

"I'm listening," I said, holding my breath.

"Well, I had an Agent Levengood come see me this morning

with their report. He told me I can't keep it, but he wanted to see me personally to give me the results. I told him about you, Chief, and all of your cooperation in the matter, and asked him to stay over 'til tomorrow...at the state's expense, of course...to give you a chance to come here and see him in person. Can you make it?"

"You betcha," I said, my voice squeaking like a rusty door hinge. "I appreciate that, Captain," I said, bringing it back down.

"There's just one thing..." he went on, "...he's got to be out of here by two tomorrow afternoon, three at the latest. Can you be here by noon?"

"I definitely will, sir."

"Good man!" he said. "Oh and, Chief... You'd better prepare yourself. It's heavy...very heavy." That set my mind to working. Could it be heavier than anything I'd already seen? I doubted it.

"I will, Captain."

"Good. I'll see you at noon then, Chief."

"You got it," I said and he rang off. I called Warren Newman to get him to cover me the next day telling him I'd just been called to Albany on a "highway expansion matter."

CHAPTER 16

Mahjong, Anyone?

"There is no fear in love, but perfect love casteth out fear: because fear hath torment. He that feareth is not made in perfect love."

1 John-4:18

I left the next morning straight from home and arrived in Albany just before eleven thirty. I knew where the State Police complex was, so all I had to do was find St. George's office. I walked through the door by noon. There was a pretty young girl in uniform at the desk with lots of sandy hair clipped up on the back her head.

"Chief Terrence Chagford to see Captain St. George," I said as I walked up to her.

"Yes." she said smiling. "He's been expecting you. You can go right in," and pointed to the door behind her. I steeled myself as best as I could and went in.

"Chief! So glad you could make it," St. George said, smiling as he stood up, coming around his desk to shake my hand.

"Good to see you too, Captain," I said.

"This is Agent Grover Levengood from Washington," The Captain said motioning to a tall, squarely built black man in a black business suit. Agent Levengood rose to greet me with his hand out. He was not forty, I would have guessed, with smooth dark features, a bright smile and glasses.

"It's a pleasure to meet you, Chief Chagford. I've heard a great deal about you." I looked to St. George who winked at me and smiled.

"Thank you for staying over to see me, Agent. It was very kind of you," I said, trying to sound as professional as I did back in the day.

"Not at all. Brothers under the badge and all that," he said, waving it off. "But we should get right down to it if you don't mind. I'm under somewhat of a deadline. I'm meeting my wife in Manhattan for dinner and a show. A friend of mine in our office there scored two tickets to *The Producers* for me and I owe my wife a night out. She's been dying to see it. I'd rather see *Rent*, myself, so maybe if we have the time, we can still catch a Sunday matineé," he said, flashing his bright toothy smile again.

"I understand completely," I said, smiling back as I sat down. "Go ahead...Shoot."

"Well, as I'm sure you already know, there were twenty-seven sets of remains recovered from the site." His tone changed to serious, professional. I nodded. "All of them were female. All of them between the ages of sixteen and thirty...and Caucasian.

"There was evidence in some of the older victims of a pelvic condition common among prostitutes, so we've made that leap as to most, if not all of them. At the very least they were of a lower class, poorer background. The teeth are very telling in that respect. From the marks evident on some of the bones, it appears that at least some of them were dismembered and then reassembled for burial." I made an involuntary groan of disgust at that, but didn't say anything. I just wanted him to get on with it.

"My people tell me that, as far as they can tell based on the evidence, they all were 'done' over approximately a twenty-year period, which they estimate to be from around 1901 to 1924, give or take, and although it's tough to be completely accurate, they believe that the ones exhumed from under the shed floor were 'done' first, then extrapolated in burials from there outward."

"Okay. I'm with you," I said, nodding. *Jeez, it's getting hot in here,* I thought while he went on.

"Now, for the Mahjong tiles. They were made of ivory,

which means they predated the plastic age and were rather expensive when they were made and purchased. We estimate between 1850 and 1900, but I'll get to that more, later. Each set of bones had a tile associated with it, either under the skull or under the pelvic area, which we believe to mean that 'our man' placed them there either before, during or after death, in the mouth or...the genital areas of the victims.

"Our researchers tell us that these tiles, by themselves, have no occult significance, so they believe that they were used as a personal tag or signature, the source of which I'll also get to in a moment. Next, as to identifying 'our man,' we sent an agent to Jennisburg to do some discreet research into the house and the chain of title according to our time line." I was way ahead of him there, but I listened and nodded patiently.

"The house was built in 1901 by a man named Dr. Charles Lawson Eccleston. Your local paper of the day identified him as an English national. He's our man. From there we went to the immigration records to determine his date of entry to the United States to be 1899."

Touché, old girl, I thought, reminded of Grace's amateur detective work

"From there we looked for any similar crimes between 1900 and 1901...and we found two," he said, in an almost mechanical tone that I remembered from my old days with 'the Government.'

"Two women were found strangled and floating in the East river in 1900. Each had a tile lodged either in the throat or...rectum." My eyebrows rose at that.

"We found an article describing an incident later in 1900 of a mob attack somewhere downtown, naming Dr. Eccleston along with a Russian woman émigré named Romanovsy, where a man was hanged in the street. His name was Kakospharmakos, a Greek émigré. At the time, there appeared to be some occult connection.

"According to our other research, the Russian woman was some sort of a psychic and the Greek was reputed to be a devil worshiper who supposedly specialized in conjuring demons or some such nonsense. He was exiled from his own country because of it."

Levengood flipped the pages of the report in his hands,

gleaning from it as he went along. "On this point, depending how one looks at these things, either as clever or just plain freaky, the Greek's Ellis Island papers state his full name to be Andros Kakospharmakos, which, when translated from Greek to English, means 'devil conjuring man,' so I guess we may never know who he really was." The short hairs on my neck bristled at that as I recalled the scribbling on the walls of the house, the symbols, the five pointed inverted star...and the false door Martin tried to walk through to get away.

"From there we did a background search of Dr. Eccleston in England. The records there reflect that he was born the son of an affluent family from Cornwall in 1871. When the boy was five years old, his father died rather young of typhus while traveling in the Far East for the British government, leaving his mother a young widow of significant means until the time her death, which was about the same time 'our doctor' entered college in London.

"Dr. Eccleston graduated with honors and was apparently well poised for a successful medical career. That's where our personal information ends. However, when we searched for similar crimes in England in conjunction with Scotland Yard historians, we came up with two, a prostitute and a dance hall girl in1888 and 1889. These two were poisoned, but they had the tiles to connect them to our guy."

"Confidentially speaking, the current Scotland Yard historians were of the opinion that the cases were...swept under the carpet, in a manner of speaking. At the time, the Scotland Yard police had just finished taking a good shellacking over the 'Jack the Ripper' killings and were in no hurry to have another mess on their hands, so when there were no more similar murders, they let it go."

Beads of sweat began building on my forehead. It was getting like an oven in there, and the thought of "The Good Doctor," as he'd identified himself to Martin, skulking around the damp, gas-lit streets of London at the same time as 'Jack the Ripper' before coming to my little town almost blew what was left of my fucking mind.

"Knowing what we now know about these types of killers..." Levengood continued. "...we know that, unless he was dead, he wasn't going to stop killing, so we checked for other similar killings in the capitals of Western Europe. The next hit we got was in Paris between 1891 and 1893. There were four, two street prostitutes, another dance hall girl, and the last was something they had back then called a 'courtesan,' what we might call today a celebrated, high priced call girl or escort." As he spoke, my mind raced back to my meeting with Cash Hasher and a chill ran through my limbs despite the increasingly tropical temperature in that room.

"It appears that these girls were celebrities back then and rather well regarded in certain circles of Parisian society. This is where we think he overstepped himself. The police reports on the death of that one indicated that they were looking for an 'English Gentleman' for questioning in the matter. We think that this may have caused him to run again, but there was a difference with the Paris cases. He was escalating in violence by then. The Paris women had their throats cut and, once again, the tiles were the identifying markers in the places on the bodies we've been discussing."

At that, I had to take out my handkerchief and wipe my head. St. George must have picked up on my distress because he poured me a glass of cold water from a pitcher on his desk. It seemed incredibly hot in that room, and then I realized it wasn't just me. I could see he was starting to sweat, too.

"We got more hits in Madrid over a five-year period from 1894 to 1899, seven of them. The M.O. was the same, prostitutes and dance hall girls. The Spanish police at the time were the least modern in police practice, thought and philosophy as compared to the London and Paris forces. They really didn't pay much attention to it all. The girls were found in slum areas, sketchy reports were made, and then forgotten. Once again, the tiles were the linking factor. These girls had their throats cut as well, but they also had symbols carved into their flesh and at least two had numerous cigar burns around the breast area. Unfortunately, the reports didn't contain any descriptions of the symbols, but given the nature of our other information, we believe they had a 'satanic' connotation."

You better fucking believe it, Agent, I thought, forcing myself to recall the image of 'the thing' in the basement, raising its hands and mumbling to itself in that fucked-up language.

"There also was some evidence of dismemberment in Spanish cases, an arm here, a leg there, an ear...fingers. We assume by then it was trophy time." As Levengood spoke those particular words, I found myself thrown back to the image of the Spanish girl on the table who called herself 'Iris,' the one who warned me, "He's behind you!" and my hands began to shake. I just held tight to the arms of the chair, like I was on a very bumpy plane ride, and let him go on.

"He came to New York City in the same year he left Spain." Levengood said, becoming visibly uneasy himself, squirming and shifting uncomfortably in his chair. I could see beads of sweat rising on his forehead by then, too. "We've concluded that, because New York was the most modern city he'd 'worked' in, he managed to rein himself in on the violent aspect of the killings to avoid detection. That's why he took to strangling the two in New York."

My head swam as I tried to count up the numbers and still absorb what Levengood was telling me. He took a short break to drain the tall glass of water in front of him. St. George poured more for all of us as we all wiped our brows in almost comic unison, then Levengood was back to flipping pages and speaking.

"It seems that after the mob incident in New York, he decided to take to the country, finding your quiet, little village and making a home for himself there. Location was probably the deciding factor. Your town was not too close to the city, allowing him to hide quite effectively, yet not too far from adequate hunting grounds for his favorite types of 'young ladies'. We think he brought the girls there from New York City, Albany, Buffalo...even possibly Boston, anywhere within a few hours' trip where he could find prostitutes or desperate women. He would have been much too clever to have troubled himself with local girls and arousing suspicion around the house." Then he paused and took a sip from his glass.

"Is there more?" I asked, not really wanting to know, but feeling compelled to ask, nevertheless.

"Not factually," he said. "Those were all the killings we could find, but we did come up with some other related information which you might find interesting."

"Go ahead. I'm listening."

"Of course, we had our profilers look at the thing. They came up with some preliminary thoughts that may pull the whole thing together for you. They believe that the seeds of this sort of violence against women begins early in life, the fact that he targeted mostly prostitutes bringing in a sexual element.

"They believe that it was possible that his young, widowed mother may have had an abnormally large sexual appetite and may have brought her lovers into the house where the child probably witnessed the acts. The mother may have even forced him to watch, or even participate. Incest isn't even out of the question. The extent and violence of this sort of behavior transcends your garden variety promiscuity, so whatever she was doing had to have been well beyond the usual societal norms and inordinately intense for the child, to say the least."

"They believe that the link to the tiles stems from the dead father, who most likely sent them back from the Far East before he died, as a gift for the boy...probably his last gift. They further believe that the mother may have taken out her frustrations at her widowhood on the child by forcing him to take the tiles in his mouth to prevent his crying while he witnessed her acts...and that possibly as her sexual mania escalated, may have taken to forcing the tiles into the child's rectum as a punishment."

My stomach revolted into a knot as I listened to him tell that part. My hands were numb from gripping the arms of my chair, white knuckled. "Dear God!" was all I could say.

"By the time he'd reached puberty and could defend himself from her aggression, it was too late. He was already programmed for what he would later become. There may have been a period of relative normalcy by then, but the fact that the mother died shortly before he went to London to study medicine strongly suggests that he may have caused her death. Also, the fact that what may have been his first prostitute killings were accomplished by poison further supports the possibility that he may have 'done' the mother by poison because her death was listed generically as consumption at age thirty-nine."

I had to wipe my face again by then and noticed that St. George was sweating again as well. It'd gotten so hot in there.

"The bottom line is that my people believe that the tiles, coming from the father, represented a phallic symbol for our boy, becoming, more or less, a part of him or an extension of his manhood. The fact that he used them the way he did, leaving them in the places he did, further supports that theory. The fact that he used them in crimes against women suggests revenge against the mother, in essence, doing to her what she did to him and ripping her apart for it, over and over again." Levengood stopped to take another drink and we all mopped our brows, dripping from the heat, before he continued,

"But there is one other thing that my people found rather interesting. It seems that this Russian woman, Romanovsky, was a rather prominent medium of the time. Apparently she was some sort of…cult celebrity, I guess we would call it today. She was invited into the best homes…the wealthy…the influential. Her books can still be found in the old archives of libraries in New York and London, and there are numerous mentions of her in prominent biographies of the day along with even more newspaper accounts of her exploits and alleged spiritual accomplishments." At that, Levengood let go the tight smirk of a disbeliever.

"When we traced her, we found that she was appearing in every major city where our man was conducting his…'hobby'. We think he may have followed her from London to Paris. As a matter of fact, there was some documentation to show that in 1893, 'Madame Romanovsky,' as she was called, was accused of conning the jewels out of a certain Countess something or other, and was told if she returned the jewels she would only be deported, rather than jailed. As a result of the scandal, she fled to Madrid, as did our boy. I should tell you here that, as strange occurrences will happen, Countess 'whatever' went into a coma and died shortly before 'The Madame' left the country. Then she was on to New York, as I said, in 1898."

"But the thing that made my people scratch their heads was, 'why would a man with such obvious deep hatred and penchant for violence toward women, then align himself so closely to a woman?' Was she a mother figure? No. If that were it, he would have killed her immediately. He wouldn't have been able to control himself. It wasn't that. Then they examined the existing photographs of her. There are quite a few of them still around in books and newspapers, like I said, she was quite a phenomenon." Levengood shifted in his chair took another drink and handed me a photograph.

I studied the photograph closely. Madame Romanovsky was a large woman, strong looking, and stout, not beautiful or feminine in any sense of the word. She had large, peasant-like features and a mop of frizzy, unkempt hair tied in a knot at the top of her head. Her eyes were dark and piercing, almost hypnotic. They seemed to jump right off the page at you from the photograph. She was very eccentric looking with string upon string of beads around her neck, large dangling earrings, rings on every finger, and she was smoking a cigar. Levengood went on with his report as I looked at the picture before passing it to St. George.

"When they examined it all closely, it came to them. Maybe she wasn't a woman at all, but a man living as a woman. It made sense. The deception would have made it a great deal easier to gain access to the affluent homes without presenting a threatening appearance that a man might, and it would explain why they could be so close and she could still be safe. We'll never be able to prove it one way or another without an exhumation, but at this point but what real purpose would it serve?

"The upshot of the closeness of their relationship would be that it certainly explains why she bought the house. She bought it to keep the bodies from being discovered. She had to have known about his activities, if not participating in them herself. Maybe she even helped procure our little lovelies for him. It's even possible that she found it useful to obtain some of the by-products of his hobby for her own occult activities. It wouldn't be unheard of, hair, skin, blood and fingernails are supposed to be very powerful in a number of occult rituals. In any event, there is no doubt that, at the least, she covered for his crimes."

I thought my head was going explode. I needed some Advil, a strong drink, a pill, anything. God, it was so hot in that room. It was all too much for my tiny, small town mind to take in. Levengood must have read my mind.

"You look like you could use a drink, Chief," he said,

smiling as he wiped his forehead again, trying to lighten things up.

"I know I sure could," St George said.

"...but hold on, Chief, I'm almost finished. Then we can each take the drink of our choice," Levengood said, smiling again.

"The only issue remaining for us is what happened to Dr. Eccleston. There are no official records anywhere here in New York State, but we did come across what we're certain was his end. In searching for similar crimes in New York State, we came across a report of a drowning in Lake George in 1924 listed as an apparent suicide due to 'lunacy' of a man the age Eccleston would have been and fitting his general description. It seems he was fished out of the lake by a couple of summer guests from a nearby resort. When the autopsy was performed, the coroner found the tiles in his throat, stomach and rectum. Just between us..." he said leaning forward, "...we know it was him. The only question is did he 'do' himself, or did the freak show he associated with 'do' him to get him out of the way because he was getting out of hand and they were afraid he'd bring the law down on them? Either way, it coincides with the timeline for the end of the Jennisburg killings, so it's enough for us." Levengood put up his hands and made a slight shrug.

"That's it..." he paused, thinking to himself for a few seconds, then said, "...but based on all we've discovered...and I hate to lay this on you, Chief, but...it looks like your little town has the dubious honor of having played host to the country's first recorded serial killer." I squirmed in my chair, my mind reeling, spiraling out of control. I wiped my face again.

"So what happens now? I mean, I have a town to think of...most of our trade depends on our country quaintness," I asked him.

Levengood shrugged again. "Nothing happens," he said matter of factly. "...I don't think New York State has an interest in scaring away tourists and attracting ghouls. Does it Captain?" he asked, blithely looking at St. George.

"Not that I know of," St. George said, shrugging and throwing up his hands.

"Who knows about this in your area, Chief?" Levengood

asked me.

"Just me...thanks, in great part, to the discretion of Captain St. George here," I said giving him the credit due him.

"Well, as far as the federal government is concerned, the matter is purely academic. It's only useful to us for research purposes into the mind of a serial killer and early cultist activity. I'm sure the folks down there are going to have a field day for years to come analyzing this one, but as far as you and your town are concerned, we have no duty to publicize the matter, or disseminate any information unless someone comes asking, and if no one comes asking...then that's the end of it." With that, Levengood was up out of his chair putting the report in his briefcase.

"I hope you don't mind if I run now, Chief...Captain. I wouldn't want to keep the wife waiting too long, you know." He smiled politely, clearly rushed and nodding to each of us. St. George and I were up on our feet as well.

"Thank you so much for all your help Agent Levengood...and for staying to see me," I said, shaking his hand firmly for a long time.

"Not a problem, Chief. Like I said, brothers under the badge and all. It was my pleasure to help." Then it was St. George's turn to shake his hand.

"Thanks for staying, Grover. I hope you enjoy the show."

"Take care, Captain. I'm sure we will," he said and was out the door.

After Levengood was gone, we sat back down again, St. George and I, to grasp all that we were just told. "That business about his mother and the Russian woman was news to me," he said wiping his face again and pouring us more water. "You going to be alright, Chief?" he asked.

"Yeah, it's just going to take a little while to get my head around all this," I said and took a nice long drink of that gloriously cold water.

"Is there anything I can do for you?" he asked me, genuinely concerned.

"Nah. I'll be okay. You've done plenty already, and I can't thank you enough for it," I said sincerely. He smiled a big, honest smile.

"My pleasure, Chief...but you know that they're going to dig up that woman's body anyway, right?" he said, grinning.

"Yep...and after seeing that picture, I'm sure they're right in their assumption. It all makes some sort of bizarre sense now," I said, feeling some stability come back to my stomach.

"Yeah, I know what you mean. Crazy as hell, isn't it?" St. George said, shaking his head. I got up and put out my hand to him.

"If there is ever...ever...anything I can ever do for you, Captain... please don't think twice about it. You have yourself one serious friend in Gordon County."

He took my hand, shaking it hard. "Same goes here, Chief. Don't hesitate if you ever need anything," he said with a big, friendly smile, blue eyes shining. It came to me then, the thing about St. George that had been hiding in the back of my mind, eluding my attempts to put my finger on it. His demeanor reminded me of my father.

When I got to the outer office, I asked the girl in uniform if there was a washroom nearby and she pointed down the hall. I washed my hands and face over and over, frantically. What I needed then was a cigarette and a good strong cup of coffee...maybe even treat myself to an espresso since I was in town. Right then, I needed time to absorb everything, so I got my coffee and went to sit in the nearest park to smoke for awhile, letting the bracing cold bring my temperature down. I was numbed by the whole thing, but beyond numb, sick but beyond sick.

I didn't even feel the cold. I just kept going over in my head what Levengood had told me, replaying it like a broken record. It was all too horrendous, too unthinkable and too...inhuman to be real. But it was. It was real. I knew it in the deepest part of my existence. There was no denying it ever again.

Then it seemed that out of all the chaos whirling around in my mind, a single cogent thought came through. It was about Grace and Jenny and 'the man.' I'd figured out another part of it from what Levengood had said about 'the mother.' It feared women, and it hated them because it feared them. That's why it had no real influence over Jenny and didn't hurt her or Grace, even though she had the bracelet all those years. It feared them, so the best it could do was to scare them. They were women filled with love. It couldn't get to them. All it could do was to frighten them away from its real prey, Norman Harper, Martin Welliver...and maybe even me. In the end, I knew it to be the coward that it was, and that knowledge pleased me immensely. *Tick!*

CHAPTER 17

Le Pendu

"Shall I tell you what real evil is? To cringe to the things that are called evil, to surrender to them our freedom, in defiance of which we ought to face any suffering."

-Seneca
Roman Philosopher
Mid 1st Century AD

I headed home around 4:00 P.M., the time in the park and the cold taking its toll on me, the sweat in my damp clothes freezing to my skin. It wasn't until after I'd been driving for awhile that I felt the tremors in my hands begin again, mild at first, nothing I couldn't control, but then it started to rain.

An hour into the trip the tremors began to get worse...and so did the rain. It looked like I was headed into a storm front that was coming east, and it seemed that, as the rain got worse, so did the shakes, or vice versa...whichever.

As I drove on, it began to reverberate throughout my whole body, getting more intense with each mile marker. About a half an hour away from home, it got so bad it started to overtake me and I got scared...terrified, actually. The rain was pounding, I was shaking uncontrollably and couldn't see. I thought I was going to die, my heart was going to just stop. I couldn't hold it off any longer. Shaking violently from the inside out, I barely had the control it took to pull over, but when I saw the rest stop a few hundred feet ahead, I somehow managed it. I thought that even if I was going to die, it would be unforgivable to take anyone else with me.

I made it to the parking lot...to a space in the back, before it over took me completely...like one enormous epileptic fit or like my body was being riddled by a hail of invisible bullets. I was done for.

Then I smelled something strange, mild at first but getting stronger by the second, a horrible dead smell like wet animals decomposing, but different from the smell in the house. I grabbed the steering wheel and held on for dear life, listening to the rain pounding wildly on the car.

Suddenly another sound was added to the rain pounding on the hood. My blood curdled in my veins. It was the sound of wings flapping, heavy, wet flapping, like a gigantic mythical bird, and another smell...burning...stinging, acrid smoke of a fire, burning sulphur and seared flesh. It surrounded me...then an image appeared before my eyes. I was standing before the wall in the basement of the house again, reading the words.

"COME FLY WITH ME...BE A MONSTER AMONG MEN...AND I WILL MAKE YOU THE FINEST OF YOUR KIND.... FEAR ME...BRING HIM BACK OR WE WILL EAT YOUR SOUL."

My stomach convulsed with fear as violently as I ever expected it could, beyond what I felt in the house, beyond what I felt in the basement, inconceivable, apocalyptic fear. What was left of my mind worked beyond the breadth of its capacity to face the revelation that it was real. It was the thing that'd made Eccleston the 'finest of his kind.' I knew it in that flash of that second. Then I felt it. It was in the car with me, in the back seat. The atmosphere in the car raised to boiling hot, the windows steaming to opaque, the heat, the smell and my own death grip of fear, stifling me, choking me.

I closed my eyes and started to pray. "Holy Mary, Mother of God. Pray for us sinners now and at the hour of our death." I couldn't breathe. I was going to die. *Oh, dear God. I'm going to die right here, right now, in this highway rest stop.* My mind shot in every direction, looking for some escape, the throes of death beginning to settle in my fingers and toes. I squeezed my eyes tight, grasping the steering wheel with all my might, waiting for it to kill me. "Holy Mary, Mother of God," I prayed again. "Pray for us sinners now and at the hour of our death."

I heard the sound of heavy breathing, snorting, behind my head, like overheated horses after a long, strenuous run. It whispered to me...a horrible, rasping voice. I felt its scalding breath scorching the skin on the back of my neck.

"So you're a Backgammon man, are you, Chief? I can work with that." It said, mocking me with a thick, wet, black sounding chuckle.

Oh, my God. It's been watching me, listening to everything I've said, screamed through my mind.

"Did you know I knew your father, Chief Terry? Well I did. I watched him die with a shriveled dick...like a pussy...a coward. I watched him cry like a little girl as he wallowed in his own piss and shit, afraid to die, afraid to leave his poor little boy alone in the cold cruel world without him," it snickered snidely in my ear. "He called you name, you know. It was the last word he ever spoke before that final pump of blood carried away the last of his pathethic, useless life with it. Terrrryyyy!" it said in a high pitched, girlish whine, mocking my dad. The blood rushed to my head making it feel like it would split like a melon, an erupting volcano unleashing a lifetime of pent-up hatred, spewing its fire into the atmosphere.

"DON'T YOU TALK ABOUT MY FATHER!" I screamed at it, banging my head and hands on the steering wheel. Then I heard those sick words in my ear.

"Do you want to die like that too, Chief Terry? It doesn't have to be that way, if you play nice. Pray to me. Make me your god. COME FLY WITH ME...I WILL GIVE YOU WINGS AND MAKE YOU A MONSTER AMONG MEN...THE FINEST OF YOUR KIND... AND YOU'LL NEVER HAVE TO BE AFRAID, OR HURT, OR CRY EVER AGAIN."

It wanted me. It wanted me to become like . . . it. *Oh my God! It wanted me!*

Another convulsion overtook me with the dawning realization of it. It wanted me to replace the Eccelston I'd destroyed. I didn't know what to do. *Why me? Had I sunk so low, my spirit become so weakened by the corrosion of my life that it thought I'd be easy prey?* It was more than I could absorb, or deal with, or understand.

Then, from the most secret hidden places of my being, all gathering together to form a single thought, it came to me, and I did what that thought told me. I thought of all the love I'd known, raising the mirror of my life that I'd avoided for so long to finally, really see myself.

I knew my fate then. I was going to die, right there in that car, in that parking lot, and I decided that if it was going to die, I wanted it to happen with that love my heart. I visualized it so it appeared before my closed eyes. I saw my mother's eyes, felt her arms around me, heard her voice me telling me that she loved me. I heard Lila's voice when she told me she and Eli wanted to name their baby after me, feeling her cool hand lovingly touch my face, then the awkward warmth of Eli's arms as he threw them around me at the airport and after the wedding.

I remembered the look in Martin's eyes that night by the fire when I'd tried to fix him, saw the shine in his broad smile as I came in the door from Mexico, so happy to see me, and the heartfelt conviction in his voice when he told me he wouldn't let me suffer alone.

I saw the compassion in Jenny's eyes when she told me about Jeff's brother, knowing I would understand, and the gratitude in Jeff's face after Jenny's attack. I thought of Cordelia Weston, the feeling of her tears on my skin that day she came to see me in the hospital, then Angelica and our painful parting in the dream.

I thought of Grace, feeling her kissed fingertips touch mine the last time I saw her. Finally, I saw my father's face, smiling at me and tussling my hair as he hummed his song to me, tucking me in at night.

It was all there. They were all there balling up inside me, like a towering snowball rolling down hill, gaining monumental strength, and force, and mass, as it went. They were all there gathering around me at the moment of my death until finally, I was ready. If I had to die, I was going to face it like a man, but not just any man, a man who had known the richness love in his life, drunk freely from the font of human emotion, and returned that love with all the force his sad heart could pump forth.

I opened my eyes to look at it in the rearview mirror. I saw it, and it saw me. I saw its eyes, huge, blazing, yellow eyes with slits for pupils like a gigantic cat, and I said to it in my most steely, determined voice.

"No! You will not have me!" Then without thinking, I roared at it without taking my eyes from it, like an enraged jungle lion, finally uncaged after suffering years of torment at the hands of its captor, screaming at the top of my lungs, banging my hands against the wheel again. "YOOOUUUU WIIILLL NOOOOOOOTTTT HAAAVVEE MEEEE, YOOOUUU BBAAAASSSTTTAAAARRDDD!"

It laughed at me, a deep, bellowing, black laughter, snickering at my poor, pitiable resolve, daring to face its overwhelming power.

"Tsk, tsk, tsk...such a waste. You'd've made quite a catch, Chief. I could have done so very much with you... Oh, well, so be it," it hissed in a voice designed to trick me into believing I was insignificant to it, nominal and unimportant. Then I saw its huge tongue, black and split like a serpent, come winding through the protective grill behind my head, dissolving it as it worked its way through. I watched it in the rearview mirror, horrified as it wound and coiled itself around my neck, feeling its thick, slimy skin on my throat, winding and squeezing the breath out of me and...I closed my eyes. I was ready to die, and for the first time in my life, I was not afraid.

Good-bye and please remember how very much I love you all, I said to myself as I felt myself begin to choke from its reeking stench, the pressure draining my life away from me, going gray. Then just I was about to lose consciousness, I heard an enormous thud come from behind me, the sound of a direct slamming blow striking hard muscle mass covered by thick wet flesh, and an ear splitting, high pitched squeal.

My neck jerked and the thing slithered back from around my neck. The pressure was gone, but the car began to rock and thump violently, vibrating and quaking all around me, ready to come apart in pieces around me at any second. There was more high pitched screaming, the sickening squeal of animals in pain, like pigs in a slaughterhouse, and the sound of more blows being landed, rapidly, one after another mixed with the sound of claws scraping and scratching against metal. Through it all, I heard the sound of a voice, deep, gruff and gravelly, grunting and growling with driving physical exertion.

Suddenly the sounds abruptly ceased and the shaking stopped. It was all gone. I couldn't open my eyes, but I heard the sound of flight outside the car, the slapping of those gigantic wings in the rain, hovering above my head, then disappearing into the distance as I sat there holding my throat, gasping for breath. I collapsed over on the wheel, helpless.

Then I noticed something in the air had changed. It was the smell. The foul smell of that 'thing' was gone, replaced by something else, the familiar smell of Old Spice aftershave. I opened my eyes and the car filled with a brilliant burst of intense white light, blinding me. I rubbed my eyes to clear them and looked in the rearview mirror to make sure 'it' was gone.

In the half shadow thrown by the parking lot lamppost I saw a figure in the back seat. I could see the wide, muscular shoulders and the blue uniform I had seen and touched so many times as a child, but I couldn't see his face. It was covered in shadow and thick white mist rising from the floor, but it was him. He leaned forward and put his hand through the grill. I felt his warm, strong hand on my shoulder and heard that familiar voice say quietly, lovingly in my ear, "You're my whole life, sport."

Instinctively, I reached back and touched his hand, but before I could open my mouth to speak there was another flash of blinding white light, and when my eyes cleared...he was gone. I was alone in the car...but not alone. I was myself...but more than myself.

After my breath returned, I lifted my left hand. It was steady, like a rock. I couldn't believe it, then my right. It was steady, too. It was like a miracle. I got out of the car and stood beside it for some minutes, letting the cold rain soak me as it came down in sheets, washing me, cleansing me. I lifted my face to the sky and let it pour down on me, showering me.

As I stood there, I heard my own voice in my head. *You've won, Terry. You've faced death without fear. For the first time in your whole broken life, you've finally won and no small battle at that. No third place this time. No bringing up the rear for you this time. You are a man again.*

Even more than that, my father had found me and I him. He still loved me, and for the first time since I was seventeen years old, I was whole again. I was a whole man. He had not left me after all, but had given me the breath life, again. *Tick!*

❋ ❋ ❋

I headed into the rest stop Men's Room and dried off my face and hands. There was a shaggy old man at the urinal next to the sink. He looked at me over the neck high partition.

"Really comin' down out there, ain't it, son? Looks like it got you good," he said, grinning at me. I looked at him and laughed, probably sounding to him like some escaped lunatic.

"Looks like it did," I answered, all the while thinking . . . *No, 'it' didn't! NO 'IT' DIDN'T!*

❋ ❋ ❋

I didn't go straight home after that. There was still more I had to do. I knew it then. I couldn't carry the knowledge of it all by myself anymore. It was keeping the knowledge to myself, holding it so tightly inside me for so long that made it think it could have me, so I went to the only place I could. I went over to Martin's. He was the only one who would understand...the only one I could share it with. I knocked on his door. He opened it looking at me with a mix of surprise and awe.

"Chief! You're soaked. Come on in. Take your boots and jacket off," he said and limped upstairs. A few minutes later he came back with a pile of clothes, dragging his leg...badly, and using the cane. "Take these and go in there. Change out of those wet things." He pointed to the room to the right of the entry hall. I went into the unfinished office and started to change into a pair of his sweats and a shirt. They were snug around my thighs, shoulders and chest, but they were warm and comfortable...and a relief. I heard his voice call through the door, "You're just in time. I've been cooking all day. You'll stay and eat, won't you?"

When I came out, I could smell the cooking...a wonderful, sweet and spicy aroma. I could hear him singing as he cooked. It caught me off guard at first. "I left a good job in the city. Workin' for the man every night and day, and I never lost one minute of sleepin' worryin' 'bout the way things might have been. Big wheel keep on turnin'…oooohhhh Proud Mary keep on burnin'. 'cause we're rollin, rollin', rollin' yeah, rollin', rollin' on the river…roooolllliiinnin' ooonnn the riiivvveeerrr."

I was stunned. *Mah man!* Martin had some soul. *You go, Martin!* I thought with a quiet laugh to myself. Then I thought of the words he was singing, what McNeill had said about 'synchronicity,' and knew then that he was healing. It was the first time I was sure, really sure and…I found some peace in that.

I went and sat down at the table where Grace and I had sat on Christmas Eve, watching him through the open kitchen door. It hurt me to see him limp so badly and have to use the cane again. It'd been a while. I hated what I had to do next too, but it was only fair, right for both of us. I went to the kitchen doorway, drew in a deep breath and let it out in a long sigh.

"Martin, we've got to talk." I must have sounded as somber as I felt.

"Uh oh!…That doesn't sound good," he said turning the fire down under the pot to low. He sat down at the kitchen table, looking up at me. "It's back, isn't it? It's gonna hurt us…isn't it, Terry?" His eyes were wide, glazed and dark…sad.

"No, it's not back and it can't hurt us…it's over…but I…I can't carry it by myself anymore, Martin. I hate to put it on you…but you're all I have…and I can't carry it all by myself, not anymore. I just can't." I said dully, dreading every word I'd have to say. His expression changed from guarded relief to fond sympathy. He shook his head.

"I knew there was more that you were holding back. I know you. I know it's your way. I understand you better than you think… Now it's time for you to understand me," he said pointing his finger at me. "I've told you before, I'd never let you go it alone, Terry. I meant it before, and I mean it now. You can't protect me forever, you know."

"But…I can try, if I want to. Can't I?" I asked stubbornly. He looked to the sky smiling, threw up his hands then let it pass.

"Alright then…out with it. Let's have it. I'm ready. I can take it. Whatever it is, we'll get through it together. I promise." His eyes were dark and brooding, but not fearful. They were strong...determined... and very much alive. I was glad for his strength. I needed it so much right then.

I began with that day in my office with Kittridge and St. George. He listened intently, hanging on every word. Then I moved onto the days out at the site. His face registered the shock and disgust I would have expected. He got pale, as I knew by then was his nature, but he didn't falter.

"Terry, how could you not tell me all this?" he asked, quietly mystified, his voice lowered to almost a mumble.

"You were doing so well...you seemed so happy, and I was feeling so...sick inside. I didn't want you to feel it, too... not until I had an end to it and it couldn't hurt you anymore."

I told him about the meeting with Levengood and St. George that afternoon and what I'd learned there. Stark, speechless astonishment wrote itself all over his face as I spoke, like he'd been kicked in the stomach, wincing more and more as I got closer to the end and the part of how they think it got that way...and the body in the lake. I didn't mention my roadside experience. It could have all been in my head or a figment of my imagination from the shock of what I'd learned...*or not*...but whatever it was, I was clean now. I knew it. I felt it in my heart and soul...and in my body. I was clean, and it would never touch me again, so I kept that part to myself.

When I was done, Martin got up slowly from the table and went over to his pot on the stove, stirring it...not saying a word.

"I see you've got the cane again," I said, trying to get him to speak to me.

"It's just the rain...nothing to worry about," he said and went quiet again. I got a little concerned, so I went to the heart of it.

"Say something, will ya?"

"What's left to say? That's the end. Isn't it?" he asked, his voice frighteningly calm.

"Yes, that's the end of it. The house is gone. The bones are gone. The tiles are gone. The thing is gone. There's nothing left but our memories of it." He turned around to look at me then, a fire in his eyes that I'd never seen before, his color coming up with his temper.

"Good!" he shouted, gesturing with his hand, one finger pointing away at the air, "because I am not going to waste one more fucking minute of my life on that filthy, disgusting creature and it's foul, inhuman practices...not one more minute. And you know what, Terry? I'm gonna take my lead from your mother here and lay it on the line."

He was pointing at me then. "Neither are you! I don't ever expect I'll say 'no' to you ever again in my life, except for this once and I'm saying it. I'm saying 'No.' I don't care how it got that way, or where it is now. I don't care about those fucking possessed tiles...or anything else about it. It's taken all that it's going to ever take from me...and from you! That's the end of it, and I'm not fucking sorry it is!"

"Now you listen to me! I've made a fine dinner here and there's no one in this world I'd rather share it with than you, the bravest, strongest, most deeply loving man I've ever known in my life, and nothing is going to spoil it...not for me...or for you. Nothing! Not now, and not ever again. Do you understand?" His tone changed from full rant to half pleading. "Please tell me you understand what I'm saying to you here, Chief?"

It wouldn't have been fair for me to try and stop him, not that I knew what to say anyway. Besides, he'd earned his due by then. My legs started bouncing uncontrollably with nervous tension under the table. I looked down at my feet.

"Yes, I understand," I said meekly, the color coming up in my face, burning the tops of my ears and flushing me all over. It was clear that the lawyer was not to be contradicted here and would have his way on this, so I looked up to let him finish.

"And you know why?" he asked me, shouting again like a raving madman, veins bulging in the sides of his head and neck, but still barely able to contain the smile brewing behind it all.

"Why?" I asked quietly, not knowing what to expect next.

"Because I fucking said so, and Martin Welliver has been through too much in his goddamn life to hold with any crap!" he shouted, jabbing his finger at me. "You got me, Chief?" Then he let go, laughing loudly, honestly.

I laughed myself as soon as I realized he was quoting me back to myself from that night by the fire. "Touché, Counselor! Yes, *sir,* Mr. Welliver," I said, holding up my hands in feigned surrender. Then his tone and expression changed again, back to serious as he came closer to me, hesitating for a moment.

"So...do you think...you could ever...?" he asked uncertainly, almost inaudibly. It hit me then, like a crack of lightning, splitting me in two. I went back to looking down at my feet, feeling further on the edge of myself than I ever had before. I saw my folded hands in front of me, reminding me of what it was like seeing and feeling his blood on them in the men's room that first night at the hospital, thinking, *I'm coming with you*, as I watched it swirl down the drain.

Suddenly, a bolt of delirium shot up through me, into my brain, making me sweat, dizzying me almost to the point of a faint. I felt the light, tentative touch of his hand stoke the back of my head, making the short hairs of my buzzcut bristle and heard him groan as he got down on one knee in front of me. I looked up.

He wasn't so much smiling as...beaming...radiantly, his big, shining eyes searching mine, and for one brief, flickering second of infinity, I though I could see the world there. *God help me!* I thought, then said the next thing that came into my head, working desperately not to reveal the humbling state of my shame-laden awkwardness.

"I already do...but Martin, I'm so very hungry. Can we please eat now? I don't think I can stand it any longer."

※ ※ ※

Famished, I ate as fast as he could serve me and more wolfishly than I thought I was ever capable, until I'd had my fill and then some. I just couldn't seem to get enough, and learned what he said that night was right, the dinner was fine, the finest I'd ever had. Later, as we smoked over coffee and dessert, he asked me if he could have my two bronze medals. He said he was very proud of all I'd accomplished and thought it would be a good idea to display them in the library with some of my old action shots from the Games in an area devoted exclusively to Olympic athletes and sports heroes to show young people how much they could achieve.

I returned his request with my widest crooked smile, sitting back like a big, ol' porch dog who'd just been well fed, because, by then, I'd realized he'd sacrificed himself, unconditionally and completely...to save me, much in the way I'd sacrificed myself to save him all those months leading up to that night. He'd earned my undying loyalty and respect. Independent of anything he may have been before, he was Martin Welliver of Jennisburg, New York, and to that end, there wasn't anything he could've asked of me that I wouldn't have done for him, so if it was my bronze medals he wanted, it was my bronze medals he would have.

"They're all yours." *Tick!*

❋ ❋ ❋

When I went to leave that night, he took my hand, put two Valium in it and said, "These are the last two, but after tonight, I don't think either of us will need them anymore. Take them and get a good night's sleep, Chief. You've earned it...and let it all go. Please, just let it go. If you don't, it'll eat you alive inside and we'll all lose, and as selfish as it may sound, if anything were ever to happen to you... Please don't ever leave me, Terry. Promise me...please," he said haltingly, his voice placid in the darkness of the doorway as he came close to me, putting his head on my shoulder.

"I promise," I said and pulled him closer, feeling his heartbeat quicken against my chest. "Don't worry. I always keep my promises. Don't I?" I whispered, feeling a confidence in myself that I don't think I've ever felt before. That's when I realized that I'd finally beaten it, all of it, the booze, the drugs, the pain, all my fears both old and new, and the demons I'd had lived with so long, both from within and without. We've never talked about any of it after that night, the house or anything connected with it. For us, it would always just 'be.' *Tick!*

Walking down to the car, I stopped for a moment, turning to watch Martin close the door behind him and felt...free. For the first time in my life, I was free to be just myself. I'd never felt that before. At that very moment, I could swear I caught the faintest whiff of Grace's scent, 'My Sin,' she'd called it, and I remembered James Gibb relaying her last words to me. "She just said to tell you that you'll be alright." I looked up toward sky, my eyes welling with the relief that I was no longer 'dangling' like a 'hanging man' in so many ways, saying to myself, and whoever else might be listening, "Thank you, Gracie." Then I popped the two pills into my mouth, swallowed them dry, and went home for a well deserved night's sleep, a long time in coming. *Tick!*

CHAPTER 18

Heir Apparent

"The conquest of fear lies in the moment of its acceptance."
Unknown.

The following week, the miniature models arrived from McNeill along with some photos of himself at work, biographical material and reviews. The models were just what I'd envisioned. He did a nice job capturing the poses I wanted. I had Martin send my approval to him as soon as he could while I got my friends at the local paper to start a special piece on McNeill, Grace's bequests to the library and the bronze statue then under construction.

I told them the statue was the gift of an 'anonymous donor,' and asked them to concentrate on featuring the plans for the work on the library, Martin's place as the new director and McNeill's work, in particular. It was a big deal for the local and they ate it up. It wasn't hard to get the regional paper to agree to do the same and make a spread of it. The editor-in-chief was a second cousin to our Mrs. Mayor and had heard about the bequest and the statue well before I had even gotten there. The fix was in. *Gotta love it.*

Along with the models, McNeill included a long, handwritten note saying that he'd gotten an intern from the university to come on and help with the project for school credit, so he was sure he'd be able to deliver on time. That I might have expected, for him to deliver on time. What I didn't expect was the last part.

He wrote that Grace was a beautiful woman who had lived a long life, deserving to be remembered for the library she'd built, but he wrote that Angelica was only a little girl who died tragically and far too soon through the violence of an unforgivable act of mindless hate. He said that, when I told him the story, he felt the thing he called 'synchronicity,' and since I was giving my heart and money to have her remembered, he wanted to give his hands, only charging me for the materials it took to make her. He just wanted to know the location so he could visit it if he had the chance. I knew I was right about him when I met him. He's a 'good Joe' that McNeill.

Lila and Eli came back from their honeymoon tanned and happy. She wasn't too thrilled about my 'forcing her' to take my 'unofficial' part-time proposition, but, in the end, she saw the sense in it when I explained it to her 'properly'. Her only condition was that she be allowed to keep a police radio at home with the extra dispatch equipment. That I could agree to…piece of cake.

The following weeks were only eventful in the sense that I closed on the Woodville house and hired some local guys to take down the upstairs dividing wall to make it into one big loft bedroom. I also had them sand, stain and finish all the hardwood floors in the living room, dining room and small back room that I planned to make my office. I was having carpet put in upstairs and on the stairs as well, a dark sage green, calm, quiet and soothing. I had painters come in after the work upstairs was done to make it a nice quiet…and yes, soothing, pale sage color. The kitchen and bathrooms didn't need any real work, just some minor painting and a thorough cleaning. I expected it all to be done by the end of May, and it was.

The closing on my old house was set for the end of May as well, so I needed to get started on cleaning, sorting and packing. I decided to take as little of my old stuff with me as possible. A fresh, new start was what was needed. I didn't need my bedroom set, dining room or kitchen sets, so all that was left to pack were my personal belongings, my living room furniture and desk things. As I expected, Lila had enlisted Jenny to help and we began going through things on the average of about two afternoons a week. I told Lila that anything I was going to leave or throw out that she might want for her flea market sales she could have. She took my dishes, flatware and most of my pots and pans.

The only things I kept were my automatic coffee maker, which I love, and one of a kind items like can openers, cooking utensils and such, until I could get new ones. I gave her all my linens because my mother had volunteered to get me new ones. I really have so little taste in those matters.

I went through my bookshelves, keeping only my favorites, no more than a dozen or so out of maybe a hundred. I let Lila take the rest for her flea marketing. It was all wonderfully ordinary...gloriously commonplace, until I heard Lila call out, "Chief! You want to keep this or not?"

I looked up and saw that she had the paperweight in her hand. The one I crushed the last tile with. I felt myself make an involuntary expression of disgust, closely followed by a loud groan of much pain remembered. *Did I really want a constant reminder of 'the thing' in my new house? Did I really want to look at it every day and have to think about it all...everyday?* I asked myself and thought of what Martin had said on the last night we talked about such things. "Please, just let it go," he'd said and made me promise. So I did...I let it go.

"You take it Lila...but don't sell it cheap. I brought it back from Europe. I got it in Spain, but I know it's Italian...and kind of old. Don't take less than twenty...twenty-five dollars for it."

"You sure you don't want to keep it, Chief?" she asked again, looking at it like it might be valuable, or mean something special to me. I thought about it again, briefly.

"Nah . . . it's kind of ugly. Don'tcha think? I never really liked it anyway. You take it."

Lila had a great system going there. She marked the boxes with colored tape, blue for the things she'd take and red for the things I'd take to the new house. The rest went in the trash or stayed with the house. We started lining up the boxes according to color alongside the front door for the final move with the truck. The paperweight made me think though,...about this...my little therapy essay and what to do with it.

I couldn't bring myself to throw it away. It holds my heart

and soul…all the things that have helped me survive my darkest days, so I decided to keep it. When I'm done, I'll wrap it and tie it to keep it in behind my books where I won't have to look at it, but still know it was safe, so if for some strange reason in my old age I wanted to revisit those days, it would be there…in case I ever got too complacent with myself, or forgot who I was, or how I'd gotten here, if I forgot what life meant or the strength of love. No, this I could not let go. It was me. It is me!

❋ ❋ ❋

McNeill delivered on time. When the statues arrived at the library, Sheila Woolf called me, excited. I had the delivery men put the crate that held the figure of Grace and her bench in the general location of where I wanted it, then had them take Anglica and her bench to the Woodville house. Martin and I inspected the figure of Grace and were mightily impressed. McNeill had gotten it. It *was* Grace…just as I'd know her when I was young—beautiful…confident…graceful. We covered it with a tarp until it could be installed permanently and agreed on a date for the unveiling ceremony Martin had been planning. It was to be two weeks from that day, a Saturday afternoon.

I wrote to McNeill expressing my most sincere pleasure and gratitude. I included the final payment and told him how much it would please me if he and a guest would attend the unveiling and stay the weekend…as my guests, and asked him to let me know if he would be coming so I could hold the copies of his articles for him. If he couldn't make it, I'd send them on, but I did hope he'd want to come as much as I wanted him there. He called Lila when he got my letter a few days later and said he'd be here. That pleased me, very much.

The Saturday of the unveiling arrived and the weather was perfect. It was as bright, shiny and as warm a day as early spring could bring in our area. McNeill arrived the afternoon before with his date, a young woman…significantly younger than he was, and a model. She was very beautiful with long dark hair and sky blue eyes with thick dark lashes. Her name was Autumn Summers…or at least that was the name she was using. I couldn't resist the urge to have some fun with it, thinking to myself…

Hey, Autumn Summers whaddaya doin' this Winter. Corny, I know, but a guy has got to have some fun sometimes.

People started to gather about eleven forty-five for the ceremony to begin at noon. On my way over, I stopped in front of Marchand's Flower Shop to look at their spring display when I felt a tug on my sleeve at my elbow. I turned around to find Martha Portensky standing there squinting her eyes at me comically.

"Martha, how are you? Long time no see," I said good-naturedly. I should have known that the squinty eyes meant something.

"Draf's and unlevel floors huh, Chief Terry?... My foot!" she said, squinting her eyes even more to emphasize her point until they looked like two piss holes in the snow. "I jus' hope you salted the earth when it was done."

"Why Martha, I don't know what you mean. You don't think I had anything to do with it do you? The reports all say it was burglars," I said with a voice of exaggerated surprise, widening my eyes innocently.

Martha was no threat to me, so why not make light of it for her sake. "I don't know and I don't care," she said, looking like she was ready to stomp her foot at me. "I'm jus' glad to be rid of it!"

I took a different tack then. "Well, you know Martha, Mr. Welliver is living over at Grace Coutraire's place now and he's setting up a law practice. He could probably use some help over there getting things straightened out...and he did pay you in advance." I said, raising an eyebrow. She put her bony fingers to her lips, thinking for a moment.

"Yes, I did hear somethin' 'bout that," she said looking back to me. "You know you're right, Chief. Maybe I should speak to him 'bout it. I only ever seen it from the outside, but I'm sure it's a beautiful place inside."

I had her going then. "Well, Mr. Welliver is over at the Library right now. They're ready to unveil the statue of Grace any minute." I said, nudging her some.

"I'm on my way over there right now," she said with a glint in her eye. "I think I will talk to him about helpin' him out. Thanks for tellin' me, Chief." she said, smiling at me and nodding. I was glad. I still felt awful about the way I had treated her in the Market last winter.

"No problem, Martha. I'm glad I could help," I said, and she was off. Once she was gone, I laughed to myself. It wouldn't hurt for Martin to have some company over there, even though, after her experiences over at the 'other' house, Martha would probably be looking for spooks around every corner.

※ ※ ※

By noon, everyone was assembled and ready to go. The Mayor was there, of course, and the members of the Town Council with the new member making her first public appearance in office. Martin was dressed in his new suit. His hair had gotten long and wavy by then, and he wore it slicked back. He'd also grown a goatee and was wearing a pair of gold rimmed glasses that I'd never seen before. I guess we all hide our weaknesses whenever we can. He brought a new cane too, dark wood with a brass knob. He wasn't limping and the weather was fine, so I chuckled to myself that he was taking on an affectation, but I'm sure it just gave him an added sense of security so he wouldn't worry about stumbling in public. I thought the whole thing made him look very 'artsy.' Grace would've liked that. Sheila Woolf was there dressed smartly in a long grey skirt, frilly white blouse with an elegant black jacket and she wearing Grace's pearls, which did suit her very well. She looked lovely, but she was no Grace Coutraire. In the end, I don't imagine that many are.

Everyone lined up on the front lawn of the library along the left side of the tarp-covered statue, the Mayor, Martin, McNeill and Sheila as the town gathered around to see the statue. The Council members were lined up behind them, including the newest member wearing a simple black dress under a short gray tailored jacket with lions in her ears and on her breast, her hair done in the style Grace wore and smelling of 'My Sin.' At least this time, I knew that what I was smelling was real and was more relieved than I could tell to be able to say that. Martin had ordered coffee, tea, juice and soft drinks to be served on the opposite side of the Library's front lawn along with an assortment of finger sandwiches. *Nice touch*, I thought, but couldn't help wondering if any were made with 'tapénade.'

When the time arrived, the Mayor said a few words introducing Martin as the new Library Director. Martin stepped up to address the crowd and said what a nice way it was for him to meet the town, how honored he was to be named to the position, and how he was pleased to be the one to preside over the first of the many new improvements that the library would have in the coming few years due to Grace's generous bequest. He went on to say that, thanks to the donor, who wished to remain anonymous, he was pleased to introduce the sculptor who brought life to the statue of Grace Coutraire for all to see as they entered the 'Coutraire Library' and be reminded of her dedication and generosity to the future life of the library...Mr. Evan Killough McNeill. Martin's a very good public speaker. I don't know why I should have been surprised by that. He was a lawyer, after all.

McNeill stepped forward in a grand artistic gesture, taking a deep bow while the assembled on-lookers applauded. There were probably about two hundred or more by then. I stood way in the back to watch. When McNeill stepped back into the line, Martin introduced Sheila as the Head Librarian, whom they all knew, "...and who would do us the honor of unveiling the piece."

Sheila stepped forward, uncertainly pulling the tarp from the figure in short tenuous tugs. There was an immediate collective gasp and applause from all in attendance, and it was more than justified. With the light shining through the gaps between the tree branches, the effect was magnificent. Grace's figure glistened prominently and was everything I had asked for and expected, not a dull boring figure, but a lively, flowing rendition of someone we all knew, respected and in some cases, loved.

I stayed awhile to listen to the murmurs of approval and comments of how McNeill had really captured the 'Grace' that most of us knew. There was also some comment on who the 'anonymous donor' may have been. That was my cue to leave, but before I did, I watched the line of the Mayor, Martin, McNeill and Sheila begin to shake hands as the on-lookers filed past them making compliments, not unlike the receiving line at a wedding.

It was the town's chance to finally acquaint itself in the light of day with 'the mysterious Martin Welliver from New York'. The same Martin Welliver who'd had that awful accident last winter. The same Martin Wellliver whose house burned down only a few months ago and who had just put up a new sign in front of Grace's old house, "Martin Welliver, Esq., Attorney-At- Law, General Practice." The whole town was intrigued and couldn't wait to meet him, and it was clear from what I could see that he was meeting it all with aplomb and didn't need me, so I went back to the station and put my head down on my desk to take a nap.

Tick!

As I began to doze off, a strange thought occurred to me...about how much like Grace Martin was. They were both sophisticated and stylish with impeccable taste and manners. They both loved the arts and loved to be surrounded by beautiful things, while at the same time having an inscrutable affinity for those who were so very different from themselves in so many ways, like Lance Jamison...and me.

Both Grace and Martin had held out their hearts to me...bare, vulnerable and unafraid of judgment as if they knew something that I didn't, that they would be safe there. I thought how pleased Grace would be to know that Martin had succeeded her at the library and how secure she would feel knowing that her life's work was now in his capable hands. I also realized for the first time that, since his recovery, Martin had taken to wearing high quality, old fashioned Bay Rum, a scent that would identify him to me whenever he was anywhere in the vicinity, and always remind me of him when he wasn't.

In the end, it was Martin's day and I couldn't have been more proud to see him have it...Martin's Day...and Grace's. I hadn't let them down after all...either of them. Now there was only one thing left for me to do.

Tick!

❀ ❀ ❀

The next morning, I stopped by to see McNeill off. He'd been scarce since the ceremony the afternoon before. I guess he was too busy watching 'the seasons change' or something like that, to leave his room. When I knocked on his door, Autumn Summers answered it in a towel. I must confess, she was quite a girl. I thought of Cashmere Hasher opening her door to me wearing only her robe all those months ago and smiled slyly to myself.

"Evan, the Chief is here," she called over her shoulder. McNeill came to the door fully dressed and stepped out into the hall to speak to me.

"I was going to stop by and see you before we left, Chief...to say thank you for the opportunity and your hospitality."

"My pleasure," I said. "I'm very pleased with the results...and I brought you your copies of the articles I promised you. There are ten copies of each." He looked surprised.

"Well, you are a man of your word, Chief." he said, taking the bundles I'd brought and putting them just inside the door.

"As are you, Mr. McNeill," I said, extending my hand to shake his. "I'll send you some word on where you can find Angelica as soon as I have an exact address."

"I'd like that very much, Chief," he said, pumping my hand firmly. I could see in his eyes that he was the man I thought him to be. I knew that he would visit the church someday. It had to do with something called 'synchronicity.'

CHAPTER 19

Act of Contrition

"What power has love but forgiveness?"
                                        -William Carlos Williams,
                                        20th Century American Poet

I spent the early part of the following week making preparations for the trip. I had to make arrangements for the bronze of Angelica to be shipped to Memphis on the same flight I was taking that coming Saturday. Once that was done, I hired a U-Haul and had Joe Rogan help me lift the crate into the truck. On Saturday morning, I drove to Albany by myself. After I arrived in Memphis, I rented another U-Haul, taking the crate with the figure of Angelica with me to the hotel where I'd already made arrangements with the owner to get a local man to help me carry it and set it up. It turned out to be his nephew, a big, muscular, black haired man of about thirty with a mustache, goatee and tattoos named Orson 'you can call me Bud' Bartholomew. I thought he was probably an ex-con, but I was very grateful for him, nonetheless. It made my job much easier. He was young and strong and I was...well...not so young and not so strong anymore.

I called ahead to the church to check on the service times for that Sunday. I didn't want to arrive before the early service, or while people were gathering. I mailed a note that afternoon to the minister telling him how to set the marble bench permanently in cement to keep it from being toppled or stolen. I knew it wouldn't arrive until after I'd been and gone but, notwithstanding my own feelings, I knew the rest of the world hadn't changed very much in the last few years and wanted to do what I could to prevent anyone from ever hurting her again.

That Sunday morning, I put on my grey suit and Bud and I went to the church. I drove the truck and had Bud follow me in his bathroom tile green '69 Chevy pick-up to the recently rebuilt "New Jesus Christ of Hope Baptist Church." It was bigger and more beautiful than the old one had been, but was still all white, all clapboard...and could accommodate a much larger congregation. I was pleased to see it had grown so much.

By the time we arrived, the service was in progress giving us the time we needed to uncrate and carry the bronze and marble bench to the spot I thought to be most suitable. Like Grace, it was on the lawn on the left side of the walkway about fifty feet from the entrance. Luckily, the ground was level and the lawn well trimmed.

Bud and I carried the bench to the spot I'd chosen, pressing it down to make sure it was stable, then went and got the bronze. I carried her head and he carried her feet. It wasn't as heavy as I would have thought, or maybe it was just that Bud was bearing the bulk of the load.

Once the bronze was in place on the bench, Bud got out his tool belt and fastened it with the bolts McNeill had installed to fix it immovable on the bench. With that done, I gave him a fifty and sent him on his way with a handshake and my thanks. I couldn't help but notice the twin rebel flag bumper stickers he had on the back of the truck as he drove away and wondered what he must have thought about coming to a black church to pay respects, so to speak, finding myself thinking hopefully that, *Maybe the world has changed some after all, even if only just a little bit.*

Then I returned to the task at hand, standing for a moment facing the door, working to collect myself for what I knew was coming. I was afraid again. I could feel it welling up inside me, another tidal wave gaining momentum with each second I delayed. But then I heard the music coming from inside, powerful, soulful, God praising gospel, the clapping of hundreds of hands, the stomping of hundreds of feet, all with one single, unified purpose. The whole building shook with it.

I took the time to listen intently, opening myself up to it, letting it engulf me and swell up inside me, displacing the fear, turning back that tidal wave. Overwhelmed with inspiration, beauty and faith, it gave me a sense of strength and peace, both of which I needed to go in and do what I had to do.

I picked up my feet, one at a time, taking it slowly, step by step. I opened the door and let the power of the music embrace me as I walked in slowly, my head down, taking a seat in the far end of the last empty pew. Then the music changed, becoming slow, deep and harmonious.

Before I knew it, my face was wet, streaming, all of it coming out... flooding out of me...a river of sorrow releasing itself, emptying into a gulf of relief...all the pain and guilt...the sadness and grief...fear and shame, everything I had felt and held on to so tightly for so long came pouring out of me. The tidal wave was suddenly going in the other direction. There was no controlling it. I didn't want to control it anymore. It was my release, so I just let it go.

I could only imagine what the congregation must have thought. "What is this crazy white man doing carrying on like that in the back of our church?" But I couldn't care. A few minutes later, I felt a presence next to me, taking my hand and I looked up. It was Cordelia Weston. Her eyes were streaming with tears as she looked at me. All I could do was shake my head.

"I'm so sorry...I'm so sorry," I sobbed, unrestrained. She squeezed my hand, putting her other arm around me.

"Mr. Chagford, it's not your fault...no more than it was mine. We both tried our best to save her." I was rocking again, back and forth. She rocked with me. "It's alright, baby," she said weeping. "She's with God now. God called her home. She had to go. It's what He wanted. You have to believe that...I do," she said, looking at me with the most forgiving, heartfelt look in her eyes.

"You poor man. You've been carrying this around with you for so long...I can see it in your face, and in your eyes, wearing it on your life." She held me tight and touched my face. "I don't want that for you, and I know she wouldn't want that either."

My heart hurt so badly, I thought it would splinter into bits. Then the music stopped. She took out her handkerchief and gave it to me. I wiped my face, a sense of peace washing over me. She took my hand again and held it while the minister made his closing remarks. When it was over, we stood up and walked out together. I wanted to know if she'd approve of what I'd done. I needed to know.

We stepped out of the door and over to the side. When she saw the bronze, her eyes went wide with surprise. She turned to look at my face, her hand over her mouth, crying again then walking over to be close to it, she gently touched the face. Then she came back to me, putting her arms around me, holding me tight. All I could do was sob in her arms.

"Thank you so much for bringing my baby back to me," she said in my ear as we held each other. "She's beautiful...isn't she?" she asked me through her tears.

"Yes," I said, "she is...my beautiful, little angel." Mrs. Weston pulled back and put her hand to my face. It was soft and warm...and gentle and sweet.

"You're a good man, Mr. Chagford...a fine man. It would be a sin for you to hurt anymore over this. I don't want that, and neither would my baby." Choked with emotion, all I could do was nod.

"Promise me, Mr. Chagford...please promise me that you'll believe what I believe. My girl is happy and at peace with God...that's what's important now...for us both. Will you promise me that?" she said, searching for my eyes. I nodded again.

"Yes, ma'am...I promise," I said with a deep heaving sigh, taking her hand and letting it trail as I turned, not wanting to let go and lose that connection.

❋ ❋ ❋

I walked in the bright sunlight down the sidewalk back toward to the parking lot. About halfway there, I stopped and turned to look back at Mrs. Weston and the statue. She was surrounded by the minister and her friends from the congregation. They were all hugging and smiling as they looked at the little bronze girl, some touching her, and I turned again to go. After I had taken a few steps, a breeze blew, soft and warm. I put my face up to catch it. When it blew again, I smelled it. There was baby powder on the breeze. I stopped in my tracks. It was Angelica. She was there with me. I could smell her. I could feel her near me. I raised my head again to inhale as much of it as I could. It blew again, this time carrying with it a small voice.

"I love you, Terrence," it said.

"I love you too, baby," I said to the breeze, and then she was gone.

I wiped my face again with the handkerchief Mrs. Weston had given me and started back to the truck. When I got in, I sat for a while with the engine running, thinking to myself before heading down the road. After I had gone a respectable distance, I turned on the radio. It was playing my old song. The one I was thinking of when I saw Martin's car go off the bridge, and so many times before and since.

"In the clearing stands a boxer and a fighter by his trade and he carries the reminders of ev'ry glove that laid him down or cut him till he cried out In his anger and his shame 'I am leaving, I am leaving' but the fighter still remains…"

It was over. It was really, finally, all over. The only task left before me was to go home, take care of my people the best that I knew how… and make whatever peace I could with the rest of my life. My clock had finally righted itself, my hour had finally come. *Tick!*

EPILOGUE

A Strange Occurrence

As is usual with most published materials, there is a great deal of preparation to be done before a text ever reaches the presses, not the least of which are the final edits and contract details. In the end, the final work done on this volume took place in New York City over a period of several months, during which I attended a number of meetings. Of those meetings, the last seemed to be the most trivial, but after the close of that last meeting when all of the final 'i's were dotted and 't's crossed, I had an experience which may or may not have some bearing on the content of the text which I will relate to the reader here as the subject of this Epilogue.

On the evening of that last meeting, we had closed rather late, sometime after 10:00 P.M. As had become my habit, I left the building and walked to the Port Authority Bus Terminal Parking Garage to think and breathe before getting my car to head back to Montclair. When I pulled out of the parking garage I discovered that, in the interim from my entering the building, it had begun to rain, lightly at first, but increasingly heavy as I entered and passed through the Lincoln Tunnel.

By the time I got on to the New Jersey Turnpike South, it was after 11:00 P.M. and coming down in buckets. Knowing that I had a relatively short ride to my exit, I tried to take it slow and ride it out when I began feeling oddly uncomfortable. With each quarter mile that I drove, an uneasy feeling I can only describe as 'oppressive' grew in the atmosphere around me. With the rain pounding on the car and an almost complete loss of visibility, I found that all I could do was hold tight to the steering wheel and hope for the best.

Stubborn until the end, I refused to pull over to the side of the road until the worst of the rain had passed, even though the atmosphere inside the car began to make it difficult for me to breathe. The pressure on my chest from the thickness of the air around me made me think that I might be having a heart attack. Then, just as my limbs began to go numb and my stomach tightened with the fear of my own mortality, the car swerved out of my control and began to shake violently. Scared out of my wits to either stop where I was or continue on, I decided to try and make it to the next rest stop, which I knew to be only a couple hundred feet ahead of me. Thankfully, I arrived at the rest stop safely a few moments later. Once I was securely off the road, I stopped, threw the car into park and got out in the pouring rain. I stood there for a few seconds paralyzed with fear of…the unknown, I guess, but when I looked down, I felt like a complete idiot. My rear left tire was flat. I'd had a blow out.

After standing there shaking my head, feeling like a child afraid of its own shadow for awhile, I got back into the car to call AAA. When I got back in my seat and reached for my cell phone, it was there again, that same 'oppressive' feeling I'd had all during the ride, but this time it was combined with the feeling that I wasn't alone, that I was being watched by a presence in the car with me. Then I heard something move in the back seat. Automatically, I looked up into the rear view mirror to see what was behind me. A shadow moved, formless and swift, and I noticed that my briefcase was on the floor, not on the seat where I'd left it. There was someone in that car with me, or something. I got out of the car as fast as I could and ran to the Service Area without looking back to call my wife from a pay phone to come pick me up. The next day, I had AAA go out to fix the flat and bring the car back to my house. I put it up for sale that day and sold it a week later for half its value, having never gotten back in it again.

I leave it here for the reader as I left it there for myself. But before I do, I'd like to dedicate the following passage to "the Chief" in the hope that if he someday reads this, he will approve of what I have done and know how much I so very truly admire him.

Daniel Vincent Carruthers
October 2005

✸ ✸ ✸

"The balance of a man's sanity can very often be found swinging from a tether like a pendulum, the ultimate result depending, first, on the quality of his heart. Where a forgiving heart may produce an accepting creature that opens like a flower upon the touch of the kind hand of friendship, a foul heart produces a dangerous one that would eat it instinctually, like a wild beast, without provocation. At times, it is possible for a man's heart to swing alternately in each direction without affixing to either extreme. In those cases, it is the revelation of his soul that determines the path of his illness, whether his diseased soul has not yet progressed to the stage where it deprives him of the strength to open it, like an inviting door, to reveal the chancre of its weakness to the light and air that would heal it, or has progressed beyond that point, to the stage where it must keep it closed, afraid to reveal the depraved shadows of its weakness, preferring it, instead, to fester and rot in the darkness that dwells there. Beyond that, any result can only rest in the outcome of the battle between angels and demons, and, in that instance, may God forgive us all our limitations and failure to understand ourselves."

-15th Century Dutch Physician,
left anonymously out of fear of
retaliation by the Inquisition.

Moon River

"Moon River, wider than a mile,

I'm crossing you in style some day.
Oh, dream maker, you heart breaker,
wherever you're going I'm going your way.
Two drifters off to see the world.
There's such a lot of world to see.
We're after the same rainbow's end—
waiting 'round the bend,
my Huckleberry friend,
Moon River and me."

Music by Henry Mancini,
Lyrics by Johnny Mercer.